PENGUIN ⟨🐧⟩ CLASSICS

THE WOODLANDERS

THOMAS HARDY was born in a cottage in Higher Bockhampton, near Dorchester, on 2 June 1840. He was educated locally and at sixteen was articled to a Dorchester architect, John Hicks. In 1862 he moved to London and found employment with another architect, Arthur Blomfield. He now began to write poetry and published an essay. By 1867 he had returned to Dorset to work as Hicks's assistant and began his first (unpublished) novel, *The Poor Man and the Lady*.

On an architectural visit to St Juliot in Cornwall in 1870 he met his first wife, Emma Gifford. Before their marriage in 1874 he had published four novels and was earning his living as a writer. More novels followed and in 1878 the Hardys moved from Dorset to the London literary scene. But in 1885, after building his house at Max Gate near Dorchester, Hardy again returned to Dorset. He then produced most of his major novels: *The Mayor of Casterbridge* (1886), *The Woodlanders* (1887), *Tess of the D'Urbervilles* (1891), *The Pursuit of the Well-Beloved* (1892) and *Jude the Obscure* (1895). Amidst the controversy caused by *Jude the Obscure*, he turned to the poetry he had been writing all his life. In the next thirty years he published over nine hundred poems and his epic drama in verse, *The Dynasts*.

After a long and bitter estrangement, Emma Hardy died at Max Gate in 1912. Paradoxically, the event triggered some of Hardy's finest love poetry. In 1914, however, he married Florence Dugdale, a close friend for several years. In 1910 he had been awarded the Order of Merit and was recognized, even revered, as the major literary figure of the time. He died on 11 January 1928. His ashes were buried in Westminster Abbey and his heart at Stinsford in Dorset.

PATRICIA INGHAM is General Editor of all Hardy's fiction in the Penguin Classics Edition. She is a Fellow of St Anne's College, Reader in English and *The Times* Lecturer in English Language, Oxford University. She has written extensively on the Victorian novel and on Hardy in particular. Her most recent publications include *Dickens, Women and Language* (1992) and *The Language of Gender and Class: Transformation in the Victorian Novel* (1996). She has also edited Elizabeth Gaskell's *North and South* and Thomas Hardy's *The Pursuit of the Well-Beloved and The Well-Beloved* for Penguin Classics.

CONTENTS

ACKNOWLEDGEMENTS

This edition is dedicated to the late Mary Bonney.

I am grateful for specific material to the Dorset County Museum, Roger Crisp, Michael Inwood, Gabriele Taylor, and the library staff of St Anne's College, particularly David Smith, Martina Mangels and Alison Corley. I am most indebted to Jenny Harrington and Shannon Russell. To all of these I offer thanks.

GENERAL EDITOR'S PREFACE

This edition uses, with one exception, the first edition in *volume* form of each of Hardy's novels and therefore offers something not generally available. Their dates range from 1871 to 1897. The purpose behind this choice is to present each novel as the creation of its own period and without revisions of later times, since these versions have an integrity and value of their own. The outline of textual history that follows is designed to expand on this statement.

All of Hardy's fourteen novels, except *Jude the Obscure* (1895) which first appeared as a volume in the Wessex Novels, were published individually as he wrote them (from 1871 onwards). Apart from *Desperate Remedies* (1871) and *Under the Greenwood Tree* (1872), all were published first as serials in periodicals, where they were subjected to varying degrees of editorial interference and censorship. *Desperate Remedies* and *Under the Greenwood Tree* appeared directly in volume form from Tinsley Brothers. By 1895 ten more novels had been published in volumes by six different publishers.

By 1895 Hardy was sufficiently well-established to negotiate with Osgood, McIlvaine a collected edition of all earlier novels and short story collections plus the volume edition of *Jude the Obscure*. *The Well-Beloved* (radically changed from its serialized version) was added in 1897, completing the appearance of all Hardy's novels in volume form. Significantly this collection was called the 'Wessex Novels' and contained a map of 'The Wessex of the Novels' and authorial prefaces, as well as frontispieces by Macbeth-Raeburn of a scene from the novel sketched 'on the spot'. The texts were heavily revised by Hardy, amongst other things, in relation to topography, to strengthen the 'Wessex' element so as to suggest that this half-real half-imagined location had been coherently conceived from the beginning, though of course he knew that this was not so. In practice 'Wessex' had an uncertain and ambiguous development in the earlier editions. To trace the growth of Wessex in the novels as they appeared it is necessary to read them in their original pre-1895 form. For the 1895–6 edition represents a substantial layer of reworking.

Similarly, in the last fully revised and collected edition of 1912–13, the Wessex Edition, further alterations were made to topographical detail and photographs of Dorset were included. In the more open climate of opinion then prevailing, sexual and religious references were sometimes (though not always) made bolder. In both collected editions there were also many changes of other kinds. In addition, novels and short story volumes were grouped thematically as 'Novels of Character and Environment', 'Romances and Fantasies' and 'Novels of Ingenuity' in a way suggesting a unifying master plan underlying all texts. A few revisions were made for the Mellstock Edition of 1919–20, but to only some texts.

It is various versions of the 1912–13 edition which are generally available today, incorporating these layers of alteration and shaped in part by the critical climate when the alterations were made. Therefore the present edition offers the texts as Hardy's readers first encountered them, in a form of which he in general approved, the version that his early critics reacted to. It reveals Hardy as he first dawned upon the public and shows how his writing (including the creation of Wessex) developed, partly in response to differing climates of opinion in the 1870s, 1880s and early 1890s. In keeping with these general aims, the edition will reproduce all contemporary illustrations where the originals were line drawings. In addition, for all texts which were illustrated, individual volumes will provide an appendix discussing the artist and the illustrations.

The exception to the use of the first volume editions is *Far from the Madding Crowd*, for which Hardy's holograph manuscript will be used. That edition will demonstrate in detail just how the text is 'the creation of its own period': by relating the manuscript to the serial version and to the first volume edition. The heavy editorial censoring by Leslie Stephen for the serial and the subsequent revision for the volume provide an extreme example of the processes that in many cases precede and produce the first book versions. In addition, the complete serial version (1892) of *The Well-Beloved* will be printed alongside the volume edition, since it is arguably a different novel from the latter.

To complete the picture of how the texts developed later, editors trace in their Notes on the History of the Text the major changes in 1895–6 and 1912–13. They quote significant alterations in their explanatory notes and include the authorial prefaces of 1895–6 and 1912–13. They also indicate something of the pre-history of the texts in manuscripts where these are available. The editing of the short stories will be separately dealt with in the two volumes containing them.

Patricia Ingham
St Anne's College, Oxford

1840 2 June: Thomas Hardy born, Higher Bockhampton, Dorset, eldest child of a builder, Thomas Hardy, and Jemima Hand, who had been married for less than six months. Younger siblings: Mary, Henry, Katharine (Kate), to whom he remained close.

1848–56 Schooling in Dorset.

1856 Hardy watched the hanging of Martha Browne for the murder of her husband. (Thought to be remembered in the death of Tess Durbeyfield.)

1856–60 Articled to Dorchester architect, John Hicks; later his assistant.

late 1850s Important friendship with Horace Moule (eight years older, middle-class and well-educated), who became his intellectual mentor and encouraged his self-education.

1862 London architect, Arthur Blomfield, employed him as a draughtsman. Self-education continued.

1867 Returned to Dorset as a jobbing architect. He worked for Hicks on church restoration.

1868 Completed his first novel *The Poor Man and the Lady* but it was rejected for publication (see 1878).

1869 Worked for the architect Crickmay in Weymouth, again on church restoration.

1870 After many youthful infatuations thought to be referred to in early poems, met his first wife, Emma Lavinia Gifford, on a professional visit to St Juliot in north Cornwall.

1871 *Desperate Remedies* published in volume form by Tinsley Brothers.

1872 *Under the Greenwood Tree* published in volume form by Tinsley Brothers.

1873 *A Pair of Blue Eyes* (previously serialized in *Tinsleys' Magazine*). Horace Moule committed suicide.

1874 *Far from the Madding Crowd* (previously serialized in the *Cornhill*

Magazine). Hardy married Emma and set up house in London (Surbiton). They had no children, to Hardy's regret; and she never got on with his family.

1875 The Hardys returned to Dorset (Swanage).

1876 *The Hand of Ethelberta* (previously serialized in the *Cornhill Magazine*).

1878 *The Return of the Native* (previously serialized in *Belgravia*). The Hardys moved back to London (Tooting). Serialized version of part of first unpublished novel appeared in *Harper's Weekly* in New York as *An Indiscretion in the Life of an Heiress*. It was never included in his collected works.

1880 *The Trumpet-Major* (previously serialized in *Good Words*). Hardy ill for many months.

1881 *A Laodicean* (previously serialized in *Harper's New Monthly Magazine*). The Hardys returned to Dorset.

1882 *Two on a Tower* (previously serialized in the *Atlantic Monthly*).

1885 The Hardys moved for the last time to a house, Max Gate, outside Dorchester, designed by Hardy and built by his brother.

1886 *The Mayor of Casterbridge* (previously serialized in the *Graphic*).

1887 *The Woodlanders* (previously serialized in *Macmillan's Magazine*).

1888 *Wessex Tales*.

1891 *A Group of Noble Dames* (tales). *Tess of the D'Urbervilles* (previously serialized in censored form in the *Graphic*). It simultaneously enhanced his reputation as a novelist and caused a scandal because of its advanced views on sexual conduct.

1892 Hardy's father, Thomas, died. Serialized version of *The Well-Beloved*, entitled *The Pursuit of the Well-Beloved* in the *Illustrated London News*. Growing estrangement from Emma.

1892–3 *Our Exploits at West Poley*, a long tale for boys, published in an American periodical, the *Household*.

1893 Met Florence Henniker, one of several society women with whom he had intense friendships. Collaborated with her on *The Spectre of the Real* (published 1894).

1894 *Life's Little Ironies* (tales).

1895 *Jude the Obscure*, a savage attack on marriage which worsened relations with Emma. Serialized previously in *Harper's New*

Monthly Magazine. It received both eulogistic and vitriolic reviews. The latter were a factor in his ceasing to write novels.

1895–6 First Collected Edition of novels: Wessex Novels (16 volumes), published by Osgood, McIlvaine. This included the first book edition of *Jude the Obscure.*

1897 *The Well-Beloved* (rewritten) published as a book; added to the Wessex Novels as vol. XVII. From now on he published only the poetry he had been writing since the 1860s. **No more novels**.

1898 *Wessex Poems and Other Verses.* Hardy and Emma continued to live at Max Gate but were now estranged and 'kept separate'.

1901 *Poems of the Past and the Present.*

1902 Macmillan became his publishers.

1904 Part 1 of *The Dynasts* (epic-drama in verse on Napoleon). Hardy's mother, Jemima, 'the single most important influence in his life', died.

1905 Met Florence Emily Dugdale, his future second wife, then aged 26. Soon a friend and secretary.

1906 Part 2 of *The Dynasts.*

1908 Part 3 of *The Dynasts.*

1909 *Time's Laughingstocks and Other Verses.*

1910 Awarded Order of Merit, having previously refused a knighthood.

1912–13 Major collected edition of novels and verse, revised by Hardy: The Wessex Edition (24 volumes). 27 November: Emma died still estranged. This triggered the writing of Hardy's finest love-lyrics about their early time in Cornwall.

1913 *A Changed Man and Other Tales.*

1914 10 February: married Florence Dugdale (already hurt by his poetic reaction to Emma's death). *Satires of Circumstance. The Dynasts: Prologue and Epilogue.*

1915 Mary, Hardy's sister, died. His distant young cousin, Frank, killed at Gallipoli.

1916 *Selected Poems.*

1917 *Moments of Vision and Miscellaneous Verses.*

1919–20 Mellstock Edition of novels and verse (37 volumes).

1922 *Late Lyrics and Earlier with Many Other Verses.*

1923 *The Famous Tragedy of the Queen of Cornwall* (drama).

1924 Dramatized *Tess* performed at Dorchester. Hardy infatuated with the local woman, Gertrude Bugler, who played Tess.

1925 *Human Shows, Far Phantasies, Songs and Trifles.*

1928 Hardy died on 11 January. His heart was buried in Emma's grave at Stinsford, his ashes in Westminster Abbey. *Winter Words in Various Moods and Metres* published posthumously. Hardy's brother, Henry, died.

1928–30 Hardy's autobiography published (on his instructions) under his second wife's name.

1937 Florence Hardy (his second wife) died.

1940 Hardy's last sibling, Kate, died.

This map is from the Wessex Novels Edition, 1895–6

The following abbreviations are used for texts frequently cited throughout the edition.

Collected Letters: R. L. Purdy and M. Millgate (eds.), *The Collected Letters of Thomas Hardy*, 7 vols. (Oxford: Clarendon Press, 1978–88)

Life: Thomas Hardy, *The Life and Work of Thomas Hardy*, ed. Michael Millgate (London: Macmillan, 1982)

Literary Notebooks: L. Björk (ed.), *The Literary Notebooks of Thomas Hardy*, 2 vols. (London: Macmillan, 1985)

Personal Notebooks: R. Taylor (ed.), *The Personal Notebooks of Thomas Hardy* (London: Macmillan, 1979)

Poems: S. Hynes (ed.), *The Complete Poetical Works of Thomas Hardy*, 5 vols. (Oxford: Clarendon Press, 1982–95)

Many years after publication in 1887, Hardy described *The Woodlanders* as 'a woodland story' which he now found 'quaint and fresh'. The innocent title suggests a rural idyll harking back to his early novel *Under the Greenwood Tree* (1872). Contemporary critics, however, whether approving or hostile, did not read it in this mild way. They found it strong meat: a 'vivid drama'; 'his best and most powerful work'; 'as disagreeable as it is powerful'.[1] Hardy's apparent assumption of the text's simple directness denies the complexity and sophistication of the work to which the critics were more understandably responding in different ways.

But the detachment of a title that refuses to comment does capture an important aspect of the novel: its engagement with a major paradigm which both obsessed most intellectual disciplines in the nineteenth century and implied scientific distancing. In the early part of the twentieth century, linguistic structuralism as outlined by Saussure became a model metaphorically applied to a range of subjects from anthropology to literary criticism, fashion and sport. In the nineteenth century scientific and other enquiries used as their overarching explanatory metaphor that of decoding a new or strange language. In describing his revolutionary discoveries Charles Lyell used the figure of linguistic decipherment for his interpretation of the history of geological formations and their implications for the age of the universe. Algernon Mantell, from whose popularizing of Lyell's work Hardy learned the geology which remained a lifelong interest, did the same. He wrote in 1838:

Before we can attain that elevation from which we may look down upon and comprehend the mysteries of the natural world . . . we must learn to read the records of creation *in a strange language*.[2]

Forms of the metaphor were often repeated by students of language.

William Whitney wrote in 1867 that 'a noteworthy and often remarked similarity exists between the facts of geology and those of linguistic study'.[3] The figure was in common currency when Charles Darwin, in writing 'On the Imperfection of the Geological Record' in *The Origin of Species* (1859), asserted that:

For my part, following out Lyell's metaphor, I look at the natural geological record, as a history of the world imperfectly kept, and written *in a changing dialect* . . . [my emphasis].[4]

The interchange of geological, botanical, zoological and linguistic phenomena as the vehicles of metaphor in scientific disciplines came as naturally as breathing because of the common methods of research. All these studies depended on the accumulation of observable facts and the laborious interpretation of what could be deduced from them about the origins and history of the things involved. The methods of Lyell and Darwin might be generally described in words that Hardy used of his own work as 'humbly recording diverse readings of . . . phenomena'. The works of such scientists as these effectively secularized the long Christian tradition of seeing the physical world as everywhere the inscription of the Word of God. Patristic and medieval allegorists had explicated this Word in innumerable treatises and sermons for the faithful. And even in the nineteenth century efforts were made by some, including Mantell, to reconcile the Christian and the scientific viewpoints.

Darwin himself kept a tactful silence. Geologists, biologists and students of language alike were preoccupied with the same questions: What is the origin of this? and, How did it develop? These were areas which for centuries had been assumed necessarily to have a spiritual or metaphysical dimension, but no longer. Hardy was keenly interested in geological discoveries and Darwinian accounts of evolutionary development. He was also obsessed with language itself and what was being discovered about it. For him this mainly meant vocabulary/lexis. His concern was above all with meaning, both denotative and associative or connotative. He studied earlier dictionaries such as John Walker's *A Rhyming Dictionary of the English Language* (first published in 1775) of which he owned a nineteenth-century edition (1865) and to which he added a list of some 400 words.[5] He was an eager purchaser of the successive volumes of *The Oxford English Dictionary on Historical Principles* (1884–1928), now known as the *OED*. Letters were exchanged with the editors and Hardy added lists of dialect 'words omitted' to his copy of the dictionary. His own vocabulary was deliberately extended, particularly in his poetry which deployed words from many registers. Glossing the dialect words in the 1908 *Selected Poems of William Barnes*, the poet who wrote in the Dorset dialect, he reveals his sensitivity to fine shades of meaning. Hardy writes that his glosses of dialect words are

a sorry substitute for the full significance the original words bear to those who read them without translation, and know their delicate ability to express the doings, joys and jests, troubles, sorrows, needs and sickness of life in the rural world as elsewhere.[6]

There is much evidence that Hardy studied the history of words closely and energetically. It is also clear that he took a romantic view of the meaning of words as something about which one has 'a feeling before it gets defined'.[7]

By the time he wrote *The Woodlanders* he had given much attention to the subject of decoding language and other phenomena. This novel, as much as *The Moonstone* or *The Woman in White*, is a narrative that attempts to decipher the mysterious codes represented by all events and individuals. The codes relate to questions which occupied Hardy throughout his career as a novelist: what are the implications of evolution, the significance of social class and the nature and future of women? Social class, particularly in relation to talented men of working-class origin, had been a recurrent theme. It had begun in *The Poor Man and the Lady* (unpublished in full) and been transferred by textual cannibalism into *Desperate Remedies* (1871), *Under the Greenwood Tree* (1872) and *A Pair of Blue Eyes* (1873). It is later found in *A Laodicean* (1881) and *Two on a Tower* (1882). It was to reach its apotheosis in the last novel with Jude Fawley in *Jude the Obscure* (1895). Apart from *The Mayor of Casterbridge* (1886), women had been prominent in all his novels.

The importance of the written word is enacted by the reliance of the narrative dynamic on written forms: in letters, legal documents, the marriage service and, in one instance, graffiti. Episodes involving documents are the characteristic events of the narrative and the triggers for many changes and crises. Grace Melbury's return from a genteel school to a less genteel home, which initiates her emotional entanglements, is announced in a letter to her father. Her revived engagement to the rustic Giles Winterborne is threatened when he reads a letter indicating that he will lose his house on the death of John South. Grace's father, now bent on a socially upward marriage for her, shows Grace 'a heap of papers'. These title-deeds and bonds which she is to inherit are one means of persuading her that her 'sphere ought not to be middling', as it would be if she married Giles. After South's death and a letter from Felice Charmond confirming the loss of his property, Giles writes to Melbury, giving up Grace. She remorsefully corrects graffiti scrawled on his house to read 'Oh, Giles, you've lost your dwelling-place / And therefore, Giles, you'll *keep* your Grace.' Giles misreads it as the work of 'some idle boy' and ignores unknowingly the chance of reconciliation it offers.

The marriage of Grace to the local doctor, Edred Fitzpiers, and his liaison with Felice are also mapped out by a series of significant documents. At their first meeting he ingratiates himself with Grace by tearing up an agreement to purchase the corpse of her servant, Grammer Oliver, for dissection. This brings them into a relationship which results in marriage. Similarly a note from Felice summoning him to treat her is the reason for his meeting her. It is speedily followed by an affair which causes him to cancel by letter the purchase of a medical practice elsewhere which would remove him from her vicinity. A forgotten turnpike ticket leads his wife to realize that he has been visiting Felice. And when the discovery of his liaison results in injury at the hands of Grace's father, Fitzpiers elopes with his mistress and sends his wife 'the coldest of marital epistles'. This for a time ends the marriage.

There follows an abortive and painful attempt by Melbury to procure a divorce for Grace through the agency of a shifty lawyer's clerk, Beaucock. The supposed mechanism for the divorce is cited by Beaucock as the new law embodied in 'the new statute, twenty and twenty-one Vic., cap. eighty-five'. This creates a period of hope and uncertainty when Melbury writes to Grace and Giles from London, encouraging them to re-establish their relationship. Another letter ends their new happiness as Beaucock writes warning Giles that divorce is impossible.

Meantime Fitzpiers, to release himself from a now stale affair, taunts Felice with a letter from Marty South revealing that Felice's 'magnificent pile of hair' was made up 'of the writer's rather than her own'. Their separation enables Fitzpiers to initiate a reconciliation with Grace by a letter 'in the gentlest language'. He follows this with another carefully sentimental letter on St Valentine's Day. Grace, brooding on what to do, re-reads the marriage service. She finds the promises she made at her wedding 'a staggerer for a gentle woman of strong devotional sentiment'. Thus staggered, she succumbs again to Fitzpiers that night. The written word is dangerous and its consequences are unpredictable.

Within this strange framework of lives acted out and partly determined by reading or misreading, by using or misusing what is written, the narrative works to arrive at a reading (or understanding) of locations, events and even individuals with a Darwinian persistence. This mirrors Hardy's own practice in the *Life* when he notes in January 1886:

Cold weather brings out upon the faces of people, the *written* marks of their habits, vices, passions, and memories, as warmth brings out our paper writing in sympathetic [i.e. invisible] ink [my emphasis]. (p. 183)

The icy temperature allows him to reinterpret the true nature of the splotches in the face of a drunkard and to recognize what seemed a 'hectic flush' as a clear sign of disease.[8]

This interpretation of signs closely resembles Darwin's method of proceeding as, for instance, when he elicits the meaning of his observation that a severe winter killed as many as 80 per cent of the game birds in his grounds. Such a loss, he argues, is unexpected, given the fact that epidemics which kill 10 per cent of a human population would be regarded as extraordinarily severe. He concludes that although climate might seem to be irrelevant to evolutionary development, in so far as it 'chiefly acts in reducing food, it brings on the most severe struggle between the individuals . . .'[9] and so increases the mortality rate.

Like Darwin and other nineteenth-century scientists, the narrator in *The Woodlanders* presents himself as decoding meaning from the data he observes. In his case these are not only natural objects but artifacts. He notices carvings of initials on a door in Melbury's house and can read into them 'bygone generations' who lived here in past times. Giles, obsessed with watching Grace and her father, fingers these indentations mechanically and without interpreting them. Similarly the narrator can read off from the possession by a household of a coffin-stool as much as he could distinguish about the status of a squire or nobleman from his possession of 'old helmets or shields'. The stool means that 'the social position of the household in the past' was that of a 'well-to-do villager, whose tenure was by copy of court-roll'. Like Darwin's flora and fauna or Lyell's rocks, these present objects can be translated into their past history.

The countrymen and women share with the narrator this knowledge of the local language in which meaning is encoded. Giles, when not distraught, can observe his surroundings with the precision of a Sherlock Holmes (whose first adventure appeared in print in the same year as *The Woodlanders*). He can interpret even the 'mud picture' of footprints, which reveal to him that Grace and her father have passed that way. Examining the muddy soil, he sees 'amongst the large sole-and-heel tracks an impression of a slighter kind from a boot that was obviously not local'. He can make the inference since he knows 'all the cobblers' patterns in that district because they were very few to know'.

Giles is the most skilful of readers amongst the villagers but he is matched by John South's daughter, Marty, who is also familiar with the language of the woodlands in which they have always lived:

The casual glimpses which the ordinary population bestowed upon that wondrous world of sap and leaves called the Hintock woods had been with these two, Giles and Marty, a clear gaze. They had been possessed of its finer mysteries as of commonplace knowledge; had been able *to read its hieroglyphs as ordinary writing* . . . together they had, with the run of the years, mentally collected those remoter *signs and symbols* which seen in few were *of runic obscurity*, but all together made an *alphabet* [my emphases].

The suggestion of a visible past which only these two can perceive is captured by the assertion that they alone have the secret of the ancient and angular runic alphabet which was carved on stone or wood before writing on skin or parchment was known.

Other indigenous inhabitants of the woods know the current forms of the local signs and symbols because they have had to learn them in order to carry on a daily existence:

The countryman, who is obliged to judge the time of day from changes in external nature, sees a thousand successive tints and traits in the landscape which are never discerned by him who hears the regular chime of a clock, because they are never in request.

This gives them the key to interpreting each other as they 'use their eyes' on the taciturn Giles, after the loss of his property:

The infinitesimal movement of muscle, curve, hair, and wrinkle, which when accompanied by a voice goes unregarded, is watched and *translated* in the lack of it, till virtually the whole surrounding circle of familiars is charged with the reserved one's moods and meanings [my emphasis].

The presence of a common code for human beings and growing things makes possible the translation of one into the other. Occasionally the transposition is of man into nature, and even more occasionally it is benign. Grace remembers Giles in this way:

He rose upon her memory as the fruit-god and the wood-god in alternation: sometimes leafy and smeared with green lichen, . . . sometimes cider-stained and starred with apple-pips.

More usually the transposition is of nature into the human and it is to show a common blight. A sunless day emerges 'like a dead-born child', with a 'bleared white visage'. At Little Hintock can be seen 'pale dangling arms of ivy which had crept through the joints of the tiles and were groping in vain for some support, their leaves being dwarfed and sickly for want of sunlight'. Trees reveal 'old amputations' and are wrinkled 'like an old crone's face'. Sometimes they seem to be 'in a cold sweat' like 'haggard grey phantoms'. At dusk the surfaces of plants appear like 'weak, lidless eyes'. On older trees 'huge lobes of fungi grow like lungs'.

Outsiders like Edred Fitzpiers, Felice Charmond and her anonymous lover who insults Giles by offering money in return for kindness, do not know what local *mores* mean. They are unfamiliar with the implications of the villagers' actions and appearances. Fitzpiers mistakes Giles' melancholy taciturnly for dislike of Grace. He accepts Grace's false confession of infidelity at face value and finds her more alluring because of it. Felice misinterprets the bells on Giles' huge timber-load, before which she is compelled to back her two carriages, as triumphalist and not as a warning of approach which, if heeded, could have prevented their confrontation. Fitzpiers is bored by a winter spent in the country because he lacks the grammar and lexicon which would enable him to read its present significance and its past history. Such linguistic tools would be provided by 'an almost exhaustive biographical or historical acquaintance with every object, animate or inanimate, within the observer's horizon'. Such knowledge would allow him to perceive 'whose feet have traversed the fields which look so grey from his windows, . . . whose creaking plough has turned those sods from time to time; whose hands planted the trees . . . whose horses and hounds have torn through that underwood.' This reinscribing of the past would in turn allow him to read into his surroundings 'bygone domestic dramas of love, jealousy, revenge, or disappointment, that have been enacted in the cottages, the mansions, the street, or on the green'. Similarly, to Felice, her dead husband's collection of man-traps are museum objects. To Tim Tangs, the husband of Fitzpiers' village mistress, Suke Damson, they are an appropriate form of revenge for a poacher of wives as once for the poachers of game.

The behavioural language of these middle-class individuals, who are aliens both socially and geographically, is equally unfamiliar and baffling to the native woodlanders. To the latter Felice as a landowner is a deity who controls their fate and also, confusingly, a 'wicked woman' who sits down to dinner 'in a gown no higher than her elbows'.

They take Fitzpiers to be 'some rare kind of gentleman and doctor', 'descended from the clouds' and he confounds them by marrying Grace Melbury, one of themselves. For the narrator what distinguishes these outsiders is a high degree of self-awareness, a perception of themselves as social performers. Their appearance and behaviour is not, like the woodlanders, as unaffected as that of a plant or tree; it is theatrical. They see themselves as taking part in a high drama. Like Othello, they perceive themselves as third persons observed by others. They adjust what they say, do and wear accordingly. This theatricality is made clear. Felice has been 'a play-actress' in poorer days and uses the skill of 'her art' to disguise Fitzpiers when he needs to leave the neighbourhood unnoticed. She stages her first encounter with him so as to appear a seductively wicked, cigarette-smoking *femme fatale*, reclining elegantly on her couch. Her deep purple clothing is in fact a dressing gown which, as a form of undress, signals sexual accessibility. She is later aware that the pretence of Fitzpiers visiting her only as a doctor is seen by the country people as 'a farce'. Fitzpiers similarly over-acts the part of a conventional romantic lover towards Grace, saying 'I almost wept when I awoke and found that you had appeared to me in Time, but not in Space, alas!' The narrator notes ironically: 'At moments there was something theatrical in the delivery of Fitzpiers's effusion; yet it would have been inexact to say it was intrinsically theatrical.'

Grace, still half a village girl, vainly attempts to produce the appropriate response 'like an inexperienced actress, who having at last taken up her position on the boards, and spoken her speeches, does not know how to move off'. The melodramatic scenario is picked up by the third outsider to appear in the area. Felice's jealous ex-lover and her future assassin is observed by Giles on Midsummer Eve walking through the woods in evening dress making 'strange gestures, like those of one who is rehearsing a scene to himself'. Possibly the scene he is rehearsing does eventually take place when he shoots Felice with fatal results. But their theatricality and melodramatic behaviour ties together Fitzpiers, Felice and the stranger from South Carolina, giving them a group identity. What they perceive is not the result of disinterested observation of externals but of preconceived notions about themselves.

Typically it is Fitzpiers who theorizes this when he explains to Giles how he interprets the act of falling in love. It is, he asserts, 'joy accompanied by an idea which we project against any suitable object in the line of our vision, just as the rainbow iris is projected against an oak, ash, or elm tree indifferently.' If some other approximately suitable woman had appeared when Grace did, he would have 'fallen in love' with her instead. This denial of the importance of external facts, their precise detail, is the opposite of what the working class is seen as doing. Like Humpty Dumpty the middle-class characters are in the position of making things mean what they want them to mean and using their social skills and independence to sustain and exploit their fictions.

It appears that a determining factor in how people decipher the signs about them is social class. While the woodlanders can interpret what they know in both inanimate and human phenomena, they are vulnerable to the self-interested flexibility of their 'superiors'. When Melbury shows Felice that Fitzpiers' adultery is destructive to others, her picture of it as a grand passion is disturbed. She is temporarily aware that others see the play she is acting in as sordid. But confidence in her theatrical identity as victim of tragic passion soon returns. Giles, on the other hand, recognizes that his love for Grace is hopeless but cannot change it. His inflexibility leads to his death from which no good comes to anyone. Grace, who oscillates between the two classes, finally learns the middle-class art of compromise as she returns to Fitzpiers and the self-deception which allows her to feel it as dutiful.

The inscription of the natural world and its human population as one large evolutionary text requiring decoding draws in humanity in a way that Darwin himself did not dare to in 1859. When he made an attempt in *The Descent of Man*, after dealing with physical evolution, he landed himself in the difficulties necessitated by dealing with a human moral sense which devalued self-interest:

The greatest difficulty which presents itself, when we are driven to the above conclusion on the origins of man is the high standard of intellectual power and of moral disposition which he has attained.[10]

The problem was compounded by the kind of language into which his account of evolution had to be translated. In *The Origin of Species* he had needed a transparent medium which would not distort his data. But the one medium available was loaded with emotional associations and moral and social values. Pointing this out in 1959, one critic concluded that Darwin's difficulty arose because he

did not have the word 'ecology'. He was in fact an ecological thinker, and in ecology words like 'competition' and 'cooperation' are too inexact, too value-weighted, too metaphorical and too anthropomorphic to be used at all.[11]

The irony of time has ensured that the word 'ecology' is itself now value-weighted, and has illustrated the fact that there is no method of sterilizing words to keep them value-free.

Darwin did attempt such sterilization of the meaning of words. In Chapter Three of *The Origin of Species* he writes that he uses its title 'Struggle for Existence' 'in a large and metaphorical sense' and attempts to restrict the meaning of the metaphor:

Two canine animals in a time of dearth, may be truly said to struggle with each other which shall get food and live. But a plant on the edge of a desert is said to struggle for life against the drought, though more properly it should be said to be dependent on the moisture.[12]

This spelling out of how far the metaphor is supposed to go cannot drain away the suggestion of agency in the phrase 'struggle for existence' which clashes with Darwin's thesis that those who are only *by chance* best adapted to their physical environment survive. The word 'survive' itself has, for him, to be limited to 'continuing to exist and producing progeny'.

The untrappable nature of meaning, the inability of the individual scientist to make signs mean what s/he wants them to mean, was increased by the free use made by scientists of language reverberating with echoes from many literary and religious discourses. Their narratives allude to other more overtly imaginative or 'fictional' narratives. Typically, Mantell in *The Wonders of Geology* (1839) wrote:

In the shapeless pebble that we tread upon, in the rude mass of rock or clay, the uninstructed eye would in vain seek for novelty or beauty; like the adventurer in the Eastern fable, the inquirer finds the cavern closed to his entrance, and the rock refusing to give up the treasures entombed within its stony sepulchre, till the talisman is obtained that can dissolve the enchantment, and unfold the marvellous secrets which have so long lain hidden.[13]

The talisman of course is an understanding of geology such as Mantell possesses.

Once human beings are woven into the evolutionary picture, the moral values and emotional associations that attach to the ideas of struggle, survival and being the fittest to survive become inescapable. Unlike Darwin, Hardy does not resist them but engages with the problems they present. This extension of the implications of evolution replaces Darwin's question 'How did this come to be so?' with new ones. Hardy questions not the How but 'the Whence and Wherefore of things' (General Preface to 1912 edition). Though he claimed never to have aimed at 'objectless [i.e. pointless] consistency' in his answers, he did not deny that he asked these questions.[14] His most overt probing of them occurs in *The Woodlanders*, where the sense of evolutionary development is omnipresent. In this context, key concepts are examined in the light of the moral dimension which Darwin had tried to erase from his language. Even his arguments in *The Descent of Man* work towards this erasure as he tries to subsume humanity's moral sense, in particular their valuing of selflessness, under 'the social instinct'. But in the strict terms of *The Origin of Species* self-interest is a positive good and selflessness is not valuable: the survival of the genetic line is the only form of success. In Hardy's text, however, the crucial notion of adaptation, the formula for survival, is reconsidered.

This is made clear by an earlier title suggested for the story by Hardy: 'Fitzpiers at Hintock'.[15] The juxtaposition of man and environment, of aristocratic foreign name and rural location, is the naming of an experiment in evolution. It is Grace who crystallizes this view of him as 'a tropical plant in a hedgerow', a plant that might be expected to wither, away from its exotic habitat. But Fitzpiers' distinctive characteristic is his potent sexuality, a factor in evolution which Darwin discusses in the second edition of *The Descent of Man* when he quotes approvingly Schopenhauer's statement that:

The final aim of all love-intrigues, be they comic or tragic, is really of more importance than all other ends in human life. What it all turns upon is the composition of the next generation.[16]

Fitzpiers' power of sexual attraction secures him a varied range of partners: Suke Damson, Felice and Grace. This power is so 'irresistible' and 'coercive' that it affects Grace 'like a dram' of liquor. Even he notices her 'curious susceptibility to his presence', which she is unable to conceal and is not entirely willing to feel. Despite his opportunistic seduction of Suke, his infidelity to Grace, and his fatal desertion of the pregnant Felice, he is left finally with a newly reconciled wife, the prospect of Melbury's money and a medical practice bought with an inheritance from a female relative – also presumably won by his masculine charm.

So pointed is Fitzpiers' sexual, social, and financial success that it evoked adverse criticism, at the time of the novel's publication, from those moralists who expected sin not to pay, at least in fiction:

Mr. Hardy ought not to have allowed this sensual and selfish liar, good-natured in an easy way though he certainly was, to be received back into his wife's favour and made happy on terms so easy as are here imposed on him.[17]

By its elaboration of Fitzpiers' sexual misdemeanours and his providential escape from the all-too-appropriate man-trap, the text draws attention to the way that lack of a moral sense can work as an aid to social survival and financial success. The moral sense, far from being a social instinct, is shown as an evolutionary irrelevance or even a hindrance.

On the other hand 'depravity', which in contemporary terms would have been an apt description of Fitzpiers' conduct, is not seen as a simple concept. It is for instance complicated by a view that temporarily possesses the narrator's mind as he decodes death and decay in the woodland and translates it into human terms:

Here, as everywhere, the Unfulfilled Intention, which makes life what it is, was as obvious as it could be among the depraved crowds of a city slum. The leaf was deformed, the curve was crippled, the taper was interrupted; the lichen ate the vigour of the stalk, and the ivy slowly strangled to death the promising sapling.

The opening of this passage accepts a reworking of the idea of the 'undeserving poor' to give it the evolutionary tinge which had some currency in the 1880s and 1890s. It alludes to the argument that the existence of a 'lower' level of poor, which had been a part of class ideology since the 1850s, was the result of interference with the evolutionary process by medical and sanitary improvements. White wrote in 1887 that because of improved conditions in large towns since the early nineteenth century 'thousands of such persons who would have died even fifty years ago' now survive.[18] This involves an equation of physical defectiveness and moral depravity as well as the implication that without interference natural processes will destroy the depraved, a view not easily reconciled with Fitzpiers' success.

Like other 'unadjusted impressions', depravity as an evolutionary mistake is emotionally evoked in a particular context of natural decay but takes no permanent place in the text. Both Fitzpiers and the city slum dwellers, however, do survive to problematize the idea that 'survival' applied to human beings can continue to mean only 'continuing to survive and producing progeny'. In practice, in relation to humanity the term commonly refers to more than the merely physical. Human survival is often seen as a sign of will-power or even stoicism. 'I'll survive' can be a brave assertion of the kind uttered in Hardy's novels by semi-heroic figures like Henchard in *The Mayor of Casterbridge*. His claim that 'My punishment is not greater than I can bear' is a poetic translation of the colloquial 'I'll survive'.

In *Tess of the D'Urbervilles* the narrator follows Angel Clare's thoughts on what constitutes a valuable moral character:

Who was the moral man? Still more pertinently who was the moral woman? The beauty or ugliness of a character lay not only in its achievements, but its aims and impulses; its true history lay not among things done but among things willed. (Chapter 49)

By this standard the kind of survival to be valued is moral survival, the maintenance of integrity such as Giles and Marty achieve. The ending of the narrative seems to reinforce this view. Marty eulogizes Giles over his grave:

Now, my own own love . . . you are mine and on'y mine; for she has forgot 'ee at last . . . If ever I forget your name let me forget home and heaven . . . But no, no, my love, I never can forget 'ee; for you was a *good* man, and did good things!

Then the narrator transfigures Marty in terms reminiscent of Wordsworth's 'The Solitary Reaper'. She is seen as a 'solitary and silent girl' with 'the marks of poverty and toil effaced by the misty hour', who

touched sublimity at points, and looked almost like a being who had rejected with indifference the attribute of sex for the loftier quality of abstract humanism.

The location of this scene at the end of the narrative gives it prominence. So too does the language, weighted with religious and poetic terms of approval. The enigmatic phrase 'abstract humanism' suggests both an ungendered figure and a being symbolizing humanistic ideals of (inexpedient) fidelity and selflessness.

But it would be unwise to read this as a general conclusion to a story concerned with what Darwin was prepared to recognize as 'love intrigues', the intricate network of sexual relationships. Like other ardent passages in Hardy's novels, the finale is strangely local. It is at odds with Marty's earlier sense of frustration and failure, her taunting graffiti and her destructive letter to Fitzpiers. Her bitterness seems to require Giles' death in order to remove it. What she is dedicating herself to in her semi-religious monologue is an empty and pointless life to be spent grieving for a man who rejected her, a technical 'possession' of him made possible by Grace's desertion. Similarly Giles embraces failure almost willingly. The increasing passivity and quietism of his reactions to Grace and Melbury's treatment as the revision of the text proceeded, along with the decrease in his ability to criticize Grace's heartless behaviour, define him as an oversimple organism. He is almost a natural victim. So there are no definitive answers to the moral Whence and Wherefore of things in this text.

For the evolutionary paradigm is not the only key to interpretation that Hardy uses. He also tries some of the touchstones of philosophy, poetry, drama: concepts of tragedy, ideas of Nemesis or vengeance. What he finds difficult to theorize is precisely the injustice of life that early critics of this novel accused him of underwriting. Little Hintock is not merely the setting for the working out of a Darwinian narrative but for a story which, in another equally valid perspective, is a drama 'of truly Sophoclean grandeur' in which momentarily Giles and Marty (as Iphigenia) seem to be involved. It is also a social drama in which miscommunication and incompatible mores between differing social groups precipitate trouble. Or is it an illustration of life's little ironies emanating from an unspecified source which can turn Felice's melodramatic play-acting into the real thing when she is shot by a rejected lover? The same irony can shadow happy moments or benign seasons with the inevitability of disillusion. 'Relentless Jehovah' or more often an unspecified Nemesis may be behind it all.

A factor in this polyvalent story of gloom is that of gender, which overrides even social class. Hardy's gradual arrival at the view that women get the worst of it in the long run which is to appear so powerfully in *Tess of the D'Urbervilles* and *Jude the Obscure* is a constant here. It is not assumed to be something explicable in terms of physiology; it is a social fact. Marty South, Suke Damson, Felice Charmond and Grace Fitzpiers (née Melbury) come from different social strata, spanning much of the social scale. All four women are at the disposition of men. Marty's poverty and later homelessness is the result of her father's mismanagement of affairs. Since she is neither rich nor beautiful, her passionate feelings and her sexuality are redundant. The only decisions available to her are limited and negative: the selling of her only claim to sexual attractiveness, her lustrous hair, to the already well-endowed Felice; the provision of a weapon that Fitzpiers can use – to discard a mistress of whom he is tired. Suke Damson comes from the same class as Marty but has all the sexual allure that the other girl lacks. Her willingness to take her pleasure with a handsome stranger in a convenient hayfield suggests a woman with some control over her life. But unlike her partner in the hayfield, she becomes emotionally dependent on him to the point where it sours an expedient marriage to a man of her own class. In fact her husband's jealousy of Fitzpiers causes him to lay the man-trap which becomes the trigger for another woman, Grace, to fall into her unfaithful husband's arms. Felice Charmond too is, as she says, carried like a cork 'upon the waves of masculine desire'. The first example of this is her landowning husband who brings her to the remote village in which she now finds herself a widow. Her elopement and apparent physical and emotional escape with Fitzpiers ends in her disgrace and death at the hands of another man while Fitzpiers is able to recapture his respectability.

Grace is first turned into a social mongrel by the genteel education imposed by her father and which she only belatedly explains was a painful experience: 'I was always a little despised by the other girls at school, because they knew where I came from, and that my parents were not in so good a station as theirs.' Beautiful, educated and with a rich father, she appears a likely candidate for social success and happiness. But pressured and manipulated by him, overcome by physical susceptibility, she drifts into a disastrous marriage. Marrying Fitzpiers is intended by Melbury to satisfy his own vicarious cravings for social advancement. It leaves Grace after her husband's elopement and the failed divorce attempt 'neither married nor single'. She is regarded even by her father as ruined by this state. He is ready to believe that a return to the despised Fitzpiers is 'the most respectable thing to do'.

Strikingly, Grace is the only individual who seems to have learnt anything of value from the events of the narrative. She gives at times an impression of increased maturity. This is when Fitzpiers is rumoured to be seriously injured and his mistresses, Suke and Felice, rush to visit his bedside. Ironically she accepts that they share her right to be there: 'You have a perfect right to go in there; who can have a better than either of you?' At this point a new feeling not previously predictable is created by a dispassionate assessment of the farcical situation:

A tenderness spread over Grace like a dew. It was well enough, conventionally, to address either one of them in the wife's regulation terms of virtuous sarcasm, as woman, creature or thing. But life, what was it, and who was she?

She now sees the women unconventionally as victims of the same man who 'had never really behaved towards either of them anyhow but selfishly'. Then she weeps: 'The tears which his possibly critical situation could not bring to her eyes surged over at the contemplation of these fellow-women.'

Her unconventionality extends to a feeling that she is no longer morally bound to Fitzpiers. This is a view that would be unsurprising in a 'new woman' like Sue Bridehead but one which is quite unforeseen in the previously orthodox Grace. However, like Sue Bridehead, she regresses from this liberal position. This does not happen because of guilt induced by some catastrophe on the scale of the deaths of Sue and Jude's children but because of what seems a combination of expediency and physical attraction to Fitzpiers. She rationalizes these reactions to herself as a belated recognition of the 'force' of her marriage vows. This priggish gloss allows her to return to her husband. It is now that her hitherto transparent motives are no longer on view. Her expectations of the future are not revealed. In the text used in this edition, significant comment is left to one of the search party of woodlanders after the missing Grace has been found at a hotel reconciled with her husband: 'She's got him quite tame. But how long 'twill last I can't say.' In the 1887 edition a comment was added by Melbury: 'Well – he's her husband . . . but it's a forlorn hope for her and God knows how it will end!' This was extended to a prediction in 1896:

'Well – he's her husband – and let her take him back to her bed if she will! . . . But let her bear in mind that the woman walks and laughs somewhere at this very moment whose neck he'll be coling next year as he does hers tonight; and as he did Felice Charmond's last year; and Suke Damson's the year afore!'

It is possible to see Grace's regression as a piece of cynicism, a kind of weakness or a re-emergence of the view of women's nature and role inculcated by social conditioning. What does not seem to be in doubt is that she will get the worst of it in the long run, in spite of her apparent ability at an earlier stage to overcome the restrictions of convention. Gender, at least in this text, is an inescapable fate.

Notes

1. R. G. Cox, *Thomas Hardy, The Critical Heritage* (New York: Barnes and Noble, 1970), pp. 152, 153, 142.

2. G. A. Mantell, *The Wonders of Geology or a Fundamental Exposition of Geological Phenomena* (London: Relfe and Fletcher, 1838), p. 2.

3. W. Whitney, *Language and the Study of Language* (N. Trübner & Company, 1867), p. 282.

4. Charles Darwin, *The Origin of Species by Means of Natural Selection or the Preservation of Favoured Races in the Struggle for Life*, ed. J. W. Burrow (London: Penguin Books, 1968), p. 316.

5. D. Taylor, *Hardy's Literary Language and Victorian Philology* (Oxford: Clarendon Press, 1993), p. 306.

6. W. Barnes, *Selected Poems*, ed. Thomas Hardy (London: Henry Frowde, 1908), pp. vii–viii.

7. Taylor, *Hardy's Literary Language*, p. 119.

8. M. Millgate (ed.), *The Life and Work of Thomas Hardy* (London: The Macmillan Press, 1982), p. 183.

9. Darwin, *The Origin of Species*, p. 121.

10. Charles Darwin, *The Descent of Man and Selection in Relation to Sex* (London: John Murray, 1871), p. 390.

11. M. Peckham, 'Darwinism and Darwinisticism', *Victorian Studies*, 3 (1956), p. 20.

12. Darwin, *The Origin of Species*, p. 116.

13. Mantell, *The Wonders of Geology*, p. 3.

14. Thomas Hardy, *General Preface*, Wessex Edition I (1912).

15. D. Kramer, 'Revisions and Vision: Thomas Hardy's *The Woodlanders*', *Bulletin of the New York Public Library*, vol. 75 (April 1971), p. 201.

16. Darwin, *The Descent of Man*, (Second edition, 1874) p. 609.

17. Cox, *Thomas Hardy*, pp. 143–4.

18. G. S. Jones, *Outcast London, A Study in the Relationship between Classes in Victorian Society* (Oxford: Clarendon Press, 1971), p. 287.

FURTHER READING

Biographical Material

Gibson, J., *Thomas Hardy: Interviews and Recollections* (London: Macmillan Press, 1999).

Millgate, M., *Thomas Hardy: A Biography* (Oxford: Oxford University Press, 1982). The definitive biography and only reliable one.

—— (ed.), *The Life and Work of Thomas Hardy* (London: The Macmillan Press, 1982). An edition of the work published by Hardy's second wife Florence but which is largely by Hardy himself.

Critical Edition

Kramer, D., ed., *The Woodlanders* (Clarendon Press, 1981).

Books on Hardy's Novels

Boumelha, P., *Thomas Hardy and Women: Sexual Ideology and Narrative Form* (Brighton: Harvester Press, 1982).

Butler, L. St. J., *Alternative Hardy* (London: The Macmillan Press, 1989).

Dave, J. C., *The Human Predicament in Hardy's Novels* (Atlantic Highlands, N.J.: Humanities Press, 1985).

Fisher, J., *The Hidden Hardy* (London: The Macmillan Press, 1992).

Frederico, A., *Masculine Identity in Hardy and Gissing* London and Toronto: Associated University Presses, 1991), especially chapter 3.

Garson, M., *Hardy's Fables of Integrity: Women, Body, Text* (Oxford: Clarendon Press, 1991).

Goode, J., *Thomas Hardy: The Offensive Truth* (Oxford: Basil Blackwell, 1988).

Ingham, P., *Authors in Context: Thomas Hardy* (Oxford: Oxford University Press, 2003).

——, *Thomas Hardy* (Hemel Hempstead: Harvester Wheatsheaf, 1989).

Morgan, R., *Women and Sexuality in the Novels of Thomas Hardy* (London and New York: Routledge, 1988).

Widdowson, P., *Hardy in History: A Study in Literary Sociology* (London: Routledge, 1989).

Articles on The Woodlanders

Ball, D., 'Tragic Contradiction in Hardy's *The Woodlanders*', *Ariel*, 18 (1987), pp. 17–25.

Boumelha, P., 'The Patriarchy of Class: *Under the Greenwood Tree, Far from the Madding Crowd* and *The Woodlanders*' in D. Kramer (ed.), *Cambridge Companion to Thomas Hardy* (Cambridge: Cambridge University Press, 1999), pp. 130–45.

Buckler, W., 'Towards a Poetics of Hardy's Novels: *The Woodlanders*', *Dickens Studies Annual*, 14 (1985), pp. 327–36.

Giordano, F. R. jr., 'The Martyrdom of Giles Winterborne', *Thomas Hardy Annual*, 2 (1984), pp. 61–78.

Glance, J. C., 'The Problem of the Man-trap in Hardy's *The Woodlanders*', *Victorian Newsletter*, 78 (Fall 1990), pp. 26–9.

Higgins, L., 'Strange Webs of Melancholy: Shelleyan Echoes in *The Woodlanders*', *Thomas Hardy Annual*, 5 (1987), pp. 38–46.

Kramer, D., '*Revisions and Vision*: Thomas Hardy's *The Woodlanders*', *Bulletin of the New York Public Library*, 75 (1971), pp. 195–230, 248–82.

Morrison, R. D., 'Love and Evolution in Thomas Hardy's *The Woodlanders*', *Kentucky Philological Review*, 6 (1991), pp. 32–7.

Peck, J., 'Hardy's *The Woodlanders*: The Too Transparent Web', *English Literature in Transition*, 24(3) (1981), pp. 147–54.

Quéré, H. and Sénéchal, J., 'Hardy's Alternatives in *The Woodlanders*, chapter 39', *Alternative Hardy*, ed. L. St. J. Butler (Macmillan, 1989), pp. 173–203.

Radford, A., 'The Unmarried Fertility Figure in Hardy's *The Woodlanders* (1887)', *Victorian Newsletter*, 99 (2001), pp. 24–32.

Skilling, M. R., 'Investigations into the Country of *The Woodlanders*', *Thomas Hardy Journal*, 5.8(3), pp. 62–7.

The idea which was the germ of *The Woodlanders*, according to Hardy himself, dates back to some ten years earlier. In 1875, because of the success of his rural novel *Far from the Madding Crowd* (1874), he was pressed by the *Cornhill Magazine* for another work. In response, as he tells in his autobiographical writing, he began on 'a woodland story he had thought of (which later took shape in *The Woodlanders*)' (*Life*, p. 105). But he put it aside to 'make a plunge in a new and untried direction' in *The Hand of Ethelberta* (*Life*, p. 105). Only in 1884, after agreeing to produce a new serialized novel for *Macmillan's Magazine*, did he turn to it again. The definitive account of the history of the text was published by Dale Kramer in 1981.[1] The present edition is much indebted to this.

After some delay in writing it, *The Woodlanders* was completed on 4 February 1887 (*Life*, p. 192); was first published in monthly serial parts (without illustrations) from May 1886 to April 1887; and simultaneously but in weekly parts in America in *Harper's Bazaar*. The first English (three) volume edition appeared from Macmillan in March 1887; and the American one from Harper & Brothers in the same year. Immediately after this it appeared from Macmillan in a cheap one-volume format in August 1887.

So during the year 1886–7 Hardy was busy not only writing but revising his text. The manuscript (now in the Dorset County Museum) which was used as printers' copy already shows layers of revision. And when he received proofs of the English serial, Hardy added revisions to one set before despatching them to Harper's for their serial. Then he made more revisions to another set for use in the American and volume edition. For the English serial itself, he revised a third set further for *Macmillan's Magazine*; and for the English (three) volume edition he made yet more alterations.

The next major revision took place eight years or so later when

Hardy's new publishers Osgood, McIlvaine brought out the first collected edition of his novels, The Wessex Novels (1895–6) in which *The Woodlanders*, dated 1896, appeared as volume VII. The title of the collection indicates one important feature of this edition. It was now that Hardy revised place names and distances in the texts to lend topographical coherence and a new kind of identity to the concept of his half-imagined, half-real region of Wessex that had gradually emerged over twenty-five years of novel writing. The name was taken from the ancient Anglo-Saxon kingdom of Wessex over which Alfred the Great had ruled. But it is not the case that all places referred to can be certainly identified with actual locations in Dorset and the surrounding areas. One example of this uncertainty is the location of Little Hintock itself. Hardy, having identified it as having 'more of *Melbury Osmond* in it than of Minterne',[2] corrected this to 'a hamlet anywhere within 2 miles' of Melbury Osmond.[3] Some twenty-five years later he 'confessed' that 'I do not know myself where the hamlet is more precisely' than as it is explained in the narrative (1912 Preface to *The Woodlanders*) – by stating that it is overlooked by 'High Stoy' and 'Bubb-Down Hill'.[4]

After a later change of publishers to Macmillan (who reprinted the Wessex Novels as the Uniform Edition in 1903), a new collected version was published in 1912–13. This is the Wessex Edition, the last complete edition to be revised by Hardy himself, and *The Woodlanders* appeared as volume VI in 1912. (For the Mellstock Edition of 1919–20, only *A Pair of Blue Eyes* was significantly altered by the author.)

These are the authoritative texts of *The Woodlanders* and they constitute a single line of development. There are very many revisions but all are relatively minor. Some of them are evidently the result of changes of mind, others relate partly to standards of taste or propriety prevailing over some twenty-five years (1887–1912), particularly in sexual matters and religious reference.

The manuscript shows many deletions, substitutions and additions. Edred Fitzpiers was Edgar Fitz Rayne until part way through the text when he became Edgar Fitzpiers. He survived as Edgar into the serial version and became Edred only in 1887. Giles, on the other hand, was only briefly an original Ambrose. The manuscript also includes an account of a meeting in chapter 30 between Fitzpiers and Felice Charmond in church watched angrily by Melbury, which was not printed until Kramer included it in his edition in 1981.

The largest revision of the text, however, was made for the 1887 three-volume first English edition. The extent of such changes is surprising in view of Hardy's bland statements in letters to Frederick Macmillan in February 1887. He spoke only of possibly shortening 'passages that seem tedious'[5] and of dealing with 'a few discrepancies here and there in the serial issue'.[6] True, the alterations did not include major changes in the plot but they did affect characterization. Further, revisions relating to individual characters naturally affected the balance between them. This was a topic on which Hardy revealed an explicit interest when he wrote about the illustrations for *The Return of the Native* to Arthur Hopkins, indicating the relative importance of the characters by numbering them from one to five.[7]

The most noticeable of these adjustments are to the character of Giles Winterborne who is a distinctly harder man before the 1887 text. In earlier versions he shows a 'dry' rather than a 'shy' self-control (1887 i.124); before Grace Melbury's return from her fashionable school he is said to be not only 'doubtful' (as in 1887) but 'a trifle cynical' (i.76) about her father's account of her newly acquired superiority. When Melbury shows reluctance to allow him contact with his daughter, Giles earlier reflected with some 'causticity of humour' on the man's wavering about the betrothal that he himself encouraged in the first place, rather than 'regretted' it. In the pre-1887 texts the 'wary grimness' (i.294) with which he evades Fitzpiers' questions about the unknown girl he has seen is attributed to his character as much as to circumstances which are the only cause in 1887. This tougher earlier version of Giles could view the newly returned Grace critically and consider himself 'not altogether her fool' (i.79). He could address her sarcastically 'with mock awe' (i.166) when she talked over his head. Grace herself felt that her regret over the attraction Fitzpiers has for her was made worse by 'the silent almost sarcastic criticism apparent in Winterborne's air towards her' (ii.105). The omission of these references in 1887 results in a loss of detachment and awareness in Giles that leaves him a meek and passive character.

One result of Giles' passivity and consequent humility is to throw Fitzpiers' proactiveness into sharper relief. This is especially so because in the 1887 text Fitzpiers (who seems to have started off in the manuscript as some kind of land-agent) is given an enhancement of social status which is further increased in 1912. In 1887 it takes the form of a minor character's assertion that 'Though he belongs to the oldest, ancientest family in the county [later 'country'], he's stooped to make hisself useful like any common genius' (i.117). While passivity makes Giles' love for Grace more idealistic, in 1887 Fitzpiers originally intends only 'a vulgar intimacy' (ii.38) with her, in contrast to the earlier reading 'a vulgar flirtation'. He becomes a more complex character as Giles becomes simpler.

The balance between the two central female figures, Grace Melbury and Felice Charmond, also shifts. Felice, a rich landowner and *femme fatale*, becomes less dominant in 1887, a decline continued in the 1896 edition. In the manuscript she had been specifically described as 'the daughter of an eminent painter'; in 1887 this claim is no longer made. It is merely stated that she does not care about the mysterious merit attaching to 'family antiquity' (i.150). Though she is only twenty-eight her lush beauty is described in 1887 as 'not a little worn' (ii.294). An addition to 1887 refers to a rumour that her death was not entirely the result of a shot from a jealous ex-lover but 'from the effect of fright upon her condition at the time' (iii.233). This reference to a possible pregnancy has an ambiguous force: it characterizes her as a typical fallen woman at the same time as stressing her vulnerability.

Grace, on the other hand, develops from 1887 onwards more positively away from the stereotype of the chaste wife. Even though married to Fitzpiers she shows some signs of sexual feeling for Giles. This becomes increasingly evident in later texts but the beginnings show in the latter part of the 1887 version. Hoping for a divorce from the unfaithful Fitzpiers, she speaks not 'archly' as in early versions, but 'invitingly' (iii.87) to Giles when pressing him to take a solitary walk with her. Later, when he knows but she does not that divorce is impossible, she urges him to kiss her: ' "Then why don't you do what you want to?" She was almost pouting at his hesitation' (iii.119). In 1887 this was not to be expected from a heroine already married to another man, but the text is in general franker than in earlier versions over sexual matters. Fitzpiers' seduction of Suke Damson in the hayfield has extra references to their lying on the hay together. And the chapter which describes it reinstates the sentence which was found in the manuscript but omitted from the serial: 'It was daybreak before Fitzpiers and Suke Damson re-entered Little Hintock' (ii.82).

In the version of the novel which appeared in 1896 as a volume of the Wessex Novels, further revisions are made, in line with those in 1887. Significantly several show Grace moving further away from the stereotype of passive and asexual femininity in a way that alters the balance between her and Felice yet more. Some such changes occur in scenes where the two are together. When the two women are lost and distraught in the wood together, Felice makes a confession which she can only whisper. In earlier versions this elicits from Grace 'Can it be – can it be!' To this is added in 1896 an exclamation of extraordinary frankness for the time: 'He's had you' (ii.325). Later after Fitzpiers' accident his former mistress, Suke, and his current mistress, Felice, rush to the Melburys' house to be at his side. To Grace's speech as she lets them into Fitzpiers' empty bedroom is added in 1896: 'Wives all, let's enter together!' (iii.39). Where in earlier texts she had pitied the two as 'fellow-women' she now sees in them 'fellow-women whose relations with him were as close as her own – without its conventionality' (iii.40).

Grace's feelings for Giles also become explicit in the episode where she hides in his hut while he sleeps outside and develops the fever which kills him. When finally she suspects his illness and summons him, in 1887 she merely urges him to come in. To this is added in 1896: 'I want you here!' and to her second summons 'I don't mind what they say or what they think any more' is added a desperate: 'Come to me!' (iii.169).

In this edition too Felice is downgraded further by an added reference to her past promiscuity. The jealous lover who finally kills her had formerly been described as 'that continental follower on whom she had once smiled'. To this is added in 1896 that he is one 'among others too numerous to name' (ii.302).

The increase in sexual frankness in 1896 extends beyond this development of character. After Giles' death in the hut Fitzpiers in 1887 says to Grace, 'You say you have been living here'; in 1896, 'You say you have been living here with him' (iii.198). When she allows her father to infer that she and Giles were lovers he had lamented, 'What has come upon us', to which he now adds in 1896, 'through your giving yourself to him' (iii.206).

But perhaps the most important addition to this version is that made in the section after Grace returns to her unfaithful husband. It is one which projects the narrative beyond the limits of the novel through Melbury's prediction of the Fitzpiers' future. The one-volume English edition (1887) had already inserted: 'Well – he's her husband,' Melbury said to himself. 'But it's a forlorn hope for her; and God knows how it will end!' In 1896 this became:

'Well – he's her husband,' Melbury said to himself, 'and let her take him back to her bed if she will! . . . But let her bear in mind that the woman walks and laughs somewhere at this very moment whose neck he'll be coling next year as he does hers tonight; and as he did Felice Charmond's last year; and Suke Damson's the year afore! . . . It's a forlorn hope for her; and God knows how it will end' (iii.308).

The last version of the text in the 1912 Wessex Edition (volume VI) carries on the development in detail which began in 1887. The speech in which Grace summons Giles to join her in the hut had already been changed to a direct invitation in 1896 and is now further coloured by the addition of 'dearest' (iii.169). Even Marty, finding herself alone at Giles' grave, is allowed to recognize not just as in earlier versions 'where Mrs. Fitzpiers was then' but that 'Mrs. Fitzpiers was by that time in the arms of another man' (iii.315).

And at this stage the elaboration of Fitzpiers' aristocratic lineage continues. Two explicit references are added about his being descended through his mother from 'the Lords Baxby of Sherton' (ii.109) and so to an 'extinct earldom' (iii.88). Peripheral to the narrative are alterations which attribute the pulling down of Winterborne's house to Felice Charmond's agent and using it to illustrate 'the landlords' principle at this date of getting rid of cottages wherever possible' (ii.176).

The Wessex Edition is known for its overall revision of dialect forms (such as changing *ye* to *'ee*). This cannot properly be described as making the language of dialect speakers more authentic or realistic.[8] Hardy is not attempting to transpose/translate their speech into dialect but employing common conventions as to such use in literature. This he makes explicit in 1878 when he writes that: 'If a writer attempts to exhibit on paper the precise accents of a rustic speaker he disturbs the proper balance of a true representation.'[9]

In revising this aspect of earlier versions of the novels, Hardy had removed some authentic but obtrusive dialect forms from particular speakers. In 1912 he was quite prepared to insert or alter such noticeable forms occasionally, as he does twice with Grammer Oliver's language in *The Woodlanders*. Presumably this was done to achieve what he perceived as 'the proper balance' in relation to the speaker's social position and to the immediate context.

The present edition uses the first English (three) volume edition for both substantives and accidentals. It emends only obvious errors. Readings from the later texts are given in the Notes.

Notes

1. Thomas Hardy, *The Woodlanders*, ed. Dale Kramer (Oxford: Clarendon Press, 1981); and Dale Kramer, 'Revisions and Vision: Thomas Hardy's *The Woodlanders*', *Bulletin of the New York Public Library*, 75 (1971), 195–230, 248–82.
2. *Letters*, i.163.
3. *Letters*, i.164.
4. 1912 Preface to *The Woodlanders*.
5. *Letters*, i.161.
6. *Letters*, i.162.
7. *Letters*, i.52.
8. Patricia Ingham, 'Dialect in the Novels of Hardy and George Eliot' in G. Watson (ed.), *Literary English since Shakespeare* (London: Oxford University Press, Oxford, New York, 1971), pp. 347–63.
9. *Athenaeum*, 30 November 1878, p. 688.

THE WOODLANDERS

BY

THOMAS HARDY

IN THREE VOLUMES

VOL. I.

London

MACMILLAN AND CO.

AND NEW YORK

1887

VOLUME I

The rambler who, for old association's sake, should trace the forsaken coach-road running almost in a meridional line from Bristol to the south shore of England, would find himself during the latter half of his journey in the vicinity of some extensive woodlands, interspersed with apple-orchards. Here the trees, timber or fruit-bearing as the case may be, make the wayside hedges ragged by their drip and shade, their lower limbs stretching in level repose over the road, as though reclining on the insubstantial air. At one place, where Rubdon Hill is crossed, a bank slopes up to the trees on the left hand, while on the right spreads a deep and silent vale. The spot is lonely, and when the days are darkening the many gay ones now perished who have rolled over the hill, the blistered soles that have trodden it, and the tears that have wetted it, return upon the mind of the loiterer.

The physiognomy of a deserted highway expresses solitude to a degree that is not reached by mere dales or downs, and bespeaks a tomb-like stillness more emphatic than that of glades and pools. The contrast of what is with what might be, probably accounts for this. To step, for instance, at the place under notice, from the edge of the plantation into the adjoining pale thoroughfare, and pause amid its emptiness for a moment, was to exchange by the act of a single stride the simple absence of human companionship for an incubus of the forlorn.

At this spot, on the lowering evening of a by-gone winter's day, there stood a man who had thus indirectly entered upon the scene from a stile hard by, and was temporarily influenced by some such feeling of being suddenly more alone than before he had emerged upon the highway.

It could be seen by a glance at his rather finical style of dress that he did not belong to the country proper; and from his air, after a while, that though there might be a sombre beauty in the scenery, music in the breeze, and a wan procession of coaching ghosts in the sentiment of this old turnpike-road, he was mainly puzzled about the way.

He looked north and south, and mechanically prodded the ground with his walking-stick. A closer glance at his face corroborated the testimony of his clothes. Nothing irradiated it; the expression enthroned there was absolute submission to and belief in a little assortment of forms and habitudes.

At first not a soul appeared who could enlighten him as he desired, or seemed likely to appear that night. But presently a slight noise of labouring wheels, and the steady dig of a horse's shoe-tips became audible; and there loomed, in the notch of hill and plantation that the road formed here, a carrier's van drawn by a single horse.

The vehicle was half full of passengers, mostly women. He held up his stick at its approach, and the woman who was driving drew rein.

"I've been trying to find a short way to Little Hintock[1] this last half hour, Mrs. Dollery," he said. "But though I've been to Great Hintock and Hintock House half a dozen times, I am at fault about the small village. You can help me, I dare say?"

She assured him that she could – that as she went to Great Hintock her van passed near it – that it was only up the lane branching out of the road into which she was about to turn. "Though," continued Mrs. Dollery, " 'tis such a little small place that, as a town gentleman, you'd need have a candle and lantern to find it if ye don't know where 'tis. Bedad! I wouldn't live there if they'd pay me to. Now at Great Hintock you do see the world a bit."

He mounted and sat beside her, with his feet outwards, where they were ever and anon brushed over by the horse's tail.

This van was rather a movable attachment of the roadway than an extraneous object, to those who knew it well. The old horse, whose hair was of the roughness and colour of heather, whose leg-joints, shoulders, and hoofs were distorted by harness and drudgery from colthood – though if all had their rights he ought, symmetrical in outline, to have been picking the herbage of some Eastern plain[2] instead of tugging here – had trodden this road almost daily for twenty years. Even his subjection was not made congruous throughout, for, the harness being too short, his tail was not drawn through the crupper, so that the breeching slipped awkwardly to one side. He knew every subtle incline of the six or seven miles of ground between Hintock and Sherton Abbas – the market town to which he journeyed – as accurately as any surveyor could have learnt it by a Dumpy level.[3]

The vehicle had a square black tilt which nodded with the motion of the wheels, and at a point in it over the driver's head was a hook to which the reins were hitched at times, forming a catenary curve[4] from the horse's shoulders. Somewhere about the axles was a loose chain, whose only known purpose was to clink as it went. Mrs. Dollery, having to hop up and down many times in the service of her passengers, wore, especially in windy weather, short leggings under her gown for modesty's sake; and instead of a bonnet a felt hat tied down with a handkerchief, to guard against an ear-ache to which she was frequently subject. In the rear of the van was a glass window which she cleaned with her pocket-hand kerchief every market-day before starting. Looking at the van from the back, the spectator could thus see, through its interior, a square piece of the same sky and landscape that he saw without, but intruded on by the profiles of the seated passengers, who, as they rumbled onward, their lips moving and heads nodding in animated private converse, remained in happy unconsciousness that their mannerisms and facial peculiarities were sharply defined to the public eye.

This hour of coming home from market was the happy one, if not the happiest, of the week for them. Snugly ensconced under the tilt they could forget the sorrows of the world without, and survey life and recapitulate the incidents of the day with placid smiles.

The passengers in the back part formed a group to themselves, and while the newcomer spoke to the proprietress, they indulged in a confidential chat about him as about other people, which the noise of the van rendered inaudible to himself and Mrs. Dollery sitting forward.

" 'Tis Barber Percomb – he that's got the waxen woman[5] in his window," said one "What business can bring him out here at this time, and not a journeyman haircutter, but a master-barber that's left off his pole[6] because 'tis not genteel?"

They listened to his conversation, but the barber, though he had nodded and spoken genially, seemed indisposed to gratify the curiosity that he had aroused; and the unrestrained flow of ideas which had animated the inside of the van before his arrival was checked thenceforward.

Thus they rode on till they turned into a half-invisible little lane, whence, as it reached the verge of an eminence, could be discerned in the dusk, about half a mile to the right, gardens and orchards sunk in a concave, and, as it were, snipped out of the woodland. From this self-contained place rose in stealthy silence tall stems of smoke, which the eye of imagination could trace downward to their root on quiet hearthstones, festooned overhead with hams and flitches. It was one of those sequestered spots outside the gates of the world where may usually be found more meditation than action, and more listlessness than meditation; where reasoning proceeds on narrow premisses, and results in inferences wildly imaginative; yet where, from time to time, no less than in other places, dramas of a grandeur and unity truly Sophoclean[7] are enacted in the real, by virtue of the concentrated passions and closely-knit interdependence of the lives therein.

This place was the Little Hintock of the master-barber's search. The coming night gradually obscured the smoke of the chimneys, but the position of the wood-environed community could still be distinguished by a few faint lights, winking more or less ineffectually through the leafless boughs and the undiscernible songsters they bore, in the form of balls of feathers, at roost among them.

Out of the lane followed by the van branched a yet smaller lane, at the corner of which the barber alighted, Mrs. Dollery's van going on to the larger village, whose superiority to the despised smaller one as an exemplar of the world's movements was not particularly apparent in its means of approach.

"A very clever and learned young doctor, who, they say, is in league with the devil, lives in the place you be going to – not because there's anybody for'n to cure there, but because 'tis the middle of his district."

The observation was flung at the barber by one of the women at parting, as a last attempt to get at his errand that way.

But he made no reply, and without further pause plunged towards the umbrageous nook, and paced cautiously over the dead leaves which nearly buried the road or street of the hamlet. As very few people except themselves passed this way after dark, a majority of the denizens of Little Hintock deemed window-curtains unnecessary; and on this account their visitor made it his business to stop opposite the casements of each cottage that he came to, with a demeanour which showed that he was endeavouring to conjecture, from the persons and things he observed within, the whereabouts of somebody or other who resided here.

Only the smaller dwellings interested him; one or two houses, whose size, antiquity, and rambling appurtenances signified that notwithstanding their remoteness they must formerly have been, if they were not still, inhabited by people of a certain social standing, being neglected by him entirely. Smells of pomace, and the hiss of fermenting cider, which reached him from the back quarters of other tenements, revealed the recent occupation of some of the inhabitants, and joined with the scent of decay from the perishing leaves under foot.

Half a dozen dwellings were passed without result. The next, which stood opposite a tall tree, was in an exceptional state of radiance, the flickering brightness from the inside shining up the chimney and making a luminous mist of the emerging smoke. The interior, as seen through the window, caused him to draw up with a terminative air and watch. The house was rather large for a cottage, and the door, which opened immediately into the living-room, stood ajar, so that a riband of light fell through the opening into the dark atmosphere without. Every now and then a moth, decrepit from the late season, would flit for a moment across the outcoming rays and disappear again into the night.

CHAPTER II

In the room from which this cheerful blaze proceeded he beheld a girl seated on a willow chair, and busily working by the light of the fire, which was ample and of wood. With a bill-hook[1] in one hand,

and a leather glove, much too large for her, on the other, she was making spars, such as are used by thatchers, with great rapidity. She wore a leather apron for this purpose, which was also much too large for her figure. On her left hand lay a bundle of the straight, smooth hazel rods called spar-gads – the raw material of her manufacture; on her right a heap of chips and ends – the refuse – with which the fire was maintained; in front, a pile of the finished articles. To produce them she took up each gad, looked critically at it from end to end, cut it to length, split it into four, and sharpened each of the quarters with dexterous blows, which brought it to a triangular point precisely resembling that of a bayonet.

Beside her, in case she might require more light, a brass candlestick stood on a little round table, curiously formed of an old coffin-stool, with a deal top nailed on, the white surface of the latter contrasting oddly with the black carved oak of the substructure. The social position of the household in the past was almost as definitively shown by the presence of this article as that of an esquire or nobleman by his old helmets or shields. It had been customary for every well-to-do villager, whose tenure was by copy of court-roll,[2] or in any way more permanent than that of the mere cotter, to keep a pair of these stools for the use of his own dead; but changes had led to the discontinuance of the custom, and the stools were frequently made use of in the manner described.

The young woman laid down the bill-hook for a moment and examined the palm of her right hand, which, unlike the other, was ungloved, and showed little hardness or roughness about it. The palm was red and blistering, as if this present occupation were not frequent enough with her to subdue it to what it worked in.[3] As with so many right hands born to manual labour, there was nothing in its fundamental shape to bear out the physiological conventionalism that gradations of birth, gentle or mean, show themselves primarily in the form of this member. Nothing but a cast of the die of destiny had decided that the girl should handle the tool; and the fingers which clasped the heavy ash haft might have skilfully guided the pencil or swept the string, had they only been set to do it in good time.

Her face had the usual fulness of expression which is developed by a life of solitude. Where the eyes of a multitude continuously beat like waves upon a countenance they seem to wear away its individuality; but in the still water of privacy every tentacle of feeling and sentiment shoots out in visible luxuriance, to be interpreted as readily as a printed book by an intruder. In years she was no more than nineteen or twenty, but the necessity of taking thought at a too early period of life had forced the provisional curves of her childhood's face to a premature finality. Thus she had but little pretension to beauty, save in one prominent particular – her hair. Its abundance made it almost unmanageable; its colour was, roughly speaking, and as seen here by firelight, brown; but careful notice, or an observation by day, would have revealed that its true shade was a rare and beautiful approximation to chestnut.

On this one bright gift of Time to the particular victim of his now before us the newcomer's eyes were fixed; meanwhile the fingers of his right hand mechanically played over something sticking up from his waistcoat pocket – the bows of a pair of scissors, whose polish made them feebly responsive to the light from within the house. In her present beholder's mind the scene formed by the girlish spar-maker composed itself into an impression-picture[4] of extremest type, wherein the girl's hair alone, as the focus of observation, was depicted with intensity and distinctness, while her face, shoulders, hands, and figure in general, were a blurred mass of unimportant detail, lost in haze and obscurity.

He hesitated no longer, but tapped at the door and entered. The young woman turned at the crunch of his boots on the sanded floor, and exclaiming, "Oh, Mr. Percomb, how you frightened me!" quite lost her colour for a moment.

He replied, "You should shut your door – then you'd hear folk open it."

"I can't," she said; "the chimney smokes so. Mr. Percomb, you look as unnatural away from your wigs as a canary in a thorn-hedge. Surely you have not come out here on my account – for –"

"Yes – to have your answer about this." He touched her hair with his cane, and she winced. "Do you agree?" he continued. "It is necessary that I should know at once, as the lady is soon going away, and it takes time to make up."

"Don't press me – it worries me. I was in hopes you had thought no more of it. I can *not* part with it – so there!"

"Now look here, Marty," said the other, sitting down on the coffin-stool table. "How much do you get for making these spars?"

"Hush – father's up stairs awake, and he don't know that I am doing his work."

"Well, now tell me," said the man more softly. "How much do you get?"

"Eighteenpence a thousand," she said reluctantly.

"Who are you making them for?"

"Mr. Melbury, the timber-dealer, just below here."

"And how many can you make in a day?"

"In a day and half the night, three bundles – that's a thousand and a half."

"Two and threepence." Her visitor paused. "Well, look here," he continued, with the remains of a computation in his tone, which computation had been to fix the probable sum of money necessary to outweigh her present resources, and her woman's love of comeliness, "here's a sovereign[5] – a gold sovereign, almost new." He held it out between his finger and thumb. "That's as much as you'd earn in a week and a half at that rough man's work, and it's yours for just letting me snip off what you've got too much of."

The girl's bosom moved a very little. "Why can't the lady send to some other girl who don't value her hair – not to me?" she exclaimed.

"Why, simpleton, because yours is the exact shade of her own, and 'tis a shade you can't match by dyeing. But you are not going to refuse me now I've come all the way from Sherton on purpose?"

"I say I won't sell it – to you or anybody."

"Now listen," and he drew up a little closer beside her. "The lady is very rich, and won't be particular to a few shillings; so I will advance to this on my own responsibility – I'll make the one sovereign two, rather than go back empty-handed."

"No, no, no!" she cried, beginning to be much agitated. "You are a tempting me. You go on like the Devil to Dr. Faustus in the penny book.[6] But I don't want your money, and won't agree. Why did you come? I said when you got me into your shop and urged me so much that I didn't mean to sell my hair!" The speaker was hot and stern.

"Marty, now hearken. The lady that wants it wants it badly. And, between you and me, you'd better let her have it. 'Twill be bad for you if you don't."

"Bad for me? Who is she then?"

The wig-maker held his tongue, and the girl repeated the question.

"I am not at liberty to tell you. And as she is going abroad soon it makes no difference who she is at all."

"She wants it to go abroad wi'?" He assented by a nod.

The girl regarded him reflectively. "Now, Mr. Percomb," she said, "I know who 'tis. 'Tis she at the House – Mrs. Charmond!"

"That's my secret. However, if you agree to let me have it, I'll tell you in confidence."

"I'll certainly not let you have it unless you tell me the truth. It is Mrs. Charmond."

The man dropped his voice. "Well – it is. You sat in front of her in church the other day, and she noticed how exactly your hair matches her own. Ever since then she's been hankering for it, to help out hers, and at last decided to get it. As she won't wear it till she goes off abroad, she knows nobody will recognise the change. I'm commissioned to get it for her, and then it is to be made up. I shouldn't have vamped all these miles for any less important employer. Now, mind 'tis as much as my business with her is worth if it should be known that I've let out her name; but honour between us two, Marty, and you'll say nothing that would injure me?"

"I don't wish to tell upon her," said Marty coolly. "But my hair is my own, and I'm going to keep it."

"Now that's not fair, after what I've told you," said the nettled emissary. "You see, Marty, as you are in the same parish, and in one of this lady's cottages, and your father is ill, and wouldn't like to turn out, it would be as well to oblige her. I say that as a friend. But I won't press you to make up your mind to-night. You'll be coming to market to-morrow, I dare say, and you can call then. If you think it over you'll be inclined to bring what I want, I know."

"I've nothing more to say," she answered.

Her companion saw from her manner that it was useless to urge her further by speech. "As you are a trusty young woman," he said, "I'll put these sovereigns up here, for ornament, that you may see how handsome they are. Bring the article to-morrow, or return the sovereigns." He stuck them edgewise into the frame of a small mantel looking-glass. "I hope you'll bring it; for your sake and mine. I should have thought she could have suited herself elsewhere; but as it's her fancy it must be indulged if possible. If you cut it off yourself mind how you do it, so as to keep all the locks one way." He showed her how this was to be done.

"But I sha'n't," she replied with laconic indifference. "I value my looks too much to spoil 'em. She wants my curls to get another lover with; though if stories are true she's broke the heart of many a noble gentleman already."

"Lord, it's wonderful how you guess things, Marty," said the barber. "I've had it from those that know that there certainly is some foreign gentleman in her eye. However, mind what I ask."

"She's not going to get him through me."

Percomb had retired as far as the door; he came back, planted his cane on the coffin-stool, and looked her in the face. "Marty South," he said with deliberate emphasis, "*you've got a lover yourself*, and that's why you won't let it go!"

She reddened so intensely as to pass the mild blush that suffices to heighten beauty; she put the yellow leather glove on one hand, took up the hook with the other, and sat down doggedly to her work without turning her face to him again. He regarded her head for a moment, went to the door, and with one look back at her departed on his way homeward.

Marty pursued her occupation for a few minutes; then suddenly laying down the bill-hook, she jumped up and went to the back of the room, where she opened a door which disclosed a staircase so whitely scrubbed that the grain of the wood was well-nigh sodden away by cleansing. At the top she gently approached a bedroom, and without entering said, "Father, do you want anything?"

A weak voice inside answered in the negative, adding, "I should be all right by to-morrow if it were not for the tree!"

"The tree again – always the tree! Oh, father, don't worry so about that. You know it can do you no harm."

"Who have ye had talking to ye down stairs?"

"A Sherton man called – nothing to trouble about," she said soothingly. "Father," she went on, "can Mrs. Charmond turn us out of our house if she's minded to?"

"Turn us out? No. Nobody can turn us out till my poor soul is turned out of my body. 'Tis lifehold,[7] like Giles Winterborne's. But when my life drops 'twill be hers – not till then." His words on this subject so far had been rational and firm enough. But now he lapsed into his moaning strain: "And the tree will do it – that tree will soon be the death of me."

"Nonsense, you know better. How can it be?" She refrained from further speech, and descended to the ground floor again.

"Thank Heaven, then," she said to herself, "what belongs to me I keep."

CHAPTER III

The lights in the village went out, house after house, till there only remained two in the darkness. One of these came from a residence on the hill-side, of which there is something to be said later on; the other shone from the window of Marty South. Precisely the same extinguished effect was produced here, however, by her rising when the clock struck ten and hanging up a thick cloth curtain. The door it was necessary to keep ajar in hers as in most cottages, because of the smoke; but she obviated the effect of the riband of light through the chink by hanging a cloth over that also. She was one of those people who, if they have to work harder than their neighbours, prefer to keep the necessity a secret as far as possible; and, but for the slight sounds of wood-splintering which came from within, no wayfarer would have perceived that here the cottager did not sleep as elsewhere.

Eleven, twelve, one o'clock struck; the heap of spars grew higher, and the pile of chips and ends more bulky. Even the light on the hill had now been extinguished; but still she worked on. When the temperature of the night without had fallen so low as to make her chilly, she opened a large blue umbrella to ward off the draught from the door. The two sovereigns confronted her from the looking-glass in such a manner as to suggest a pair of jaundiced eyes on the watch for an opportunity. Whenever she sighed for weariness she lifted her gaze towards them, but withdrew it quickly, stroking her tresses for a moment, as if to assure herself that they were still secure. When the clock struck three she arose and tied up the spars she had last made in a bundle resembling those that lay against the wall.

She wrapped round her a long red woollen cravat, and opened the door. The night in all its fulness met her flatly on the threshold, like the very brink of an absolute void, or the ante-mundane Ginnung-Gap[1] believed in by her Teuton forefathers. For her eyes were fresh from the blaze, and here there was no street lamp or lantern to form a kindly transition between the inner glare and the outer dark. A lingering wind brought to her ear the creaking sound of two over-crowded branches in the neighbouring wood, which were rubbing each other into wounds, and other vocalised sorrows of the trees, together with the screech of owls, and the fluttering tumble of some awkward woodpigeon ill-balanced on its roosting bough.

But the pupils of her young eyes soon expanded, and she could see well enough for her purpose. Taking a bundle of spars under each arm, and guided by the serrated line of tree-tops against the sky, she went some hundred yards or more down the lane till she reached a long open shed, carpeted around with the dead leaves that lay about everywhere. Night, that strange personality, which within walls brings ominous introspectiveness and self-distrust, but under the open sky banishes such subjective anxieties as too trivial for thought, gave to

Marty South a less perturbed and brisker manner now. She laid the spars on the ground within the shed and returned for more, going to and fro till her whole manufactured stock was deposited here.

This erection was the waggon-house of the chief man of business hereabout, Mr. George Melbury, the timber, bark, and copse-ware merchant for whom Marty's father did work of this sort by the piece. It formed one of the many rambling outhouses which surrounded his dwelling, an equally irregular block of building, whose immense chimneys could just be discerned even now. The four huge waggons under the shed were built on those ancient lines whose proportions have been ousted by modern patterns, their shapes bulging and curving at the base and ends like Trafalgar line-of-battle ships,[2] with which venerable hulks, indeed, these vehicles evidenced a constructive spirit curiously in harmony. One was laden with sheep-cribs, another with hurdles, another with ash-poles, and the fourth, at the foot of which she had placed her thatching-spars, was half full of similar bundles.

She was pausing a moment with that easeful sense of accomplishment which follows work done that has been a hard struggle in the doing, when she heard a woman's voice on the other side of the hedge say anxiously, "George!"

In a moment the name was repeated, with "Do come indoors! What are you doing there?"

The cart-house adjoined the garden, and before Marty had moved she saw enter the latter from the timber-merchant's back door an elderly woman sheltering a candle with her hand, the light from which cast a moving thorn-pattern of shade on Marty's face. Its rays soon fell upon a man whose clothes were carelessly thrown on, standing in advance of the speaker. He was a thin, slightly stooping figure, with a small nervous mouth, and a face cleanly shaven; and he walked along the path with his eyes bent on the ground. In the pair Marty South recognised her employer Melbury and his wife. She was the second Mrs. Melbury, the first having died shortly after the birth of the timber-merchant's only child.

" 'Tis no use to stay in bed!" he said as soon as she came up to where he was pacing restlessly about. "I can't sleep. I keep thinking of things."[3]

"What things?"

He did not answer.

"The lady at the Great House?"

"No."

"The turnpike bonds?"[4]

"No. Though I wish I hadn't got 'em."

"The ghosts of the Two Brothers?"[5]

He shook his head.

"Not about Grace?"

"Yes. 'Tis she."

(Grace was the speaker's only daughter.)

"Why worry about her?"

"First, I cannot think why she doesn't answer my letter. She must be ill."

"No, no. Things only appear so gloomy in the night time."

"Second, I have not invested any money specially for her, to put her out of the reach of poverty if my affairs fail."

"They are safe. Besides, she is sure to marry well."

"You are wrong. That's my third trouble. I have a plan in my head about her, and according to my plan she won't marry well."

"A plan for her not to marry well?" said his wife, surprised.

"In one sense. It is a plan for her to marry a particular person, and he is poor. It is Giles Winterborne."

"Giles Winterborne? Well, it is all right. Love will make up for his want of money. He adores the very ground she walks on."

(Marty South started, and could not tear herself away.)

"Yes," said the timber-merchant; "I know that well. There will be no lack of that with him. But since I have educated her so well, and so long, and so far above the level of the daughters hereabout, it is *wasting her* to give her to a man of no higher standing than he."

"Then why do it?" she asked.

"Ah! – now you've hit it! Lucy, it is in obedience to a solemn resolve I made . . . I made it because I did his father a terrible wrong; and it has been a weight on my conscience ever since that time, till this scheme of making amends occurred to me through seeing that Giles liked her."

"Wronged his father?" asked Mrs. Melbury.

"Yes, grievously wronged him," said her husband.

"Well, don't think of it to-night," she urged. "Come indoors."

"No, no; the air cools my head. I shall not stay long."

He was silent awhile; then he told her that his first wife, his daughter's mother, was first the promised of Winterborne's father, who loved her tenderly, till he, the speaker, won her away from him by a trick, because he wanted to marry her himself. He went on to say that the other man's happiness was ruined by it; that though he married Winterborne's mother, it was but a half-hearted business with him. Melbury added that he was afterwards very miserable at what he had done; but that as time went on, and the children grew up, and seemed to be attached to each other, he determined to do all he could to right the wrong by letting his daughter marry the lad; not only that, but to give her the best education he could afford, so as to make the gift as valuable a one as it lay in his power to bestow. "I still mean to do it," said Melbury.

"Then do," said she.

"But all these things trouble me," said he; "for I feel I am sacrificing her for my own sin; and I think of her, and often come down here and look at this."

"Look at what?" asked his wife.

He took the candle from her hand, held it to the ground, and removed a tile which lay in the garden-path. " 'Tis the track of her shoe that she made when she ran down here the day before she went away all those months ago. I covered it up when she was gone; and when I come here and look at it, I ask myself again, why should she be sacrificed to a poor man?"

"It is not altogether a sacrifice," said the woman. "He is in love with her, and he's honest and upright. If she encourages him, what can you wish for more?"

"I wish for nothing definite. But there's a lot of things possible for her. Why, Mrs. Charmond is wanting some refined young lady, I hear, to go abroad with her – as companion or something of the kind. She'd jump at Grace."

"That's all uncertain. Better stick to what's sure."

"True, true," said Melbury; "and I hope it will be for the best. Yes, let me get 'em married up as soon as I can, so as to have it over and done with." He continued looking at the imprint, while he added, "Suppose she should be dying, and never make a track on this path any more?"

"She'll write soon, depend upon't. Come, 'tis wrong to stay here and brood so."

He admitted it, but said he could not help it. "Whether she write or no, I shall fetch her in a few days." And thus speaking he covered the track, and preceded his wife indoors.

Melbury perhaps was an unlucky man in having within him the sentiment which could indulge in this foolish fondness about the imprint of a daughter's footstep. Nature does not carry on her government with a view to such feelings; and when advancing years render the opened hearts of those who possess them less dexterous than formerly in shutting against the blast, they must suffer "buffeting at will by rain and storm"[6] no less than little celandines.

But her own existence, and not Mr. Melbury's, was the centre of Marty's consciousness, and it was in relation to this that the matter struck her as she slowly withdrew.

"That, then, is the secret of it all," she said. "And Giles Winterborne is not for me, and the less I think of him the better."

She returned to her cottage. The sovereigns were staring at her from the looking-glass as she had left them. With a preoccupied countenance, and with tears in her eyes, she got a pair of scissors, and began mercilessly cutting off the long locks of her hair, arranging and tying them with their points all one way, as the barber had directed. Upon the pale scrubbed deal of the coffin-stool table they stretched like waving and ropy weeds over the washed white bed of a stream.

She would not turn again to the little looking-glass out of humanity to herself, knowing what a deflowered visage[7] would look back at her, and almost break her heart; she dreaded it as much as did her own ancestral goddess the reflection in the pool after the rape of her locks by Loke[8] the Malicious. She steadily stuck to business, wrapped the hair in a parcel, and sealed it up; after which she raked out the fire and went to bed, having first set up an alarum made of a candle and piece of thread, with a stone attached.

But such a reminder was unnecessary to-night. Having tossed about till five o'clock, Marty heard the sparrows walking down their long holes in the thatch above her sloping ceiling to their exits at the eaves; whereupon she also arose, and descended to the ground floor again.

It was still dark, but she began moving about the house in those automatic initiatory acts and touches which represent among house-wives the installation of another day. While thus engaged she heard the rumbling of Mr. Melbury's waggons, and knew that there, too, the day's toil had begun.

An armful of gads thrown on the still hot embers caused them to blaze up cheerfully, and bring her diminished head-gear into sudden prominence as a shadow. At this a step approached the door.

"Are folk astir here yet?" inquired a voice she knew well.

"Yes, Mr. Winterborne," said Marty, throwing on a tilt bonnet, which completely hid the recent ravages of the scissors. "Come in!"

The door was flung back, and there stepped in upon the mat a man, not particularly young for a lover, nor particularly mature for a person of affairs – each of which functions he in some degree discharged. There was reserve in his glance, and restraint upon his mouth. He carried a horn lantern which hung upon a swivel, and, wheeling as it dangled, marked grotesque shapes upon the shadier part of the walls.

He said that he had looked in on his way down, to tell her that they did not expect her father to make up his contract if he was not well. Mr. Melbury would give him another week, and they would go their journey with a short load that day.

"They are done," said Marty, "and lying in the cart-house."

"Done?" he repeated. "Your father has not been too ill to work after all, then?"

She made some evasive reply. "I'll show you where they be, if you are going down," she added.

They went out and walked together, the pattern of the air-holes in the top of the lantern being thrown upon the mist overhead, where they appeared of giant size, as if reaching the tent-shaped sky. They had no remarks to make to each other, and they uttered none. Hardly anything could be more isolated or more self-contained than the lives of these two walking here in the lonely hour before day, when grey shades, material and mental, are so very grey. And yet, looked at in a certain way, their lonely courses formed no detached design at all, but were part of the pattern in the great web of human doings[9] then weaving in both hemispheres, from the White Sea to Cape Horn.[10]

The shed was reached, and she pointed out the spars. Winterborne regarded them silently, then looked at her.

"Now, Marty, I believe —" he said, and shook his head.

"What?"

"That you've done the work yourself."

"Don't you tell anybody, will you, Mr. Winterborne?" she pleaded by way of answer. "Because I am afraid Mr. Melbury may refuse my work if he knows it is mine."

"But how could you learn to do it? 'Tis a trade."

"Trade!" said she. "I'd be bound to learn it in two hours."

"Oh, no, you wouldn't, Mrs. Marty." Winterborne held down his lantern, and examined the cleanly split hazels as they lay. "Marty," he said with dry admiration, "your father with his forty years of practice never made a spar better than that. They are too good for the thatching of houses; they are good enough for the furniture. But I won't tell. Let me look at your hands – your poor hands!"

He had a kindly manner of a quietly severe tone; and when she seemed reluctant to show her hands he took hold of one and examined it as if it were his own. Her fingers were blistered.

"They'll get harder in time," she said. "For if father continues ill I shall have to go on wi' it. Now I'll help put 'em up in waggon."

Winterborne without speaking set down his lantern, lifted her like a doll as she was about to stoop over the bundles, placed her behind him, and began throwing up the bundles himself. "Rather than you should do it I will," he said. "But the men will be here directly. Why, Marty – whatever has happened to your head? Lord, it has shrunk to nothing – it looks like an apple upon a gate-post!"

Her heart swelled, and she could not speak. At length she managed to groan, looking on the ground, "I've made myself ugly – and hateful – that's what I've done!"

"No, no," he answered. "You've only cut your hair – I see now."

"Then why must you needs say that about apples and gate-posts?"

"Let me see!"

For answer she ran off into the gloom of the sluggish dawn. He did not attempt to follow her. When she reached her father's door she stood on the step and looked back. Mr. Melbury's men had arrived, and were loading up the spars; and their lanterns appeared from the distance at which she stood to have wan circles round them, like eyes weary with watching. She observed them for a few seconds as they set about harnessing the horses, and then went indoors.

CHAPTER IV

There was now a distinct manifestation of morning in the air, and presently the bleared white visage of a sunless winter day emerged like a dead-born child.[1] The woodlanders everywhere had already bestirred themselves, rising at this time of the year at the far less dreary hour of absolute darkness. It had been above an hour earlier, before a single bird had untucked his head, that twenty lights were struck in as many bedrooms, twenty pairs of shutters opened, and twenty pairs of eyes stretched to the sky to forecast the weather for the day.

Owls that had been catching mice in the outhouses, rabbits that had been eating the winter-greens in the gardens, and stoats that had been sucking the blood of the rabbits, discerning that their human neighbours were on the move, discreetly withdrew from publicity, and were seen and heard no more till nightfall.

The daylight revealed the whole of Mr. Melbury's homestead, of which the waggon-sheds had been an out-lying erection. It formed three sides of an open quadrangle, and consisted of all sorts of buildings, the largest and central one being the dwelling itself. The fourth side of the quadrangle was the public road.

It was a dwelling-house of respectable, roomy, almost dignified aspect, which, taken with the fact that there were the remains of other such buildings hereabout, indicated that Little Hintock had at some time or other been of greater importance than now, as its old name of Hintock St. Osmond also testified. The house was of no marked antiquity; yet of well-advanced age; older than a stale novelty, but no canonised antique; faded, not hoary; looking at you from the still distinct middle-distance of the early Georgian time,[2] and awakening on that account the instincts of reminiscence more decidedly than the remoter, and far grander, memorials which have to speak from the misty reaches of mediævalism. The faces, dress, passions, gratitudes, and revenges of the great-great-grandfathers and grandmothers who had been the first to gaze from those rectangular windows, and had stood under that keystoned doorway, could be divined and measured by homely standards of to-day. It was a house in whose reverberations queer old personal tales were yet audible if properly listened for; and not, as with those of the castle and cloister, silent beyond the possibility of echo.

The garden-front remained much as it had always been, and there was a porch and entrance that way. But the principal house-door opened on the square yard or quadrangle towards the road, formerly a regular carriage entrance; though the middle of the area was now made use of for stacking timber, faggots, bundles, and other products of the wood. It was divided from the lane by a lichen-coated wall, in which hung a pair of gates, flanked by piers out of the perpendicular, with a round white ball on the top of each.

The building on the left of the inclosure was a long-backed erection, now used for spar-making, sawing, crib-framing, and copseware manufacture in general. Opposite were the waggon-sheds where Marty had deposited her spars.

Here Winterborne had remained after the girl's abrupt departure, to see that the loads were properly made up. Winterborne was connected with the Melbury family in various ways. In addition to the sentimental relationship which arose from his father having been the first Mrs. Melbury's lover, Winterborne's aunt had married and emigrated with the brother of the timber-merchant many years before – an alliance that was sufficient to place Winterborne, though the poorer, on a footing of social intimacy with the Melburys. As in most villages so secluded as this, intermarriages were of Hapsburgian frequency[3] among the inhabitants, and there were hardly two houses in Little Hintock unrelated by some matrimonial tie or other.

For this reason a curious kind of partnership existed between Melbury and the younger man – a partnership based upon an unwritten code, by which each acted in the way he thought fair towards the other, on a give-and-take principle. Melbury, with his timber and copse-ware business, found that the weight of his labour came in winter and spring. Winterborne was in the apple and cider trade, and his requirements in cartage and other work came in the autumn of each year. Hence horses, waggons, and in some degree men, were handed over to him when the apples began to fall; he in return, lending his assistance to Melbury in the busiest wood-cutting season, as now.

Before he had left the shed a boy came from the house to ask him to remain till Mr. Melbury had seen him. Winterborne thereupon crossed over to the spar-house where some journeymen were already at work, two of them being travelling spar-makers from White-Hart Lane, who, when the fall of the leaf began, made their appearance regularly, and when winter was over disappeared in silence till the season came again.

Firewood was the one thing abundant in Little Hintock; and a blaze of gad-ends made the outhouse gay with its light, which vied with that of the day as yet. In the hollow shades of the roof could be seen pale dangling arms of ivy which had crept through the joints of the tiles and were groping in vain for some support, their leaves being dwarfed and sickly for want of sunlight;[4] others were pushing in with such force at the eaves as to lift from their supports the shelves that were fixed there.

Besides the itinerant journey-workers there were also present John Upjohn, Melbury's regular man; a neighbour engaged in the hollow-turnery trade; Old Timothy Tangs and young Timothy Tangs, top and bottom sawyers at work in Mr. Melbury's pit outside; Farmer Cawtree, who kept the cider-house, and Robert Creedle, an old man who worked for Winterborne, and stood warming his hands; these latter having been enticed in by the ruddy blaze, though they had no particular business there. None of them call for any remark, except perhaps Creedle. To have completely described him it would have been necessary to write a military memoir, for he wore under his smock-frock a cast-off soldier's jacket that had seen hot service, its collar showing just above the flap of the frock; also a hunting memoir, to include the top-boots that he had picked up by chance; also chronicles of voyaging and shipwreck, for his pocket-knife had been given him by a weather-beaten sailor. But Creedle carried about with him on his uneventful rounds these silent testimonies of war, sport, and adventure, and thought nothing of their associations or their stories.

Copse-work, as it was called, being an occupation which the secondary intelligence of the hands and arms could carry on without requiring the sovereign attention of the head, the minds of its professors wandered considerably from the objects before them; hence the tales, chronicles, and ramifications of family history which were recounted here were of a very exhaustive kind.

Winterborne, seeing that Melbury had not arrived, stepped back again outside the door; and the conversation interrupted by his momentary presence flowed anew, reaching his ears as an accompaniment to the regular dripping of the fog from the plantation boughs around.

The topic at present handled was a highly popular and frequent one – the personal character of Mrs. Charmond, the owner of the surrounding woods and groves.

"My brother-in-law told me, and I have no reason to doubt it," said Creedle, "that she'd sit down to her dinner with a frock hardly higher than her elbows. 'Oh, you wicked woman!' he said to himself when he first see her, 'you go to your church, and sit, and kneel, as if your knee-jints were greased with very saint's anointment, and tell off your hear-us-good-Lords as pat as a business man counting money; and yet you can eat your victuals such a figure as that!' Whether she's a reformed character by this time I can't say; but I don't care who the man is, that's how she went on when my brother-in-law lived there."

"Did she do it in her husband's time?"

"That I don't know – hardly, I should think, considering his temper. Ah —!" Here Creedle threw grieved remembrance into physical form by slowly resigning his head to obliquity and letting his eyes water. "That man! 'Not if the angels of heaven come down, Creedle,' he said, 'shall you do another day's work for me!' Yes – he would as soon take a winged creature's name in vain as yours or mine! Well, now I must get these spars home-along, and to-morrow, thank God, I must see about using 'em."

An old woman now entered upon the scene. She was Mr. Melbury's servant, and passed a great part of her time in crossing the yard between the house-door and the spar-shed, whither she had come now for fuel. She had two facial aspects – one, of a soft and flexible kind, which she used indoors; the other, with stiff lines and corners, which she assumed when bustling among the men outside.

"Ah, Grammer Oliver," said John Upjohn, "it do do my heart good to see a old woman like you so dapper and stirring, when I bear in mind that, after fifty, one year counts as two did aforc! But your smoke didn't rise this morning till twenty minutes past seven by my beater; and that's late, Grammer Oliver."

"If you was a full-sized man, John, I might take notice of your scornful meanings. But really a woman couldn't feel hurt if such smallness were to spit fire and brimstone itself at her. Here," she added, holding out a spar-gad to one of the workmen, from which dangled a long black-pudding, "here's something for thy breakfast, and if you want tea you must fetch it from indoors."

"Mr. Melbury is late this morning," said the bottom-sawyer.

"Yes. 'Twas a dark dawn," said Mrs. Oliver. "Even when I opened the door, so late as I was, you couldn't have told poor men from gentlemen, or John from a reasonable-sized object. And I don't think maister's slept at all well to-night. He's anxious about his daughter; and I know what that is, for I've cried bucketfuls for my own."

When the old woman had gone Creedle said:–

"He'll fret his heart green if he don't soon hear from that maid of his. Well, learning is better than houses and lands. But to keep a maid at school till she is taller out of pattens than her mother was in 'em[5] – 'tis tempting Providence."

"It seems no time ago that she was a little playward girl," said young Timothy Tangs.

"I can mind her mother," said the hollow-turner. "Alway a teuny, delicate piece; her touch upon your hand was as soft as wind. She was inoculated for the small-pox and had it beautifully fine, just about the time that I was out of my apprenticeship – ay, and a long apprenticeship 'twas. I served that master of mine six years and three hundred and fourteen days."

The hollow-turner pronounced the days with emphasis, as if, considering their number, they were a rather more remarkable fact than the years.

"Mr. Winterborne's father walked with her at one time," said old Timothy Tangs. "But Mr. Melbury won her. She was a child of a woman, and would cry like rain if so be he huffed her. Whenever she and her husband came to a puddle in their walks together he'd take her up like a halfpenny doll and put her over without dirting her a speck. And if he keeps the daughter so long at boarding school he'll make her as nesh as her mother was. But here he comes."

Just before this moment Winterborne had seen Melbury crossing the court from his door. He was carrying an open letter in his hand, and came straight to Winterborne. His gloom of the preceding night had quite gone.

"I'd no sooner made up my mind, Giles, to go and see why Grace didn't come or write than I get a letter from her – 'My dear father,' says she, 'I'm coming home tomorrow (that's to-day), but I didn't think it worth while to write long beforehand.' The little rascal, and didn't she! Now, Giles, as you are going to Sherton market to-day with your apple-trees, why not join me and Grace there, and we'll drive home all together?"

He made the proposal with cheerful energy; he was hardly the same man as the man of the small dark hours. Even among the moodiest, the tendency to be cheered is stronger than the tendency to be cast down; and a soul's specific gravity[6] stands permanently less than that of the sea of troubles[7] into which it is thrown.

Winterborne, though not demonstrative, replied to this suggestion with alacrity. There was not much doubt that Marty's grounds for cutting off her hair were substantial enough, if this man's eyes had been a reason for keeping it on. As for the timber-merchant, it was plain that his invitation had been given solely in pursuance of his scheme for uniting the pair. He had made up his mind to the course as a duty, and was strenuously bent upon following it out.

Accompanied by Winterborne he now turned towards the door of the spar-house, when his footsteps were heard by the men as aforesaid.

"Well, John, and Robert," he said, nodding, as he entered. "A rimy morning."

" 'Tis, sir," said Creedle, energetically, for not having as yet been able to summon force sufficient to go away and begin work he felt the necessity of throwing some into his speech. "I don't care who the man is, 'tis the rimiest morning we've had this fall."

"I heard you wondering why I've kept my daughter so long at boarding-school," resumed Mr. Melbury, looking up from the letter which he was reading anew by the fire, and turning to them with the suddenness that was a trait in him. "Hey?" he asked with affected shrewdness. "But you did, you know. Well now, though it is my own business more than anybody else's, I'll tell ye. When I was a boy another boy – the pa'son's son – along with a lot of others, asked me, 'Who dragged Whom round the walls of What?'[8] and I said, 'Sam Barrett, who dragged his wife in a chair round the tower when she went to be churched.' They laughed at me so much that I went home ashamed, and couldn't sleep for shame; and I cried that night till my pillow was wet; till I thought to myself – 'They may laugh at me for my ignorance, but that was father's fault, and none o' my making, and I must bear it. But they shall never laugh at my children, if I have any: I'll starve first!' Thank God I've been able to keep her at school at the figure of near a hundred a year;[9] and her scholarship is such that she has stayed on as governess for a time. Let 'em laugh now if they can: Mrs. Charmond herself is not better informed than my girl Grace."

There was something between high indifference and humble emotion in his delivery, which made it difficult for them to reply. Winterborne's interest was of a kind which did not show itself in words; listening, he stood by the fire, mechanically stirring the embers with a spar-gad.

"You'll be, then, ready, Giles?" Melbury continued, awaking from a reverie. "Well, what was the latest news at Shottsford yesterday, Mr. Cawtree?"

"Oh, well, Shottsford is Shottsford still – you can't victual your carcase there unless you've got money; and you can't buy a cup of genuine there, whether or no . . . But as the saying is 'Go abroad and you'll hear news of home.' It seems that our new neighbour, this young Doctor What's-his-name, is a strange, deep, perusing gentleman; and there's good reason for supposing he has sold his soul to the wicked one."

" 'Od name it all," murmured the timber-merchant, unimpressed by the news, but reminded of other things by the subject of it; "I've got to meet a gentleman this very morning, and yet I've planned to go to Sherton Abbas for the maid."

"I won't praise the doctor's wisdom till I hear what sort of bargain he's made," said the top-sawyer.

" 'Tis only an old woman's tale," said Cawtree. "But it seems that he wanted certain books on some mysterious black art, and in order that the people hereabout should not know anything about them, he ordered 'em direct from London, and not from the Sherton bookseller. The parcel was delivered by mistake at the pa'son's, and as he wasn't at home his wife opened it, and went into hysterics when she read 'em, thinking her husband had turned heathen, and 'twould be the ruin of the children. But when he came he knew no more about 'em than she; and found they were this Mr. Fitzpiers's property. So he wrote, 'Beware!' outside, and sent 'em on by the sexton."

"He must be a curious young man," mused the hollow-turner.

"He must," said Timothy Tangs.

"Nonsense," said Mr. Melbury, authoritatively, "he's only a gentle-man fond of science, and philosophy, and poetry, and, in fact, every kind of knowledge; and being lonely here he passes his time in making such matters his hobby."

"Well," said old Timothy, " 'tis a strange thing about doctors that the worse they be the better they be. I mean that if you hear anything of this sort about 'em, ten to one they can cure ye as nobody else can."

"True," said Cawtree, emphatically. "And for my part I shall take my custom from old Jones and go to this one directly I've anything the matter inside me. That last medicine old Jones gave me had no taste in it at all."

Mr. Melbury, as became a well-informed man, did not listen to these recitals, being, moreover, preoccupied with the business appointment which had come into his head. He walked up and down, looking on the floor – his usual custom when undecided. That stiffness about the arm, hip, and knee-joint, which was apparent when he walked, was the net product of the divers sprains and over-exertions that had been required of him in handling trees and timber when a young man, for he was of the sort called self-made, and had worked hard. He knew the origin of every one of these cramps; that in his left shoulder had come of carrying a pollard, unassisted, from Tutcombe Bottom home; that in one leg was caused by the crash of an elm against it when they were felling; that in the other was from lifting a bole. On many a morrow after wearying himself by these prodigious muscular efforts, he had risen from his bed fresh as usual; and confident in the recuperative power of his youth, he had repeated the strains anew. But treacherous Time had been only hiding ill results when they could be guarded against, for greater effect when they could not. Now in his declining years the store had been unfolded in the form of rheumatisms, pricks, and spasms, in every one of which Melbury recognised some act, which, had its consequence been contemporaneously made known, he would wisely have abstained from repeating.

On a summons by Grammer Oliver to breakfast he went to the kitchen, where the family breakfasted in winter to save house-labour; and sitting down by the fire looked a long time at the pair of dancing shadows cast by each fire-iron and dogknob on the whitewashed chimney-corner – a yellow one from the window, and a blue one from the fire.

"I don't quite know what to do to-day," he said to his wife at last. "I've recollected that I promised to meet Mrs. Charmond's steward in Round Wood at twelve o'clock, and yet I want to go for Grace."

"Why not let Giles fetch her by himself? 'Twill bring 'em together all the quicker."

"I could do that – but I always have gone, without fail, every time hitherto, and perhaps she'll be disappointed if I stay away."

"You may be disappointed, but I don't think she will, if you send Giles," said Mrs. Melbury drily.

"Very well – I'll send him."

Melbury was often persuaded by the quietude of his wife's words when strenuous argument would have had no effect. This second Mrs. Melbury was a placid woman, who had been nurse to his child Grace after her mother's death. Little Grace had clung to the nurse with much affection; and ultimately Melbury, in dread lest the only woman who cared for the girl should be induced to leave her, persuaded the mild Lucy to marry him. The arrangement – for it was little more – had worked satisfactorily enough; Grace had thriven, and Melbury had not repented.

He returned to the spar-house and found Giles near at hand, to whom he explained the change of plan. "As she won't arrive till five o'clock, you can get your business very well over in time to receive her," said Melbury. "The green gig[10] will do for her; you'll spin along quicker with that, and won't be late upon the road. Her boxes can be called for by one of the waggons."

Winterborne, knowing nothing of the timber-merchant's restitutory aims, quietly thought all this to be a kindly chance. Wishing, even more than her father, to despatch his apple-tree business in the market before Grace's arrival, he prepared to start at once.

Melbury was careful that the turn-out should be seemly. The gig-wheels, for instance, were not always washed during winter-time before a journey, the muddy roads rendering that labour useless; but they were washed to-day. The harness was blacked, and when the grey horse had been put in, and Winterborne was in his seat ready to start, Mr. Melbury stepped out with a blacking-brush and with his own hands touched over the yellow hoofs of the animal.

"You see, Giles," he said as he blacked, "coming from a fashionable school she might feel shocked at the homeliness of home; and 'tis these little things that catch a dainty woman's eye if they are neglected. We, living here alone, don't notice how the whitey-brown creeps out of the earth over us; but she, fresh from a city – why, she'll notice everything!"

"That she will," said Giles.

"And scorn us if we don't mind."

"Not scorn us."

"No, no, no – that's only words. She's too good a girl to do that. But when we consider what she knows, and what she has seen since she last saw us, 'tis as well to meet her views. Why, 'tis a year since she was in this old place, owing to her going abroad in the summer; and naturally we shall look small, just at first – I only say just at first."

Mr. Melbury's tone evinced a certain exultation in the very sense of that inferiority he affected to deplore; for this advanced and refined being, was she not his own all the time? Not so Giles; he felt doubtful.[11] He looked at his clothes with misgiving; but said nothing.

It was his custom during the planting season to carry a specimen apple-tree to market with him as an advertisement of what he dealt in. This had been tied across the gig; and mounting in front he drove away, the twigs nodding with each step of the horse. Melbury went indoors. Before the gig had passed out of sight Mr. Melbury reappeared and shouted after –

"Here, Giles," he said, breathlessly following with some wraps, "it may be very chilly to-night, and she may want something extra about her. And Giles," he added, when the young man put the horse in motion once more; "tell her that I should have come myself, but I had particular business with Mrs. Charmond's agent which prevented me. Don't forget."

He watched Winterborne out of sight under the boughs, where cobwebs glistened in the now clearing air, lengthening and shortening their shine like elastic needles; he saw the woodpigeons rise as Giles drove past them; and said to himself with a jerk – a shape into which emotion with him often resolved itself – "There now, I hope the two will bring it to a point, and have done with it! 'Tis a pity to let such a girl throw herself away upon him – a thousand pities! . . . And yet 'tis my duty, for his father's sake."

CHAPTER V

Winterborne sped on his way to Sherton Abbas without elation and without discomposure. Had he regarded his inner self spectacularly, as lovers are now daily more wont to do, he might have felt pride in the discernment of a somewhat rare power in him – that of keeping not only judgment but emotion suspended in difficult cases. But he noted it not.[1]

Arrived at the entrance to a long flat lane, which had taken the spirit out of many a pedestrian in times when, with the majority, to travel meant to walk, he saw before him the trim figure of a young woman in pattens, journeying with that steadfast concentration which means purpose and not pleasure. He was soon near enough to see that she was Marty South. Click, click, click, went the pattens; and she did not turn her head.

Yet she had seen him, and shrank from being overtaken by him thus; but as it was inevitable, she braced herself up for his inspection by closing her lips so as to make her mouth quite unemotional, and by throwing an additional firmness into her tread.

"Why do you wear pattens, Marty? The turnpike is clean enough although the lanes are muddy."

"They save my boots."

"But twelve miles in pattens – 'twill twist your feet off. Come, get up and ride with me."

She hesitated, removed her pattens, knocked the gravel out of them against the wheel, and mounted in front of the nodding specimen apple-tree. She had so arranged her bonnet with a full border and trimmings that her lack of long hair did not much injure her appearance; though Giles of course saw that it was gone, and may have guessed her motive in parting with it, such sales though infrequent being not unheard of in that locality.

But nature's adornment was still hard by, in fact, within two feet of him. In Marty's basket was a brown-paper packet, and in the packet the chestnut locks, which, by reason of the barber's request for secrecy, she had not ventured to intrust to other hands.

Giles asked, with some hesitation, how her father was getting on.

He was better, she said; he would be able to work in a day or two; he would be quite well but for his craze about the tree falling on him.

"You know why I don't ask for him so often as I might, I suppose?" said Winterborne. "Or don't you know?"

"I think I do."

"Because of the houses?"

She nodded.

"Yes. I am afraid it may seem that my anxiety is about those houses which I should lose by his death, more than about him. Marty, I do feel anxious about the houses, since half my income depends upon them; but I do likewise care for him; and it almost seems wrong that houses should be leased for lives, so as to lead to such mixed feelings."

"After father's death they will be Mrs. Charmond's?"

"They'll be hers."

"They are going to keep company with my hair," she thought.

Thus talking they reached the town. By no pressure would she ride up the street with him. "That's the right of another woman," she said with playful malice as she put on her pattens. "I wonder what you are thinking of! Thank you for the lift in that handsome gig. Good-bye."

He blushed a little, shook his head at her, and drove on ahead into the streets; the churches, the abbey, and other buildings on this clear bright morning having the linear distinctness of architectural drawings, as if the original dream and vision of the conceiving master-mason were for a few minutes flashed down through the centuries to an unappreciative age. Giles saw their eloquent look on this day of transparency, but could not construe it. He turned into the inn-yard.

Marty, following the same track, marched promptly to the hair-dresser's. Percomb was the chief of his trade in Sherton Abbas. He had the patronage of such county offshoots as had been obliged to seek the shelter of small houses in that ancient town, of the local clergy, and so on; for some of whom he had made wigs, while others among them had compensated for neglecting him in their lifetime by patronising him when they were dead, and letting him shave their corpses. On the strength of all this he had taken down his pole, and called himself "Perruquier to the aristocracy."

Nevertheless this sort of support did not quite fill his children's mouths, and they had to be filled. So behind his house there was a little yard reached by a passage from the back street, and in that yard was a pole, and under the pole a shop of quite another description than the ornamental one in the front street. Here on Saturday nights from seven till ten he took an almost innumerable succession of twopences from the farm-labourers who flocked thither in crowds from the country. And thus he lived.

Marty, of course, went to the front shop, and handed her packet to him silently.

"Thank you," said the barber quite joyfully. "I hardly expected it after what you said last night."

She turned aside, while a tear welled up and stood in each eye at this reminder.

"Nothing of what I told you," he whispered. "But I can trust you, I see."

She had now reached the end of this distressing business; and went listlessly along the street to attend to other errands. These occupied her till four o'clock, at which time she re-crossed the market-place. It was impossible to avoid re-discovering Winterborne every time she passed that way, for standing, as he always did at this season of the year, with his specimen apple-tree in the midst, the boughs rose above the heads of the farmers, and brought a delightful suggestion of orchards into the heart of the town.

When her eye fell upon him for the last time he was standing somewhat apart, holding the tree like an ensign,[2] and looking on the ground instead of pushing his produce as he ought to have been doing. He was, in fact, not a very successful seller either of his trees or of his cider, his habit of speaking his mind when he spoke at all militating against this branch of his business.

While she regarded him he lifted his eyes in a direction away from Marty, and his face kindled with recognition and surprise. She followed his gaze, and saw walking across to him a flexible young creature in whom she perceived the features of her she had known as Miss Grace Melbury, but now looking glorified and refined to much above her former level. Winterborne, being fixed to the spot by his apple-tree, could not advance to meet her: he held out his spare hand with his hat in it, and with some embarrassment beheld her coming on tip-toe through the mud to the middle of the square where he stood.

Miss Melbury, as Marty could see, had not been expected by Giles so early. Indeed, her father had named five o'clock as her probable time, for which reason that hour had been looming out all the day in his forward perspective, like an important edifice on a dull plain. Now here she was come, he knew not how, and his arranged welcome stultified.

His face became gloomy at her necessity for stepping into the road, and more still at the little look of embarrassment she showed at having to perform the meeting with him under an apple-tree ten feet high in the middle of the market-place. Having had occasion to take off the new gloves she had bought to come home in, she held out to him a hand graduating from pink at the tips of the fingers to white at the palm; and the reception formed a scene, with the tree over their heads, which was not by any means an ordinary one in Sherton Abbas streets.

Nevertheless the greeting in her looks and on her lips had a restrained shape, which perhaps was not unnatural. For true it was that Giles Winterborne, though well-attired and well-mannered for a yeoman, looked rough beside her. It had sometimes dimly occurred to him, in his ruminating silences at Little Hintock, that external phenomena – such as the lowness or height or colour of a hat, the fold of a coat, the make of a boot, or the chance attitude or occupation of a limb at the instant of view – may have a great influence upon feminine opinion of a man's worth, so frequently founded on non-essentials; but a certain causticity of mental tone towards himself and the world in general had prevented to-day, as always, any enthusiastic action on the strength of that reflection, and her momentary instinct of reserve at first sight of him was the penalty he paid for his laxness.

He gave away the tree to a bystander, as soon as he could find one who would accept the cumbersome gift, and the twain moved on towards the inn at which he had put up. Marty made as if to step forward for the pleasure of being recognised by Miss Melbury; but abruptly checking herself she glided behind a carrier's van, saying dryly, "No; I baint wanted there;" and critically regarded Winterborne's companion.

It would have been very difficult to describe Grace Melbury with precision, either then or at any time. Nay, from the highest point of view, to precisely describe a human being, the focus of a universe, how impossible! But, apart from transcendentalism,[3] there never probably lived a person who was in herself more completely a *reductio ad absurdum*[4] of attempts to appraise a woman, even externally, by items of face and figure.

Speaking generally, it may be said that she was sometimes beautiful, at other times not beautiful, according to the state of her health and spirits.

In simple corporeal presentment she was of a fair and clear complexion, rather pale than pink, slim in build and elastic in movement. Her look expressed a tendency to wait for others' thoughts before uttering her own: possibly also to wait for others' deeds before her own doing. In her small, delicate mouth, which had hardly settled down to its matured curves, there was a gentleness that might hinder sufficient self-assertion for her own good. She had well-formed eyebrows which, had her portrait been painted, would probably have been done in Prout's or Vandyke brown.

There was nothing remarkable in her dress just now, beyond a natural fitness, and a style that was recent for the streets of Sherton. But, had it been the reverse, and quite striking, it would have meant just as little. For there can be hardly anything less connected with a woman's personality than drapery which she has neither designed, manufactured, cut, sewed, nor even seen, except by a glance of approval when told that such and such a shape and colour must be had because it has been decided by others as imperative at that particular time.

What people therefore saw of her in a cursory view was very little; in truth, mainly something that was not she. The woman herself was a shadowy conjectural creature who had little to do with the outlines presented to Sherton eyes: a shape in the gloom, whose true quality could only be approximated by putting together a movement now and a glance then, in that patient attention which nothing but watchful loving-kindness ever troubles to give.

There was a little delay in their setting out from the town, and Marty South took advantage of it to hasten forward, with the view of escaping them on the way, lest they should feel compelled to spoil their *tête-à-tête* by asking her to ride. She walked fast, and one-third of the journey was done, and the evening rapidly darkening, before she perceived any sign of them behind her. Then, while ascending a hill, she dimly saw their vehicle drawing near the lowest part of the incline, their heads slightly bent towards each other, drawn together, no doubt, by their souls; as the heads of a pair of horses well in hand are drawn in by the rein. She walked still faster.

But between these and herself there was a carriage, apparently a brougham,[5] coming in the same direction, with lighted lamps. When it overtook her – which was not soon on account of her pace – the scene was much darker, and the lights glared in her eyes sufficiently to hide the details of the equipage.

It occurred to Marty that she might take hold behind this carriage and so keep along with it, to save herself from the patronage of being overtaken and picked up for pity's sake by the coming pair. Accordingly, as the carriage drew abreast of her in climbing the long ascent, she walked close to the wheels, the rays of the nearest lamp penetrating her very pores. She had only just dropped behind when the carriage stopped, and to her surprise the coachman asked her, over his shoulder, if she would ride. What made the question more surprising was that it came in obedience to an order from the interior of the vehicle.

Marty gladly assented, for she was weary, very weary, after working all night and keeping afoot all day. She mounted beside the coachman, wondering why this good fortune had happened to her. He was rather a great man in aspect, and she did not like to inquire of him for some time.

At last she said, "Who has been so kind as to ask me to ride?"

"Mrs. Charmond," replied her statuesque companion.

Marty was stirred at the name, so closely connected with her last night's experiences. "Is this her carriage?" she whispered.

"Yes; she's inside."

Marty reflected, and perceived that Mrs. Charmond must have recognised her plodding up the hill under the blaze of the lamp; recognised, probably, her stubbly poll (since she had kept away her face), and thought that those stubbles were the result of her own desire.

Marty South was not so very far wrong. Inside the carriage a pair of bright eyes looked from a ripe handsome face, and though behind those bright eyes was a mind of unfathomed mysteries, beneath them there beat a heart capable of quick, extempore warmth – a heart which could indeed be passionately and imprudently warm on certain occasions. At present, after recognising the girl, she had acted on a mere impulse, possibly feeling gratified at the denuded appearance which signified the success of her agent in obtaining what she had required.

" 'Tis wonderful that she should ask ye," observed the magisterial coachman presently. "I have never known her do it before, for as a rule she takes no interest in the village folk at all."

Marty said no more, but occasionally turned her head to see if she could get a glimpse of the Olympian creature[6] who, as the coachman had truly observed, hardly ever descended from her clouds into the Tempe-vale[7] of the parishioners. But she could discern nothing of the lady. She also looked for Miss Melbury and Winterborne. The nose of their horse sometimes came quite near the back of Mrs. Charmond's carriage. But they never attempted to pass it till the latter conveyance turned towards the park gate, when they sped by. Here the carriage drew up that the gate might be opened; and in the momentary silence Marty heard a gentle oral sound, soft as a breeze.

"What's that?" she whispered.

"Mis'ess yawning."

"Why should she yawn?"

"Oh, because she's been used to such wonderful good life, and finds it dull here. She'll soon be off again on account of it."

"So rich and so powerful, and yet to yawn!" the girl murmured. "Then things don't fay with she any more than with we!"

Marty now alighted; the lamp again shone upon her, and as the carriage rolled on, a voice said to her from the interior, "Good night."

"Good night, ma'am," said Marty. But she had not been able to see the woman who began so greatly to interest her – the second person of her own sex who had operated strongly on her mind that day.

CHAPTER VI

Meanwhile Winterborne and Grace Melbury had also undergone their little experiences.

As he drove off with her out of the town the glances of people fell upon them, the younger thinking that Mr. Winterborne was in a pleasant place, and wondering in what relation he stood towards her. Winterborne himself was unconscious of this. Occupied solely with the idea of having her in charge, he did not notice much with outward eye.

Their conversation was in briefest phrase for some time, Grace being somewhat disconcerted, through not having understood till they were about to start that Giles was to be her sole conductor, in place of her father. When they were in the open country he spoke.

"Don't Brownley's farm-buildings look strange to you, now they have been moved bodily from the hollow where the old ones stood to the top of the hill?"

She admitted that they did, though she should not have seen any difference in them if he had not pointed it out.

"They had a good crop of bitter-sweets, they couldn't grind them all" – nodding towards an orchard where some heaps of apples had been left lying ever since the ingathering.

She said "Yes," but looking at another orchard.

"Why, you are looking at John-apple-trees! You know bitter-sweets – you used to well enough?"

"I am afraid I have forgotten, and it is getting too dark to distinguish."

Winterborne did not continue. It seemed as if the knowledge and interests which had formerly moved Grace's mind had quite died away from her. He wondered whether the special attributes of his image in the past had evaporated like these other things.

However that might be, the fact at present was merely this, that where he was seeing John-apples and farm-buildings she was beholding a much contrasting scene:[1] a broad lawn in the fashionable suburb of a fast city, the evergreen leaves shining in the evening sun, amid which bounding girls, gracefully clad in artistic arrangements of blue, brown, red, and white, were playing at games, with laughter and chat, in all the pride of life, the notes of piano and harp trembling in the air from the open windows adjoining. Moreover they were girls – and this was a fact which Grace Melbury's delicate femininity could not lose sight of – whose parents Giles would have addressed with a deferential Sir or Madam. Beside this visioned scene the homely farmsteads did not quite hold their own from her present twenty-year point of survey. For all his woodland sequestration Giles knew the primitive simplicity of the subject he had started, and now sounded a deeper note.

" 'Twas very odd what we said to each other years ago; I often think of it. I mean our saying that if we still liked each other when you were twenty and I twenty-five, we'd —"

"It was child's tattle."

"H'm?" said Giles suddenly.

"I mean we were young," said she more considerately. That abrupt manner of his in making inquiries reminded her that he was unaltered.

"Yes . . . I beg your pardon, Miss Melbury; your father *sent* me to meet you to-day."

"I know it, and I am glad of it." And she looked at him affectionately.

He seemed satisfied with her and went on – "At that time you were sitting beside me at the back of your father's covered car, when we were coming home from gipsying, all the party being squeezed in together as tight as sheep in an auction-pen. It got darker and darker, and I said – I forget the exact words – but I put my arm round your waist, and there you let it stay till your father, sitting in front, suddenly stopped telling his story to Farmer Bollen, to light his pipe. The flash shone into the car, and showed us all up distinctly; my arm flew from your waist like lightning, yet not so quickly but that some of 'em had seen, and laughed at us. Yet your father, to our amazement, instead of being angry, was mild as milk, and seemed quite pleased. Have you forgot all that, or haven't you?"

She owned that she remembered it very well, now that he mentioned the circumstances. "But I must have been in short frocks,"[2] she said slily.

"Come now, Miss Melbury, that won't do! Short frocks indeed! You know better as well as I."

Grace thereupon declared that she would not argue with an old friend she valued so highly as she valued him, but if it were as he said, then she was virtually no less than an old woman now, so far did the time seem removed from her present.

"But old feelings come to life again in some people," she added softly.

"And in others they have never died!" said he.

"Ah – they are Love's very *ownest* and best, I suppose! I don't pretend to rank so high as they."

"It's not a they – it's a he."

Grace sighed.

"Shall I tell you all about Bath or Cheltenham, or places on the Continent that I visited last summer?" she said.

"With all my heart."

She then described places and persons, avoiding, however, what he most wished to hear – everything specially appertaining to her own existence. When she had done she said gaily, "Now do you tell me in return what has happened in Hintock since I have been away."

"Anything to keep the conversation away from her and me," said Giles within him.

It was true; cultivation had so far advanced in the soil of Miss

Melbury's mind as to lead her to talk of anything save of that she knew well, and had the greatest interest in developing – herself. She had fallen from the good old Hintock ways.

He had not proceeded far with his somewhat bald narration when they drew near a carriage that had been preceding them for some time in the dusk. Miss Melbury inquired if he knew whose carriage it was.

Winterborne, although he had seen it, had not taken it into account. On examination he said it was Mrs. Charmond's.

Grace watched the vehicle and its easy roll, and seemed to feel more nearly akin to it than to the one she was in.

"Pooh – we can polish off the mileage as well as they, come to that," said Winterborne, reading her mind; and rising to emulation at what it bespoke he whipped on the horse. This it was which had brought the nose of Mr. Melbury's old grey close to the back of Mrs. Charmond's much eclipsing vehicle.

"There's Marty South sitting up with the coachman," said he, discerning her by her dress.

"Ah, poor Marty! I must ask her to come to see me this very evening. How does she happen to be riding there?"

"I don't know. It is very singular."

Thus these people with converging destinies went along the road together, till Winterborne, leaving the track of the carriage, turned into Little Hintock, where almost the first house was the timber-merchant's. Pencils of light streamed out of the windows sufficiently to show the white laurestinus flowers, and glance against the polished leaves of laurel. The interior of the rooms could be seen distinctly, warmed up by the fire-flames, which in the parlour were reflected from the pictures and book-case, and in the kitchen from the utensils and ware.

"Let us look at the dear place for a moment before we call them," she said.

In the kitchen dinner was preparing; for though Melbury dined at one o'clock at other times, to-day the meal had been kept back for Grace. A rickety old spit was in motion, its end being fixed in the fire-dog, and the whole kept going by means of a cord conveyed over pulleys along the ceiling to a large stone suspended in a corner of the room. Old Grammer Oliver came and wound it up with a rattle like that of a mill.

In the parlour a colossal shade of Mrs. Melbury's head fell on the wall and ceiling; but before the girl had regarded this room many moments their presence was discovered, and her father and stepmother came out to welcome her.

The character of the Melbury family was of that kind which evinces some shyness in showing strong emotion among each other; a trait frequent in rural households, and one curiously inverse to most of the peculiarities distinguishing villagers from the people of towns. Thus hiding their warmer feelings under commonplace talk all round, Grace's reception produced no extraordinary demonstrations. But that more was felt than was enacted appeared from the fact that her father, in taking her indoors, quite forgot the presence of Giles without, as did also Grace herself.

He said nothing; but took the gig round to the yard and called out from the spar-house the man who attended to these matters, when there was no conversation among the spar-makers to particularly engage him. Winterborne then returned to the door with the intention of entering the house.

The family had gone into the parlour, and were still absorbed in themselves. The fire was as before the only light, and it irradiated Grace's face and hands so as to make them look wondrously smooth and fair beside those of the two elders; shining also through the loose hair about her temples as sunlight through a brake. Her father was surveying her in a dazed conjecture, so much had she developed and progressed in manner and stature since he last had set eyes on her.

Observing these things Winterborne remained dubious by the door, mechanically tracing with his fingers certain time-worn letters carved in the jambs, – initials of bygone generations of householders who had lived and died there.

No, he declared to himself, he would not enter and join the family; they had forgotten him, and it was enough for today that he had brought her home. Still, he was a little surprised that her father's eagerness to send him for Grace should have resulted in such indifference as this.

He walked softly away into the lane towards his own house, looking back when he reached the turning, from which he could get a last glimpse of the timber-merchant's roof. He hazarded guesses as to what Grace was saying just at that moment, and murmured with some self-derision, "nothing about me!" He looked also in the other direction, and saw against the sky the thatched hip and solitary chimney of Marty's cottage, and thought of her too, struggling bravely along under that humble shelter, among her spar-gads and pots and skimmers.

At the timber-merchant's, in the meantime, conversation flowed; and as Giles Winterborne had rightly enough deemed, on subjects in which he had no share. Among the excluding matters there was, as chief, the effect upon Mr. Melbury of the womanly mien and manners of his daughter, which took him so much unawares that it thrust the image of her conductor homeward back into quite the obscurest cellarage of his brain.

Another was his interview with Mrs. Charmond's agent that morning, at which the lady herself had been present for a few minutes. Melbury had purchased some standing timber from her a long time before, and now that the date had come for felling it he was left to pursue almost his own course. This was what the household were actually talking of during Giles's cogitation without.

"So thoroughly does she trust me," said Melbury, "that I might fell, top, or lop, on my own judgment, any stick o' timber whatever in her wood, and fix the price o't, and settle the matter. But name it all, I wouldn't do such a thing. However, it may be useful to have this good understanding with her . . . I wish she took more interest in the place, and stayed here all the year round."

"I am afraid 'tis not her regard for you, but her dislike of Hintock, that makes her so easy about the trees," said Mrs. Melbury.

When dinner was over, Grace took a candle and began to ramble pleasurably through the rooms of her old home, from which she had latterly become well-nigh an alien. Each nook and each object revived a memory, and simultaneously modified it. The chambers seemed lower than they had appeared on any previous occasion of her return, the surfaces of both walls and ceilings standing in such near relations to the eye that it could not avoid taking microscopic note of their irregularities and old fashion. Her own bedroom wore at once a look more familiar than when she had left it, and yet a face estranged. The world of little things therein gazed at her in helpless stationariness, as though they had tried and been unable to make any progress without her presence.[3] Over the place where her candle had been accustomed to stand, when she had used to read in bed till the midnight hour, there was still the brown spot of smoke. She did not know that her father had taken especial care to keep it from being cleaned off.

Having concluded her perambulation of this now uselessly commodious edifice, Grace began to feel that she had come a long journey since the morning; and when her father had been up himself, as well as his wife, to see that her room was comfortable and the fire burning, she prepared to retire for the night.

No sooner, however, was she in bed than her momentary sleepiness took itself off, and she wished she had stayed up longer. She amused herself by listening to the old familiar noises that she could hear to be still going on down stairs, and by looking towards the window as she lay. The blind had been drawn up, as she used to have it when a girl, and she could just discern the dim tree-tops against the sky on the neighbouring hill. Beneath this meeting-line of light and shade nothing was visible save one solitary point of light, which blinked as the tree-twigs waved to and fro before its beams.

From its position it seemed to radiate from the window of a house on the hill-side. The house had been empty when she was last at home, and she wondered who inhabited the place now.

Her conjectures, however, were not intently carried on, and she was watching the light quite idly, when it gradually changed colour, and at length shone blue as sapphire. Thus it remained several minutes, and then it passed through violet to red.

Her curiosity was so widely awakened by the phenomenon that she sat up in bed, and stared steadily at the shine. An appearance of this sort, sufficient to excite attention anywhere, was no less than a marvel in Hintock, as Grace had known the hamlet. Almost every diurnal and nocturnal effect in that woodland place had hitherto been the direct result of the regular terrestrial roll[4] which produced the season's changes; but here was something dissociated from these normal sequences, and foreign to local knowledge.

It was about this moment that Grace heard the household below preparing to retire, the most emphatic noise in the proceeding being that of her father bolting the doors. Then the stairs creaked, and her father and mother passed her chamber. The last to come was Grammer Oliver.

Grace slid out of bed, ran across the room, and lifting the latch said, "I am not asleep, Grammer. Come in and talk to me."

Before the old woman had entered Grace was again under the bedclothes. Grammer set down her candlestick, and seated herself on the edge of Miss Melbury's coverlet.

"I want you to tell me what light that is I see on the hill-side," said Grace.

Mrs. Oliver looked across. "Oh, that," she said, "is from the doctor's. He's often doing things of that sort. Perhaps you don't know that we've a doctor living here now – Mr. Fitzpiers by name?"

Grace admitted that she had not heard of him.

"Well then, miss, he's come here to get up a practice. Though he belongs to the oldest, ancientest family in the county, he's stooped to make hisself useful like any common genius.[5] I know him very well, through going there to help 'em scrub sometimes, which your father said I might do if I wanted to in my spare time. Being a bachelor-man he've only lodgings. Oh, yes, I know him very well. Sometimes he'll talk to me as if I were his own mother."

"Indeed."

"Yes. 'Grammer,' he said one day when I asked him why he came here where there's hardly anybody living, 'I'll tell you why I came here. I took a map, and I marked on it where Dr. Jones's practice ends to the north of this district, and where Mr. Taylor's ends on the south, and little Jimmy Green's on the east, and somebody else's to the west. Then I took a pair of compasses, and found the exact middle of the country that was left between these bounds, and that middle was Little Hintock; so here I am.' . . . But, Lord, there: poor young man!"

"Why?"

"He said, 'Grammer Oliver, I've been here three months, and although there are a good many people in the Hintocks and the villages round, and a scattered practice is often a very good one, I don't seem to get many patients. And there's no society at all; and I'm pretty near melancholy mad,' he said, with a great yawn. 'I should be quite if it were not for my books, and my lab – laboratory, and what not. Grammer, I was made for higher things.' And then he'd yawn and yawn again."

"Was he really made for higher things, do you think? Is he clever?"

"Well, no. How can he be clever? He may be able to jine up a broken man or woman after a fashion, and put his finger upon an ache if you tell him nearly where 'tis; but these young men – they should live to my time of life, and then they'd see how clever they were at five-and-twenty! And yet he's a projick, a real projick, and says the oddest of rozums. 'Ah, Grammer,' he said at another time, 'Let me tell you that Everything is Nothing.[6] There's only Me and Not Me[7] in the whole world.' And he told me that no man's hands could help what they did, any more than the hands of a clock . . . Yes, he's a man of strange meditations, and his eyes seem to see as far as the north star."

"He will soon go away, no doubt."

"I don't think so."

Grace did not say "Why?" and Grammer hesitated. At last she went on, "Don't tell your father or mother, miss, if I let you know a secret?"

Grace gave the required promise.

"Well, he talks of buying me; so he won't go away just yet."

"Buying you – how?"

"Not my soul – my body, when I'm dead. One day when I was there cleaning, he said, 'Grammer, you've a large brain – a very large organ of brain,' he said. 'A woman's is usually four ounces less than a man's; but yours is man's size.' Well, then – hee, hee! – after he'd flattered me a bit like that, he said he'd give me ten pounds to have me as a natomy after my death. Well, knowing I'd no chick nor chiel left, and nobody with any interest in me, I thought, faith, if I can be of any use to my fellow-creatures after I'm gone they are welcome to me; so I said I'd think it over, and would most likely agree and take the ten pounds. Now this is a secret, miss, between us two. The money would be very useful to me; and I see no harm in it."

"Of course there's no harm. But oh, Grammer – how can you think to do it? I wish you hadn't told me."

"I wish I hadn't – if you don't like to know it, miss. But you needn't mind. Lord, hee, hee! I shall keep him waiting many a year yet, bless ye!"

"I hope you will, I am sure."

The girl thereupon fell into such deep reflection that conversation languished, and Grammer Oliver taking her candle wished Miss Melbury good-night.

The latter's eyes rested on the distant glimmer, around which she allowed her reasoning fancy to play in vague eddies that shaped the doings of the philosopher behind that light on the lines of intelligence just received. It was strange to her to come back from the world to Little Hintock and find in one of its nooks, like a tropical plant in a hedgerow, a nucleus of advanced ideas and practices which had nothing in common with the life around. Chemical experiments, anatomical projects, and metaphysical conceptions had found a strange home here.

Thus she remained thinking, the imagined pursuits of the man behind the light intermingling with conjectural sketches of his personality, till her eyes fell together with their own heaviness, and she slept.

CHAPTER VII

Kaleidoscopic dreams of a weird alchemist-surgeon, Grammer Oliver's skeleton, and the face of Giles Winterborne, brought Grace Melbury to the morning of the next day. It was fine. A north wind was blowing – that not unacceptable compromise between the atmospheric cutlery of the eastern blast and the spongy gales of the west quarter. She looked from her window in the direction of the light of the previous evening, and could just discern through the trees the shape of the surgeon's house. Somehow, in the broad, practical daylight, that unknown and lonely gentleman seemed to be shorn of much of the interest which had invested his personality and pursuits in the hours of darkness, and as Grace's dressing proceeded he faded from her mind.

Meanwhile Winterborne, though half-assured of her father's favour, was rendered a little restless by Miss Melbury's behaviour. Despite his shy self-control,[1] he could not help looking continually from his own door towards the timber-merchant's in the probability of somebody's emergence therefrom.

His attention was at length justified by the appearance of two figures, that of Mr. Melbury himself, and Grace beside him. They stepped out in a direction towards the densest quarter of the wood, and Winterborne walked contemplatively behind them, till all three were soon under the trees.

Although the time of bare boughs had now set in, there were sheltered hollows amid the Hintock plantations and copses in which a more tardy leave-taking than on windy summits was the rule with the foliage. This caused here and there an apparent mixture of the seasons; so that in some of the dells they passed by holly-berries in full red growing beside oak and hazel whose leaves were as yet not far removed from green, and brambles whose verdure was rich and deep as in the month of August. To Grace these well-known peculiarities were as an old painting restored.

Now could be beheld that change from the handsome to the curious which the features of a wood undergo at the ingress of the winter months. Angles were taking the place of curves, and reticulations of surfaces – a change constituting a sudden lapse from the ornate to the primitive on Nature's canvas,[2] and comparable to a retrogressive step from the art of an advanced school of painting to that of the Pacific Islander.

Winterborne followed, and kept his eye upon the two figures as they threaded their way through these sylvan masses. Mr. Melbury's long legs, his gaiters drawn in to the bone at the ankles, his slight stoop, his habit of getting lost in thought and arousing himself with an exclamation of "Hah!" accompanied with an upward jerk of the head, composed a personage recognisable by his neighbours as far as he could be seen. It seemed as if the squirrels and birds knew him. One of the former would occasionally run from the path to hide behind the arm of some tree, which the little animal carefully edged round *pari passu*[3] with Melbury and his daughter's movement onward, assuming a mock manner, as though he were saying, "Ho, ho; you are only a timber-merchant, and carry no gun!"

They went noiselessly over mats of starry moss, rustled through interspersed tracts of leaves, skirted trunks with spreading roots, whose mossed rinds made them like hands wearing green gloves; elbowed old elms and ashes with great forks, in which stood pools of water that overflowed on rainy days, and ran down their stems in green cascades. On older trees still than these huge lobes of fungi grew like lungs. Here, as everywhere, the Unfulfilled Intention, which makes life what it is, was as obvious as it could be among the depraved crowds of a city slum.[4] The leaf was deformed,[5] the curve was crippled, the taper was interrupted; the lichen ate the vigour of the stalk, and the ivy slowly strangled to death the promising sapling.

They dived amid beeches under which nothing grew, the younger boughs still retaining their hectic leaves, that rustled in the breeze with a sound almost metallic, like the sheet-iron foliage of the fabled Jarnvid wood.[6] Some flecks of white in Grace's drapery had enabled Giles to keep her and her father in view till this time; but now he lost sight of them, and was obliged to follow by ear – no difficult matter, for on the line of their course every wood-pigeon rose from its perch with a continued clash, dashing its wings against the branches with well-nigh force enough to break every quill. By taking the track of this noise he soon came to a stile.

Was it worth while to go further? He examined the doughy soil at the foot of the stile, and saw amongst the large sole-and-heel tracks an impression of a slighter kind, from a boot that was obviously not local, for Winterborne knew all the cobblers' patterns in that district, because they were very few to know. The mud-picture was enough to make him swing himself over and proceed.

The character of the woodland now changed. The bases of the smaller trees were nibbled bare by rabbits, and at divers points heaps of fresh-made chips, and the newly-cut stool of a tree, stared white through the undergrowth. There had been a large fall of timber this year, which explained the meaning of some sounds that soon reached him.

A voice was shouting intermittently in a sort of human bark, reminding Giles that there was a sale of trees and faggots that very day. Melbury would naturally be present. Thereupon Winterborne remembered that he himself wanted a few faggots, and entered upon the scene.

A large group of buyers stood round the auctioneer, or followed him when, between his pauses, he wandered on from one lot of plantation produce to another, like some philosopher of the Peripatetic school[7] delivering his lectures in the shady groves of the Lyceum. His companions were timber-dealers, yeomen, farmers, villagers, and others; mostly woodland men, who on that account could afford to be curious in their walking-sticks, which consequently exhibited various monstrosities of vegetation, the chief being corkscrew shapes in black and white thorn, brought to that pattern by the slow torture of an encircling woodbine during their growth, as the Chinese have been said to mould human beings into grotesque toys by continued compression in infancy.[8] Two women, wearing men's jackets on their gowns, conducted in the rear of the halting procession a pony-cart containing bread and cheese, with a barrel of strong ale for the select, and cider in milking-pails, into which anybody dipped who chose.

The auctioneer adjusted himself to circumstances by using his walking-stick as a hammer, and knocked down the lot on any convenient object that took his fancy, such as the crown of a little boy's head, or the shoulders of a bystander who had no business there except to taste the brew; a proceeding which would have been deemed humorous but for the air of stern rigidity which the auctioneer's face preserved, tending to show that the eccentricity was a result of that absence of mind which is engendered by the press of affairs, and no freak of fancy at all.

Mr. Melbury stood slightly apart from the rest of the Peripatetics, and Grace beside him, clinging closely to his arm; her modern attire looking almost odd where everything else was old-fashioned, and throwing over the familiar garniture of the trees a homeliness that seemed to demand improvement by the addition of a few contemporary novelties also. Grace seemed to regard the selling with the interest which attaches to memories revived after an interval of obliviousness.

Winterborne went and stood close to them; the timber-merchant spoke, and continued his buying; Grace merely smiled. To justify his presence there Winterborne began bidding for timber and faggots that he did not want, pursuing the occupation in an abstracted mood, in which the auctioneer's voice seemed to become one of the natural sounds of the woodland.

A few flakes of snow descended, at the sight of which a robin, alarmed at these signs of imminent winter, and seeing that no offence was meant by the human invasion, came and perched on the tip of the faggots that were being sold, and looked into the auctioneer's face, whilst waiting for some chance crumb from the bread-basket. Standing a little behind Grace, Winterborne observed how one flake would sail downward and settle on a curl of her hair, and how another would choose her shoulder, and another the edge of her bonnet, which took up so much of his attention that his biddings proceeded incoherently; and when the auctioneer said every now and then, with a nod towards him, "Yours, Mr. Winterborne," he had no idea whether he had bought faggots, poles, or log-wood.

He regretted[9] that her father should show such inequalities of temperament as to keep Grace tightly on his arm to-day, when he had quite lately seemed anxious to recognise their betrothal as a fact. And thus musing, and joining in no conversation with other buyers except when directly addressed, he followed the assemblage hither and thither till the end of the auction, when Giles for the first time realised what his purchases had been. Hundreds of faggots, and divers lots of timber, had been set down to him, when all he had required had been a few bundles of spray for his man Robert Creedle's use in baking and lighting fires.

Business being over, he turned to speak to the timber-merchant. But Melbury's manner was short and distant; and Grace too looked vexed and reproachful. Winterborne then discovered that he had been unwittingly bidding against her father, and picking up his favourite lots in spite of him. With a very few words they left the spot, and pursued their way homeward.

Giles was extremely blank at what he had done, and remained standing under the trees, all the other men having strayed silently away. He saw Melbury and his daughter pass down a glade without looking back. While they moved slowly through it a lady appeared on horseback in the middle distance, the line of her progress converging upon that of Melbury's. They met, Melbury took off his hat, and she reined in her horse. A conversation was evidently in progress between Grace and her father and this equestrian, in whom he was almost sure that he recognised Mrs. Charmond, less by her outline than by the livery of the groom who had halted some yards off.

The interlocutors did not part till after a prolonged pause, during which much seemed to be said. When Melbury and Grace resumed their walk it was with something of a lighter tread than before.

Winterborne then pursued his own course homeward. He was unwilling to let coldness grow up between himself and the Melburys for any trivial reason, and in the evening he went to their house. On drawing near the gate his attention was attracted by the sight of one of the bedrooms blinking into a state of illumination. In it stood Grace lighting several candles, her right hand elevating the taper, her left hand on her bosom, her face thoughtfully fixed on each wick as it kindled, as if she saw in every flame's growth the rise of a life to maturity. He wondered what such unusual brilliancy could mean to-night.

On getting indoors he found her father and stepmother in a state of suppressed excitement, which at first he could not comprehend.

"I am sorry about my biddings to-day," said Giles. "I don't know what I was doing. I have come to say that any of the lots you may require are yours."

"Oh, never mind – never mind," replied the timber merchant with a slight wave of his hand. "I have so much else to think of that I nearly had forgot it. Just now, too, there are matters of a different kind from trade to attend to, so don't let it concern ye."

As the timber-merchant spoke, as it were, down to him from a higher plane than his own, Giles turned to Mrs. Melbury.

"Grace is going to the House to-morrow," she said quietly. "She is looking out her things now. I dare say she is wanting me this minute to assist her." Thereupon Mrs. Melbury left the room.

Nothing is more remarkable than the independent personality of the tongue now and then. Mr. Melbury knew that his words had been a sort of boast. He decried boasting, particularly to Giles; yet whenever the subject was Grace, his judgment resigned the ministry of speech in spite of him.

Winterborne felt surprise, pleasure, and also a little apprehension at the news. He repeated Mrs. Melbury's words.

"Yes," said paternal pride, not sorry to have dragged out of him what he could not in any circumstances have kept in. "Coming home from the woods this afternoon we met Mrs. Charmond out for a ride. She spoke to me on a little matter of business and then got acquainted with Grace. 'Twas wonderful how she took to Grace in a few minutes; that freemasonry of education made 'em close at once. Naturally enough she was amazed that such an article – ha – ha! – could come out of my house. At last it led on to Mis'ess Grace being asked to the House. So she's busy hunting up her frills and furbelows to go in." As Giles remained in thought without responding, Melbury continued: "But I'll call her down stairs?"

"No, no; don't do that, since she's busy," said Winterborne.

Melbury, feeling from the young man's manner that his own talk had been too much at Giles and too little to him, repented at once. His face changed, and he said, in lower tones, with an effort: "She's yours, Giles, as far as I am concerned."

"Thanks – my best thanks, sir. But I think, since it is all right between us about the biddings, that I'll not interrupt her now. I'll step homeward, and call another time."

On leaving the house he looked up at the bedroom again. Grace, surrounded by a sufficient number of candles to answer all purposes of self-criticism was standing before a cheval glass that her father had lately bought expressly for her use; she was bonneted, cloaked, and gloved, and glanced over her shoulder into the mirror, estimating her aspect. Her face was lit with the natural elation of a young girl hoping to inaugurate on the morrow an intimate acquaintance with a new, interesting, and powerful friend.

CHAPTER VIII

The inspiriting appointment which had led Grace Melbury to indulge in a six-candle illumination for the arrangement of her attire carried her over the ground the next morning with a springy tread. Her sense of being properly appreciated on her own native soil seemed to brighten the atmosphere and herbage around her, as the glow-worm's lamp irradiates the grass. Thus she moved along, a vessel of emotion, going to empty itself on she knew not what.

Twenty minutes' walking through copses, over a stile, and along an upland lawn, brought her to the verge of a deep glen, in which Hintock House[1] appeared, immediately beneath her eye. To describe it as standing in a hollow would not express the situation of the manor-house; it stood in a hole. But the hole was full of beauty. From the spot which Grace had reached, a stone could easily have been thrown over or into the birds'-nested chimneys of the mansion. Its walls were surmounted by a battlemented parapet; but the grey lead roofs were quite visible behind it, with their gutters, laps, rolls,[2] and skylights, together with incised letterings and shoe-patterns cut by idlers thereon.

The front of the house was an ordinary manorial presentation of Elizabethan windows, mullioned and hooded,[3] worked in rich snuff-coloured freestone from local quarries. The ashlar of the walls, where not overgrown with ivy and other creepers, was coated with lichen of every shade, intensifying its luxuriance with its nearness to the ground till, below the plinth, it merged in moss.

Above the house to the back was a dense plantation, the roots of whose trees were above the level of the chimneys. The corresponding high ground on which Grace stood was richly grassed, with only an old tree here and there. A few sheep lay about, which as they ruminated looked quietly into the bedroom windows.

The situation of the house, prejudicial to humanity, was a stimulus to vegetation, on which account an endless shearing of the heavy-armed ivy went on, and a continual lopping of trees and shrubs. It was an edifice built in times when human constitutions were damp-proof, when shelter from the boisterous was all that men thought of in choosing a dwelling-place, the insidious being beneath their notice; and its hollow site was an ocular reminder by its unfitness for modern lives of the fragility to which these have declined.

The highest architectural cunning could have done nothing to make Hintock House dry and salubrious; and ruthless ignorance could have done little to make it unpicturesque. It was vegetable nature's own home; a spot to inspire the painter and poet of still life – if they did not suffer too much from the relaxing atmosphere – and to draw groans from the gregariously disposed.

Grace descended the green escarpment by a zigzag path into the drive, which swept round beneath the slope. The exterior of the house had been familiar to her from her childhood, but she had never been inside, and the approach to knowing an old thing in a new way was a lively experience.

It was with a little flutter that she was shown in; but she recollected that Mrs. Charmond would probably be alone. Up to a few days before this time that lady had been accompanied in her comings, stayings, and goings by a relative, believed to be her aunt; latterly, however, these two ladies had separated, owing, it was supposed, to a quarrel; and Mrs. Charmond had been left desolate. Being presumably a woman who did not care for solitude, this deprivation might possibly account for her sudden interest in Grace.

Mrs. Charmond was at the end of a gallery opening from the hall when Miss Melbury was announced, and saw her through the glass doors between them. She came forward with a smile on her face, and told the young girl it was good of her to come.

"Ah! you have noticed those," she said, seeing that Grace's eyes were attracted by some curious objects against the walls. "They are man-traps.[4] My husband was a connoisseur in man-traps and spring-guns and such articles, collecting them from all his neighbours. He knew the histories of all these – which gin had broken a man's leg which gun had killed a man. I don't like them here; but I've never yet given directions for them to be taken away." She added playfully, "Man-traps are of rather ominous significance where a person of our sex lives, are they not?"

Grace was bound to smile; but that side of womanliness was one which her inexperience had no great zest in contemplating.

"They are interesting, no doubt, as relics of a barbarous time happily past," she said, looking thoughtfully at the varied designs of the instruments.

"Well, we must not take them too seriously," said Mrs. Charmond with an indolent turn of her head, and they moved on inwards.

When she had shown her visitor different articles in cabinets that she deemed likely to interest her, some tapestries, wood carvings, ivories, miniatures, and so on – always with a mien of listlessness which might either have been constitutional, or partly owing to the situation of the place – they sat down to an early cup of tea.

"Will you pour it out, please? Do," she said, leaning back in her chair, and placing her hand above her forehead, while her almond eyes – those long eyes so common to the angelic legions of early Italian art – became longer, and her voice more languishing. She showed that oblique-mannered softness which is perhaps most frequent in women of darker complexion and more lymphatic temperament than Mrs. Charmond's was; women who lingeringly smile their meanings to men rather than speak them, who inveigle rather than prompt, and take advantage of currents rather than steer.

"I am the most inactive woman when I am here," she said. "I think sometimes I was born to live and do nothing, nothing, nothing but float about, as we fancy we do sometimes in dreams. But that cannot be really my destiny, and I must struggle against such fancies."

"I am so sorry you do not enjoy exertion – it is quite sad! I wish I could tend you and make you very happy."

There was something so sympathetic, so responsive in the sound of Grace's voice, that it impelled people to play havoc with their customary reservations in talking to her. "It is tender and kind of you to feel that," said Mrs. Charmond. "Perhaps I have given you the notion that my languor is more than it really is. But this place oppresses me, and I have a plan of going abroad a good deal. I used to go with a relative, but that arrangement has dropped through."

Regarding Grace with a final glance of criticism she seemed to make up her mind to consider the young girl satisfactory, and continued:

"Now I am often impelled to record my impressions of times and places. I have often thought of writing a *New Sentimental Journey*.[5] But I cannot find energy enough to do it alone. When I am at different places in the south of Europe I feel a crowd of ideas and fancies thronging upon me continually; but to unfold writing materials, take up a cold steel pen, and put these impressions down systematically on cold smooth paper – that I cannot do. So I have thought that if I always could have somebody at my elbow with whom I am in sympathy, I might dictate any ideas that come into my head. And directly I had made your acquaintance the other day it struck me that you would suit me so well. Would you like to undertake it? You might read to me, too, if desirable. Will you think it over, and ask your parents if they are willing?"

"Oh, yes," said Grace. "I am almost sure they would be very glad."

"You are so accomplished, I hear; I should be quite honoured by such intellectual company."

Grace, modestly blushing, deprecated any such idea.

"Do you keep up your lucubrations at Little Hintock?"

"Oh, no . . . Lucubrations are not unknown at Little Hintock; but they are not carried on by me."

"What – another student in that retreat?"

"There is a surgeon lately come, and I have heard that he reads a great deal – I see his light sometimes through the trees late at night."

"Oh, yes – a doctor – I believe I was told of him. It is a strange place for him to settle in."

"It is a convenient centre for a practice, they say. But he does not confine his studies to medicine, it seems. He investigates theology, and metaphysics, and all sorts of subjects."

"What is his name?"

"Fitzpiers. He represents a very old family, I believe, the Fitzpierses of Buckbury-Fitzpiers – not a great many miles from here."

"I am not sufficiently local to know the history of the family. I was never in the country till my husband brought me here."

Mrs. Charmond did not care to pursue this line of investigation. Whatever mysterious merit might attach to family antiquity, it was one which[6] her adaptable, wandering, *weltbürgerliche*[7] nature had grown tired of caring about – a peculiarity that made her a contrast to her neighbours.

"It is of rather more importance to know what the man is himself than what his family is," she said, "if he is going to practise upon us as a surgeon. Heaven send him skill! Have you seen him?"

Grace had not. "I think he is not a very old man," she added.

"Has he a wife?"

"I am not aware that he has."

"Well, I hope he will be useful here. I must get to know him when I come back. It will be very convenient to have a medical man – if he is clever – in one's own parish. I get dreadfully nervous sometimes, living in such an outlandish place; and Sherton is so far to send to. No doubt you feel Hintock to be a great change after watering-place life."

"I do. But it is home. It has its advantages and its disadvantages." Grace was thinking less of the solitude than of the attendant circumstances.

They chatted on for some time, Grace being set quite at her ease by her entertainer. Mrs. Charmond was far too well-practised a woman not to know that to show a marked patronage to a sensitive young girl who would probably be very quick to discern it was to demolish her dignity rather than to establish it in that young girl's eyes. So being violently possessed with her idea of making use of this

gentle acquaintance, ready and waiting at her own door, she took
great pains to win her confidence at starting.

Just before Grace's departure the two chanced to pause before a
mirror which reflected their faces[8] in immediate juxtaposition, so as
to bring into prominence their resemblances and their contrasts. Both
looked attractive as glassed back by the faithful reflector; but Grace's
countenance had the effect of making Mrs. Charmond appear more
than her full age. There are complexions which set off each other to
great advantage, and there are those which antagonise, the one killing
or damaging its neighbour unmercifully.

This was unhappily the case here. Mrs. Charmond fell into a
meditation, and replied abstractedly to a cursory remark of her companion's. However she parted from her young friend in the kindliest
tones, promising to send and let her know as soon as her mind was
made up on the arrangement she had suggested.

When Grace had ascended nearly to the top of the adjoining slope
she looked back, and saw that Mrs. Charmond still stood at the door
meditatively regarding her.

Often during the previous night, after his call on the Melburys,
Winterborne's thoughts had run upon Grace's announced visit to
Hintock House. Why had he not proposed to walk with her part of
the way? Something told him that she might not, on such an occasion,
have cared for his company.

He was still more of that opinion when, standing in his garden next
day, he saw her go past on the journey with such a pretty pride in the
event. He wondered if her father's ambition, which had purchased
for her the means of intellectual light and culture far beyond those of
any other native of the village, would conduce to the flight of her
future interests above and away from the local life which was once to
her movement of the world.

Nevertheless, he had her father's permission to win her if he could;
and to this end it became desirable to bring matters soon to a crisis.
If she should think herself too good for him, he must let her go, and
make the best of his loss. The question was how to quicken events
towards an issue.

He thought and thought, and at last decided that as good a way as any would be to give a Christmas party, and ask Grace and her parents to come as chief guests.

These ruminations were occupying him when there became audible a slight knocking at his front door. He descended the path, and looked out, and beheld Marty South, dressed for out-door work.

"Why didn't you come, Mr. Winterborne?" she said. "I've been waiting there hours and hours, and at last I thought I must try to find you."

"Bless my soul, I'd quite forgot," said Giles.

What he had forgotten was that there were a thousand young fir-trees[9] to be planted in a neighbouring spot which had been cleared by the woodcutters, and that he had arranged to plant them with his own hands. He had a marvellous power of making trees grow. Although he would seem to shovel in the earth quite carelessly there was a sort of sympathy between himself and the fir, oak, or beech that he was operating on; so that the roots took hold of the soil in a few days. When, on the other hand, any of the journeymen planted, although they seemed to go through an identically similar process, one quarter of the trees would die away during the ensuing August.

Hence Winterborne found delight in the work even when, as at present, he contracted to do it on portions of the woodland in which he had no personal interest. Marty, who turned her hand to anything, was usually the one who performed the part of keeping the trees in a perpendicular position whilst he threw in the mould.

He accompanied her towards the spot, being stimulated yet further to proceed with the work by the knowledge that the ground was close to the wayside along which Grace must pass on her return from Hintock House.

"You've a cold in the head, Marty," he said as they walked. "That comes of cutting off your hair."

"I suppose it do. Yes; I've three headaches going on in my head at the same time."

"Three headaches!"

"Yes, Mr. Winterborne; a rheumatic headache in my poll, a sick headache over my eyes, and a misery headache in the middle of my brain. However, I came out, for I thought you might be waiting and grumbling like anything if I was not there."

The holes were already dug, and they set to work. Winterborne's fingers were endowed with a gentle conjuror's touch in spreading the roots of each little tree, resulting in a sort of caress under which the delicate fibres all laid themselves out in their proper directions for growth. He put most of these roots towards the south-west; for, he said, in forty years' time, when some great gale is blowing from that quarter, the trees will require the strongest holdfast on that side to stand against it and not fall.

"How they sigh directly we put 'em upright, though while they are lying down they don't sigh at all," said Marty.

"Do they?" said Giles. "I've never noticed it."

She erected one of the young pines into its hole, and held up her finger; the soft musical breathing instantly set in which was not to cease night or day till the grown tree should be felled – probably long after the two planters should be felled themselves.

"It seems to me," the girl continued, "as if they sigh because they are very sorry to begin life in earnest – just as we be."

"Just as we be?" He looked critically at her. "You ought not to feel like that, Marty."

Her only reply was turning to take up the next tree; and they planted on through a great part of the day, almost without another word. Winterborne's mind ran on his contemplated evening-party, his abstraction being such that he hardly was conscious of Marty's presence beside him.

From the nature of their employment, in which he handled the spade and she merely held the tree, it followed that he got good exercise and she got none. But she was a heroic girl, and though her outstretched hand was chill as a stone, and her cheeks blue, and her cold worse than ever, she would not complain whilst he was disposed to continue work. But when he paused she said, "Mr. Winterborne, can I run down the lane and back to warm my feet?"

"Why, yes, of course," he said, awakening anew to her existence. "Though I was just thinking what a mild day it is for the season. Now I warrant that cold of yours is twice as bad as it was. You had no business to chop that hair off, Marty; it serves you almost right. Look here, cut off home at once."

"A run down the lane will be quite enough."

"No it won't. You ought not to have come out to-day at all."

"But I should like to finish the —"

"Marty, I tell you to go home," said he peremptorily. "I can manage to keep the rest of them upright with a stick or something."

She went away without saying any more. When she had gone down the orchard a little distance she looked back. Giles suddenly went after her.

"Marty, it was for your good that I was rough, you know. But warm yourself in your own way, I don't care."

When she had run off he fancied he discerned a woman's dress through the holly bushes which divided the coppice from the road. It was Grace at last, on her way back from the interview with Mrs. Charmond. He threw down the tree he was planting, and was about to break through the belt of holly when he suddenly became aware of the presence of another man, who was looking over the hedge on the opposite side of the way upon the figure of the unconscious Grace.

The stranger appeared as a handsome and gentlemanly personage of six or eight and twenty, and he was quizzing her through an eyeglass. Seeing that Winterborne was noticing him he let his glass drop with a click upon the rail which protected the hedge, and walked away in the opposite direction.

Giles knew in a moment that this must be Mr. Fitzpiers. When he was gone Winterborne pushed through the holly, and emerged close beside the interesting object of their contemplation.

CHAPTER IX

"I heard the bushes move long before I saw you," she began. "I said first, 'it is some terrible beast'; next, 'it is a poacher'; next, 'it is a friend!' "

He regarded her with a slight smile, weighing, not her speech, but the question whether he should tell her that she had been flatteringly watched by a gentleman. He decided in the negative.

"You have been to the House?" he said. "But I need not ask." The fact was that there shone upon Miss Melbury's face a species of exaltation, which saw no environing details; not even Giles's occupation; only his bare presence.

"Why need you not ask?"

"Your face is like the face of Moses[1] when he came down from the Mount."

She reddened a little and said, "How can you be so profane, Giles Winterborne?"

"How can you think so much of that class of people? Well, I beg pardon, I didn't mean to speak so freely. How do you like her house and her?"

"Exceedingly. I had not been inside the walls since I was a child, when it used to be let to strangers, before Mrs. Charmond's late husband bought the property. She is *so* nice!" And Grace fell into such an abstracted gaze at the mental image of Mrs. Charmond and her niceness that it almost conjured up a vision of that lady to Giles himself.

"She has only been here a month or two it seems, and cannot stay much longer, because she finds it so lonely and damp in winter. She is going abroad. Only think, she would like me to go with her!"

Giles's features stiffened a little at the news. "Indeed; what for? But I won't keep you standing here. Hoi, Robert!" he cried to a swaying collection of old clothes in the distance, which composed the figure of Creedle, his man. "Go on filling in there till I come back."

"I'm a coming, sir; I'm a coming."

"Well, the reason is this," continued she as they went on together, "Mrs. Charmond has a delightful side to her character – a desire to record her impressions of travel, like Alexandre Dumas and Méry, and Sterne[2] and others. But she cannot find energy enough to do it herself." And Grace proceeded to explain Mrs. Charmond's proposal at large. "My notion is that Méry's style will suit her best, because he writes in that soft, emotional, luxurious way she has," Grace said musingly.

"Indeed!" said Winterborne, sighing. "Suppose you talk over my head a little longer, Miss Grace Melbury."

"Oh, I didn't mean it!" she said repentantly looking into his eyes. "And as for myself, I hate French books. And I love dear old Hintock, *and the people in it*, fifty times better than all the Continent. But the scheme; I think it an enchanting notion, don't you, Giles?"

"It is well enough in one sense, but it will take you away," said he, mollified.

"Only for a short time. We should return in May."

"Well, Miss Melbury; it is a question for your father."

Winterborne walked with her nearly to her house. He had awaited her coming, mainly with the view of mentioning to her his proposal to have a Christmas party; but homely Christmas gatherings in the jovial Hintock style seemed so primitive and uncouth beside the lofty matters of her converse that he refrained.

As soon as she was gone he turned back towards the scene of his planting, and could not help saying to himself as he walked, that this engagement of his was a very unpromising business. Her outing to-day had not improved it. A woman who could go to Hintock House, and be friendly with its mistress; enter into the views of its mistress, talk like her, and dress not much unlike her: why, she would hardly be contented with him, a yeoman, immersed in tree planting, even though he planted them well. "And yet she's a true-hearted girl," he said, thinking of her words about Hintock. "I must bring matters to a point, and there's an end of it."

When he reached the place of work he found that Marty had come back, and dismissing Creedle he went on planting silently with the girl as before.

"Suppose, Marty," he said after a while, looking at her extended arm, upon which old scratches from briars showed themselves purple in the cold wind, "Suppose you know a person, and want to bring that person to a good understanding with you, do you think a Christmas party of some sort is a warming-up thing, and likely to be useful in hastening on the matter?"

"Is there to be dancing?"

"There might be, certainly."

"Will He dance with Her?"

"Well, yes."

"Then it might bring things to a head, one way or the other, I won't be the maid to say which."

"It shall be done," said Winterborne, not to her, though he spoke the words quite loudly. And as the day was nearly ended, he added, "Here, Marty, I'll send up a man to plant the rest to-morrow. I've other things to think of just now."

She did not inquire what other things, for she had seen him walking with Grace Melbury. She looked towards the western sky, which was now aglow like some vast foundry wherein new worlds were being cast. Across it the bare bough of a tree stretched horizontally, revealing every twig against the evening fire, and showing in dark profile every beck and movement of three pheasants that were settling themselves down on it in a row to roost.

"It will be fine to-morrow," said Marty, observing them with the vermilion light of the sun in the pupils of her eyes, "for they are a-croupied down nearly at the end of the bough. If it were going to be stormy they'd squeeze close to the trunk. The weather is almost all they have to think of, isn't it, Mr. Winterborne? and so they must be lighter-hearted than we."

"I dare say they are," said Winterborne.

Before taking a single step in the preparations, Winterborne, with no great hopes, went across that evening to the timber-merchant's to ascertain if Grace and her parents would honour him with their presence. Having first to set his nightly gins in the garden, to catch the rabbits that ate his winter-greens, his call was delayed till just after the rising of the moon, whose rays reached the Hintock houses but fitfully as yet, on account of the trees. Melbury was crossing his yard on his way to call on some one at the larger village, but he readily turned and walked up and down with the young man.

Giles, in his self-deprecatory sense of living on a much smaller scale than the Melburys did, would not for the world imply that his invitation was to a gathering of any importance. So he put it in the mild form of "Can you come in for an hour when you have done business, the day after to-morrow; and Mrs. and Miss Melbury, if they have nothing more pressing to do?"

Melbury would give no answer at once. "No, I can't tell you to-day," he said. "I must talk it over with the women. As far as I am concerned, my dear Giles, you know I'll come with pleasure. But how do I know what Grace's notions may be? You see, she has been away amongst cultivated folks a good while; and now this acquaintance with Mrs. Charmond – well, I'll ask her. I can say no more."

When Winterborne was gone the timber-merchant went on his way. He knew very well that Grace, whatever her own feelings, would either go or not go, according as he suggested; and his instinct was, for the moment, to suggest staying at home. His errand took him near the church, and the way to his destination was equally easy across the churchyard or outside it. For some reason or other he chose the former way.

The moon was faintly lighting up the grave-stones, and the path, and the front of the building. Suddenly Mr. Melbury paused, turned in upon the grass, and approached a particular headstone, where he read, "In memory of John Winterborne," with the subjoined date and age. It was the grave of Giles's father.

The timber-merchant laid his hand upon the stone, and was human-ised. "Jack, my wronged friend!" he said, "I'll be faithful to my plan of making amends to thee."

When he reached home that evening, he said to Grace and Mrs.

Melbury, who were working at a little table by the fire, "Giles wants us to go down and spend an hour with him the day after to-morrow; and I'm thinking, that as 'tis Giles who asks us, we'll go."

They assented without demur; and the timber-merchant sent Giles the next morning an answer in the affirmative.

Winterborne, in his modesty, had mentioned no particular hour in his invitation to the Melburys, though he had to the inferior guests, therefore Mr. Melbury and his family, expecting no other people, chose their own time, which chanced to be rather early in the afternoon, by reason of the somewhat quicker despatch than usual of the timber-merchant's business that day.

They showed their sense of the unimportance of the occasion by walking quite slowly to the house, as if they were merely out for a ramble, and going to nothing special at all; or at most intending to pay a casual call and take a cup of tea.

At this hour stir and bustle pervaded the interior of Winterborne's domicile from cellar to apple-loft. He had planned an elaborate high tea[3] for six o'clock or thereabouts, and a good roaring supper to come on about eleven. Being a bachelor of rather retiring habits, the whole of the preparations devolved upon himself and his trusty man and familiar Robert Creedle, who did everything that required doing, from making Giles's bed to catching moles in his field. He was a survival from the days when Giles's father held the homestead, and Giles was a playing boy.

These two, with a certain dilatoriness which appertained to both, were now in the heat of preparation in the bakehouse, expecting nobody before six o'clock. Winterborne was standing before the brick oven in his shirt-sleeves, tossing in thorn sprays, and stirring about the blazing mass with a long-handled, three-pronged, Beelzebub kind of fork,[4] the heat shining out upon his streaming face and making his eyes like furnaces; the thorns crackling and sputtering; while Creedle, having ranged the pastry dishes in a row on the table till the oven should be ready, was pressing out the crust of a final apple-pie with a rolling-pin. A great pot boiled on the fire; and through the open door of the back-kitchen a boy was seen seated on the fender, emptying the snuffers and scouring the candlesticks, a row of the latter standing upside down on the hob to melt out the grease.

Looking up from the rolling-pin, Creedle saw passing the window first the timber-merchant, in his second-best suit, next Mrs. Melbury in her best silk, and behind them Grace in the fashionable attire which, lately brought home with her from the Continent, she had worn on her visit to Mrs. Charmond's. The eyes of the three had been attracted through the window to the proceedings within by the fierce illumination which the oven threw out upon the operators and their utensils.

"Lord, Lord; if they baint come a'ready!" said Creedle.

"No – hey?" said Giles, looking round aghast; while the boy in the background waved a reeking candlestick in his delight.

As there was no help for it Winterborne hastily rolled down his shirt-sleeves and went to meet them in the doorway.

"My dear Giles, I see we have made a mistake in the time," said the timber-merchant's wife, her face lengthening with concern.

"Oh, it is not much difference. I hope you'll come in."

"But this means a regular randyvoo!" said Mr. Melbury accusingly, as he glanced round and pointed towards the viands in the bakehouse with his stick.

"Well, yes," said Giles.

"And – not Great Hintock band, and dancing, surely?"

"I told three of 'em they might drop in if they'd nothing else to do," Giles mildly admitted.

"Now, why the name didn't ye tell us afore that 'twas going to be a bouncing kind of thing?[5] How should I know what folk mean if they don't say? Now, shall we come in, or shall we go home, and come back-along in a couple of hours?"

"I hope you'll stay, if you'll be so good as not to mind, now you are here! I shall have it all right and tidy in a very little time. I ought not to have been so backward; but Creedle is rather slow."

Giles spoke quite anxiously for one of his undemonstrative temperament; for he feared that if the Melburys once were back in their own house they would not be disposed to turn out again.

" 'Tis we ought not to have been so forward; that's what 'tis," said Mr. Melbury testily. "Don't keep us here in your best sitting-room;

lead on to the bakehouse, man. Now we are here we'll help ye get ready for the rest. Here, mis'ess, take off your things, and help him out in his baking, or he won't get done to-night. I'll finish heating the oven, and set you free to go and skiver up them ducks." His eye had passed with pitiless directness of criticism into yet remoter recesses of Winterborne's awkwardly built premises, where the aforesaid birds were hanging.

"And I'll help finish the tarts," said Grace cheerfully.

"I don't know about that," said her father. " 'Tisn't quite so much in your line as it is in your mother-law's[6] and mine."

"Of course I couldn't let you, Grace!" said Giles, with some distress.

"I'll do it, of course," said Mrs. Melbury, taking off her silk train, hanging it up to a nail, carefully rolling back her sleeves, pinning them to her shoulders, and stripping Giles of his apron for her own use.

So Grace pottered idly about while her father and his wife helped on the preparations. A kindly pity of his household management, which Winterborne saw in her eyes whenever he caught them, depressed him much more than her contempt would have done.

Creedle met Giles at the pump after a while, when each of the others was absorbed in the difficulties of a *cuisine* based on utensils, cupboards, and provisions that were strange to them. He groaned to the young man in a whisper, "This is a bruckle het, maister, I'm much afeard! Who'd ha' thought they'd ha' come so soon!"

The bitter placidity of Winterborne's look hinted the misgivings he did not care to express. "Have you got the celery ready?" he asked quickly.

"Now, that's a thing I never could mind; no, not if you'd pay me in silver and gold!" said Creedle. "And I don't care who the man is, I says that a stick of celery that isn't scrubbed with the scrubbing-brush, is not clean."

"*Very* well, very well! I'll attend to it. You go and get 'em comfortable indoors."

He hastened to the garden, and soon returned, tossing the stalks to Creedle, who was still in a tragic mood. "If ye'd ha' married, d'ye see, maister," he murmured, "this calamity couldn't have happened to us!"

Everything being at last under way, the oven set, and all done that could insure the supper turning up ready at some time or other, Giles and his friends entered the parlour, where the Melburys again dropped into position as guests, though the room was not nearly so warm and cheerful as the blazing bakehouse. Others now arrived, among them Farmer Cawtree, and the hollow-turner, and tea went off very well.

Grace's disposition to make the best of everything, and to wink at deficiencies in Winterborne's way of living, was so uniform and persistent that he suspected her of seeing even more deficiencies than he was aware of. That suppressed sympathy which had showed in her face ever since her arrival told him as much too plainly.

"This muddling style of housekeeping is what you've not lately been used to, I suppose?" he said when they were a little apart.

"No; but I like it; it reminds me so pleasantly that everything here in dear old Hintock is just as it used to be. The oil is – not quite nice; but everything else is."

"The oil?"

"On the chairs, I mean; because it gets on one's dress. Still, mine is not a new one."

Giles found that the boy, in his zeal to make things look bright, had smeared the chairs with some greasy furniture-polish, and refrained from rubbing it dry in order not to diminish the mirror-like effect that the mixture produced as laid on. Giles apologised and scolded the boy; but he felt that the fates were against him.

CHAPTER X

Supper-time came, and with it the hot-baked meats from the oven, laid on a snowy cloth fresh from the press, and reticulated with folds as in Flemish Last-Suppers.[1] Creedle and the boy fetched and carried with amazing alacrity; the latter, to mollify his superior, and make things pleasant, expressing his admiration of Creedle's cleverness when they were alone.

"I s'pose the time when you learnt all these knowing things, Mr. Creedle, was when you was in the militia?"

"Well, yes. I seed the world that year somewhat, certainly, and mastered many arts of strange dashing life. Not but that Giles has worked hard in helping me to bring things to such perfection to-day. 'Giles,' says I, though he's maister. Not that I should call'n maister by rights, for his father growed up side by side with me, as if one mother had twinned us and been our nourishing."

"I s'pose your memory can reach a long way back into history, Mr. Creedle?"

"Oh, yes. Ancient days, when there was battles, and famines, and hang-fairs,[2] and other pomps, seem to me as yesterday. Ah, many's the patriarch I've seed come and go in this parish! There, he's calling for more plates. Lord, why can't 'em turn their plates bottom upward for pudding, as we bucks used to do in former days!"

Meanwhile in the adjoining room Giles was presiding in a half unconscious state. He could not get over the initial failures in his scheme for advancing his suit; and hence he did not know that he was eating mouthfuls of bread and nothing else, and continually snuffing the two candles next him till he had reduced them to mere glimmers drowned in their own grease. Creedle now appeared with a specially prepared dish, which he served by elevating the little three-legged pot that contained it, and tilting the contents into a platter, exclaiming simultaneously, "Draw back, gentlemen and ladies, please!"

A splash followed. Grace gave a quick involuntary nod and blink, and put her handkerchief to her face.

"Good heavens, what did you do that for, Creedle?" said Giles, sternly, jumping up.

" 'Tis how I do it when they baint here, maister," mildly expostulated Creedle, in an aside audible to all the company.

"Well yes – but –" replied Giles. He went over to Grace, and hoped none of it had gone into her eye.

"Oh, no," she said. "Only a sprinkle on my face. It was nothing."

"Kiss it and make it well," gallantly observed Mr. Cawtree.

Miss Melbury blushed.

The timber-merchant replied quickly, "Oh, it is nothing! She must bear these little mishaps." But there could be discerned in his face something which said, "I ought to have foreseen all this, and kept her away."

Giles himself, since the untoward beginning of the feast, had not quite liked to see Grace present. He wished he had not asked such people as Cawtree and the hollow-turner. He had done it, in dearth of other friends, that the room might not appear empty. In his mind's eye, before the event, they had been the mere background or padding of the scene; but somehow in the reality they were the most prominent personages there.

After supper they played cards; Cawtree and the hollow-turner monopolising the new packs for an interminable game, in which a lump of chalk was incessantly used – a game those two always played wherever they were, taking a solitary candle and going to a private table in a corner with the mien of persons bent on weighty matters. The rest of the company on this account were obliged to put up with old packs for their round game, that had been lying by in a drawer ever since the time that Giles's grandmother was alive. Each card had a great stain in the middle of its back, produced by the touch of generations of damp and excited thumbs, now fleshless in the grave; and the kings and queens wore a decayed expression of feature, as if they were rather an impecunious dethroned race of monarchs hiding in obscure slums than real regal characters. Every now and then the comparatively few remarks of the players at the round game were harshly intruded on by the measured jingle of Farmer Cawtree and the hollow-turner from the back of the room:–

> "And I' will hold' a wa'-ger with you'
> That all' these marks' are thirt'-y-two!"

accompanied by rapping strokes with the chalk on the table; then an exclamation, an argument, a dealing of the cards; then the commencement of the rhymes anew.

The timber-merchant showed his feelings by talking with a reserved weight in his words, and by praising the party in a patronising tone, when Winterborne expressed his fear that he and his were not enjoying themselves.

"Oh yes, yes; pretty much. What handsome glasses those are! I didn't know you had such glasses in the house. Now, Lucy [to his wife], you ought to get some like them for ourselves." And when they had abandoned cards, and Winterborne was talking to Melbury by the fire, it was the timber-merchant who stood with his back to the mantel in a proprietary attitude; from which post of vantage he critically regarded Giles's person, rather as a superficies than as a solid with ideas and feelings inside it; saying, "What a splendid coat that one is you have on, Giles. I can't get such coats. You dress better than I."

After supper there was a dance, the bandsmen from Great Hintock having arrived some time before. Grace had been away from home so long, and was so drilled in new dances, that she had forgotten the old figures, and hence did not join in the movement. Then Giles felt that all was over. As for her, she was thinking, as she watched the gyrations, of a very different measure that she had been accustomed to tread with a bevy of sylph-like creatures in muslin, in the music-room of a large house, most of whom were now moving in scenes widely removed from this, both as regarded place and character.

A woman she did not know came and offered to tell her fortune with the abandoned cards. Grace assented to the proposal, and the woman told her tale unskilfully, for want of practice, as she declared.

Mr. Melbury was standing by, and exclaimed contemptuously, "Tell her fortune, indeed! Her fortune has been told by men of science – what do you call 'em? Phrenologists.[3] You can't teach her anything new. She's been too far among the wise ones to be astonished at anything she can hear among us folks in Hintock."

At last the time came for breaking up, Melbury and his family being the earliest to leave, the two card-players still pursuing their game doggedly in the corner, where they had completely covered Giles's mahogany table with chalk scratches. The Melburys walked home, the distance being short and the night clear.

"Well, Giles is a very good fellow," said Mr. Melbury, as they struck down the lane under boughs which formed a black filigree in which the stars seemed set.

"Certainly he is," said Grace, quickly, and in such a tone as to show that he stood no lower, if no higher, in her regard than he had stood before.

When they were opposite an opening through which, by day, the doctor's house could be seen, they observed a light in one of his rooms, although it was now about two o'clock.

"The doctor is not abed yet," said Mrs. Melbury.

"Hard study, no doubt," said her husband.

"One would think that, as he seems to have nothing to do about here by day, he could at least afford to go to bed early at night. 'Tis astonishing how little we see of him."

Melbury's mind seemed to turn with much relief to the contemplation of Mr. Fitzpiers after the scenes of the evening. "It is natural enough," he replied. "What can a man of that sort find to interest him in Hintock? I don't expect he'll stay here long."

His thoughts then reverted to Giles's party, and when they were nearly home he spoke again, his daughter being a few steps in advance: "It is hardly the line of life for a girl like Grace, after what she's been accustomed to. I didn't foresee that, in sending her to boarding-school, and letting her travel, and what not, to make her a good bargain for Giles, I should be really spoiling her for him. Ah 'tis a thousand pities! But he ought to have her – he ought!"

At this moment the two exclusive, chalk-mark men, having at last really finished their play, could be heard coming along in the rear, vociferously singing a song to march-time, and keeping vigorous step to the same in far-reaching strides –

> "She may go, oh!
> She may go, oh!
> She may go to the devil for me!"[4]

The timber-merchant turned indignantly to Mrs. Melbury. "That's the sort of society we've been asked to meet," he said. "For us old folk it didn't matter; but for Grace – Giles should have known better!"

*

Meanwhile, in the empty house from which the guests had just cleared out, the subject of their discourse was walking from room to room surveying the general displacement of furniture with no ecstatic feeling; rather the reverse, indeed. At last he entered the bakehouse, and found there Robert Creedle sitting over the embers, also lost in contemplation. Winterborne sat down beside him.

"Well, Robert, you must be tired. You'd better get on to bed."

"Ay, ay, Giles – what do I call ye? Maister, I would say. But 'tis well to think the day *is* done, when 'tis done."

Winterborne had abstractedly taken the poker, and with a wrinkled forehead was ploughing abroad the wood-embers on the wide hearth, till it was like a vast scorching Sahara, with red-hot boulders lying about everywhere. "Do you think it went off well, Creedle?" he asked.

"The victuals did; that I know. And the drink did; that I steadfastly believe, from the holler sound of the barrels. Good honest drink 'twere, the headiest mead I ever brewed; and the best wine that berries could rise to; and the briskest Horner-and-Cleeves cider ever wrung down, leaving out the spice and sperrits I put into it, while that egg-flip would ha' passed through muslin, so little criddled 'twere. 'Twas good enough to make any king's heart merry – ay, to make his whole carcase smile! Still, I don't deny I'm afeard some things didn't go well with He and his." Creedle nodded in a direction which signified where the Melburys lived.

"I'm afraid, too, that it was a failure there!"

"If so, 'twere doomed to be so. Not but what that snail might as well have come upon anybody else's plate as hers."

"What snail?"

"Well, maister, there was a little small one upon the edge of her plate when I brought it out; and so it must have been in her few leaves of winter-green."

"How the deuce did a snail get there?"

"That I don't know no more than the dead; but there my gentleman was."

"But, Robert, of all places, that was where he shouldn't have been."

"Well, 'twas his native home, come to that; and where else could we expect him to be? I don't care who the man is, snails and caterpillars always will lurk in close to the stump of cabbages in that tantalising way."

"He wasn't alive, I suppose?" said Giles, with a shudder on Grace's account.

"Oh, no. He was well boiled. I warrant him well boiled. God forbid that a *live* snail should be seed on any plate of victuals that's served by Robert Creedle ... But Lord, there; I don't mind 'em myself – them green ones; for they were born on cabbage, and they've lived on cabbage, so they must be made of cabbage. But she, the close-mouthed little lady, she didn't say a word about it; though 'twould have made good small conversation as to the nater of such creatures; especially as wit ran short among us sometimes."

"Oh, yes – 'tis all over!" murmured Giles to himself, shaking his head over the glooming plain of embers, and lining his forehead more than ever. "Do you know, Robert," he said, "that she's been accustomed to servants and everything superfine these many years? How, then, could she stand our ways?"

"Well, all I can say is, then, that she ought to hob-and-nob elsewhere. They shouldn't have schooled her so monstrous high, or else bachelor-men shouldn't give randys, or if they do give 'em, only to their own race."

"Perhaps that's true," said Winterborne, rising and yawning a sigh.

CHAPTER XI

" 'Tis a pity – a thousand pities!" her father kept saying next morning at breakfast, Grace being still in her bedroom.

Here was the fact, which could not be disguised: since seeing what an immense change her last twelve months of absence had produced in his daughter, after the heavy sum per annum that he had been spending for several years upon her education, he was reluctant to let her marry Giles Winterborne, indefinitely occupied as woodsman, cider-merchant, apple-farmer, and what-not, even were she willing to marry him herself.

But how could he, with any self-respect, obstruct Winterborne's suit at this stage, and nullify a scheme he had laboured to promote – was, indeed, mechanically promoting at this moment? A crisis was approaching, mainly as a result of his contrivances; and it would have to be met.

"She will be his wife, if you don't upset her notion that she's bound to accept him as an understood thing," said Mrs. Melbury. "Bless you, she'll soon shake down here in Hintock and be content with Giles's way of living, which he'll improve with what money she'll have from you. 'Tis the strangeness after her genteel life that makes her feel uncomfortable at first. Why, when *I* saw Hintock the first time I thought I never could like it. But things gradually get familiar, and stone floors seem not so very cold and hard, and the hooting of owls not so very dreadful, and loneliness not so very lonely, after a while."

"Yes, I believe ye. That's just it. I *know* Grace will gradually sink down to our level again, and catch our manners and way of speaking, and feel a drowsy content in being Giles's wife. But I can't bear the thought of dragging down to that old level as promising a piece of maidenhood as ever lived – fit to ornament a palace wi', that I've taken so much trouble to lift up. Fancy her white hands getting redder every day, and her tongue losing its pretty up-country curl in talking, and her bounding walk becoming the regular Hintock shail-and-wamble."

"She may shail; but she'll never wamble," replied his wife decisively.

When Grace came down stairs he complained of her lying in bed so late; not so much moved by a particular objection to that form of indulgence as discomposed by these other reflections.

The corners of her pretty mouth dropped a little down. "You used to complain with justice when I was a girl," she said; "but I am a woman now, and can judge for myself . . . But it is not that; it is something else!" Instead of sitting down she went outside the door.

He was sorry. The petulance that relatives show towards each other is in truth directed against that intangible Cause which has shaped the situation no less for the offenders than the offended, but is too elusive to be discerned and cornered by poor humanity in irritated mood. Melbury followed her. She had rambled on to the paddock, where the white frost lay, making the grass rustle like paper-shavings under their feet; and where starlings in flocks of twenties and thirties were walking about, watched by a comfortable family of sparrows perched in a line along the string-course of the chimney, and preening themselves in the rays of the sun.

"Come in to breakfast, my girl," he said. "And as to Giles, use your own mind. Whatever pleases you will please me."

"I am promised to him, father; and I cannot help thinking that in honour I ought to marry him, whenever I do marry."

He had a strong suspicion that somewhere in the bottom of her heart there pulsed an old simple indigenous feeling favourable to Giles, though it had become overlaid with implanted tastes. "Very well," he said. "But I hope I sha'n't lose you yet. Come in to breakfast. What did you think of the inside of Hintock House the other day?"

"I liked it much."

"Different from friend Winterborne's?"

She said nothing; but he who knew her was aware that she meant by her silence to reproach him with drawing cruel comparisons.

"Mrs. Charmond has asked you to come again – when, did you say?"

"She thought Tuesday; but would send the day before to let me know if it suited her." And with this subject upon their lips they entered to breakfast.

Tuesday came, but no message from Mrs. Charmond. Nor was there any on Wednesday. In brief, a fortnight slipped by without a sign, and it looked suspiciously as if Mrs. Charmond was not going further in the direction of "taking up"[1] Grace at present.

Her father reasoned thereon. Immediately after his daughter's two indubitable successes with Mrs. Charmond – the interview in the wood and the visit to the House – she had attended Winterborne's party. No doubt the out-and-out joviality of that gathering had made it a topic in the neighbourhood, and that every one present as guests had been widely spoken of – Grace, with her exceptional qualities, above all. What then so natural as that Mrs. Charmond should have heard the village news, and become quite disappointed in her expectations of Grace at finding she kept such company?

Full of this *post hoc* argument,[2] Mr. Melbury overlooked the infinite throng of other possible reasons and unreasons for a woman changing her mind. For instance, while knowing that his Grace was attractive, he quite forgot that Mrs. Charmond had also great pretensions to beauty.

So it was settled in his mind that her sudden mingling with the villagers at the unlucky Winterborne's was the cause of her most grievous loss, as he deemed it, in the direction of Hintock House.

" 'Tis a great sacrifice!" he would repeat to himself. "I am ruining her for conscience' sake!"

It was one morning later on, while these things were agitating his mind, that something darkened the window just as they finished breakfast. Looking up they saw Giles in person, mounted on horseback, and straining his neck forward, as he had been doing for some time, to catch their attention through the window. Grace had been the first to see him, and involuntarily exclaimed, "There he is – and a new horse!"

On their faces, as they regarded Giles, were written their suspended thoughts and compound feelings concerning him, could he have read them through those old panes. But he saw nothing: his features just now were, for a wonder, lit up with a red smile at some other idea. So they rose from breakfast and went to the door, Grace with an anxious, wistful manner, her father in a reverie, Mrs. Melbury placid and inquiring.

"We have come out to look at your horse," she said.

It could be seen that he was pleased at their attention, and explained that he had ridden a mile or two to try the animal's paces. "I bought her," he added, with warmth so severely repressed as to seem indifference, "because she has been used to carry a lady."

Still Mr. Melbury did not brighten. Mrs. Melbury said, "And is she quiet?"

Winterborne assured her that there was no doubt of it. "I took care of that. She's fifteen, and very clever for her age."

"Well, get off and come in," said Melbury brusquely; and Giles dismounted accordingly.

This event was the concrete result of Winterborne's thoughts during the past week or two. The want of success with his evening-party he had accepted in as philosophic a mood as he was capable of; but there had been enthusiasm enough left in him one day at Sherton Abbas market to purchase this mare, which had belonged to a neighbouring parson with several daughters, and was offered him to carry either a gentleman or a lady, and to do odd jobs of carting and agriculture at a pinch. This obliging quadruped seemed to furnish Giles with a means of reinstating himself in Melbury's good opinion as a man of considerateness, by throwing out equestrian possibilities to Grace.

The latter looked at him with intensified interest this morning, in the mood which is altogether peculiar to woman's nature, and which, when reduced into plain words, seems as impossible as the penetrability of matter – that of entertaining a tender pity for the object of her own unnecessary coldness. The imperturbable poise which marked Winterborne in general was enlivened now by a freshness and animation that set a brightness in his eye and on his cheek. Mrs. Melbury asked him to have some breakfast, and he pleasurably replied that he would join them, not perceiving that they had all finished the meal, and that the note piped by the kettle denoted it to be nearly empty; so that fresh water had to be brought in, and a general renovation of the table carried out. Neither did he know, so full was he of his tender ulterior object in buying that horse, how the morning was slipping away, nor how he was keeping the family from dispersing about their duties.

Then he told throughout the humorous story of the horse's purchase, looking particularly grim at some fixed object in the room, a way he always looked when he narrated anything that amused him. While he was still thinking of the scene he had described, Grace rose and said, "I have to go and help my mother now, Mr. Winterborne."

"H'm?" he ejaculated, turning his eyes suddenly upon her.

She repeated her words with a slight blush of awkwardness; whereupon Giles, becoming suddenly conscious, too conscious, jumped up, saying, "To be sure, to be sure!" and wished them quickly good morning.

Nevertheless he had upon the whole strengthened his position, with her at least. Time, too, was on his side, for (as her father saw with some regret) already the homeliness of Hintock life was fast becoming effaced from her observation as a singularity; as the momentary strangeness of a face from which we have for years been separated insensibly passes off with renewed intercourse, and tones itself down into identity with the lineaments of the past.

Thus Mr. Melbury went out of the house still unreconciled to the sacrifice of the gem he had been at such pains in mounting. He fain could hope, in the secret nether chamber of his mind, that something would happen, before the balance of her feeling had quite turned in Winterborne's favour, to relieve his conscience and preserve her on her elevated plane.[3]

CHAPTER XII

It was a day of rather bright weather for the season. Miss Melbury went out for a morning walk, and her ever-regardful father, having an hour's leisure, offered to walk with her.

The breeze was fresh and quite steady, filtering itself through the denuded mass of twigs without swaying them, but making the point of each ivy-leaf on the trunks scratch its underlying neighbour restlessly. Grace's lips sucked in this native air of hers like milk. They soon reached a place where the wood ran down into a corner, and went outside it towards comparatively open ground. Having looked round about, they were intending to re-enter the copse when a fox quietly emerged with a dragging brush, trotted past them tamely as a domestic cat, and disappeared amid some dead fern. They walked on, her father merely observing, after watching the animal, "They are hunting somewhere near."

Further up they saw in the mid-distance the hounds running hither and thither, as if the scent lay cold that day. Soon divers members of the hunt appeared on the scene, and it was evident from their movements that the chase had been stultified by general puzzle-headedness as to the whereabouts of the intended victim. In a minute a gentleman farmer panting with Actæonic excitement,[1] rode up to the two pedestrians, and Grace being a few steps in advance he addressed her, asking if she had seen the fox.

"Yes," said she. "I saw him some time ago – just out there."

"Did you cry Halloo?"

"I said nothing."

"Then why the devil didn't you, or get the old buffer to do it for you?" said the man as he cantered away.

She looked rather disconcerted at this reply, and observing her father's face saw that it was quite red.

"He ought not to have spoken to ye like that!" said the old man in the tone of one whose heart was bruised, though it was not by the epithet applied to himself. "And he wouldn't if he had been a gentleman. 'Twas not the language to use to a woman of any niceness. You so well read and cultivated – how could he expect ye to go shouting a view-halloo like a farm tomboy! Hasn't it cost me near a hundred a year to lift you out of all that, so as to show an example to the neighbourhood of what a woman can be? Grace, shall I tell you the secret of it? 'Twas because *I* was in your company. If a blackcoated squire or pa'son had been walking with you instead of me he wouldn't have spoken so."

"No, no, father; there's nothing in you rough or ill-mannered!"

"I tell you it is that! I've noticed, and I've noticed it many times, that a woman takes her colour from the man she's walking with. The woman who looks an unquestionable lady when she's with a polished-up fellow, looks a tawdry imitation article when she's hobbing and nobbing[2] with a homely blade. You sha'n't be treated like that for long, or at least your children sha'n't. You shall have somebody to walk with you who looks more of a dandy than I – please God you shall!"

"But, my dear father," she said, much distressed, "I don't mind at all. I don't wish for more honour than I already have!"

"A perplexing and ticklish possession is a daughter," according to a Greek poet,[3] and to nobody was one ever more so than to Melbury. As for Grace, she began to feel troubled; she did not perhaps wish, there and then, to unambitiously devote her life to Giles Winterborne, but she was more and more uneasy at being the social hope of the family.

"You would like to have more honour, if it pleases me?" asked her father in continuation of the subject.

Despite her feeling she assented to this. His reasoning had been not without weight upon her.

"Grace," he said, just before they had reached the house, "if it costs me my life you shall marry well! To-day has shown me that whatever a young woman's niceness, she stands for nothing alone. You shall marry well."

He breathed heavily, and his breathing was caught up by the breeze, which seemed to sigh a soft remonstrance.

She looked calmly at him. "And how about Mr. Winterborne?" she asked. "I mention it, father, not as a matter of sentiment, but as a question of keeping faith."

The timber-merchant's eyes fell for a moment. "I don't know – I don't know," he said. " 'Tis a trying strait. Well, well; there's no hurry. We'll wait and see how he gets on."

That evening he called her into his room, a snug little apartment behind the large parlour. It had at one time been part of the bakehouse, with the ordinary oval brick oven in the wall; but Mr. Melbury in turning it into an office had built into the cavity an iron safe, which he used for holding his private papers. The door of the safe was now open, and his keys were hanging from it.

"Sit down, Grace, and keep me company," he said. "You may amuse yourself by looking over these." He threw out a heap of papers before her.

"What are they?" she asked.

"Securities of various sorts." He unfolded them one by one. "Papers worth so much money each. Now here's a lot of turnpike bonds, for one thing. Would you think that each of these pieces of paper is worth two hundred pounds?"

"No, indeed, if you didn't say so."

" 'Tis so then. Now here are papers of another sort. They are for different sums in the three per cents. Now these are Port-Breedy Harbour bonds.[4] We have a great stake in that harbour, you know, because I send off timber there. Open the rest at your pleasure. They'll interest ye."

"Yes, I will, some day," said she rising.

"Nonsense, open them now. You ought to learn a little of such matters. A young lady of education should not be ignorant of money affairs altogether. Suppose you should be left a widow some day, with your husband's title deeds and investments thrown upon your hands —"

"Don't say that, father. Title deeds; it sounds so vain!"

"It does not. Come to that, I have title deeds myself. There, that piece of parchment represents houses in Sherton Abbas."

"Yes, but — " She hesitated, looked at the fire, and went on in a low voice, "If what has been arranged about me should come to anything, my sphere will be quite a middling one."

"Your sphere ought not to be middling," he exclaimed. "You said you never felt more at home, more in your element, anywhere than you did that afternoon with Mrs. Charmond, when she showed you her house, and all her knick-knacks, and made you stay to tea so nicely in her drawing-room, surely you did!"

"Yes, I did say so," admitted Grace.

"Was it true?"

"Yes, I felt so at the time. The feeling is less strong now, perhaps."

"Ah! Now, though you don't see it, your feeling at the time was the right one, because your mind and body were just in full and fresh cultivation, so that going there with her was like meeting like. Since then you've been staying with us, and have fallen back a little, and so you don't feel your place so strongly. Now do as I tell you, and look over these papers, and see what you'll be worth some day. For they'll all be yours, you know; who have I got to leave 'em to but you?

Perhaps when your education is backed up by what these papers represent, and that backed up by another such a set and their owner, men such as that fellow was this morning may think you a little more than a buffer's girl."

So she did as commanded, and opened each of the folded representatives of hard cash that her father put before her. To sow in her heart cravings for social position was obviously his strong desire, though in direct antagonism to a better feeling which had hitherto prevailed with him, and had, indeed, only succumbed that morning during the ramble.

She wished that she was not his worldly hope; the responsibility of such a position was too great. She had made it for herself mainly by her appearance and attractive behaviour to him since her return. "If I had only come home in a shabby dress, and tried to speak roughly, this might not have happened," she thought. She deplored less the fact, however, than the contingencies.

Her father then insisted upon her looking over his cheque book and reading the counterfoils. This also she obediently did, and at last came to two or three which had been drawn to defray some of the late expenses of her clothes, board, and education.

"I, too, cost a good deal, like the horses and waggons and corn!" she said, looking up sorrily.

"I didn't want you to look at those; I merely meant to give you an idea of my investment transactions. But if you do cost as much as they, never mind. You'll yield a better return."

"Don't think of me like that!" she begged. "A mere chattel."[5]

"A what? Oh, a dictionary word.[6] Well, as that's in your line I don't forbid it, even if it tells against me," he said good-humouredly. And he looked her proudly up and down.

A few minutes later Grammer Oliver came to tell them that supper was ready, and in giving the information she added incidentally, "So we shall soon lose the mistress of Hintock House for some time, I hear, Maister Melbury. Yes, she's going off to foreign parts to-morrow, for the rest of the winter months; and be-chok'd if I don't wish I could do the same, for my wind-pipe is furred like a flue."

When the old woman had left the room, Melbury turned to his

daughter and said, "So, Grace, you've lost your new friend, and your chance of keeping her company and writing her travels is quite gone from ye!"

Grace said nothing.

"Now," he went on emphatically, " 'tis Winterborne's affair has done this. Oh yes, 'tis. So let me say one word. Promise me that you will not meet him again without my knowledge."

"I never do meet him, father, either without your knowledge or with it."

"So much the better. I don't like the look of this at all. And I say it not out of harshness to him, poor fellow, but out of tenderness to you. For how could a woman, brought up delicately as you have been, bear the roughness of a life with him?"

She sighed; it was a sigh of sympathy with Giles, complicated by a sense of the intractability of circumstances.

At that same hour, and almost at that same minute, there was a conversation about Winterborne in progress in the village street, opposite Mr. Melbury's gates, where Timothy Tangs the elder and Robert Creedle had accidentally met.

The sawyer was asking Creedle if he had heard what was all over the parish, the skin of his face being drawn two ways on the matter – towards brightness in respect of it as news, and towards concern in respect of its bearings.

"Why that poor little lonesome thing, Marty South, is likely to lose her father. He was almost well, but is much worse again; a man all skin and grief he ever were; and if he leave Little Hintock for a better land, won't it make some difference to your good man Winterborne, neighbour Creedle?"

"Can I be a prophet in Hintock?"[7] said Creedle. "I was only shaping of such a thing yesterday in my poor long-seeing way! It is upon John South's life that all Mr. Winterborne's houses hang. If so be South die and so make his decease, thereupon the law ordains that the houses fall without the least chance of absolution into Her hands at the House. I told him so; but the words of the faithful be only as wind!"[8]

CHAPTER XIII

The news was true. The life – the one fragile life – that had been used as a measuring-tape of time[1] by law, was in danger of being frayed away. It was the last of a group of lives which had served this purpose, at the end of whose breathings the small homestead occupied by South himself, the larger one of Giles Winterborne, and half a dozen others that had been in the possession of various Hintock village families for the previous hundred years, and were now Winterborne's, would fall in and become part of the encompassing estate.

Winterborne walked up and down his garden next day thinking of the contingency. The sense that the paths he was pacing, the cabbage-plots, the apple-trees, his dwelling, cider-cellar, wring-house, stables, weathercock, were all slipping away over his head and beneath his feet as if they were painted on a magic lantern slide, was curious. In spite of John South's late indisposition he had not anticipated danger.

Whilst he was here in the garden somebody came to fetch him. It was Marty herself, and she showed her distress by her unconsciousness of a cropped poll.

"Father is still so much troubled in his mind about that tree," she said. "You know the tree I mean, Mr. Winterborne? the tall one in front of the house that he thinks will blow down and kill us. Can you come and see if you can persuade him out of his notion? I can do nothing."

He accompanied her to the cottage, and she conducted him up stairs. John South was pillowed up in a chair between the bed and the window, exactly opposite the latter, towards which his face was turned.

"Ah, neighbour Winterborne," he said. "I wouldn't have minded if my life had only been my own to lose; I don't vallie it in much of itself, and can let it go if 'tis required of me. But to think what 'tis worth to you, a young man rising in life, that do trouble me! It seems a trick of dishonesty towards ye to go off at fifty-five! I could bear up, I know I could, if it were not for the tree – yes, the tree 'tis that's killing me. There he stands, threatening my life every minute that the wind do blow. He'll come down upon us, and squat us dead; and what will ye do when the life on your property is taken away!"

"Never you mind me – that's of no consequence," said Giles. "Think of yourself alone."

He looked out of the window in the direction of the woodman's gaze. The tree was a tall elm, familiar to him from childhood, which stood at a distance of two-thirds its own height from the front of South's dwelling. Whenever the wind blew, as it did now, the tree rocked, naturally enough; and the sight of its motion, and sound of its sighs, had gradually bred the terrifying illusion in the woodman's mind. Thus he would sit all day, in spite of persuasion, watching its every sway, and listening to the melancholy Gregorian melodies[2] which the air wrung out of it. This fear it apparently was, rather than any organic disease, which was eating away the health of John South.

As the tree waved South waved his head, making it his fugleman with abject obedience. "Ah, when it was quite a small tree," he said, "and I was a little boy, I thought one day of chopping it off with my hook to make a clothes-line prop with. But I put off doing it, and then I again thought that I would; but I forgot it, and didn't. And at last it got too big, and now 'tis my enemy, and will be the death of me. Little did I think, when I let that sapling stay, that a time would come when it would torment me, and dash me into my grave."

"No, no," said Winterborne and Marty soothingly. But they thought it possible that it might hasten him into his grave, though in another way than by falling.

"I tell you what," added Winterborne; "I'll climb up this afternoon, and shroud off the lower boughs, and then it won't be so heavy, and the wind won't affect it so."

"She won't allow it – a strange woman come from nobody knows where – she won't have it done."

"You mean Mrs. Charmond? Oh, she doesn't know there's such a tree on her estate. Besides, shrouding is not felling, and I'll risk that much."

He went out, and when afternoon came he returned, took a bill-hook from the shed, and with a ladder climbed into the lower part of the tree, where he began lopping off – "shrouding" as they called it at Hintock – the lowest boughs. Each of these quivered under his attack, bent, cracked, and fell into the hedge. Having cut away the lowest tier he stepped off the ladder, climbed a few steps higher, and attacked those at the next level. Thus he ascended with the progress of his work far above the top of the ladder, cutting away his perches as he went, and leaving nothing but a bare stem below him.

The work was troublesome, for the tree was large. The afternoon wore on, turning dark and misty about four o'clock. From time to time Giles cast his eyes across towards the bedroom-window of South, where, by the flickering fire in the chamber, he could see the old man watching him, sitting motionless with a hand upon each arm of the chair. Beside him sat Marty, also straining her eyes towards the skyey field of his operations.

A curious question suddenly occurred to Winterborne, and he stopped his chopping. He was operating on another person's property to prolong the years of a lease by whose termination that person would considerably benefit. In that aspect of the case he doubted if he ought to go on. On the other hand he was working to save a man's life, and this seemed to empower him to adopt arbitrary measures.

The wind had died down to a calm, and while he was weighing the circumstances he saw coming along the road through the increasing mist a figure which, indistinct as it was, he knew well. It was Grace Melbury, on her way out from the house, probably for a short evening walk before dark. He arranged himself for a greeting from her, since she could hardly avoid passing immediately beneath the tree.

But Grace, though she looked up and saw him, was just at that time too full of the words of her father to give him any encouragement. The years-long regard that she had had for him was not kindled by her return into a flame of sufficient brilliancy to make her rebellious. Thinking that she might not see him, he cried, "Miss Melbury, here I am."

She turned up her head again. She was near enough to see the expression of his face, and the nails in his soles, silver-bright with constant walking. But she did not reply; and dropping her glance again went on.

Winterborne's face grew strange; he mused, and proceeded automatically with his work. Grace meanwhile had not gone far. She had reached a gate, whereon she had leant sadly, and whispered to herself, "What shall I do?"

A sudden fog came on, and she curtailed her walk, passing under the tree again on her return. Again he addressed her. "Grace," he said, when she was close to the trunk, "speak to me." She gazed straight up, shook her head without stopping, and went on to a little distance, where she stood observing him from behind the hedge.

Her coldness had been kindly meant. If it was to be done, she had said to herself, it should be begun at once. While she stood out of observation Giles seemed to recognise her meaning; with a sudden start he worked on, climbing higher into the sky, and cutting himself off more and more from all intercourse with the sublunary world. At last he had worked himself so high up the elm, and the mist had so thickened, that he could only just be discerned as a dark grey spot on the light grey zenith; he would have been altogether out of notice but for the stroke of his bill-hook, and the flight of a bough downward, and its crash upon the hedge at intervals.

It was not to be done thus, after all: plainness and candour were best. She went back a third time; he did not see her now, and she lingeringly gazed up at his unconscious figure, loth to put an end to any kind of hope that might live on in him still.

"Giles – Mr. Winterborne," she said.

His work so rustled the boughs that he did not hear.

"Mr. Winterborne!" she cried again, and this time he stopped, looked down, and replied.

"My silence just now was not accident," she said in an unequal voice. "My father says it is better for us not to think too much of that – engagement, or understanding, between us, that you know of. I, too, think that upon the whole he is right. But we are friends, you know, Giles, and almost relations."

"Very well," he answered, in an enfeebled voice which barely reached down the tree. "I have nothing to say, Grace – I cannot say anything till I've thought a while!"

She added, with emotion in her tone, "For myself I would have married you – some day – I think. But I give way, for I see it would be unwise."

He made no reply, but sat back upon a bough, placed his elbow in a fork, and rested his head upon his hand. Thus he remained till the fog and the night had completely inclosed him from her view.

Grace heaved a divided sigh, with a tense pause between, and moved onward, her heart feeling uncomfortably big and heavy, and her eyes wet. Had Giles, instead of remaining still, immediately come down from the tree to her, would she have continued in that filial, acquiescent frame of mind which she had announced to him as final? If it be true, as women themselves have declared, that one of their sex is never so much inclined to throw in her lot with a man for good and all as five minutes after she has told him such a thing cannot be, the probabilities are that something might have been done by the appearance of Winterborne on the ground beside Grace. But he continued motionless and silent in that gloomy Niflheim[3] or fog-land which involved him, and she proceeded on her way.

The spot seemed now to be quite deserted. The light from South's window made rays on the fog, but did not reach the tree. A quarter of an hour passed, and all was blackness overhead. Giles had not yet come down.

Then the tree seemed to shiver, then to heave a sigh: a movement was audible, and Winterborne dropped almost noiselessly to the ground. He had thought the matter out; and having returned the ladder and bill-hook to their places, pursued his way homeward. He would not allow this incident to affect his outer conduct any more than the danger to his leaseholds had done, and went to bed as usual.

Two simultaneous troubles do not always make a double trouble; and thus it came to pass that Giles's practical anxiety about his houses, which would have been enough to keep him awake half the night at any other time, was displaced and not reinforced by his sentimental trouble about Grace Melbury. This severance was in truth more like a burial of her than a rupture with her, but he did not realise so much at present; even when he arose in the morning he felt quite moody and stern; as yet the second note in the gamut of such emotions, a distracting regret for his loss, had not made itself heard.

A load of oak timber was to be sent away that morning to a builder whose works were in a town many miles off. The trunks were chained down to a heavy timber carriage with enormous red wheels, and four of the most powerful of Melbury's horses were harnessed in front to draw them.

The horses wore their bells that day. There were sixteen to the team, carried on a frame above each animal's shoulders, and tuned to scale, so as to form two octaves, running from the highest note on the right or off-side of the leader to the lowest on the left or near-side of the shaft-horse. Melbury was among the last to retain horse-bells in that neighbourhood; for living at Little Hintock, where the lanes yet remained as narrow as before the days of turnpike roads, these sound-signals were still as useful to him and his neighbours as they had ever been in former times. Much backing was saved in the course of a year by the warning notes they cast ahead; moreover the tones of all the teams in the district being known to the carters of each, they could tell a long way off on a dark night whether they were about to encounter friends or strangers.

The fog of the previous evening still lingered so heavily over the woods that the morning could not penetrate the trees till long after its time. The load being a ponderous one, the lane crooked, and the air so thick, Winterborne set out, as he often did, to accompany the team as far as the corner, where it would turn into a wider road.

So they rumbled on, shaking the foundations of the roadside cottages by the weight of their progress, the sixteen bells chiming harmoniously over all, till they had risen out of the valley and were descending towards the more open route, the sparks rising from their creaking skid and nearly setting fire to the dead leaves alongside.

Then occurred one of the very incidents against which the bells were an endeavour to guard. Suddenly there beamed into their eyes, quite close to them, the two lamps of a carriage, haloed by the fog. Its approach had been quite unheard by reason of their own noise.

The carriage was a covered one, while behind it could be discerned another vehicle laden with luggage.

Winterborne went to the head of the team, and heard the coachman telling the carter that he must turn back. The carter declared that this was impossible.

"You can turn if you unhitch your string-horses," said the coachman.

"It is much easier for you to turn than for us," said Winterborne. "We've five ton of timber on these wheels if we've an ounce."

"But I've another carriage with luggage at my back."

Winterborne admitted the strength of the argument. "But even with that," he said, "you can back better than we. And you ought to, for you could hear our bells half a mile off."

"And you could see our lights."

"We couldn't, because of the fog."

"Well, our time's precious," said the coachman haughtily. "You are only going to some trumpery little village or other in the neighbour-hood, while we are going straight to Italy."

"Driving all the way, I suppose?" said Winterborne sarcastically.

The contention continued in these terms till a voice from the interior of the carriage inquired what was the matter. It was a lady's voice.

She was briefly informed of the timber people's obstinacy; and then Giles could hear her telling the footman to direct the timber people to turn their horses' heads.

The message was brought, and Winterborne sent the bearer back to say that he begged the lady's pardon, but that he could not do as she requested; that though he would not assert it to be impossible, it was impossible by comparison with the slight difficulty to her party to back their light carriages. As fate would have it, the incident with Grace Melbury on the previous day made Giles less gentle than he might otherwise have shown himself, his confidence in the sex being rudely shaken.

In fine, nothing could move him, and the carriages were compelled to back till they reached one of the sidings or turn-outs constructed in the bank for the purpose. Then the team came on ponderously, and the clanging of its sixteen bells as it passed the discomfited carriages tilted up against the bank, lent a particularly triumphant tone to the

team's progress – a tone which, in point of fact, did not at all attach
to its conductor's feelings.

Giles walked behind the timber, and just as he had got past the yet
stationary carriages he heard a soft voice say, "Who is that rude man?
Not Melbury?" The sex of the speaker was so prominent in the voice
that Winterborne felt a pang of regret.

"No, ma'am. A younger man, in a smaller way of business in Little
Hintock. Winterborne is his name."

Thus they parted company. "Why, Mr. Winterborne," said the
waggoner when they were out of hearing, "that was she – Mrs.
Charmond! Who'd ha' thought it? What in the world can a woman
that does nothing be cock-watching out here at this time o' day for?
Oh, going to Italy – yes, to be sure, I heard she was going abroad.
She can't endure the winter here."

Winterborne was vexed at the incident; the more so that he knew
Mr. Melbury, in his adoration of Hintock House, would be the first
to blame him, if it became known. He accompanied the load to
the end of the lane, and then turned back with an intention to
call at South's to learn the result of the experiment of the preceding
evening.

It chanced that a few minutes before this time Grace Melbury, who
now rose soon enough to breakfast with her father, in spite of the
unwontedness of the hour, had been commissioned by him to make
the same inquiry at South's. Marty had been standing at the door
when Miss Melbury arrived. Almost before the latter had spoken,
Mrs. Charmond's carriages, released from the obstruction up the lane,
came bowling along, and the two girls turned to regard the spectacle.

Mrs. Charmond did not see them, but there was sufficient light for
them to discern her outline between the carriage windows. A noticeable
feature in her *tournure*[4] was a magnificent mass of braided locks.

"How well she looks this morning!" said Grace, forgetting Mrs.
Charmond's slight in her generous admiration. "Her hair so becomes
her worn that way. I have never seen any more beautiful!"

"Nor have I, miss," said Marty drily, and unconsciously stroking
her crown.

Grace watched the carriages with lingering regret till they were out of sight. She then learnt of Marty that South was no better. Before she had come away Winterborne approached the house, but seeing that one of the two girls standing on the doorstep was Grace he suddenly turned back again, and sought the shelter of his own home till she should have gone away.

CHAPTER XIV

The encounter with the carriages forced Winterborne's mind back again to the houses of his which would fall into Mrs. Charmond's possession in the event of South's death. He marvelled what could have induced his ancestors at Hintock, and other village people, to exchange their old copyholds for life-leases. And he was much struck with his father's negligence in not insuring South's life.

After breakfast he went up stairs, turned over his bed, and drew out a flat canvas bag which lay between the mattress and the sacking. In this he kept his leases, which had remained there unopened ever since his father's death. It was the usual hiding-place among rural lifeholders for such documents. Winterborne sat down on the bed, and looked them over. They were ordinary leases for three lives, which a member of the South family, some fifty years before this time, had accepted of the lord of the manor in lieu of certain copyholds and other rights, in consideration of having the dilapidated houses rebuilt by the said lord. They had come into his father's possession chiefly through his mother, who was a South.

Pinned to the corner of one of the indentures was a letter, which Winterborne had never seen before. It bore a remote date, the hand-writing being that of some solicitor or agent, and the signature the landholder's. It was to the effect that at any time before the last of the stated lives should drop Mr. John Winterborne, or his representative, should have the privilege of adding his own and his son's life to the life remaining on payment of a merely nominal sum; the concession being in consequence of the elder Winterborne's consent to demolish one of the houses and relinquish its site, which stood at an awkward corner of the lane, and impeded the way.

The house had been pulled down years before. Why Giles's father had not taken advantage of his privilege to insert his own and his son's lives it was impossible to say. In all likelihood death alone had hindered him in the execution of that project, the elder Winterborne having been a man who took much pleasure in dealing with house property, in his small way.

Since one of the Souths still survived there was not much doubt that Giles could do what his father had left undone, as far as his own life was concerned. This possibility cheered him much; for by those houses hung many things. Melbury's doubt of the young man's fitness to be the husband of Grace had been based not a little on the precariousness of his holdings in Little and Great Hintock. He resolved to attend to the business at once, the fine for renewal being a sum that he could easily muster.

His scheme, however, could not be carried out in a day; and meanwhile he would run up to South's as he had intended to do, to learn the result of the experiment with the tree.

Marty met him at the door. "Well, Marty," he said; and was surprised to read in her face that the case was not so hopeful as he had imagined.

"I am sorry for your labour," she said. "It is all lost. He says the tree seems taller than ever."

Winterborne looked round at it. Taller the tree certainly did seem, the gauntness of its now naked stem being more marked than before.

"It quite terrified him when he first saw what you had done to it this morning," she added. "He declares it will come down upon us and cleave us, like 'the sword of the Lord and of Gideon.' "[1]

"Well; can I do anything else?" asked he.

"The doctor says the tree ought to be cut down."

"Oh – you've had the doctor?"

"I didn't send for him. Mrs. Charmond before she left heard that father was ill, and told him to attend him at her expense."

"That was very good of her. And he says it ought to be cut down. We mustn't cut it down without her knowledge, I suppose."

He went up stairs. There the old man sat, staring at the now gaunt tree as if his gaze were frozen on to its trunk. Unluckily the tree waved afresh by this time, a wind having sprung up and blown the fog away; and his eyes turned with its wavings.

They heard footsteps – a man's, but of a lighter weight than usual. "There is Dr. Fitzpiers again," she said, and descended. Presently his tread was heard on the naked stairs.

Mr. Fitzpiers entered the sick chamber as a doctor is wont to do on such occasions, and pre-eminently when the room is that of the humble cottager; looking round towards the patient with that preoccupied gaze which so plainly reveals that he has well-nigh forgotten all about the case and the circumstances since he dismissed them from his mind at his last exit from the same apartment. He nodded to Winterborne, who had not seen him since his peep over the hedge at Grace, recalled the case to his thoughts, and went leisurely on to where South sat.

Edred Fitzpiers was, on the whole, a finely formed, handsome man. His eyes were dark and impressive, and beamed with the light either of energy or of susceptivity – it was difficult to say which; it might have been a little of both. That quick, glittering, empirical eye, sharp for the surface of things if for nothing beneath, he had not. But whether his apparent depth of vision were real, or only an artistic accident of his corporeal moulding, nothing but his deeds could reveal.

His face was rather soft than stern, charming than grand, pale than flushed; his nose – if a sketch of his features be *de rigueur*[2] for a person of his pretensions – was artistically beautiful enough to have been worth modelling by any sculptor not over busy, and was hence devoid of those knotty irregularities which often mean power; while the classical curve of his mouth was not without a looseness in its close. Either from his readily appreciative mien, or his reflective manner, his presence bespoke the philosopher[3] rather than the dandy – an effect which was helped by the absence of trinkets or other trivialities from his attire, though this was more finished and up to date than is usually the case among rural practitioners.

Strict people of the highly respectable class, knowing a little about him by report, said that he seemed likely to err rather in the possession of too many ideas than too few; to be a dreamy 'ist of some sort, or too deeply steeped in some false kind of ism.[4] However this may be, it will be seen that he was undoubtedly a somewhat rare kind of gentleman and doctor to have descended, as from the clouds, upon Little Hintock.

"This is an extraordinary case," he said at last to Winterborne, after examining South by conversation, look, and touch, and learning that the craze about the elm was stronger than ever. "Come down stairs and I'll tell you what I think."

They accordingly descended, and the doctor continued, "The tree must be cut down, or I won't answer for his life."

" 'Tis Mrs. Charmond's tree; and I suppose we must get permission?" said Giles.

"Oh – never mind whose tree it is – what's a tree beside a life! Cut it down. I have not the honour of knowing Mrs. Charmond as yet; but I am disposed to risk that much with her."

" 'Tis timber," rejoined Giles. "They never fell a stick about here without its being marked first, either by her or the agent."

"Then we'll inaugurate a new era forthwith. How long has he complained of the tree?" asked the doctor of Marty.

"Weeks and weeks, sir. The shape of it seems to haunt him like an evil spirit. He says that it is exactly his own age, that it has got human sense, and sprouted up when he was born on purpose to rule him, and keep him as its slave. Others have been like it afore in Hintock."

They could hear South's voice up stairs. "Oh, he's rocking this way; he must come! And then my poor life, that's worth houses upon houses, will be squashed out o' me. Oh! Oh!"

"That's how he goes on," she added. "And he'll never look anywhere else but out of the window, and scarcely have the curtains drawn."

"Down with it, then, and hang Mrs. Charmond," said Mr. Fitzpiers. "The best plan will be to wait till the evening, when it is dark, or early in the morning before he is awake, so that he doesn't see it fall, for that would terrify him worse than ever. Keep the blind down till I come, and then I'll assure him, and show him that his trouble is over."

The doctor departed, and they waited till the evening. When it was dusk, and the curtains drawn, Winterborne directed a couple of woodmen to bring a cross-cut saw; and the tall threatening tree was soon nearly off at its base. Next morning, before South was awake, they went and lowered it cautiously, in the direction away from the cottage. It was a business difficult to do quite silently, but it was done at last, and the elm of the same birth-year as the woodman's lay stretched upon the ground. The weakest idler that passed could now set foot on marks formerly made in the upper forks by the shoes of adventurous climbers only; once inaccessible nests could be examined microscopically; and on swaying extremities where birds alone had perched the bystanders sat down.

As soon as it was broad daylight the doctor came, and Winterborne entered the house with him. Marty said that her father was wrapped up and ready, as usual, to be put into his chair. They ascended the stairs, and soon seated him. He began at once to complain of the tree, and the danger to his life, and Winterborne's house property in consequence.

The doctor signalled to Giles, who went and drew back the printed cotton curtains. " 'Tis gone, see," said Mr. Fitzpiers.

As soon as the old man saw the vacant patch of sky in place of the branched column so familiar to his gaze, he sprang up, speechless; his eyes rose from their hollows till the whites showed all round, he fell back, and a bluish whiteness overspread him.

Greatly alarmed they put him on the bed. As soon as he came a little out of his fit, he gasped, "Oh, it is gone! – where – where?"

His whole system seemed paralysed by amazement. They were thunderstruck at the result of the experiment, and did all they could. Nothing seemed to avail. Giles and Fitzpiers went and came, but uselessly. He lingered through the day, and died that evening as the sun went down.

"D—d if my remedy hasn't killed him!" murmured the doctor.

Dismissing the subject he went down stairs. When going out of the house he turned suddenly to Giles and said, "Who was that young lady we looked at over the hedge the other day?"

Giles shook his head, as if he did not remember.

CHAPTER XV

When Melbury heard what had happened he seemed much moved, and walked thoughtfully about the premises. On South's own account he was genuinely sorry; and on Winterborne's he was the more grieved in that this catastrophe had so closely followed the somewhat harsh suggestion to Giles to draw off from his daughter.

He was quite angry with circumstances for so heedlessly inflicting on Giles a second trouble when the needful one inflicted by himself was all that the proper order of events demanded. "I told Giles's father when he came into those houses not to spend too much money on lifehold property held neither for his own life nor his son's," he exclaimed; "but he wouldn't listen to me. And now Giles has to suffer for it."

"Poor Giles!" murmured Grace.

"Now, Grace, between us two, it is very, very remarkable. It is almost as if I had foreseen this; and I am thankful for your escape, though I am sincerely sorry for Giles. Had we not dismissed him already we could hardly have found it in our hearts to dismiss him now. So I say, be thankful. I'll do all I can for him as a friend; but as a pretender to the position of my son-in-law, that can never be thought of more."

And yet at that very moment the impracticability to which poor Winterborne's suit had been reduced was touching Grace's heart to a warmer sentiment on his behalf than she had felt for years concerning him.

He, meanwhile, was sitting down alone in the familiar house which had ceased to be his; taking a calm if somewhat dismal survey of affairs. The pendulum of the clock bumped every now and then against one side of the case in which it swung, as the muffled drum to his worldly march. Looking out of the window he could perceive that a paralysis had come over Creedle's occupation of manuring the garden, owing, obviously, to a conviction that they might not be living there long enough to profit by next season's crop.

He looked at the leases again and the letter attached. There was no doubt that he had lost his houses by an accident which might easily have been circumvented if he had known the true conditions of his holding. The time for performance had now lapsed in strict law; but why should not the intention be considered by the landholder when she became aware of the circumstances, and his moral right to retain the holdings for the term of his life be conceded?

His heart sank within him when he perceived that, despite all the legal reciprocities and safeguards prepared and written, the upshot of the matter was that it depended upon the mere caprice of the woman he had met the day before in such an unfortunate way, whether he was to possess his houses for life or no.

While he was sitting and thinking a step came to the door, and Melbury appeared, looking very sorry for his position. Winterborne welcomed him by a word and a nod and went on with his examination of the parchments. His visitor sat down.

"Giles," he said, "this is very awkward, and I am sorry for it. What are you going to do?"

Giles informed him of the real state of affairs, and how barely he had missed availing himself of his chance of renewal.

"What a misfortune! Why was this neglected? Well, the best thing you can do is to write and tell her all about it, and throw yourself upon her generosity."

"I would rather not," murmured Giles.

"But you must," said Melbury.

In short, he argued so cogently that Giles allowed himself to be persuaded, and the letter to Mrs. Charmond was written and sent to Hintock House, whence, as he knew, it would at once be forwarded to her.

Melbury, feeling that he had done so good an action in coming as to extenuate his previous arbitrary conduct, went home; and Giles was left alone to the suspense of waiting for a reply from the divinity who shaped the ends of the Hintock population.[1] By this time all the villagers knew of the circumstances, and being well-nigh like one family a keen interest was the result all round.

Everybody thought of Giles; nobody thought of Marty. Had any of them looked in upon her during those moonlight nights which preceded the burial of her father they would have seen the girl absolutely alone in the house with the dead man. Her own chamber being nearest the stairs, the coffin had been placed there for convenience; and at a certain hour of the night, when the moon arrived opposite the window, its beams streamed across the still profile of South, sublimed by the august presence of death, and onward a few feet further upon the face of his daughter, lying in her little bed in the stillness of a repose almost as dignified as that of her companion – the repose of a guileless soul that had nothing more left on earth to lose, except a life which she did not over-value.

South was buried, and a week passed, and Winterborne watched for a reply from Mrs. Charmond. Melbury was very sanguine as to its tenour; but Winterborne had not told him of the encounter with her carriage, when, if ever he had heard an affronted tone on a woman's lips, he had heard it on hers.

The postman's time for passing was just after Melbury's men had assembled in the spar-house; and Winterborne, who when not busy on his own account would lend assistance there, used to go out into the lane every morning and meet the postman at the end of one of the green rides through the hazel-copse, in the straight stretch of which his laden figure could be seen a long way off. Grace also was very anxious; more anxious than her father, more perhaps than Winterborne himself. This anxiety led her into the spar-house on some pretext or other almost every morning whilst they were awaiting the answer.

Eleven times had Winterborne gone to that corner of the ride, and looked up its long straight slope through the wet greys of winter dawn. But though the postman's bowed figure loomed in view pretty regularly, he brought nothing for Giles. On the twelfth day the man of missives, while yet in the extreme distance, held up his hand, and Winterborne saw a letter in it. He took it into the spar-house before he broke the seal, and those who were there gathered round him while he read, Grace looking in at the door.

The letter was not from Mrs. Charmond herself, but from her agent at Sherton. Winterborne glanced it over and looked up.

"It's all over," he said.

"Ah!" said they all together.

"Her lawyer is instructed to say that Mrs. Charmond sees no reason for disturbing the natural course of things, particularly as she contemplates pulling the houses down," he said quietly.

"Only think of that!" said several.

Winterborne had turned away, and said vehemently to himself, "Then let her pull 'em down, and be d—d to her!"

Creedle looked at him with a face of seven sorrows,[2] saying, "Ah, 'twas that sperrit that lost 'em for ye, maister!"

Winterborne subdued his feelings, and from that hour, whatever they were, kept them entirely to himself. Yet whatever the value of taciturnity to a man among strangers, it is apt to express more than talkativeness when he dwells among friends. The countryman, who is obliged to judge the time of day from changes in external nature, sees a thousand successive tints and traits in the landscape which are never discerned by him who hears the regular chime of a clock, because they are never in request. In like manner do we use our eyes on our taciturn comrade. The infinitesimal movement of muscle, curve, hair, and wrinkle, which when accompanied by a voice goes unregarded, is watched and translated in the lack of it, till virtually the whole surrounding circle of familiars is charged with the reserved one's moods and meanings.

So with Winterborne and his neighbours after his stroke of ill-luck. He held his tongue; and they observed him, and knew that he was discomposed.

Encountering Melbury one day,[3] his manner was that of a man who abandoned all claims. "I am glad to meet ye, Mr. Melbury," he said, in a low voice, whose quality he endeavoured to make as practical as possible. "I am afraid I shall not after this be able to keep that mare I bought for the use of – a possible wife, and as I don't care to sell her, I should like, if you don't object, to give her to Miss Melbury. The horse is very quiet, and would be quite safe for her."

Mr. Melbury was rather affected at this. "You sha'n't hurt your pocket like that on our account, Giles. Grace shall have the horse, but

I'll pay you what you gave for her, and any expense you may have been put to for her keep."

He would not hear of any other terms, and thus it was arranged. They were now opposite Melbury's house, and the timber-merchant pressed Winterborne to enter, Grace being out of the way.

"Pull round the settle, Giles," said the timber-merchant as soon as they were within. "I should like to have a serious talk with you."

Thereupon he put the case to Winterborne frankly, and in quite a friendly way. He declared that he did not like to be hard on a man when he was in difficulty; but he really did not see how Winterborne could marry his daughter now, without even a house to take her to.

Giles quite acquiesced in the awkwardness of his situation, but from a momentary gasp of hope – a feeling that he would like to know Grace's mind from her own lips, he did not speak out positively even then. He accordingly departed somewhat abruptly, and went home to consider whether he would seek to bring about a meeting with her.

In the evening while he sat quietly pondering he fancied that he heard a scraping on the wall outside his house. The boughs of a monthly rose which grew there made such a noise sometimes, but as no wind was stirring he knew that it could not be the rose-tree. He took up the candle and went out. Nobody was near. As he turned the light flickered on the whitewashed rough-cast of the front, and he saw words written thereon in charcoal, which he read as follows:–

> "Oh, Giles, you've lost your dwelling-place,
> And therefore, Giles, you'll lose your Grace."

Giles went indoors. He had his suspicions as to the scrawler of those lines, but he could not be sure. What filled his heart far more than curiosity about their authorship was a terrible belief that they were turning out to be true, try to regain Grace as he might. They decided the question for him. He sat down and wrote a formal note to Melbury, stating that he shared to the full Melbury's view of his own and his daughter's promise, made some years before; he wished that it should be considered as cancelled, and they themselves quite released from any obligation on account of it.

Having fastened up this their plenary absolution,[4] he determined to get it out of his hands, and have done with it; to which end he went off to Melbury's at once. It was now so late that the family had all retired; he crept up to the house, thrust the note under the door, and stole away as silently as he had come.

Melbury himself was the first to rise the next morning, and when he had read the letter his relief was great, for he knew that Giles could have made matters unpleasant if he had chosen to work upon Grace. "Very honourable of Giles, very honourable," he kept saying to himself. "I shall not forget him. Now to keep her up to her own true level."

It happened that Grace went out for an early ramble that morning, and to go in her customary direction she could not avoid passing Winterborne's house. The morning sun was shining flat upon its white surface, and the words, which still remained, were immediately visible to her. She read them. Her face flushed to crimson. She could see Giles and Creedle talking together at the back; the charred spar-gad with which the lines had been written lay on the ground beneath the wall. Feeling pretty sure that Winterborne would observe her action, she quickly went up to the wall, rubbed out "lose" and inserted "keep" in its stead. Then she made the best of her way home without looking behind her. Giles could draw an inference now if he chose.

There could not be the least doubt that gentle Grace was warming to more sympathy with, and interest in, Winterborne than ever she had done while he was her promised lover; that since his misfortune those social shortcomings of his, which contrasted so awkwardly with her later experiences of life, had become obscured by the generous revival of an old romantic attachment to him. Though mentally trained and tilled into foreignness of view, as compared with her youthful time, Grace was not an ambitious girl, and might, if left to herself, have declined upon Winterborne without much discontent. Her feelings just now were so far from latent that the writing on the wall had quickened her to an unusual rashness.

Having returned from her walk she sat at breakfast silently. When her stepmother had left the room she said to her father, "I have made up my mind that I should like my engagement to Giles to continue."

Melbury looked much surprised.

"Nonsense," he said sharply. "You don't know what you are talking about. Look here."

He handed across to her the letter received from Giles.

She read it and said no more. Could he have seen her write on the wall? She did not know. Fate, it seemed, would have it this way, and there was nothing to do but to acquiesce.

It was a few hours after this that Winterborne who, curiously enough, had *not* perceived Grace writing, was clearing away the tree from the front of South's late dwelling. He saw Marty standing in her doorway, a slim figure in meagre black, almost without womanly contours as yet. He went up to her and said:

"Marty, why did you write that on my wall last night? It *was* you, you know."

"Because it was the truth."

"Having prophesied one thing, why did you alter it to another? Your predictions can't be worth much."

"I have not altered it."

"But you have."

"No."

"It is altered. Go and see."

She went, and read that in spite of losing his dwelling-place he would *keep* his Grace. Marty came back surprised.

"Well," she said. "Who can have made such nonsense of it?"

"Who indeed?" said he.

"I have rubbed it all out, as the point of it is quite gone."

"You'd no business to rub it out; I meant to let it stay a little longer."

"Some idle boy altered it no doubt," she murmured.

As this seemed very probable Winterborne said no more, and dismissed the matter from his mind.

From this day of his life onward for a considerable time Winterborne, though not absolutely out of his house as yet, retired into the background of human life and action thereabout – a feat not particularly difficult of performance anywhere when the doer has the assistance of a lost prestige. Grace, thinking that Winterborne saw her write,

made no further sign, and the frail barque of fidelity that she had thus
timidly launched was stranded and lost.

CHAPTER XVI

Dr. Fitzpiers lived on the slope of the hill, in a house of much less
pretension, both as to architecture and as to magnitude, than the
timber merchant's. The latter had without doubt been once the
manorial residence appertaining to the snug and modest domain of
Little Hintock, of which the boundaries were now lost by its absorption
into the adjoining estate of Mrs. Charmond. Though the Melburys
themselves were unaware of the fact, there was every reason to believe
– at least so the parson said – that the owners of that little manor had
been Melbury's own ancestors, the family name occurring in numerous
documents relating to transfers of land about the time of the civil wars.

Mr. Fitzpiers's dwelling, on the contrary, was small, box-like, and
comparatively modern. It had been occupied, and was in part occupied
still, by a retired farmer and his wife, who, on the surgeon's arrival in
quest of a home, had accommodated him by receding from their front
rooms into the kitchen quarter, whence they administered to his wants,
and emerged at regular intervals to receive from him a not unwelcome
addition to their income.

The cottage and its garden were so regular in their plan that they
might have been laid out by a Dutch designer of the time of William
and Mary.[1] In a low, dense hedge was a door, over which the hedge
formed an arch, and from the inside of the door a straight path,
bordered with clipped box, ran up the slope of the garden to the
porch, which was exactly in the middle of the house-front, with two
windows on each side. Right and left of the path were first a bed
of gooseberry-bushes; next of currant; next of raspberry; next of
strawberry; next of old-fashioned flowers; at the corners opposite the

porch being spheres of box resembling a pair of school globes. Over the roof of the house could be seen the orchard on yet higher ground, and behind the orchard the forest-trees, reaching up to the crest of the hill.

Opposite the garden door visible from the parlour window was a swing-gate leading into a field, across which there ran a footpath. The swing-gate had just been re-painted, and on one fine afternoon, before the paint was dry, and while gnats stuck dying thereon, the surgeon was standing in his room abstractedly looking out at the different pedestrians who passed along that route. Being of a philosophical stamp he perceived that the character of each of these travellers exhibited itself in a somewhat amusing manner by his or her method of handling the gate.

As regarded the men there was not much variety: they gave the gate a kick and passed through. The women were more contrasting. To them the sticky wood work was a barricade, a disgust, a menace, a treachery, as the case might be.

The first that he noticed was a bouncing young woman with her skirts tucked up and her hair wild. Fitzpiers knew her as Suke Damson. She grasped the gate without looking, giving it a supplementary push with her shoulder, when the white imprint drew from her an exclamation in language not too refined. She went to the green bank, sat down and rubbed herself in the grass, cursing the while.

"Ha! ha! ha!" laughed the doctor.

The next was a girl with her hair cropped short, in whom the surgeon recognised the daughter of his late patient, the woodman South. Moreover a black bonnet that she wore by way of mourning unpleasantly reminded him that he had ordered a tree felling which had caused her parent's death. She walked in thought, and not recklessly; but her preoccupation led her to grasp without suspicion the bar of the gate, and touch it with her arm. Fitzpiers felt sorry that she should have soiled that new black frock, poor as it was, for it was probably her only one. She looked at her hand and arm, seemed but little surprised, wiped off the disfigurement with an unmoved face, and as if without abandoning her original thoughts. Thus she went on her way.

Then there came over the green quite a different sort of personage. She walked as delicately as if she had been bred in town, and as firmly as if she had been bred in the country; she seemed one who dimly knew her appearance to be attractive, but who retained some of the charm of ignorance by forgetting self in a general pensiveness. She approached the gate.

To let such a creature touch it even with the tip of her glove was to Fitzpiers almost like letting her proceed to tragical self-destruction. He jumped up and looked for his hat, but was unable to find the right one; glancing again out of the window he saw that he was too late. Having come up she looked at the gate, picked up a little stick, and using it as a bayonet pushed open the obstacle without touching it at all.

He steadily watched her out of sight, recognising her as the very young lady whom he had seen once before and been unable to identify. Whose could that emotional face be? All the others he had seen in Hintock as yet oppressed him with their crude rusticity; the contrast offered by this suggested that she hailed from elsewhere.

Precisely these thoughts had occurred to him at the first time of seeing her; but he now went a little further with them, and considered that as there had been no carriage lately in that spot she could not have come a very long distance. She must be somebody staying at Hintock House – possibly Mrs. Charmond, of whom he had heard so much – at any rate an inmate; and this probability was sufficient to set a mild radiance in the surgeon's somewhat dull sky.

Fitzpiers sat down to the book he had been perusing. It happened to be that of a German metaphysician, for the doctor was not a practical man, except by fits, and much preferred the ideal world to the real, and the discovery of principles to their application. The young lady remained in his thoughts. He might have followed her; but he was not constitutionally active, and preferred a conjectural pursuit. However, when he went out for a ramble just before dusk he insensibly took the direction of Hintock House, which was the way Grace had been walking, her mind having run on Mrs. Charmond that day; though she had returned long since by another route.

Fitzpiers reached the edge of the glen, overlooking the manor-house.

The shutters were shut, and only one chimney smoked. The mere aspect of the place was enough to inform him that Mrs. Charmond had gone away, and that nobody else was staying there. Fitzpiers felt a vague disappointment that the young lady was not Mrs. Charmond, of whom he had heard so much; and without pausing longer to gaze at a carcase from which the spirit had flown he bent his steps homeward.

Later in the evening Fitzpiers was summoned to visit a cottage-patient about two miles distant. Like the majority of young practitioners in his vicinity he was far from having assumed the dignity of being driven his rounds by a servant in a brougham that flashed the sunlight like a mirror; his way of getting about was by means of a gig which he drove himself, hitching the rein of the horse to the gate-post, shutter-hook, or garden-paling of the domicile under visitation, or giving pennies to little boys to hold the animal during his stay – pennies which were well earned when the cases to be attended were of a certain cheerful kind that wore out the patience of the little boys.

On this account of travelling alone the night-journeys which Fitzpiers had frequently to take were dismal enough, an apparent perversity in nature ruling that whenever there was to be a birth in a particularly inaccessible and lonely place that event should occur in the night. The surgeon, having been of late years a town man, hated the solitary midnight woodland. He was not altogether skilful with the reins, and it often occurred to his mind that if in some remote depths of the trees an accident were to happen, his being alone might be the death of him. Hence he made a practice of picking up any countryman or lad whom he chanced to pass by, and under the disguise of treating him to a nice drive obtained his companionship on the journey, and his convenient assistance in opening gates.

The doctor had started on his way out of the village on the night in question when the light of his lamps fell upon the musing form of Winterborne, walking leisurely along, as if he had no object in life. Winterborne was a better class of companion than the doctor usually could get, and he at once pulled up and asked him if he would like a drive through the wood that fine night.

Giles seemed rather surprised at the doctor's friendliness, but said that he had no objection, and accordingly mounted beside Mr. Fitzpiers.

They drove along under the black boughs which formed a network upon the stars. Looking up as they passed under a horizontal bough they sometimes saw objects like large tadpoles lodged diametrically across it, which Giles explained to be pheasants at roost; and they sometimes heard the report of a gun, which reminded him that others knew what those tadpole shapes represented as well as he.

Presently the doctor said what he had been going to say for some time:

"Is there a young lady staying in this neighbourhood – a very attractive girl – with a little white boa round her neck, and white fur round her gloves?"

Winterborne, of course, knew in a moment that Grace, whom he had caught the doctor peering at, was represented by these accessories. With a wary grimness induced by the circumstances,[2] he evaded an answer by saying, "I saw a young lady talking to Mrs. Charmond the other day; perhaps it was she."

"It might have been," said Fitzpiers. "She is quite a gentlewoman – the one I mean. She cannot be a permanent resident in Hintock, or I should have seen her before. Nor does she look like one."

"She is not staying at Hintock House?"

"No; it is closed."

"Then perhaps she is staying at one of the cottages, or farmhouses?"

"Oh no – you mistake. She was a different sort of girl altogether." As Giles was nobody Fitzpiers treated him accordingly, and rhapsodised to the night in continuation:

> "She moved upon this earth a shape of brightness,[3]
>   A power, that from its objects scarcely drew
>   One impulse of her being – in her lightness
>   Most like some radiant cloud of morning dew,
>   Which wanders through the waste air's pathless blue,
>   To nourish some far desert: she did seem
>   Beside me, gathering beauty as she grew,
>   Like the bright shade of some immortal dream
> Which walks, when tempests sleep, the wave of life's dark stream."

The charm of the lines seemed to Winterborne to be somehow the result of his lost Love's charms upon Fitzpiers.

"You seem to be mightily in love with her, sir," he said, with a sensation of heartsickness, and more than ever resolved not to mention Grace by name.

"Oh, no – I am not that, Winterborne; people living insulated, as I do by the solitude of this place, get charged with emotive fluid like a Leyden jar with electric,[4] for want of some conductor at hand to disperse it. Human love is a subjective thing – the essence itself of man, as that great thinker Spinoza the philosopher says – *ipsa hominis essentia*[5] – it is joy accompanied by an idea which we project against any suitable object in the line of our vision, just as the rainbow iris is projected against an oak, ash, or elm tree indifferently. So that if any other young lady had appeared instead of the one who did appear, I should have felt just the same interest in her, and have quoted precisely the same lines from Shelley about her, as about this one I saw. Such miserable creatures of circumstance are we all!"

"Well, it is what we call being in love down in these parts, whether or no," said Winterborne.

"You are right enough if you admit that I am in love with something in my own head, and no thing-in-itself outside it at all."

"Is it part of a country doctor's duties to learn that view of things, may I ask, sir?" said Winterborne, adopting the Socratic εἰρωνεία[6] with such well-assumed simplicity that Fitzpiers answered readily –

"Oh, no. The real truth is, Winterborne, that medical practice in places like this is a very rule of thumb matter; a bottle of bitter stuff for this and that old woman – the bitterer the better – compounded from a few simple stereotyped prescriptions; occasional attendance at births, where mere presence is almost sufficient, so healthy and strong are the people; and a lance for an abscess now and then. Investigation and experiment cannot be carried on without more appliances than one has here – though I have attempted a little."

Giles did not enter into this view of the case; what he had been struck with was the curious parallelism between Mr. Fitzpiers's manner and Grace's, as shown by the fact of both of them straying into a subject of discourse so engrossing to themselves that it made them forget it was foreign to him.

Nothing further passed between himself and the doctor in relation to Grace till they were on their way back. They had stopped at a wayside inn for a glass of brandy-and-cider hot, and when they were again in motion Fitzpiers, possibly a little warmed by the liquor, resumed the subject by saying, "I should like very much to know who that young lady was."

"What difference can it make, if she's only the tree your rainbow falls on?"

"Ha, ha! True."

"You have no wife, sir?"

"I have no wife; and no idea of one. I hope to do better things than marry and settle in Hintock. Not but that it is well for a medical man to be married; and sometimes, begad, 'twould be pleasant enough in this place, with the wind roaring round the house, and the rain and the boughs beating against it. I hear that you lost your lifeholds by the death of South?"

"I did. I lost by that in more ways than one."

They had reached the top of Hintock Lane or Street, if it could be called such where three-quarters of the roadside consisted of copse and orchard. One of the first houses to be passed was Melbury's. A light was shining from a bedroom window facing lengthwise of the lane. Winterborne glanced at it, and saw what was coming. He had withheld an answer to the doctor's inquiry, to hinder his knowledge of Grace. But "who hath gathered the wind in his fists? who hath bound the waters in a garment?"[7] – he could not hinder what was doomed to arrive, and might just as well have been outspoken. As they came up to the house Grace's figure was distinctly visible, drawing the two white curtains together which were used here instead of blinds.

"Why, there she is!" said Fitzpiers. "How in the name of Heaven does she come there?"

"In the most natural way in the world. It is her home. Mr. Melbury is her father."

"Indeed – indeed – indeed! How comes he to have a daughter of that sort?"

Winterborne laughed coldly. "Won't money do anything," he said, "if you've promising material to work upon? Why shouldn't a Hintock girl, taken early from home, and put under proper instruction, become as finished as any other young lady, if she's got brains and good looks to begin with?"

"No reason at all why she shouldn't," murmured the surgeon with reflective disappointment. "Only I didn't anticipate quite that kind of origin for her."

"And you think an inch or two less of her now." There was a little tremor in Winterborne's voice as he spoke.

"Well," said the doctor with recovered warmth; "I am not so sure that I think less of her. At first it was a sort of blow; but dammy, I'll stick up for her. She's charming, every inch of her!"

"So she is," said Winterborne . . . "But not for me!"

From this ambiguous expression of the reticent woodlander, Dr. Fitzpiers inferred that Giles disliked Miss Melbury, possibly for some haughtiness in her bearing towards him, and had, on that account, withheld her name. The supposition did not tend to diminish his admiration for her.

VOLUME II

CHAPTER I

Grace's exhibition of herself, in the act of pulling-to the window curtains, had been the result of an unfortunate incident in the house that day – nothing less than the illness of Grammer Oliver, a woman who had never, till now, lain down for such a reason in her life. Like others, to whom an unbroken career of health has made the idea of keeping their bed almost as repugnant as death itself, she had continued on foot till she literally fell on the floor; and though she had, as yet, been scarcely a day off duty, she had sickened into quite a different personage from the independent Grammer of the yard and spar-house. Ill as she was, on one point she was firm. On no account would she see a doctor; in other words, Fitzpiers.

The room in which Grace had been discerned was not her own but the old woman's. On the girl's way to bed she had received a message from Grammer, to the effect that she would much like to speak to her that night.

Grace entered, and set the candle on a low chair beside the bed, so that the profile of Grammer, as she lay, cast itself in a coal-black shadow upon the whitened wall, her large head being still further magnified by an enormous turban, which was really her petticoat wound in a wreath round her temples. Grace put the room a little in order, and approaching the sick woman said,

"I am come, Grammer, as you wish. Do let us send for the doctor before it gets later."

" 'Ch[1] will not have him!" said Grammer Oliver decisively.

"Then somebody to sit up with you?"

"Can't abear it! No. I wanted to see you, Miss Grace, because 'ch have something on my mind. Dear Miss Grace, *I took that money of the doctor, after all!*"

"What money?"

"The ten pounds."[2]

Grace did not quite understand.

"The ten pounds he offered me for my head, because I've a large organ of brain. I signed a paper when I took the money, not feeling concerned about it at all. I have not liked to tell ye that it was really settled with him, because you showed such horror at the notion. Well, having thought it over more at length, I wish I hadn't done it; and it weighs upon my mind. John South's death of fear about the tree makes me think that I shall die of this . . .'Ch have been going to ask him again to let me off, but I hadn't the face."

"Why?"

"I've spent some of the money – more'n two pounds o't! It do wherrit me terribly; and I shall die o' the thought of that paper I signed with my holy cross,[3] as South died of his trouble!"

"If you ask him to burn the paper he will, I'm sure, and think no more of it."

" 'Ch have done it once already, miss. But he laughed cruel-like. 'Yours is such a fine brain, Grammer,' er[4] said, 'that science couldn't afford to lose you. Besides, you've taken my money.' . . . Don't let your father know of this, please, on no account whatever!"

"No, no. I will let you have the money to return to him."

Grammer rolled the head in question negatively upon the pillow. "Even if I should be well enough to take it to him he won't like it. Though why he should so particular want to look into the works of a poor old woman's head-piece like mine, when there's so many other folks about, I don't know. I know how he'll answer me: 'A lonely person like you, Grammer,' er woll say; 'what difference is it to you what becomes of ye when the breath's out of your body?' Oh, it do trouble me! If you only knew how he do chevy me round the chimmer in my dreams you'd pity me. How I could do it I can't think! But 'ch was always so rackless! . . . If I only had anybody to plead for me!"

"Mrs. Melbury would, I am sure."

"Ay; but he wouldn't hearken to she! It wants a younger face than hers to work upon such as he."

Grace started with comprehension. "You don't think he would do it for me?" she said.

"Oh, wouldn't he!"

"I couldn't go to him, Grammer, on any account. I don't know him at all."

"Ah, if I were a young lady," said the artful Grammer, "and could save a poor old woman's skellington from a heathen's chopper, to rest in a Christian grave, I would do it, and be glad to. But nobody will do anything for a poor old woman but push her out of the way!"

"You are very ungrateful, Grammer, to say that. But you are ill, I know, and that's why you speak so. Now believe me you are not going to die yet. Remember you told me yourself that you meant to keep him waiting many a year."

"Ay, one can joke when one is well, even in old age; but in sickness one's gaiety falters; and that which seemed small looks large; and the grim far-off seems near."

Grace's eyes had tears in them. "I don't like to go to him on such an errand, Grammer," she said brokenly. "But I will, if I must, to ease your mind!"

It was with extreme reluctance that Grace cloaked herself next morning for the undertaking. She was all the more indisposed to the journey by reason of Grammer's allusion to the effect of a pretty face upon Dr. Fitzpiers; and hence she most illogically did that which, had the doctor never seen her, would have operated to stultify the sole motive of her journey; that is to say, she put on a woollen veil which hid all her face except an occasional spark of her eyes.

Her own wish that nothing should be known of this strange and gruesome proceeding, no less than Grammer Oliver's own desire, led Grace to take every precaution against being discovered. She went out by the garden-door as the safest way, all the household having occupations at the other side. The morning looked forbidding enough when she stealthily edged forth. The battle between frost and thaw was continuing in mid-air: the trees dripped on the garden-plots, where no vegetables would grow for the dripping, though they were planted year after year with that curious mechanical regularity of country people in the face of hopelessness; the moss which covered the once broad gravel terrace was swamped; and Grace stood irresolute. Then she thought of poor Grammer, and her dreams of the doctor running after her scalpel in hand, and the possibility of a case so curiously similar to South's ending in the same way; thereupon she stepped out into the drizzle.

The nature of her errand, and Grammer Oliver's account of the compact she had made, lent a fascinating horror to Grace's conception of Fitzpiers. She knew that he was a young man; but her single object in seeking an interview with him put all considerations of his age and social aspect from her mind. Standing, as she stood, in Grammer Oliver's shoes, he was simply a remorseless Jehovah of the sciences,[5] who would not have mercy, and would have sacrifice; a man whom, save for this, she would have preferred to avoid knowing. But since, in such a small village, it was improbable that any long time could pass without their meeting, there was not much to deplore in her having to meet him now.

But, as need hardly be said, Miss Melbury's view of the doctor as a merciless, unwavering, irresistible scientist, was not quite in accordance with fact. The real Dr. Fitzpiers was a man of too many hobbies to show likelihood of rising to any great eminence in the profession he had chosen, or even to acquire any wide practice in the rural district he had marked out as his field of survey for the present. In the course of a year his mind was accustomed to pass in a grand solar sweep throughout the zodiac of the intellectual heaven.[6] Sometimes it was in the Ram, sometimes in the Bull; one month he would be immersed in alchemy, another in poesy; one month in the Twins of astrology and astronomy; then in the Crab of German literature and metaphysics. In justice to him it must be stated that he took such studies as were immediately related to his own profession in turn with the rest, and it had been in a month of anatomical ardour without the possibility of a subject that he had proposed to Grammer Oliver the terms she had mentioned to her mistress.

As may be inferred from the tone of his conversation with Winterborne, he had lately plunged into abstract philosophy with much zest; perhaps his keenly appreciative, modern, unpractical mind found this a realm more to his taste than any other. Though his aims were desultory, Fitzpiers's mental constitution was not without its admirable side; a real inquirer he honestly was; even if the midnight rays of his lamp, visible so far through the trees of Hintock, lighted rank literatures of emotion and passion[7] as often as, or oftener than, the books and *matériel* of science.[8]

But whether he meditated the Muses[9] or the philosophers, the loneliness of Hintock life was beginning to tell upon his impressionable nature. Winter in a solitary house in the country, without society, is tolerable, nay, even enjoyable and delightful, given certain conditions; but these are not the conditions which attach to the life of a professional man who drops down into such a place by mere accident. They were present to the lives of Winterborne, Melbury, and Grace; but not to the doctor's. They are old association – an almost exhaustive biographical or historical acquaintance with every object, animate and inanimate, within the observer's horizon. He must know all about those invisible ones of the days gone by, whose feet have traversed the fields which look so grey from his windows; recall whose creaking plough has turned those sods from time to time; whose hands planted the trees that form a crest to the opposite hill; whose horses and hounds have torn through that underwood; what birds affect that particular brake; what bygone domestic dramas of love, jealousy, revenge, or disappointment, have been enacted in the cottages, the mansions, the street, or on the green. The spot may have beauty, grandeur, salubrity, convenience; but if it lack memories it will ultimately pall upon him who settles there without opportunity of intercourse with his kind.

In such circumstances, maybe, an old man dreams of an ideal friend, till he throws himself into the arms of any impostor who chooses to wear that title on his face. A young man may dream of an ideal friend likewise, but some humour of the blood will probably lead him to think rather of an ideal mistress, and at length the rustle of a woman's dress, the sound of her voice, or the transit of her form across the field of his vision will enkindle his soul with a flame that blinds his eyes.

The discovery of the attractive Grace's name and family would have been enough in other circumstances to lead the doctor, if not to put her personality out of his head, to change the character of his interest in her. Instead of treasuring her image as a rarity he would at most have played with her as a toy. He was that kind of man. But situated here he could not go so far as amative cruelty. He dismissed all deferential thought about her, but he could not help taking her somewhat seriously.

He went on to imagine the impossible. So far, indeed, did he go in this futile direction that, as others are wont to do, he constructed dialogues and scenes in which Grace had turned out to be the mistress of Hintock Manor-house, the mysterious Mrs. Charmond, particularly ready and willing to be wooed by himself and nobody else.

"Well, she isn't that," he said finally. "But she's a very sweet, nice, exceptional girl."

The next morning he breakfasted alone, as usual. It was snowing with a fine-flaked desultoriness just sufficient to make the woodland grey, without ever achieving whiteness. There was not a single letter for Fitzpiers, only a medical circular and a weekly newspaper.

To sit before a large fire on such mornings, and read, and gradually acquire energy till the evening came, and then, with lamp alight, and feeling full of vigour, to pursue some engrossing subject or other till the small hours, had hitherto been his practice since arriving here. But to-day he could not settle into his chair. That self-contained position he had lately occupied, in which his whole attention was given to objects of the inner eye, all outer regard being quite disdainful, seemed to have been taken by insidious stratagem, and for the first time he had an interest without the house. He walked from one window to another, and became aware that the most irksome of solitudes is not the solitude of remoteness, but that which is just outside desirable company.

The breakfast hour went by heavily enough, and the next followed, in the same half-snowy, half-rainy style, the weather now being the inevitable relapse which sooner or later succeeds a time too radiant for the season, such as they had enjoyed in the late mid-winter at Hintock. To people at home there these changeful tricks had their interests; the strange mistakes that some of the more sanguine trees had made in budding before their month, to be incontinently glued up by frozen thawings[10] now; the similar sanguine errors of impulsive birds in framing nests that were swamped by snow-water, and other such incidents, prevented any sense of wearisomeness in the minds of the natives. But these were features of a world not familiar to Fitzpiers, and the inner visions to which he had almost exclusively attended having suddenly failed in their power to absorb him he felt unutterably dreary.

He wondered how long Miss Melbury was going to stay in Hintock. The season was unpropitious for accidental encounters with her out of doors, and except by accident he saw not how they were to become acquainted. One thing was clear – any acquaintance with her could only, with a due regard to his future, be casual, at most of the nature of a mild flirtation; for he had high aims, and they would some day lead him into other spheres than this.

Thus desultorily thinking he flung himself down upon the couch, which, as in many draughty old country houses, was constructed with a hood, being in fact a legitimate development from the settle.[11] He tried to read as he reclined, but having sat up till three o'clock that morning, the book slipped from his hand and he fell asleep.

CHAPTER II

Grace approached the house. Her knock, always soft in virtue of her nature, was softer to-day by reason of her strange errand. However, it was heard by the farmer's wife who kept the house, and Grace was admitted. Opening the door of the doctor's room the housewife glanced in, and imagining Fitzpiers absent, asked Miss Melbury to enter and wait a few minutes whilst she should go and find him, believing him to be somewhere on the premises. Grace acquiesced, went in and sat down close to the door.

As soon as the door was shut upon her she looked round the room, and started at perceiving a handsome man snugly ensconced on the couch, like a recumbent figure within some canopied mural tomb[1] of the fifteenth century, except that his hands were not exactly clasped in prayer. She had no doubt that this was the doctor.

Awaken him herself she could not, and her immediate impulse was to go and pull the broad riband with a brass rosette which hung at one side of the fireplace. But expecting the landlady to re-enter in a moment she abandoned this intention, and stood gazing in great embarrassment at the reclining philosopher.

The windows of Fitzpiers's soul being at present shuttered he probably appeared less impressive than in his hours of animation; but the light abstracted from his material features by sleep was more than counterbalanced by the mysterious influence of that state, in a stranger, upon the consciousness of a beholder so sensitive. So far as she could criticise at all, she became aware that she had encountered a specimen of creation altogether unusual in that locality. The occasions on which Grace had observed men of this stamp were when she had been far away from Hintock, and even then such examples as had met her eye were at a distance, and mainly of commoner fibre than the one who now confronted her.

She nervously wondered why the woman had not discovered her mistake and returned, and went again towards the bell-pull. Approaching the chimney her back was to Fitzpiers, but she could see him in the glass.[2] An indescribable thrill passed through her as she perceived that the eyes of the reflected image were open, gazing wonderingly at her. Under the curious unexpectedness of the sight she became as if spell-bound, almost powerless to turn her head and regard the original. However, by an effort she did turn, when there he lay asleep the same as before.

Her startled perplexity as to what he could be meaning was sufficient to lead her to precipitately abandon her errand. She crossed quickly to the door, opened and closed it noiselessly, and went out of the house unobserved. By the time that she had gone down the path and through the garden-door into the lane she had recovered her equanimity. Here, screened by the hedge, she stood and considered a while.

Drip, drip, drip, fell the rain upon her umbrella and around; she had come out on such a morning because of the seriousness of the matter in hand; yet now she had allowed her mission to be stultified by a momentary tremulousness concerning an incident which perhaps had meant nothing after all.

In the meantime her departure from the room, stealthy as it had been, had roused Fitzpiers; and he sat up. In the reflection from the mirror which Grace had beheld there was no mystery; he had opened his eyes for a few moments, but had immediately relapsed into unconsciousness, if indeed he had ever been positively awake. That somebody had just left the room he was certain, and that the lovely form which seemed to have visited him in a dream was no less than the real presentation of the person departed he could hardly doubt.

Looking out of the window a few minutes later, down the box-edged gravel-path which led to the bottom, he saw the garden-door gently open, and through it enter the young girl of his thoughts, Grace having just at this juncture determined to return and attempt the interview a second time. That he saw her coming instead of going made him ask himself if his first impression of her were not a dream indeed. She came hesitatingly along, carrying her umbrella so low over her head that he could hardly see her face. When she reached the point where the raspberry-bushes ended and the strawberry-bed began she made a little pause.

Fitzpiers feared that she might not be coming to him even now, and hastily quitting the room he ran down the path to meet her. The nature of her errand he could not divine, but he was prepared to give her any amount of encouragement.

"I beg pardon, Miss Melbury," he said. "I saw you from the window, and fancied you might imagine that I was not at home – if it is I you were coming for?"

"I was coming to speak one word to you, nothing more," she replied. "And I can say it here."

"No, no. Please do come in. Well then, if you will not come into the house, come so far as the porch!"

Thus pressed she went on to the porch, and they stood together inside it, Fitzpiers closing her umbrella for her.

"I have merely a request or petition to make," she said. "My father's servant is ill – a woman you know – and her illness is serious."

"I am sorry to hear it. You wish me to come and see her at once?"

"No, I particularly wish you not to come."

"Oh, indeed."

"Yes; and she wishes the same. It would make her seriously worse if you were to come. It would almost kill her . . . My errand is of a peculiar and awkward nature. It is concerning a subject which weighs on her mind – that unfortunate arrangement she made with you, that you might have her body — after death."

"Oh, Grammer Oliver, the old woman with the fine head. Seriously ill, is she!"

"And *so* disturbed by her rash compact! I have brought the money back – will you please return to her the agreement she signed?" Grace held out to him a couple of five-pound notes which she had kept ready tucked in her glove.

Without replying or considering the notes Fitzpiers allowed his thoughts to follow his eyes and dwell upon Grace's personality, and the sudden close relation in which he stood to her. The porch was narrow; the rain increased. It ran off the porch and dripped on the creepers, and from the creepers upon the edge of Grace's cloak and skirts.

"The rain is wetting your dress; please do come in," he said. "It really makes my heart ache to let you stay here."

Immediately inside the front door was the door of his sitting-room; he flung it open, and stood in a coaxing attitude. Try how she would Grace could not resist the supplicatory mandate written in the face and manner of this man, and distressful resignation sat on her as she glided past him into the room – brushing his coat with her elbow because of the narrowness.

He followed her, shut the door – which she somehow had hoped he would leave open – and placing a chair for her sat down.

The concern which Grace felt at the development of these common-place incidents was, of course, mainly owing to the strange effect upon her nerves of that view of him in the mirror gazing at her with open eyes when she had thought him sleeping, which made her fancy that his slumber might have been a feint based on inexplicable reasons.

She again proffered the notes; he awoke from looking at her as at a piece of live statuary, and listened deferentially as she said, "Will you then reconsider, and cancel the bond which poor Grammer Oliver so foolishly gave?"

"I'll cancel it without reconsideration. Though you will allow me to have my own opinion about her foolishness. Grammer is a very wise woman, and she was as wise in that as in other things. You think there was something very fiendish in the compact,[3] do you not, Miss Melbury? But remember that the most eminent of our surgeons in past times have entered into such agreements."

"Not fiendish – strange."

"Yes, that may be, since strangeness is not in the nature of a thing, but in its relation to something extrinsic – in this case an unessential observer."

He went to his desk, and searching awhile found a paper, which he unfolded and brought to her. A thick cross appeared in ink at the bottom – evidently from the hand of Grammer. Grace put the paper in her pocket with a look of much relief.

As Fitzpiers did not take up the money (half of which had come from Grace's own purse), she pushed it a little nearer to him. "No, no. I shall not take it from the old woman," he said. "It is more strange than the fact of a surgeon arranging to obtain a subject for dissection that our acquaintance should be formed out of it."

"I am afraid you think me uncivil in showing my dislike to the notion. But I did not mean to be."

"Oh, no, no."

He looked at her, as he had done before, with puzzled interest. "I cannot think, I cannot think," he murmured. "Something bewilders me greatly." He still reflected and hesitated. "Last night I sat up very late," he at last went on, "and on that account I fell into a little nap on that couch about half an hour ago. And during my few minutes of unconsciousness I dreamt – what do you think? – that you stood in the room."

Should she tell? She merely blushed.

"You may imagine," Fitzpiers continued, now persuaded that it had indeed been a dream, "that I should not have dreamt of you without considerable thinking about you first."

He could not be acting; of that she felt assured.

"I fancied in my vision that you stood there," he said, pointing to where she had paused. "I did not see you directly, but reflected in the glass. I thought, what a lovely creature! The design is for once carried out. Nature has at last recovered her lost union with the Idea![4] My thoughts ran in that direction because I had been reading the work of a transcendental philosopher[5] last night; and I dare say it was the dose of Idealism[6] that I received from it that made me scarcely able to distinguish between reality and fancy. I almost wept when I awoke, and found that you had appeared to me in Time, but not in Space, alas!"

At moments there was something theatrical in the delivery of Fitzpiers's effusion; yet it would have been inexact to say that it was intrinsically theatrical. It often happens that in situations of unrestraint, where there is no thought of the eye of criticism, real feeling glides into a mode of manifestation not easily distinguishable from rodomontade. A veneer of affectation overlies a bulk of truth, with the evil consequence, if perceived, that the substance is estimated by the superficies, and the whole rejected.

Grace, however, was no specialist in men's manners, and she admired the sentiment without thinking of the form. And she was embarrassed; "lovely creature" made explanation awkward to her gentle modesty.

"But can it be," said he suddenly, "that you really were here?"

"I have to confess that I have been in the room once before," faltered she. "The woman showed me in, and went away to fetch you; but as she did not return, I left."

"And you saw me asleep," he murmured, with the faintest show of humiliation.

"Yes – *if* you were asleep, and did not deceive me."

"Why do you say if?"

"I saw your eyes open in the glass, but as they were closed when I looked round upon you, I thought you were perhaps deceiving me."

"Never," said Fitzpiers fervently. "Never could I deceive you."

Foreknowledge to the distance of a year or so, in either of them, might have spoilt the effect of that pretty speech. Never deceive her! But they knew nothing, and the phrase had its day.

Grace began now to be anxious to terminate the interview, but the compelling power of Fitzpiers's atmosphere still held her there. She was like an inexperienced actress who, having at last taken up her position on the boards, and spoken her speeches, does not know how to move off. The thought of Grammer occurred to her. "I'll go at once and tell poor Grammer of your generosity," she said. "It will relieve her at once."

"Grammer's is a nervous disease, too – singular," he answered, accompanying her to the door. "One moment: look at this – it is something which may interest you."

He had thrown open the door on the other side of the passage, and she saw a microscope on the table of the confronting room. "Look into it, please; you'll be interested," he repeated.

She applied her eye, and saw the usual circle of light patterned all over with a cellular tissue of some indescribable sort. "What do you think that is?" said Fitzpiers.

She did not know.

"That's a fragment of old John South's brain, which I am investigating."

She started back, not with aversion, but with wonder as to how it should have got there. Fitzpiers laughed.

"Here am I," he said, "endeavouring to carry on simultaneously the study of physiology and transcendental philosophy, the material world and the ideal, so as to discover if possible a point of contact between them; and your finer sense is quite offended!"

"Oh, no, Mr. Fitzpiers," said Grace earnestly; "it is not so at all. I know from seeing your light at night how deeply you meditate and work. Instead of condemning you for your studies I admire you very much!"

Her face, upturned from the microscope, was so sweet, sincere, and self-forgetful in its aspect that the susceptible Fitzpiers more than wished to annihilate the lineal yard which separated it from his own. Whether anything of the kind showed in his eyes or not, Grace remained no longer at the microscope, but quickly went her way into the rain.

CHAPTER III

Instead of resuming his investigation of South's brain (which perhaps was not so interesting under the microscope as might have been expected from the importance of that organ in life) Fitzpiers reclined and ruminated on the interview. Grace's curious susceptibility to his presence, though it was as if the currents of her life were disturbed rather than attracted by him, added a special interest to her general charm.

Fitzpiers was in a distinct degree scientific, being ready and zealous to interrogate all physical manifestations, but primarily he was an idealist. He believed that behind the imperfect lay the perfect; that rare things were to be discovered amidst a bulk of commonplace; that results in a new and untried case might be different from those in other cases where the material conditions had been precisely similar. Regarding his own personality as one of unbounded possibilities, because it was his own (notwithstanding that the factors of his life had worked out a sorry product for thousands), he saw a grand speciality in his discovery at Hintock of an altogether exceptional being of the other sex.

One habit of Fitzpiers's, commoner in dreamers of more advanced age than in men of his years, was that of talking to himself. He paced round his room with a selective tread upon the more prominent blooms of the carpet, and murmured: "This phenomenal girl will be the light of my life while I am at Hintock; and the special beauty of the situation is that our attitude and relations to each other will be purely casual. Socially we can never be intimate. Anything like matrimonial intentions towards her, charming as she is, would be absurd. They would spoil the recreative character of such acquaintance.[1] And, indeed, I have other aims on the practical side of my life."

Fitzpiers bestowed a regulation thought on the advantageous marriage he was bound to make with a woman of family as good as his own, and of purse much longer. But as an object of contemplation for the present, Grace Melbury would serve to keep his soul alive, and to relieve the monotony of his days.

His first notion (acquired from the mere sight of her without converse) – that of an idle and vulgar intimacy[2] with a timber-merchant's pretty daughter, grated painfully upon him now that he had found what Grace intrinsically was. Personal intercourse with such as she could take no lower form than seemly communion, mutual explorations of the world of fancy. Since he could not call at her father's, having no practical views, cursory encounters in the lane, in the wood, coming and going to and from church, or in passing her dwelling, were what the acquaintance would have to feed on.

Such anticipated glimpses of her realised themselves in the event. Rencounters of not more than a minute's duration, frequently repeated, will build up mutual interest, even warm confidence, in a lonely place. Theirs grew as imperceptibly as the twigs budded on the trees. There never was a particular moment at which it could be said they became friends; yet a delicate understanding now existed between two who in the winter had been strangers.

Spring weather came on rather suddenly, the unsealing of buds that had long been swollen accomplishing itself in the space of one warm night. The rush of sap in the veins of the trees could almost be heard. The flowers of late April took up a position unseen, and looked as if they had been blooming a long while, though there had been no trace of them the day before yesterday; birds began not to mind getting wet. In-door people said they had heard the nightingale, to which out-door people replied contemptuously that they had heard him a fortnight before.

The young doctor's practice being scarcely so large as a London surgeon's, he frequently walked in the wood. Indeed such practice as he had he did not follow up with the assiduity that would have been necessary for developing it to exceptional proportions. One day, book in hand, he went to a part of the wood where the trees were mainly oaks. It was a calm afternoon, and there was everywhere around that sign of great undertakings on the part of vegetable nature which is apt to fill reflective human beings who are not undertaking much themselves with a sudden uneasiness at the contrast. He heard in the distance a curious sound, something like the quack of a duck, which, though it was common enough here about this time, was not common to him.

Looking through the trees Fitzpiers soon perceived the origin of the noise. The barking season had just commenced, and what he had heard was the tear of the ripping-tool as it ploughed its way along the sticky parting between the trunk and the rind. Melbury did a large business in bark, and as he was Grace's father, and possibly might be found on the spot, Fitzpiers was attracted to the scene even more than he might have been by its intrinsic interest. When he got nearer he recognised among the workmen John Upjohn, the two Timothys, and Robert Creedle, who probably had been "lent" by Winterborne; Marty South also assisted. A milking-pail of cider stood near, a half-pint cup floating on it, with which they dipped and drank whenever they passed the pail.

Each tree doomed to the flaying process was first attacked by Upjohn. With a small bill-hook he carefully freed the collar of the tree from twigs and patches of moss which encrusted it to a height of a foot or two above the ground, an operation comparable to the "little toilette"[3] of the executioner's victim. After this it was barked in its erect position to a point as high as a man could reach. If a fine product of vegetable nature could ever be said to look ridiculous it was the case now, when the oak stood naked-legged, and as if ashamed, till the axe-man came and cut a ring round it, and the two Timothys finished the work with the cross-cut saw.

As soon as it had fallen the barkers attacked it like locusts, and in a short time not a particle of rind was left on the trunk and larger limbs. Marty South was an adept at peeling the upper parts; and there she stood encaged amid the mass of twigs and buds like a great bird, running her tool into the smallest branches, beyond the furthest points to which the skill and patience of the men enabled them to proceed – branches which, in their lifetime, had swayed high above the bulk of the wood, and caught the earliest rays of the sun and moon while the lower part of the forest was still in darkness.

"You seem to have a better instrument than they, Marty," said Fitzpiers.

"No, sir," she said, holding up the tool, a horse's leg-bone fitted into a handle and filed to an edge; " 'tis only that they've less patience with the twigs, because their time is worth more than mine."

A little shed had been constructed on the spot, of thatched hurdles and boughs, and in front of it was a fire, over which a kettle sang. Fitzpiers sat down inside the shelter, and went on with his reading, except when he looked up to observe the scene and the actors.

The thought that he might settle here and become welded in with this sylvan life by marrying Grace Melbury crossed his mind for a moment. Why should he go further into the world than where he was? The secret of quiet happiness lay in limiting the aspirations; these men's thoughts were conterminous with the margin of the Hintock woodlands, and why should not his be likewise limited – a small practice among the people around him being the bound of his desires?

Presently Marty South discontinued her operations upon the quivering boughs, came out from the reclining oak, and prepared tea. When it was ready the men were called; and Fitzpiers, being in a mood to join, sat down with them.

The latent reason of his lingering here so long revealed itself when the faint creaking of the joints of a vehicle became audible, and one of the men said, "Here's he." Turning their heads they saw Melbury's gig approaching, the wheels muffled by the yielding moss.

The timber-merchant was on foot leading the horse, looking back at every few steps to caution his daughter, who kept her seat, where and how to duck her head so as to avoid the overhanging branches. They stopped at the spot where the bark-ripping had been temporarily suspended; Melbury cursorily examined the heaps of bark, and drawing near to where the workmen were sitting down, accepted their shouted invitation to have a dish of tea, for which purpose he hitched the horse to a bough.

Grace declined to take any of their beverage, and remained in her place in the vehicle, looking dreamily at the sunlight that came in thin threads through the hollies with which the oaks were interspersed.

When Melbury stepped up close to the shelter, he for the first time perceived that the doctor was present, and warmly appreciated Fitzpiers's invitation to sit down on the log beside him.

"Bless my heart, who would have thought of finding you here," he said, obviously much pleased at the circumstance. "I wonder now if my daughter knows you are so nigh at hand? I don't expect she do."

He looked out towards the gig wherein Grace sat, her face still turned sunward in the opposite direction.

"She doesn't see us," said Melbury. "Well, never mind; let her be."

Grace was indeed quite unconscious of Fitzpiers's propinquity. She was thinking of something which had little connection with the scene before her – thinking of her friend, lost as soon as found, Mrs. Charmond; of her capricious conduct, and of the contrasting scenes she was possibly enjoying at that very moment in other climes, to which Grace herself had hoped to be introduced by her friend's means. She wondered if this patronising lady[4] would return to Hintock during the summer, and whether the acquaintance which had been nipped on the last occasion of her residence there would develop on the next.

Melbury told ancient timber-stories as he sat, relating them directly to Fitzpiers, and obliquely to the men, who had heard them often before. Marty, who poured out tea, was just saying, "I think I'll take out a cup to Miss Grace," when they heard a clashing of the gig-harness, and turning round Melbury saw that the horse had become restless, and was jerking about the vehicle in a way which alarmed its occupant, though she refrained from screaming. Melbury jumped up immediately, but not more quickly than Fitzpiers; and while her father ran to the horse's head and speedily began to control him, Fitzpiers was alongside the gig assisting Grace to descend.

Her surprise at his appearance was so great that, far from making a calm and independent descent, she was very nearly lifted down in his arms. He relinquished her when she touched ground, and hoped she was not frightened.

"Oh, no, not much," she managed to say. "There was no danger – unless the mare had run under the trees where the boughs are low enough to hit my head."

"Which was by no means an impossibility, and justifies any amount of alarm."

He referred to what he thought he saw written in her face, and she could not tell him that this had little to do with the horse, but much with himself. His contiguity had, in fact, the same effect upon her as on those former occasions when he had come closer to her than usual – that of producing in her an unaccountable tendency to tearfulness.[5] Melbury soon put the horse to rights, and seeing that Grace was safe, turned again to the work-people.

His daughter's nervous distress had passed off in a few moments, and she said quite gaily to Fitzpiers as she walked with him towards the group, "There's destiny in it, you see. I was doomed to join in your picnic, although I did not intend to do so."

Marty prepared her a comfortable place, and she sat down in the circle, and listened to Fitzpiers while he drew from her father and the bark-rippers sundry narratives of their fathers', their grandfathers', and their own adventures in these woods; of the mysterious sights they had seen – only to be accounted for by supernatural agency; of white witches and black witches; and the standard story of the spirits of the Two Brothers who had fought and fallen, and had haunted Hintock House till they were exorcised by the priest, and compelled to retreat to a swamp in this very wood, whence they were returning to their old quarters at the rate of a cock's stride every New Year's Day, Old Style;[6] hence the local saying, "On new-year's tide, a cock's stride."

It was a pleasant time. The smoke from the little fire of peeled sticks rose between the sitters and the sunlight, and behind its blue films stretched the naked arms of the prostrate trees. The smell of the uncovered sap mingled with the smell of the burning wood, and the sticky inner surface of the scattered bark glistened as it revealed its pale madder hues to the eye. Melbury was so highly satisfied at having Fitzpiers as a sort of guest that he would have sat on for any length of time, but Grace, on whom Fitzpiers's eyes only too frequently alighted, seemed to think it incumbent upon her to make a show of going; and her father thereupon accompanied her to the gig.

As the doctor had helped her out of it he appeared to think that he had excellent reasons for helping her in, and performed the attention lingeringly enough.

"What were you almost in tears about just now?" he asked softly.

"I don't know," she said; and the words were strictly true.

Melbury mounted on the other side, and they drove on out of the grove, their wheels silently crushing delicate-patterned mosses, hyacinths, primroses, lords-and-ladies, and other strange and common plants, and cracking up little sticks that lay across the track. Their way homeward ran along the crest of Rubdon Hill, whence on the left they beheld a wide valley, differing both in feature and atmosphere from that of the Hintock precincts. It was the cider country, which met the woodland district on the axis of this hill. Over the vale the air was blue as sapphire – such a blue as outside that apple-valley was never seen. Under the blue the orchards were in a blaze of pink bloom, some of the richly flowered trees running almost up to where they drove along. At a gate, which opened down the incline, a man leant on his arms, regarding this fair promise so intently that he did not observe their passing.

"That was Giles," said Melbury when they had gone by.

"Was it? Poor Giles," said she.

"All that apple-blooth means heavy autumn work for him and his hands. If no blight happens before the setting, the cider yield will be such as we have not had for years."

Meanwhile, in the wood they had come from, the men had sat on so long that they were indisposed to begin work again that evening; they were paid by the ton, and their time for labour was as they chose. They placed the last gatherings of bark in rows for the curers,[7] which led them further and further away from the shed; and thus they gradually withdrew homeward as the sun went down.

Fitzpiers lingered yet. He had opened his book again, though he could hardly see a word in it, and sat before the dying fire, scarcely knowing of the men's departure. He dreamed and mused till his consciousness seemed to occupy the whole space of the woodland round, so little was there of jarring sight or sound to hinder perfect mental unity with the sentiment of the place. The idea returned upon him of sacrificing all practical aims to live in calm contentment here, and instead of going on elaborating new conceptions with infinite pains, to accept quiet domesticity according to oldest and homeliest notions. These reflections detained him till the wood was embrowned with the coming night, and the shy little bird of this dusky time had begun to pour out all the intensity of his eloquence from a bush not very far off.

Fitzpiers's eyes commanded as much of the ground in front as was open. Entering upon this he saw a figure, whose direction of movement was towards the spot where he sat. The surgeon was quite shrouded from observation by the recessed shadow of the hurdle-screen, and there was no reason why he should move till the stranger had passed by.

The shape resolved itself into a woman's; she was looking on the ground, and walking slowly as if searching for something that had been lost, her course being precisely that of Mr. Melbury's gig. Fitzpiers by a sort of divination jumped to the idea that the figure was Grace's; her nearer approach made the guess a certainty.

Yes, she was looking for something; and she came round by the prostrate trees that would have been invisible but for their white nakedness, which enabled her to avoid them easily. Thus she approached the heap of ashes, and acting upon what was suggested by a still shining ember or two she took a stick and stirred the heap, which thereupon burst into a flame. On looking around by the light thus obtained she for the first time saw the illumined face of Fitzpiers, precisely in the spot where she had left him.

Grace gave a start and a scream; she had not the least expected to find him there still. Fitzpiers lost not a moment in rising and going to her side.

"I frightened you dreadfully, I know," he said. "I ought to have spoken; but I did not at first expect it to be you. I have been sitting here ever since."

He was actually supporting her with his arm as though under the impression that she was quite overcome and in danger of falling. As soon as she could collect her ideas she gently withdrew from his grasp, and explained what she had returned for: in getting up or down from the gig, or when sitting by the hut fire, she had dropped her purse.

"Now we will find it," said Fitzpiers.

He threw an armful of last year's leaves on to the fire, which made the flame leap higher, and the encompassing shades to weave themselves into a blacker contrast, turning eve into night in a moment. By this radiance they groped about on their hands and knees, till Fitzpiers rested on his elbow, and looked at Grace.

"We almost always meet in odd circumstances," he said; "and this is one of the oddest. I wonder if it means anything?"

"Oh, no, I am sure it doesn't," said Grace in haste, quickly assuming an erect posture. "Pray don't say it any more."

"I hope there was not much money in the purse," said Fitzpiers, rising to his feet more slowly, and brushing the leaves from his trousers.

"Scarcely any. I cared most about the purse itself, because it was given me. Indeed, money is of little more use at Hintock than on Crusoe's island;[8] there's hardly any way of spending it."

They had given up the search when Fitzpiers discerned something by his foot. "Here it is!" he said. "So that your father, mother, friend, or *admirer* will not have his or her feelings hurt by a sense of your negligence after all."

"Oh, he knows nothing of what I do now."

"The admirer?" said Fitzpiers slyly.

"I don't know if you would call him that," said Grace with simplicity. "The admirer is a superficial, conditional creature, and this person is quite different."

"He has all the cardinal virtues?"[9]

"Perhaps – though I don't know them precisely."

"You unconsciously practise them, Miss Melbury, which is better. According to Schleiermacher[10] they are Self-control, Perseverance, Wisdom, and Love; and his is the best list that I know."

"I am afraid poor – " She was going to say that she feared Winterborne, the giver of the purse years before, had not much perseverance, though he had all the other three; but she determined to go no further in this direction, and was silent.

These half-revelations made a perceptible difference in Fitzpiers. His sense of personal superiority wasted away, and Grace assumed in his eyes the true aspect of a mistress in her lover's regard.

"Miss Melbury," he said suddenly; "I divine that this virtuous man you mention has been refused by you?"

She could do no otherwise than admit it.

"I did not inquire without good reason. God forbid that I should kneel in another's place at any shrine unfairly. But, my dear Miss Melbury, now that he is gone from the temple, may I draw near?"

"I – I can't say anything about that!" she cried quickly. "Because when a man has been refused you feel pity for him, and like him more than you did before."

This increasing complication added still more value to Grace in the surgeon's eyes: it rendered her adorable. "But cannot you say?" he pleaded distractedly.

"I'd rather not – I think I must go home at once."

"Oh, yes," said Fitzpiers.

But as he did not move she felt it awkward to walk straight away from him; and so they stood silently together. A diversion was created by the accident of two birds, that had either been roosting above their heads or nesting there, tumbling one over the other into the hot ashes at their feet, apparently engrossed in a desperate quarrel that prevented the use of their wings. They speedily parted, however, and flew up, with a singed smell, and were seen no more.

"That's the end of what is called love," said some one.

The speaker was neither Grace nor Fitzpiers, but Marty South, who approached with her face turned up to the sky in her endeavour to trace the birds. Suddenly perceiving Grace she exclaimed, "Oh – Miss Melbury! – I have been following they pigeons, and didn't see you. And here's Mr. Winterborne!" she continued shyly, as she looked towards Fitzpiers, who stood in the background.

"Marty," Grace interrupted; "I want you to walk home with me – will you? Come along." And without lingering longer she took hold of Marty's arm and led her away.

They went between the spectral arms of the peeled trees as they lay, and onward among the growing trees, by a path where there were no oaks, and no barking, and no Fitzpiers – nothing but copse wood, between which the primroses could be discerned in pale bunches.

"I – didn't know Mr. Winterborne was there," said Marty, breaking the silence when they had nearly reached Grace's door.

"Nor was he," said Grace.

"But, Miss Melbury – I saw him."

"No," said Grace. "It was somebody else. Giles Winterborne is nothing to me."

CHAPTER IV

The leaves over Hintock unrolled their creased tissues, and the wood-land seemed to change from an open filigree to a solid opaque body of infinitely larger shape and importance. The boughs cast green shades, which disagreed with the complexion of the girls who walked there; and a fringe of them which overhung Mr. Melbury's garden dripped on his seed-plots when it rained, pitting their surface all over as with pockmarks, till Melbury declared that gardens in such a place were no good at all. The two trees that had creaked all the winter left off creaking, the whirr of the night-hawk, however, forming a very satisfactory continuation of uncanny music from that quarter. Except at midday the sun was not seen complete by the Hintock people, but rather in the form of numerous little stars staring through the leaves.

Such an appearance it had on Midsummer eve of this year, and as the hour grew later, and nine o'clock drew on, the irradiation of the day-time became broken up by weird shadows and ghostly nooks of indistinctness. Imagination could trace amid the trunks and boughs swarthy faces and funereal figures. This was before the moon rose. Later on, when that planet was getting command of the upper heaven, and consequently shining with an unbroken face into such open glades as there were in the neighbourhood of the hamlet, it became apparent that the margin of the wood which approached the timber-merchant's premises was not to be left to the customary stillness of that reposeful time.

Fitzpiers having heard a voice or voices, was looking over his garden gate (where he now looked more frequently than into his books) fancying that Grace might be abroad with some friends. He was

irretrievably committed in heart to Grace Melbury, though he was
by no means sure that she was so far committed to him. That the Idea
had for once completely fulfilled itself in the objective substance[1]
(which he had hitherto deemed an impossibility) he was enchanted
enough to fancy must be the case at last.

It was not Grace who had passed, however, but several of the
ordinary village girls in a group; some steadily walking, some in a
mood of wild gaiety. He quietly asked his landlady, who was also in
the garden, what these girls were intending, and she informed him
that it being old Midsummer eve,[2] they were about to attempt some
spell or enchantment which would afford them a glimpse of their
future partners for life. She declared it to be an ungodly performance,
and one that she for her part would never countenance; saying which
she entered her house and retired to bed.

The young man lit a cigar, and followed the bevy of maidens slowly
up the road. They had turned into the wood at an opening between
Melbury's and Marty South's; but Fitzpiers could easily track them
by their voices, low as they endeavoured to keep their tones.

In the meantime other inhabitants of Little Hintock had become
aware of the nocturnal experiment about to be tried, and were also
sauntering stealthily after the frisky maidens. Miss Melbury had been
informed by Marty South during the day of the proposed peep into
futurity, and, being only a girl like the rest, she was sufficiently interested
to wish to see the issue. The moon was so bright and the night so calm
that she had no difficulty in persuading Mrs. Melbury to accompany
her; and thus, joined by Marty, these went onward in the same
direction.

Passing Winterborne's house they heard a noise of hammering.
Marty explained it. This was the last night on which his paternal roof
would shelter him, the days of grace since it fell into hand having
expired; and Giles was taking down his cupboards and bedsteads
with a view to an early exit next morning. His encounter with Mrs.
Charmond had cost him dearly.

When they had proceeded a little further Marty was joined by
Grammer Oliver (who was as young as the youngest in such matters),
and Grace and Mrs. Melbury went on by themselves till they had

arrived at the spot chosen by the village daughters, whose primary intention of keeping their expedition a secret had been quite defeated. Grace and her stepmother paused by a holly tree; and at a little distance stood Fitzpiers under the shade of a young oak, intently observing Grace, who was in the full rays of the moon.

He watched her without speaking, and unperceived by any but Marty and Grammer, who had drawn up on the dark side of the same holly which sheltered Mrs. and Miss Melbury on its bright side. The two former conversed in low tones.

"If they two come up in wood next Midsummer night they'll come as one," said Grammer, signifying Fitzpiers and Grace. "Instead of my skellinton he'll carry home her living carcase before long. But though she's a lady in herself, and worthy of any such as he, it do seem to me that he ought to marry somebody more of the sort of Mrs. Charmond, and that Miss Grace should make the best of Winterborne."

Marty returned no comment; and at that minute the girls, some of whom were from Great Hintock, were seen advancing to work the incantation, it being now about midnight.

"Directly we see anything we'll run home as fast as we can," said one, whose courage had begun to fail her. To this the rest assented, not knowing that a dozen neighbours lurked in the bushes around.

"I wish we had not thought of trying this," said another, "but had contented ourselves with the hole-digging[3] to-morrow at twelve, and hearing our husband's trades. It is too much like having dealings with the evil one[4] to try to raise their forms."

However, they had gone too far to recede, and slowly began to march forward in a skirmishing line through the trees, each intending to plunge alone into the deeper recesses of the wood. As far as the listeners could gather, the particular form of black art to be practised on this occasion was one connected with the sowing of hemp-seed,[5] a handful of which was carried by each girl.

At the moment of their advance they looked back, and discerned the figure of Miss Melbury who, alone of all the observers, stood in the full face of the moonlight, deeply engrossed in the proceedings. By contrast with her life of late years they made her feel as if she had receded a couple of centuries in the world's history. She was rendered doubly conspicuous by her light dress, and after a few whispered words, one of the girls (a bouncing maiden, plighted to young Timothy Tangs) asked her if she would join in, Grace with some excitement said that she would, and moved on a little in the rear of the rest.

Soon the listeners could hear nothing of their proceedings beyond the faintest occasional rustle of leaves. Grammer whispered again to Marty: "Why didn't ye go and try your luck with the rest of the maids?"

"I don't believe in it!" said Marty shortly.

"Why, half the parish is here; the silly hussies should have kept it quiet. I see Mr. Winterborne through the leaves, just come up with Robert Creedle. Marty, we ought to act the part o' Providence some-times. Do go and tell him that if he stands just behind the bush at the bottom of the slope, Miss Grace must pass down it when she comes back, and she will most likely rush into his arms; for as soon as the clock strikes they'll bundle back home along like hares. I've seen such larries before."

"Do you think I'd better?" said Marty reluctantly.

"Oh yes, he'll bless ye for it."

"I don't want that kind of blessing!"

But after a moment's thought she went, and delivered the infor-mation; and Grammer had the satisfaction of seeing Giles walk slowly to the bend in the leafy defile along which Grace would have to return.

Meanwhile Mrs. Melbury, deserted by Grace, had perceived Fitz-piers and Winterborne, and also the move of the latter. An improve-ment on Grammer's idea entered the mind of Mrs. Melbury, for she had lately discerned what her husband had not, that Grace was rapidly fascinating the surgeon. She therefore drew near to Fitzpiers.

"You should be where Mr. Winterborne is standing," she said to him significantly. "She will run down through that opening much faster than she went up it, if she is like the rest of the girls."

Fitzpiers did not require to be told twice. He went across to Win-terborne, and stood beside him. Each knew the probable purpose of the other in standing there, and neither spoke, Fitzpiers scorning to look upon Winterborne as a rival, and Winterborne adhering to the off-hand manner of indifference which had grown upon him since his dismissal.

Neither Grammer nor Marty South had seen the surgeon's manœuvre, and still to help Winterborne, as she supposed, the old woman suggested to the wood-girl that she should walk forward at the heels of Grace, and "tole" her down the required way if she showed a tendency to run in another direction. Poor Marty, always doomed to sacrifice desire to obligation, walked forward accordingly, and waited as a beacon, still and silent, for the retreat of Grace and her giddy companions, now quite out of hearing.

The first sound to break the silence was the distant note of Great Hintock clock striking the significant hour. About a minute later that quarter of the wood to which the girls had wandered resounded with the flapping of disturbed birds; then two or three hares and rabbits bounded down the glade from the same direction, and after these the rustling and crackling of leaves and dead twigs denoted the hurried approach of the adventurers, whose fluttering gowns soon became visible.

Miss Melbury, having gone forward quite in the rear of the rest, was one of the first to return, and the excitement being contagious, she ran laughing towards Marty, who still stood as a handpost to guide her; then, passing on, she flew round the fatal bush where the undergrowth narrowed to a gorge. Marty arrived at her heels just in time to see the result. Fitzpiers had quickly stepped forward in front of Winterborne, who disdaining to shift his position had turned on his heel, and then the surgeon did what he would not have thought of doing but for Mrs. Melbury's encouragement and the sentiment of an eve which effaced conventionality. Stretching out his arms as the white figure burst upon him, he captured her[6] in a moment, as if she had been a bird.

"Oh!" cried Grace in her fright.

"You are in my arms, dearest," said Fitzpiers; "and I am going to claim you, and keep you there all our two lives!"

She rested on him like one utterly mastered; and it was several seconds before she recovered from this helplessness. Subdued screams and struggles, audible from neighbouring brakes, revealed that there had been other lurkers thereabout for a similar purpose. Grace, unlike most of these companions of hers, instead of giggling and writhing, said in a trembling voice, "Mr. Fitzpiers, will you let me go?"

"Certainly," he said laughing; "as soon as you have recovered."

She waited another few moments, then quietly and firmly pushed him aside, and glided on her path, the moon whitening her hot blush away. But it had been enough; new relations between them had begun.

The case of the other girls was different, as has been said. They wrestled and tittered, only escaping after a desperate struggle. Fitzpiers could hear these enactments still going on after Grace had left him, and he remained on the spot where he had caught her, Winterborne having gone away. On a sudden another girl came bounding down the same descent that had been followed by Grace; a fine-framed young woman, with bare arms. Seeing Fitzpiers standing there, she said with playful effrontery: "May'st kiss me if 'canst catch me, Tim!"

Fitzpiers recognised her as Suke Damson, a hoydenish maiden of the hamlet, who was plainly mistaking him for her lover. He was impulsively disposed to profit by her error, and as soon as she began racing away he started in pursuit.

On she went under the boughs, now in light, now in shade, looking over her shoulder at him every few moments and kissing her hand; but so cunningly dodging about among the trees and moon-shades that she never allowed him to get dangerously near her. Thus they ran and doubled, Fitzpiers warming with the chase, till the sound of their companions had quite died away.

He began to lose hope of ever overtaking her, when all at once, by way of encouragement, she turned to a fence in which there was a stile, and leapt over it. Outside, the scene was a changed one; a meadow, where the half-made hay lay about in heaps, in the uninterrupted shine of the now high moon.

Fitzpiers saw in a moment that, having taken to open ground, she had placed herself at his mercy, and he promptly vaulted over after her. She flitted a little way down the mead, when all at once her elusive form disappeared, as if it had sunk into the earth. She had buried herself in one of the hay-cocks.

Fitzpiers, now thoroughly excited, was not going to let her escape him thus. He approached, and set about turning over the heaps one by one. As soon as he paused, tantalised and puzzled, he was directed anew by an imitative kiss which came from her hiding-place, and by snatches of a local ballad, in the smallest voice she could assume:–

"Oh, come in from the foggy, foggy dew."[7]

In a minute or two he uncovered her.

"Oh – 'tis not Tim!" said she, burying her face.

Fitzpiers, however, disregarded her resistance by reason of its mildness, stooped, and imprinted the purposed kiss, then sank down on the next hay-cock, panting with his race.

"Whom do you mean by Tim?" he asked presently.

"My young man, Tim Tangs," said she.

"Now, honour bright, did you really think it was he?"

"I did at first."

"But you didn't at last."

"I didn't at last."

"Do you much mind that it is not?"

"No," she answered slyly.

Fitzpiers kissed her again.

He did not pursue his questioning. In the moonlight Suke looked very beautiful, the scratches and blemishes incidental to her outdoor occupation being invisible under these pale rays. While they remained silent the coarse whirr of the eternal nighthawk burst sarcastically from the top of a tree at the nearest corner of the wood. Besides this not a sound of any kind reached their ears, the time of nightingales being now past, and Hintock lying at a distance of two miles at least. In the opposite direction the hay-field stretched away into remoteness till it was lost to the eye in a soft mist.

It was daybreak before Fitzpiers and Suke Damson re-entered Little Hintock.[8]

CHAPTER V

When the general stampede occurred Winterborne had also been looking on, and encountering one of the girls had asked her what caused them all to fly.

She said with solemn breathlessness that they had seen something very different from what they had hoped to see, and that she for one would never attempt such unholy ceremonies again. "We saw Satan pursuing us with his hour-glass.[1] It was terrible!"

This account being a little mixed Giles went forward towards the spot from which the girls had retreated. After listening there a few minutes he heard slow footsteps rustling over the leaves, and looking through a tangled screen of honeysuckle which hung from a bough he saw in the open space beyond a short stout man in evening dress, carrying on one arm a light overcoat and also his hat, so awkwardly arranged as possibly to have suggested the "hour-glass" to his timid observers – if this were the person whom the girls had seen. With the other hand he silently gesticulated, and the moonlight falling upon his bare brow showed him to have dark hair and a high forehead of the shape seen oftener in old prints and paintings than in real life. His curious and altogether alien aspect, his strange gestures, like those of one who is rehearsing a scene to himself, and the unusual place and hour, were sufficient to account for any trepidation among the Hintock daughters at encountering him.

He paused, and looked round, as if he had forgotten where he was; not observing Giles, who was of the colour of his environment. The latter advanced into the light. The gentleman held up his hand and came towards Giles, the two meeting half way.

"I have lost my way," said the stranger. "Perhaps you can put me in the path again." He wiped his forehead with the air of one suffering under an agitation more than that of simple fatigue.

"The turnpike-road is over there," said Giles.

"I don't want the turnpike-road," said the gentleman impatiently. "I came from that. I want Hintock House. Is there not a path to it across here?"

"Well, yes, a sort of path. But it is hard to find from this point. I'll show you the way, sir, with great pleasure."

"Thanks, my good friend. The truth is that I decided to walk across the country after dinner from the hotel at Sherton, where I am staying for a day or two. But I did not know it was so far."

"It is about a mile to the house from here."

They walked on together. As there was no path Giles occasionally stepped in front and bent aside the under-boughs of the trees to give his companion a passage, saying every now and then when the twigs, on being released, flew back like whips, "Mind your eyes, sir." To which the stranger replied, "Yes, yes," in a preoccupied tone.

So they went on, the leaf-shadows running in their usual quick succession over the forms of the pedestrians till the stranger said –

"Is it far?"

"Not much farther," said Winterborne. "The plantation runs up into a corner here, close behind the house." He added with hesitation, "You know, I suppose, sir, that Mrs. Charmond is not at home?"

"You mistake," said the other shortly. "Mrs. Charmond has been away for some time, but she's at home now."

Giles did not contradict him, though he felt sure that the gentleman was wrong.

"You are a native of this place?" the stranger said.

"Yes."

"You are happy in having a home. It is what I don't possess."

"You come from far, seemingly?"

"I come now from the south of Europe."

"Oh, indeed, sir. You are an Italian, or Spanish, or French gentleman, perhaps?"

"I am not either."

Giles did not fill the pause which ensued, and the gentleman, who seemed of an emotional nature, unable to resist friendship, at length answered the question.

"I am an Italianised American; a South Carolinian by birth," he said. "I left my native country on the failure of the Southern cause, and have never returned to it since."[2]

He spoke no more about himself, and they came to the verge of the wood. Here, striding over the fence out upon the upland sward, they could at once see the chimneys of the house in the gorge immediately beneath their position, silent, still, and pale.

"Can you tell me the time?" the gentleman asked. "My watch has stopped."

"It is between twelve and one," said Giles.

His companion expressed his astonishment. "I thought it between nine and ten at latest! Dear me – dear me!"

He now begged Giles to return, and offered him a gold coin, which looked like a sovereign, for the assistance rendered. Giles declined to accept anything, to the surprise of the stranger, who, on putting the money back into his pocket, said awkwardly, "I thought it was the custom over here. I offered it because I want you to utter no word about this meeting with me. Will you promise?"

Winterborne promised readily. He stood still whilst the other descended the slope. At the bottom the stranger looked back mistrustfully. Giles would no longer remain when he was so evidently desired to leave, and returned through the boughs to Little Hintock.

He suspected that this man, who seemed so distressed and melancholy, might be that lover and persistent wooer of Mrs. Charmond whom he had heard so frequently spoken of, and whom it was said she had treated cavalierly. But he received no confirmation of his suspicion beyond a report which reached him a few days later that a gentleman had called up the servants who were taking care of Hintock House at an hour past midnight; and on learning that Mrs. Charmond, though returned from abroad, was as yet in London, he had sworn bitterly, and gone away without leaving a card or any trace of himself.

The girls who related the story added that he sighed three times before he swore, but this part of the narrative was not corroborated. Anyhow such a gentleman drove away from Sherton next day in a carriage hired at the inn.

CHAPTER VI

The sunny, leafy week which followed the tender doings of Midsummer eve brought a visitor to Fitzpiers's door; a voice that he knew sounded in the passage. Mr. Melbury had called.

At first he had a particular objection to enter the parlour, because his boots were dusty, but as the surgeon insisted he waived the point and came in.

Looking neither to the right nor to the left, hardly at Fitzpiers himself, he put his hat under his chair and with a preoccupied gaze at the floor said, "I've called to ask you, doctor, quite privately, a question that troubles me. I've a daughter, Grace, an only daughter as you may have heard. Well, she's been out in the dew; on Midsummer eve in particular she went out in thin slippers to watch some vagary of the Hintock maids; and she's got a cough, a distinct hemming and hacking, that makes me uneasy. Now I have decided to send her away to some seaside place for a change – "

"Send her away!" Fitzpiers's countenance had fallen.

"Yes. And the question is, where would you advise me to send her?"

The timber-merchant had happened to call at a moment when Fitzpiers was at the spring-tide of a sentiment[1] that Grace was a necessity of his existence. The sudden pressure of her form upon his breast as she came headlong round the bush had never ceased to linger with him since he adopted the manœuvre for which the hour and the moonlight and the occasion had been the only excuse. Now she was to be sent away.

Ambition? – it could be postponed. Family?[2] – a common culture and reciprocity of tastes had taken the place of family parallels nowadays. He allowed himself to be carried forward on the wave of his desire.

"How strange, how very strange it is," he said, "that you should have come to me about her just now. I have been thinking every day of coming to you on the very same errand."

"Ah? You have noticed, too, that her health —"

"I have noticed nothing the matter with her health, because there is nothing. But, Mr. Melbury, I have seen your daughter several times by accident. I have admired her infinitely, and I was coming to ask you if I may become better acquainted with her – pay my addresses to her?"

Melbury was looking down as he listened, and did not see the air of half-misgiving at his own rashness that spread over Fitzpiers's face as he made this declaration.

"You have – got to know her?" said Melbury, a spell of dead silence having preceded his utterance, during which his emotion rose with almost visible effect.

"Yes," said Fitzpiers.

"And you wish to become better acquainted with her? You mean with a view to marriage – is that what you mean?"

"Yes," said the young man. "I mean, get acquainted with her, with a view to being her accepted lover; and if we suited each other, what would naturally follow."

The timber-dealer was much surprised, and fairly agitated; his hand trembled as he laid by his walking-stick.

"This takes me unawares," said he, his voice well-nigh breaking down. "I don't mean that there is anything unexpected in a gentleman being attracted by her; but it did not occur to me that it would be you. I always said," continued he, with a lump in his throat, "that my Grace would make a mark at her own level some day. That was why I educated her. I said to myself, 'I'll do it, cost what it may'; though her mother-in-law was pretty frightened at my paying out so much money year after year. I knew it would tell in the end. 'Where you've not good material to work on, such doings would be waste and vanity,' I said. 'But where you have that material, it is sure to be worth while.'"

"I am glad you don't object," said Fitzpiers, almost wishing that Grace had not been quite so cheap for him.

"If she is willing I don't object, certainly. Indeed," added the honest man, "it would be deceit if I were to pretend to feel anything else than highly honoured personally; and it is a great credit to her to have drawn to her a man of such good professional station and venerable old family. That huntsman-fellow[3] little thought how wrong he was about her! Take her and welcome, sir."

"I'll endeavour to ascertain her mind."

"Yes, yes. But she will be agreeable, I should think. She ought to be."

"I hope she may. Well, now you'll expect to see me frequently."

"Oh, yes. But, name it all – about her cough, and her going away? I had quite forgot that that was what I came about."

"I assure you," said the surgeon, "that her cough can only be the result of a slight cold, and it is not necessary to banish her to any seaside place at all."

Melbury looked unconvinced, doubting whether he ought to take Fitzpiers's professional opinion in circumstances which naturally led him to wish to keep her by him. The doctor saw this, and honestly dreading to lose sight of her, he said eagerly, "Between ourselves, if I am successful with her I will take her away myself for a month or two, as soon as we are married, which I hope will be before the chilly weather comes on. This will be so very much better than letting her go now."

The proposal pleased Melbury much. There could be hardly any danger in postponing any desirable change of air as long as the warm weather lasted, and for such a reason.

Suddenly recollecting himself he said, "Your time must be precious, doctor. I'll get home-along. I am much obliged to ye. As you will see her often, you'll discover for yourself if anything serious is the matter."

"I can assure you it is nothing," said Fitzpiers, who had seen Grace much oftener already than her father knew of.

When he was gone Fitzpiers paused, silent, registering his sensations, like a man who has made a plunge for a pearl into a medium of which he knows neither the density nor temperature.[4] But he had done it, and Grace was the sweetest girl alive.

As for the departed visitor, his own last words lingered in Melbury's ears as he walked homeward; he felt that what he had said in the emotion of the moment was very stupid, ungenteel, and unsuited to a dialogue with an educated gentleman, the smallness of whose practice was more than compensated by the former greatness of his family. He had uttered thoughts before they were weighed, and almost before they were shaped. They had expressed in a certain sense his feeling at Fitzpiers's news, but yet they were not right. Looking on the ground, and planting his stick at each tread as if it were a flagstaff, he reached his own precincts, where, as he passed through the court, he automatically stopped to look at the men working in the shed and around. One of them asked him a question about waggon-spokes.

"Hey?" said Melbury, looking hard at him. The man repeated the words.

Melbury stood; then turning suddenly away without answering, he went up the court and entered the house.

As time was no object with the journeymen, except as a thing to get passed, they leisurely surveyed the door through which he had disappeared.

"What maggot has the gaffer got in his head now?" said Tangs the elder. "Sommit to do with that chiel of his! When you've got a maid of yer own, John Upjohn, that costs ye what she costs him, that will take the squeak out of your Sunday shoes, John! But you'll never be tall enough to accomplish such as she; and 'tis a lucky thing for ye, John, as things be. Well, he ought to have a dozen – that would bring him to reason, I see 'em walking together last Sunday, and when they came to a puddle he lifted her over like a halfpenny doll. He ought to have a dozen; he'd let 'em walk through puddles for themselves then."

Meanwhile Melbury had entered the house with the look of a man who sees a vision before him. His wife was in the room. Without taking off his hat he sat down at random.

"Luce – we've done it!" he said. "Yes – the thing is as I expected. The spell, that I foresaw might be worked, has worked. She's done it, and done it well. Where is she – Grace, I mean?"

"Up in her room: what has happened?"

Mr. Melbury explained the circumstances as coherently as he could. "I told you so," he said. "A maid like her couldn't stay hid long, even in a place like this. But where is Grace? Let's have her down. Here – Gra-a-ace!"

She appeared after a reasonable interval, for she was sufficiently spoilt by this father of hers not to put herself in a hurry, however impatient his tones. "What is it, father?" said she, with a smile.

"Why, you scamp, what's this you've been doing? Not home here more than six months, yet instead of confining yourself to your father's rank making havoc in the educated classes!"

Though accustomed to show herself instantly appreciative of her father's meanings, Grace was fairly unable to look anyhow but at a loss now.

"No, no; of course you don't know what I mean, or you pretend you don't. Though for my part I believe women can see these things through a double hedge. But I suppose I must tell ye. Why, you've flung your grapnel over the doctor, and he's coming courting forthwith."

"Only think of that, my dear! Don't you feel it a triumph?" said Mrs. Melbury.

"Coming courting – I've done nothing to make him!" Grace exclaimed.

" 'Twasn't necessary that you should: 'tis voluntary that rules in these things. Well, he has behaved very honourably, and asked my consent. You'll know what to do when he gets here, I dare say. I needn't tell you to make it all smooth for him."

"You mean, to lead him on to marry me?"

"I do. Haven't I educated you for it?"

Grace looked out of the window, and at the fireplace, with no animation in her face. "Why is it settled off-hand in this way?" said she coquettishly. "You'll wait till you hear what I think of him, I suppose?"

"Oh, yes, of course. But you see what a good thing it will be."

She weighed the statement without speaking.

"You will be restored to the society you've been taken away from," continued her father; "for I don't suppose he'll stay here long."

She admitted the advantage; but it was plain that though Fitzpiers when he was present exercised a certain fascination over her, or even more, an almost psychic influence,[5] as it is called, and though his impulsive act in the wood had stirred her feelings indescribably, she had never regarded him in the light of a destined husband. "I don't know what to answer," she said. "I have learnt that he is very clever."

"He's all right, and he's coming here to see you."

A premonition that she could not resist him if he came strangely moved her. "Of course, father, you remember that it is only lately that Giles – "

"You know that you can't think of him. He has given up all claim to you."

She could not explain the subtleties of her feeling as clearly as he could state his opinion, even though she had skill in speech, and her father had none. That Fitzpiers acted upon her like a dram,[6] exciting her, throwing her into a novel atmosphere which biassed her doings until the influence was over, when she felt something of the nature of regret for the mood she had experienced[7] – could not be told to this worthy couple in words.

It so happened that on this very day Fitzpiers was called away from Hintock by an engagement to attend some medical meetings, and his visits therefore did not begin at once. A note, however, arrived from him addressed to Grace, deploring his enforced absence. As a material object this note was pretty and superfine, a note of a sort that she had been unaccustomed to see since her return to Hintock, except when a school friend wrote to her – a rare instance, for the girls were respecters of persons, and many cooled down towards the timber-dealer's daughter when she was out of sight. Thus the recipe of it pleased her, and she afterwards walked about with a reflective air.

In the evening her father, who knew that the note had come, said, "Why be ye not sitting down to answer your letter? That's what young folks did in my time."

She replied that it did not require an answer.

"Oh, you know best," he said. Nevertheless he went about his business doubting if she were right in not replying; possibly she might be so mismanaging matters as to risk the loss of an alliance which would bring her much happiness.

Melbury's respect for Fitzpiers was based less on his professional position, which was not much, than on the standing of his family in the county in bygone days. That touching faith in members of long-established families as such, irrespective of their personal condition or character, which is still found among old-fashioned people in the rural districts, reached its full perfection in Melbury. His daughter's suitor was descended from a line he had heard of in his grandfather's time as being once among the greatest, a family which had conferred its name upon a neighbouring village; how then could anything be amiss in this betrothal?

"I must keep her up to this," he said to his wife. "She sees it is for her happiness; but still she's young, and may want a little prompting from an older tongue."

CHAPTER VII

With this in view Melbury took her out for a walk, a custom of his when he wished to say anything specially impressive. Their way was over the top of that lofty ridge dividing their woodland from the cider district, whence they had in the spring beheld the miles of apple-trees in bloom. All was now deep green.

The spot recalled to Grace's mind the last occasion of her presence there, and she said, "The promise of an enormous apple-crop is fulfilling itself, is it not? I suppose Giles is getting his mills and presses ready."

This was just what her father had not come there to talk about. Without replying he raised his arm and moved his finger till he fixed it at a point.

"There," he said. "You see that plantation reaching over the hill like a great slug, and just behind the hill a particularly green sheltered bottom? That's where Mr. Fitzpiers's family were lords of the manor for I don't know how many hundred years, and there stands the village of Buckbury Fitzpiers. A wonderful property 'twas – wonderful!"

"But they are not lords of the manor there now."

"Why, no. But good and great folk fall as well as humble and foolish. The only ones representing the family now, I believe are our doctor and a maiden lady living I don't know where. You can't help being happy, Grace, in allying yourself with such a romantical family.[1] You'll feel as if you've stepped into history."

"We've been at Hintock as long as they were at Buckbury; is it not so? You say our name occurs in old deeds continually."

"Oh, yes – as yeomen, copyholders, and such like. But think how much better this will be for 'ee. You'll be living a high, perusing life,[2] such as has now become natural to you; and though the doctor's practice is small here he'll no doubt go to a dashing town when he's got his hand in, and keep a stylish carriage, and you'll be brought to know a good many ladies of excellent society. If you should ever meet me then, Grace, you can drive past me, looking the other way. I shouldn't expect you to speak to me, or wish such a thing – unless it happened to be in some lonely private place where 'twouldn't lower ye at all. Don't think such men as neighbour Giles your equal. He and I shall be good friends enough, but he's not for the like of you. He's lived our rough and homely life here, and his wife's life must be rough and homely likewise."

So much pressure could not but produce some displacement. As Grace was left very much to herself, she took advantage of one fine day before Fitzpiers's return to drive into the aforesaid vale where stood the village of Buckbury Fitzpiers. Leaving her father's man at the inn with the horse and gig, she rambled onwards to the ruins of a castle, which stood in a field hard by. She had no doubt that it represented the ancient stronghold of the Fitzpiers family.

The remains were few, and consisted mostly of remnants of the lower vaulting, supported on low stout columns surmounted by the *crochet* capital[3] of the period. The two or three arches of these vaults that were still in position had been utilised by the adjoining farmer as shelter for his calves, the floor being spread with straw, amid which the young creatures rustled, cooling their thirsty tongues by licking the quaint Norman carving, which glistened with the moisture. It was a degradation of even such a rude form of art as this to be treated so grossly, she thought, and for the first time the family of Fitzpiers assumed in her imagination the hues of a melancholy romanticism.

It was soon time to drive home, and she traversed the distance with a preoccupied mind. The idea of so modern a man in science and æsthetics as the young surgeon springing out of relics so ancient was a kind of novelty she had never before experienced. The combination lent him a social and intellectual interest which she dreaded, so much weight did it add to the strange influence[4] he exercised upon her whenever he came near her.

In an excitement which was not love, not ambition, rather a fearful consciousness[5] of hazard in the air, she awaited his return.

Meanwhile her father was awaiting him also. In his house there was an old work on medicine, published towards the end of the last century, and to put himself in harmony with events Melbury spread this work on his knees when he had done his day's business, and read about Galen, Hippocrates, and Herophilus; of the dogmatic, the empiric, the hermetical,[6] and other sects of practitioners that have arisen in history; and thence proceeded to the classification of maladies and the rules for their treatment, as laid down in this valuable book with absolute precision. Melbury regretted that the treatise was so old, fearing that he might in consequence be unable to hold as complete a conversation as he could wish with Mr. Fitzpiers, primed, no doubt, with more recent discoveries.

The day of Fitzpiers's return arrived, and he sent to say that he would call immediately. In the little time that was afforded for putting the house in order the sweeping of Melbury's parlour was as the sweeping of the parlour at the Interpreter's which well-nigh choked the Pilgrim.[7] At the end of it Mrs. Melbury sat down, folded her hands and lips, and waited. Her husband restlessly walked in and out from the timber-yard, stared at the interior of the room, jerked out "ay, ay," and retreated again.

Between four and five Fitzpiers arrived, hitching his horse to the hook outside the door.

As soon as he had walked in and perceived that Grace was not in the room, he seemed to have a misgiving. Nothing less than her actual presence could long keep him to the level of this impassioned enterprise, and that lacking he appeared as one who wished to retrace his steps.

He mechanically talked at what he considered a woodland matron's level of thought till a rustling was heard on the stairs, and Grace came in. Fitzpiers was for once as agitated as she. Over and above the genuine emotion which she raised in his heart there hung the sense that he was casting a die by impulse which he might not have thrown by judgment.

Mr. Melbury was not in the room at the moment. Having to attend to matters in the yard, he had delayed putting on his afternoon coat and waistcoat till the doctor's appearance, when, not wishing to be backward in receiving him, he entered the parlour hastily buttoning up those garments. Grace's fastidiousness was a little distressed that Fitzpiers should see by this action the strain his visit was putting upon her father; and to make matters worse for her just then, old Grammer seemed to have a passion for incessantly pumping in the back kitchen, leaving the doors open so that the banging and splashing were distinct above the parlour conversation.

Whenever the chat over the tea sank into pleasant desultoriness Mr. Melbury broke in with speeches of laboured precision on very remote topics, as if he feared to let Fitzpiers's mind dwell critically on the subject nearest the hearts of all. In truth a constrained manner was natural enough in Melbury just now, for the greatest interest of his life was reaching its crisis. Could the real have been beheld instead of the corporeal merely, the corner of the room in which he sat would have been filled with a form typical of anxious suspense, large-eyed, tight-lipped, awaiting the issue. That paternal hopes and fears so intense should be bound up in the person of one child so peculiarly circumstanced, and not have dispersed themselves over the larger field of a whole family, involved dangerous risks to future happiness.

Fitzpiers did not stay more than an hour, but that time had apparently advanced his sentiments towards Grace, once and for all, from a vaguely liquescent to an organic shape. She would not have accompanied him to the door, in response to his whispered "Come!" if her mother had not said in a matter-of-fact way, "Of course, Grace; go to the door with Mr. Fitzpiers." Accordingly Grace went, both her parents remaining in the room.

When the young pair were in the great brick-floored hall the lover took the girl's hand in his, drew it under his arm, and thus led her on to the front door, where he stealthily put his lips to her own.

She broke from him trembling, blushed, and turned aside, hardly knowing how things had advanced to this. Fitzpiers drove off, kissing his hand to her, and waving it to Melbury, who was visible through the window. Her father returned the surgeon's action with a great flourish of his own hand, and a satisfied smile.

The intoxication that Fitzpiers had, as usual, produced in Grace's brain during the visit passed off somewhat with his withdrawal. She felt like a woman who did not know what she had been doing for the previous hour; but supposed with trepidation that the afternoon's proceedings, though vague, had amounted to an engagement between herself and the handsome, coercive, irresistible Fitzpiers.

This visit was a type of many which followed it during the long summer days of that year. Grace was borne along upon a stream of reasonings, arguments, and persuasions, supplemented, it must be added, by inclinations of her own at times. No woman is without aspirations, which may be innocent enough within certain limits; and Grace had been so trained socially and educated intellectually, as to see clearly enough a pleasure in the position of wife to such a man as Fitzpiers. His material standing of itself, either present or future, had little in it to give her ambition, but the possibilities of a refined and cultivated inner life, of subtle psychological intercourse, had their charm. It was this rather than any vulgar idea of marrying well which caused her to float with the current, and to yield to the immense influence which Fitzpiers exercised over her whenever she shared his society.

Any observer would shrewdly have prophesied that whether or not she loved him as yet in the ordinary sense, she was pretty sure to do so in time.

One evening just before dusk they had taken a rather long walk together, and for a short cut homeward passed through the shrubberies of Hintock House – still deserted, and still blankly confronting with its sightless shuttered windows the surrounding foliage and slopes.

Grace was tired, and they approached the wall, and sat together on one of the stone sills – still warm with the sun that had been pouring its rays upon them all the afternoon.

"This place would just do for us, would it not, dearest?" said her betrothed, as they sat, turning and looking idly at the old façade.

"Oh, yes," said Grace, plainly showing that no such fancy had ever crossed her mind. "She is away from home still," Grace added in a minute, rather sadly, for she could not forget that she had somehow lost the valuable friendship of the lady of this bower.

"Who is? – oh, you mean Mrs. Charmond. Do you know, dear, that at one time I thought *you* lived here?"

"Indeed," said Grace. "How was that?"

He explained, as far as he could do so without mentioning his disappointment at finding it was otherwise; and then went on: "Well, never mind that. Now I want to ask you something. There is one detail of our wedding which I am sure you will leave to me. My inclination is not to be married at the horrid little church here, with all the yokels staring round at us, and a droning parson reading."

"Where then can it be? At a church in town?"

"No. Not a church at all. At a registry office. It is a quieter, snugger, and more convenient place in every way."

"Oh," said she with real distress. "How can I be married except at church, and with all my dear friends round me!"

"Yeoman Winterborne among them."

"Yes – why not? You know there was nothing serious between him and me."

"You see, dear, a noisy, bell-ringing marriage at church has this objection in our case; it would be a thing of report a long way round. Now I would gently, as gently as possible, indicate to you how inadvisable such publicity would be if we leave Hintock, and I purchase the practice that I contemplate purchasing at Budmouth – hardly more than twenty miles off. Forgive my saying that it will be far better if nobody there knows where you come from, nor anything about your parents. Your beauty and knowledge and manners will carry you anywhere if you are not hampered by such retrospective criticism."

"But could it not be a quiet ceremony, even at church?" she pleaded.

"I don't see the necessity of going there!" he said a trifle impatiently.

"Marriage is a civil contract, and the shorter and simpler it is made the better. People don't go to church when they take a house, or even when they make a will."

"Oh, Edred – I don't like to hear you speak like that."

"Well, well – I didn't mean to. But I have mentioned as much to your father, who has made no objection; and why should you?"

She deemed the point one on which she ought to allow sentiment to give way to policy – if there were indeed policy in his plan. But she was indefinably depressed as they walked homeward.

CHAPTER VIII

He left her at the door of her father's house. As he receded, and was clasped out of sight by the filmy shades, he impressed Grace as a man who hardly appertained to her existence at all. Cleverer, greater than herself, one outside her mental orbit, as she considered him, he seemed to be her ruler rather than her equal, protector, and dear familiar friend.

The disappointment she had experienced at his wish, the shock given to her girlish sensibilities by his irreverent views of marriage, together with the sure and near approach of the day fixed for committing her future to his keeping, made her so restless that she could scarcely sleep at all that night. She rose when the sparrows began to walk out of the roof-holes, sat on the floor of her room in the dim light, and by and by peeped out behind the window curtains.

It was even now day out of doors, though the tones of morning were feeble and wan, and it was long before the sun would be perceptible in this overshadowed vale. Not a sound came from any of the outhouses as yet. The tree-trunks, the road, the outbuildings, the garden, every object, wore that aspect of mesmeric fixity which the suspensive quietude of daybreak lends to such scenes. Helpless immobility seemed to be combined with intense consciousness; a meditative inertness possessed all things, oppressively contrasting with her own active emotions. Beyond the road were some cottage roofs and orchards; over these roofs and over the apple-trees behind, high up the slope, and backed by the plantation on the crest, was the house yet occupied by her future husband, the rough-cast front showing whitely through its creepers. The window-shutters were closed, the bedroom curtains closely drawn, and not the thinnest coil of smoke rose from the rugged chimneys.

Something broke the stillness. The front-door of the house she was gazing at opened softly, and there came out into the porch a female figure, wrapped in a large shawl, beneath which was visible the white skirt of a long loose garment. A grey arm, stretching from within the porch, adjusted the shawl over the woman's shoulders; it was withdrawn and disappeared, the door closing behind her.

The woman went quickly down the box-edged path between the raspberries and currants, and as she walked her well-developed form and gait betrayed her individuality. It was Suke Damson, the affianced one of simple young Tim Tangs. At the bottom of the garden she entered the shelter of the tall hedge, and only the top of her head could be seen hastening in the direction of her own dwelling.

Grace had recognised, or thought she recognised, in the grey arm stretching from the porch, the sleeve of a dressing-gown which Mr. Fitzpiers had been wearing on her own memorable visit to him. Her face fired red. She had just before thought of dressing herself and taking a lonely walk under the trees, so coolly green this early morning; but she now sat down on her bed and fell into reverie.

It seemed as if hardly any time had passed when she heard the household moving briskly about, and breakfast preparing down stairs; though, on rousing herself to robe and descend, she found that the sun was throwing his rays completely over the tree-tops, a progress in the diurnal turn denoting that at least three hours had elapsed since she last looked out of the window.

When attired she searched about the house for her father; she found him at last in the garden, stooping to examine the potatoes for signs of disease. Hearing her rustle he stood up and stretched his back and arms, saying, "Morning t'ye, Gracie. I congratulate ye. It is only a month today to the time!"

She did not answer, but, without lifting her dress, waded between the dewy rows of tall potato-green into the middle of the plot where he was.

"I have been thinking very much about my position this morning – ever since it was light," she began excitedly, and trembling so that she could hardly stand. "And I feel it is a false one. I wish not to marry Mr. Fitzpiers. I wish not to marry anybody; but I'll marry Giles Winterborne if you say I must as an alternative."

Her father's face settled into rigidity, he turned pale, and came deliberately out of the plot before he answered her. She had never seen him look so incensed before.

"Now, hearken to me," he said. "There's a time for a woman to alter her mind; and there's a time when she can no longer alter it, if she has any right eye to her parents' honour and the seemliness of things. That time has come. I won't say to ye, you *shall* marry him. But I will say, that if you refuse, I shall for ever be ashamed and a weary of ye as a daughter, and shall look upon you as the hope of my life no more. What do you know about life and what it can bring forth, and how you ought to act to lead up to best ends? Oh, you are an ungrateful maid, Grace; you've seen that fellow Giles, and he has got over ye; that's where the secret lies, I'll warrant me!"

"No, father, no! It is not Giles – it is something I cannot tell you of –"

"Well, make fools of us all; make us laughing-stocks; break it off; have your own way!"

"But who knows of the engagement as yet; how can breaking it disgrace you?"

Melbury then by degrees admitted that he had mentioned the engagement to this acquaintance and to that, till she perceived that in his restlessness and pride he had published it everywhere. She went dismally away to a bower of laurel at the top of the garden. Her father followed her.

"It is that Giles Winterborne!" he said with an upbraiding gaze at her.

"No, it is not; though for that matter you encouraged him once!" she said, troubled to the verge of despair. "It is not Giles, it is Mr. Fitzpiers."

"You've had a tiff – a lovers' tiff – that's all, I suppose?"

"It is some woman – "

"Ay, ay; you are jealous. The old story. Don't tell me. Now do you bide here. I'll send Fitzpiers to you. I saw him smoking in front of his house but a minute bygone."

He went off hastily out of the garden-gate and down the lane. But she would not stay where she was; and edging through a slit in the garden fence walked away into the wood.

Just about here the trees were large and wide apart, and there was no undergrowth, so that she could be seen to some distance; a sylph-like greenish-white creature, as toned by the sunlight and leafage. She heard a footfall crushing dead leaves behind her, and turning hastily found herself reconnoitred by Fitzpiers himself, approaching gay and fresh as the morning around them.

His remote gaze at her had been one of mild interest rather than of rapture. But she looked so lovely in the green world about her; her pink cheeks, her simple light dress, and the delicate flexibility of her movements acquired such rarity from their wild-wood setting, that his eyes kindled as he drew near.

"My darling, what is it? Your father says you are in the pouts, and jealous, and I don't know what. Ha! ha! ha! as if there were any rival to you, except vegetable nature, in this home of recluses? We know better."

"Jealous; oh, no, it is not so," said she gravely. "That's a mistake of his and yours, sir. I spoke to him so closely about the question of marriage with you that he did not apprehend my state of mind."

"But there's something wrong – eh?" he asked, eyeing her narrowly, and bending to kiss her.

She shrank away, and his purposed kiss miscarried.

"What is it?" he said, more seriously for this little defeat.

She made no answer beyond, "Mr. Fitzpiers, I have had no breakfast, I must go in."

"Come," he insisted, fixing his eyes upon her. "Tell me at once, I say."

It was the greater strength against the smaller; but she was mastered less by his manner than by her own sense of the unfairness of silence.

"I looked out of the window," she said with hesitation. "I'll tell you by and by. I must go indoors. I have had no breakfast."

By a sort of divination his conjecture went straight to the fact. "Nor I," said he lightly. "Indeed, I rose late to-day. I have had a broken night, or rather morning. A girl of the village – I don't know her name – came and rang at my bell as soon as it was light – between four and five I should think it was – perfectly maddened with an aching tooth. As nobody heard her ring she threw some gravel at my window, till at last I heard her and slipped on my dressing-gown and went down. The poor thing begged me with tears in her eyes to take out her tormentor, if I dragged her head off. Down she sat and out it came; a lovely molar, not a speck upon it; and off she went with it in her handkerchief, much contented, though it would have done good work for her for fifty years to come."

It was all so plausible – so completely explained. Knowing nothing of the incident in the wood[1] on old Midsummer eve, Grace felt that her suspicions were unworthy and absurd, and with the readiness of an honest heart she jumped at the opportunity of honouring his word. At the moment of her mental libration the bushes about the garden had moved, and her father emerged into the shady glade.

"Well, I hope it is made up?" he said cheerily.

"Oh yes," said Fitzpiers, with his eyes fixed on Grace, whose eyes were shyly bent downwards.

"Now," said her father, "tell me, the pair of ye, that you still mean to take one another for good and all; and on the strength o't you shall have another couple of hundred paid down. I swear it by the Name."

Fitzpiers took her hand. "We declare it, do we not, my dear Grace?" said he.

Relieved of her doubt, somewhat overawed, and ever anxious to please, she was disposed to settle the matter. Yet, woman-like, she would not relinquish her opportunity of asking a concession of some sort. "If our wedding can be at church, I say yes," she answered in a measured voice. "If not, I say no."

Fitzpiers was generous in his turn. "It shall be so," he rejoined gracefully. "To holy church we'll go – and much good may it do us."

They returned through the bushes indoors, Grace walking, full of thought, between the other two, somewhat comforted both by Fitzpiers's ingenious explanation and by the sense that she was not to be deprived of a religious ceremony. "So let it be," she said to herself. "Pray God it is for the best."

From this hour there was no serious recalcitration on her part. Fitzpiers kept himself continually near her, dominating any rebellious impulse, and shaping her will into passive concurrence with all his desires. Apart from his lover-like anxiety to possess her, the few golden hundreds of the timber-dealer, ready to hand, formed a warm background to Grace's lovely face, and went some way to remove his uneasiness at the prospect of endangering his professional and social chances by an alliance with the family of a simple countryman.

The interim closed up its perspective surely and silently. Whenever Grace had any doubts of her position the sense of contracting time was like a shortening chamber: at other moments she was comparatively blithe.

Day after day waxed and waned; the one or two woodmen who sawed, shaped, spokeshaved on her father's premises at this inactive season of the year, regularly came and unlocked the doors in the morning, locked them in the evening, supped, leant over their garden-gates for a whiff of evening air, and to catch any last and furthest throb of news from the outer world, which entered and expired at Little Hintock like the exhausted swell of a wave in some innermost cavern of some innermost creek of an embayed sea; yet no news interfered with the nuptial purpose at their neighbour's house.

The sappy green twig-tips of the season's growth would not, she thought, be appreciably woodier on the day she became a wife, so near was the time; the tints of the foliage would hardly have changed. Everything was so much as usual that no itinerant stranger would have supposed a woman's fate to be hanging in the balance at that summer's decline.

But there were preparations, imaginable enough by those who had special knowledge. In the remote and fashionable city of Exbury something was growing up under the hands of several persons who had never seen Grace Melbury, never would see her, or care anything about her at all; though their creation had such interesting relation to her life that it would inclose her very heart at a moment when that heart would beat, if not with more emotional ardour, at least with more emotional turbulence than at any previous time.

Why did Mrs. Dollery's van, instead of passing along at the end of the smaller village to Great Hintock direct, turn one Saturday night into Little Hintock Lane, and never pull up till it reached Mr. Melbury's gates? The gilding sheen of evening fell upon a large flat box, not less than a yard square and safely tied with cord, as it was handed out from under the tilt with a great deal of care. But it was not heavy for its size; Mrs. Dollery herself carried it into the house. Tim Tangs, the hollow-turner, Cawtree, Suke Damson, and others, looked knowing and made remarks to each other as they watched its entrance. Melbury stood at the door of the timber-shed in the attitude of a man to whom such an arrival was a trifling domestic detail with which he did not condescend to be concerned. Yet he well divined the contents of that box, and was in truth all the while in a pleasant exaltation at the proof that thus far, at any rate, no disappointment had supervened. While Mrs. Dollery remained – which was rather long, from her sense of the importance of her errand – he went into the outhouse; but as soon as she had had her say, been paid, and had rumbled away, he entered the dwelling, to find there what he knew he should find – his wife and daughter in a flutter of excitement over the wedding-gown, just arrived from the leading dressmaker of Exbury city aforesaid.

During these weeks Giles Winterborne was nowhere to be seen or heard of. At the close of his tenure in Hintock he had sold some of his furniture, packed up the rest – a few pieces endeared by associations, or necessary to his occupation – in the house of a friendly neighbour, and gone away. People said that a certain laxity had crept into his life; that he had never gone near a church latterly, and had been sometimes seen on Sundays with unblacked boots, lying on his elbow under a tree, with a cynical gaze at surrounding objects. He was likely to return to Hintock when the cider-making season came round, his apparatus being stored there, and travel with his mill and press from village to village.

The narrow interval that stood before the day diminished yet. There was in Grace's mind sometimes a certain anticipative satisfaction, the satisfaction of feeling that she would be the heroine of an hour; moreover, she was proud, as a cultivated woman, to be the wife of a cultivated man. It was an opportunity denied very frequently to young women in her position, nowadays not a few; those in whom parental discovery of the value of education has implanted tastes which parental circles fail to gratify. But what an attenuation this cold pride was of the dream of her youth, in which she had pictured herself walking in state towards the altar, flushed by the purple light and bloom of her own passion, without a single misgiving as to the sealing of the bond, and fervently receiving as her due

"The homage of a thousand hearts; the fond deep love of one."

Everything had been clear then, in imagination; now something was undefined. She had little carking anxieties; a curious fatefulness seemed to rule her, and she experienced a mournful want of some one to confide in.

The day loomed so big and nigh that her prophetic ear could in fancy catch the noise of it, hear the murmur of the villagers as she came out of church, imagine the jangle of the three thin-toned Hintock bells. The dialogues seemed to grow louder, and the ding-ding-dong of those three crazed bells more persistent. She awoke: the morning had come.

Five hours later she was the wife of Fitzpiers.

CHAPTER IX

The chief hotel at Sherton Abbas was the Earl of Wessex – a large stone-fronted inn with a yawning arch, under which vehicles were driven by stooping coachmen to back premises of wonderful commodiousness. The windows to the street were mullioned into narrow lights, and only commanded a view of the opposite houses; hence perhaps it arose that the best and most luxurious private sitting-room that the inn could afford overlooked the nether parts of the establishment, where beyond the yard were to be seen gardens and orchards, now bossed, nay encrusted, with scarlet and gold fruit, stretching to infinite distance under a luminous lavender mist. The time was early autumn,

> "When the fair apples, red as evening sky,[1]
> Do bend the tree unto the fruitful ground,
> When juicy pears, and berries of black dye
> Do dance in air, and call the eyes around."

The landscape confronting the window might indeed have been part of the identical stretch of country which the youthful Chatterton[2] had in his mind.

In this room sat she who had been the maiden Grace Melbury till the finger of fate touched her and turned her to a wife. It was two months after the wedding, and she was alone. Fitzpiers had walked out to see the abbey by the light of sunset, but she had been too fatigued to accompany him. They had reached the last stage of a long eight-weeks' tour, and were going on to Hintock that night.

In the yard between Grace and the orchards there progressed a scene natural to the locality at this time of the year. An apple-mill and press had been erected on the spot, to which some men were bringing fruit from divers points in mawn-baskets, while others were grinding them, and others wringing down the pomace, whose sweet juice gushed forth into tubs and pails. The superintendent of these proceedings, to whom the others spoke as master, was a young yeoman of prepossessing manner and aspect, whose form she recognised in a moment. He had hung his coat to a nail of the outhouse wall, and wore his shirt-sleeves rolled up beyond his elbows, to keep them unstained while he rammed the pomace into the bags of horsehair. Fragments of apple-rind had alighted upon the brim of his hat – probably from the bursting of a bag – while brown pips of the same fruit were sticking among the down upon his fine round arms, and in his beard.

She realised in a moment how he had come there. Down in the heart of the apple-country nearly every farmer kept up a cider-making apparatus and wring-house for his own use, building up the pomace in great straw "cheeses," as they were called; but here, on the margin of Pomona's plain, was a debateable land neither orchard nor sylvan exclusively, where the apple-produce was hardly sufficient to warrant each proprietor in keeping a mill of his own. This was the field of the travelling cider-maker. His press and mill were fixed to wheels instead of being set up in a cider-house; and with a couple of horses, buckets, tubs, strainers, and an assistant or two, he wandered from place to place, deriving very satisfactory returns for his trouble in such a prolific season as the present.

The back parts of the town were just now abounding with apple-gatherings. They stood in the yards in carts, baskets, and loose heaps; and the blue stagnant air of autumn which hung over everything was heavy with a sweet cidery smell. Cakes of pomace lay against the walls in the yellow sun, where they were drying to be used as fuel. Yet it was not the great make of the year as yet; before the standard crop came in there accumulated, in abundant times like this, a large superfluity of early apples, and windfalls from the trees of later harvest, which would not keep long. Thus in the baskets, and quivering in the hopper of the mill, she saw specimens of mixed dates, including the mellow countenances of streaked-jacks, codlins, costards, stubbards, ratheripes, and other well-known friends of her ravenous youth.

Grace watched the head man with interest. The slightest sigh escaped her. Perhaps she thought of the day – not so far distant – when that friend of her childhood had met her by her father's arrangement in this same town, warm with hope, though diffident, and trusting in a promise rather implied than given. Or she might have thought of days earlier yet – days of childhood – when her mouth was somewhat more ready to receive a kiss from his than was his to bestow one. However, all that was over. She had felt superior to him then, and she felt superior to him now.

She wondered why he never looked towards her open window. She did not know that in the slight commotion caused by their arrival at the inn that afternoon Winterborne had caught sight of her through the archway, had turned red, and was continuing his work with more concentrated attention on the very account of his discovery. Robert Creedle, too, who travelled with Giles, had been incidentally informed by the ostler that Dr. Fitzpiers and his young wife were in the hotel; after which news Creedle kept shaking his head and saying to himself, "Ah!" very audibly, between his thrusts at the screw of the cider-press.

"Why the deuce do you sigh like that, Robert?" asked Winterborne at last.

"Ah, maister – 'tis my thoughts – 'tis my thoughts! ... Yes, ye've lost a hundred load o' timber well seasoned; ye've lost five hundred pound in good money; ye've lost the stone-windered house that's big enough to hold a dozen families; ye've lost your share of half a dozen good waggons and their horses; – all lost! – through your letting slip she that was once yer own!"

"Good God, Creedle! you'll drive me mad!" said Giles sternly. "Don't speak of that any more!"

Thus the subject had ended in the yard. Meanwhile, the passive cause of all this loss still regarded the scene. She was beautifully dressed; she was seated in the most comfortable room that the inn afforded; her long journey had been full of variety, and almost luxuriously performed, for Fitzpiers did not study economy where pleasure was in question. Hence it perhaps arose that Giles and all his belongings seemed sorry and common to her for the moment – moving in a groove so far removed from her own of late that she could scarcely believe she had ever found congruity therein.

"No – I could never have married him!" she said, gently shaking her head. "Dear father was right. It would have been too rough a life for me." And she looked at the rings of sapphire and opal upon her white and slender fingers that had been gifts from Fitzpiers.

Seeing that Giles still kept his back turned, and with a little of the above-described pride of life – easily to be understood, and possibly excused, in a young, inexperienced woman who thought she had married well – she said at last, with a smile on her lips, "Mr. Winterborne!"

He appeared to take no heed, and she said a second time, "Mr. Winterborne!"

Even now he seemed not to hear, though a person close enough to him to see the expression of his face might have doubted it; and she said a third time, with a timid loudness, "Mr. Winterborne! What, have you forgotten my voice?" She remained with her lips parted in a welcoming smile.

He turned without surprise, and came deliberately towards the window.

"Why do you call me?" he said, with a sternness that took her completely unawares, his face being now pale. "Is it not enough that you see me here moiling and muddling for my daily bread while you are sitting there in your success, that you can't refrain from opening old wounds by calling out my name?"

She flushed, and was struck dumb for some moments; but she forgave his unreasoning anger, knowing so well in what it had its root.

"I am sorry I offended you by speaking, Giles," she replied. "Believe me, I did not intend to do that. I could hardly sit here so near you without a word of recognition."

Winterborne's heart had swollen big and his eyes grown moist by this time, so much had the gentle answer of that familiar voice moved him. He assured her hurriedly, and without looking at her, that he was not angry. He then managed to ask her, in a clumsy, constrained way, if she had had a pleasant journey, and seen many interesting sights. She spoke of a few places that she had visited, and so the time passed till he withdrew to take his place at one of the levers which pulled round the screw.

Forgotten her voice! Indeed, he had not forgotten her voice, as his bitterness showed. But though in the heat of the moment he had

reproached her keenly, his second mood was a far more tender one
– that which could regard her renunciation of such as he as her glory
and her privilege, his own fidelity notwithstanding. He could have
declared with a contemporary poet –

> "If I forget,[3]
> The salt creek may forget the ocean;
> If I forget
> The heart whence flows my heart's bright motion,
> May I sink meanlier than the worst,
> Abandoned, outcast, crushed, accurst, –
> If I forget.

> "Though you forget,
> No word of mine shall mar your pleasure;
> Though you forget, –
> You filled my barren life with treasure;
> You may withdraw the gift you gave,
> You still are queen, I still am slave,
> Though you forget."

She had tears in her eyes at the thought that she could not remind
him of what he ought to have remembered; that not herself but
the pressure of events had dissipated the dreams of their early
youth.

Grace was thus unexpectedly worsted in her encounter with her
old friend. She had opened the window with a faint sense of triumph,
but he had turned it into sadness; she did not quite comprehend the
reason why. In truth it was because she was not cruel enough in her
cruelty. If you have to use the knife, use it, say the great surgeons; and
for her own peace Grace should have handled Winterborne thoroughly
or not at all. As it was, on closing the window an indescribable – some
might have said dangerous – pity quavered in her bosom for him.

Presently her husband entered the room, and told her what a
wonderful sunset there was to be seen.

"I have not noticed it. But I have seen somebody out there that we
know," she replied, looking into the court.

Fitzpiers followed the direction of her eyes, and said he did not
recognise anybody.

"Why, Mr. Winterborne – there he is cider-making. He combines that with his other business, you know."

"Oh – that fellow,"[4] said Fitzpiers, his curiosity becoming extinct.

She, reproachfully: "What, call Mr. Winterborne a fellow, Edred? It is true I was just saying to myself that I never could have married him; but I have much regard for him, and always shall."

"Well, do by all means, my dear one. I dare say I am inhuman, and supercilious, and contemptibly proud of my poor old ramshackle family; but I do honestly confess to you that I feel as if I belonged to a different species from the people who are working in that yard."

"And from me, too, then. For my blood is no better than theirs."

He looked at her with a droll sort of awakening. It was, indeed, a startling anomaly that this woman of the tribe without should be standing there beside him as his wife, if his sentiments were as he had said. In their travels together she had ranged so unerringly at his level in ideas, tastes, and habits, that he had almost forgotten how his heart had played havoc with his principles in taking her to him.

"Ah, *you* – you are refined and educated into something quite different," he said self-assuringly.

"I don't quite like to think that," she murmured with soft regret. "And I think you under-estimate Giles Winterborne. Remember I was brought up with him till I was sent away to school, so I cannot be radically different. At any rate I don't feel so. That is no doubt my fault, and a great blemish in me. But I hope you will put up with it, Edred."

Fitzpiers said that he would endeavour to do so, and as it was now getting on for dusk they prepared to perform the last stage of their journey, so as to arrive at Hintock before it grew very late.

In less than half an hour they started, the cider-makers in the yard having ceased their labours and gone away, so that the only sounds audible there now were the trickling of the juice from the tightly-screwed press, and the buzz of a single wasp, which had drunk itself so tipsy that it was unconscious of nightfall.

Grace was very cheerful at the thought of being soon in her sylvan home; but Fitzpiers sat beside her almost silent. An indescribable oppressiveness had overtaken him with the near approach of the journey's end and the realities of life that lay there. It was two months since he married her.

"You don't say a word, Edred," she observed. "Aren't you glad to get back? I am."

"You have friends here. I have none."

"But my friends are yours."

"Oh, yes – in that sense."

The conversation languished, and they drew near the end of Hintock Lane. It had been decided that they should, at least for a time, take up their abode in her father's roomy house, one wing of which was quite at their service, being almost disused by the Melburys. Workmen had been painting, papering, and white-washing this set of rooms in the wedded pair's absence: and so scrupulous had been the timber-dealer that there should occur no hitch or disappointment on their arrival that not the smallest detail remained undone. To make it all complete a ground-floor room had been fitted up as a surgery, with an independent outer door, to which Fitzpiers's brass plate was screwed – for mere ornament, such a sign being quite superfluous where everybody knew the latitude and longitude of his neighbours for miles round.

Melbury and his wife welcomed the twain with affection, and all the house showed them deference. They went up to explore their rooms, that opened from a passage on the left hand of the staircase, the entrance to which could be shut off on the landing by a door that Melbury had hung for the purpose. A friendly fire was burning in the grate, although it was not cold. Fitzpiers said it was too soon for any sort of meal, they only having dined shortly before leaving Sherton Abbas; he would walk across to his old lodging to learn how his deputy had got on in his absence.

In leaving Melbury's door he looked back at the house. There was economy in living under that roof – and economy was desirable; but in some way he was dissatisfied with the arrangement; it immersed him so deeply in son-in-lawship to Melbury. He went on to his former residence; his *locum tenens*[5] was out, and Fitzpiers fell into conversation with his old landlady.

"Well, Mrs. Cox; what's the best news?" he asked of her with cheery weariness.

She was a little soured at losing by his marriage so profitable a tenant as the surgeon had proved to be during his residence under her roof; and the more so in there being hardly the remotest chance of her getting such another settler in the Hintock solitudes. " 'Tis what I don't wish to repeat, sir; least of all to you," she mumbled.

"Never mind me, Mrs. Cox; go ahead."

"It is what people say about your hasty marrying, Dr. Fitzpiers. Whereas they won't believe you know such clever doctrines in physic as they once supposed of ye, seeing as you could marry into Mr. Melbury's family, which is only Hintock-born, such as me."

"They are kindly welcome to their opinion," said Fitzpiers, not allowing himself to recognise that he winced. "Any thing else?"

"Yes; *she's* come home at last."

"Who's she?"

"Mrs. Charmond."

"Oh, indeed," said Fitzpiers, with but slight interest. "I've never seen her."

"She has seen you, sir, whether or no."

"Never."

"Yes. She saw you in some hotel or street for a minute or two whilst you were away travelling, and accidentally heard your name; and when she made some remark about you, Miss Ellis – that's her maid – told her you was on your wedding tour with Mr. Melbury's daughter; and she said, 'He ought to have done better than that. I fear he has spoilt his chances,' she says."

Fitzpiers did not talk much longer to this cheering housewife, and walked home with no very brisk step. He entered the door quietly, and went straight up stairs to the drawing-room extemporised for their use by Melbury in his and his bride's absence, expecting to find her there as he had left her.

The fire was burning still, but there were no lights; he looked into the next apartment fitted up as a little dining-room, but no supper was laid. He went to the top of the stairs, and heard a chorus of voices in the timber-merchant's parlour below, Grace's being occasionally intermingled.

Descending, and looking into the room from the doorway, he found quite a large gathering of neighbours and other acquaintances, praising and congratulating Mrs. Fitzpiers on her return, among them being the dairyman, Farmer Cawtree, and the relieving-officer from Great Hintock; also the road contractor, the master tanner, the exciseman,[6] and some others with their wives. Grace – girl that she was – had quite forgotten her new dignity, and her husband's; she was in the midst of them, blushing and receiving their compliments with all the pleasures of old comradeship.

Fitzpiers experienced a profound distaste for the situation. Melbury was nowhere in the room, but Melbury's wife, perceiving the doctor, came to him.

"We thought, Grace and I," she said, "that as they have called, hearing you were come, we could do no less than ask them to supper; and then Grace proposed that we should all sup together as it is the first night of your return."

By this time Grace had come round to him. "Is it not good of them to welcome me so warmly!" she exclaimed, with tears of friendship in her eyes. "After so much good feeling I could not think of our shutting ourselves up away from them in our own dining-room."

"Certainly not – certainly not," said Fitzpiers. And he entered the room with the heroic smile of a martyr.

As soon as they sat down to table Melbury came in, and seemed to see at once that Fitzpiers would much rather have received no such demonstrative reception. He thereupon privately chid his wife for her forwardness in the matter. Mrs. Melbury declared that it was as much Grace's doing as hers, after which there was no more to be said by that young woman's tender father.

By this time Fitzpiers was making the best of his position among the wide-elbowed and genial company who sat eating and drinking, laughing and joking around him; and, getting warmed himself by the good cheer, he was obliged to admit that, after all, the supper was not the least enjoyable he had ever known.

At times, however, the words about his having spoiled his opportunities, repeated to him as coming from Mrs. Charmond, haunted him like a handwriting on the wall.[7] Then his manner would become suddenly abstracted. At one moment he would mentally put an indignant query why Mrs. Charmond or any other woman should make it her business to have opinions about his opportunities; at another he thought that he could hardly be angry with her for taking an interest in the doctor of her own parish. Then he would drink a glass of grog and so get rid of the misgiving.

These hitches and quaffings were soon perceived by Grace as well as by her father; and hence both of them were much relieved when the first of the guests to discover that the hour was growing late rose and declared that he must think of moving homewards. At the words Melbury rose as alertly as if lifted by a spring; and in ten minutes they were gone.

"Now, Grace," said her husband as soon as he found himself alone with her in their private apartments, "we've had a very pleasant evening, and everybody has been very kind. But we must come to an understanding about our way of living here. If we continue in these rooms there must be no mixing in with your people below. I can't stand it, and that's the truth."

She had been sadly surprised at the suddenness of his distaste for those old-fashioned woodland forms of life which in his courtship he had professed to regard with so much interest. But she assented in a moment.

"We must be simply your father's tenants," he continued, "and our goings and comings must be as independent as if we lived elsewhere."

"Certainly, Edred – I quite see that it must be so."

"But you joined in with all those people in my absence, without knowing whether I should approve or disapprove. When I came I couldn't help myself at all."

She, sighing: "Yes – I see I ought to have waited; though they came unexpectedly, and I thought I had acted for the best."

Thus the discussion ended, and the next day Fitzpiers went on his old rounds as usual. But it was easy for so supersubtle[8] an eye as his to discern, or to think he discerned, that he was no longer regarded as an extrinsic, unfathomed gentleman of limitless potentiality, scientific and social; but as Mr. Melbury's compeer, and therefore in a degree only one of themselves. The Hintock woodlanders held with all the strength of inherited conviction to the aristocratic principle, and as soon as they had discovered that Fitzpiers was one of the old Buckbury Fitzpierses they had accorded to him for nothing a touching of hat-brims, promptness of service, and deference of approach, which Melbury had to do without though he paid for it over and over. But now, having proved a traitor to his own cause by this marriage, Fitzpiers was believed in no more as a superior hedged by his own divinity; while as doctor he began to be rated no higher than old Jones whom they had so long despised.

His few patients seemed in his two months' absence to have dwindled considerably in number, and no sooner had he returned than there came to him from the Board of Guardians[9] a complaint that a pauper had been neglected by his substitute. In a fit of pride Fitzpiers resigned his appointment as one of the surgeons to the Union,[10] which had been the nucleus of his practice here.

At the end of a fortnight he came in doors one evening to Grace, more briskly than usual. "They have written to me again about that practice in Budmouth that I once negotiated for," he said to her. "The premium asked is eight hundred pounds,[11] and I think that between your father and myself it ought to be raised. Then we can get away from this place for ever."

The question had been mooted between them before, and she was not unprepared to consider it. They had not proceeded far with the discussion when a knock came to the door, and in a minute Grammer ran up to say that a message had arrived from Hintock House requesting Dr. Fitzpiers to attend there at once. Mrs. Charmond had met with a slight accident through the overturning of her carriage.

"This is something, anyhow," said Fitzpiers, rising with an interest which he could not have defined. "I have had a presentiment that this mysterious woman and I were to be better acquainted."

The latter words were murmured to himself alone.

"Good-night," said Grace as soon as he was ready. "I shall be asleep probably when you return."

"Good-night," he replied inattentively, and went down stairs. It was the first time since their marriage that he had left her without a kiss.

CHAPTER X

CHAPTER X

Winterborne had given up his house. On this account his face was seen but fitfully in Hintock; and he would probably have disappeared from the place altogether but for his slight business connected with Melbury, on whose premises Giles kept his cider-making apparatus now that he had no place of his own to stow it in.

Coming here one afternoon on his way to a hut beyond the wood, where he now slept, he noticed that the familiar brown-thatched pinion of his paternal roof had vanished from its site, and that the walls were levelled.[1] In present circumstances he had a feeling for the spot that might have been called morbid, and when he had supped in the hut aforesaid he made use of the spare hour before bedtime to return to Little Hintock in the twilight, and ramble over the patch of ground on which he had first seen the day.

He repeated this evening visit on several like occasions. Even in the gloom he could trace where the different rooms had stood; could mark the shape of the kitchen chimney-corner in which he had roasted apples and potatoes in his boyhood, cast his bullets, and burnt his initials on articles that did and did not belong to him. The apple trees still remained to show where the garden had been, the oldest of them even now retaining the crippled slant to north-east given them by the great November gale[2] of 1824 which carried a brig bodily over the Chesil Bank.[3] They were at present bent to still greater obliquity by the heaviness of their produce. Apples bobbed against his head, and in the grass beneath he crunched scores of them as he walked. There was nobody to gather them now.

It was on the evening under notice that, half sitting, half leaning against one of these inclined trunks, Winterborne became lost in his thoughts as usual, till one little star after another had taken up a position in the piece of sky which now confronted him where his walls and chimneys had formerly raised their outlines. The house had jutted awkwardly into the road, and the opening caused by its absence was very distinct.

In the silence the trot of horses and the spin of carriage wheels became audible; the vehicle soon shaped itself against the blank sky, bearing down upon him with the bend in the lane which here occurred, and of which the house had been the cause. He could discern the figure of a woman high up on the driving-seat of a phaeton,[4] a groom being just visible behind.

Presently there was a slight scrape, then a scream. Winterborne went across to the spot, and found the phaeton half overturned, its driver sitting on the heap of rubbish which had once been his dwelling, and the man seizing the horses' heads. The equipage was Mrs. Charmond's, and the unseated charioteer that lady herself.

To his inquiry if she were hurt she made some incoherent reply to the effect that she did not know. The damage in other respects was little or none; the phaeton was righted, Mrs. Charmond placed in it, and the reins given to the servant. It appeared that she had been deceived by the removal of the house, imagining the gap caused by the demolition to be the opening of the road, so that she turned in upon the ruins instead of at the bend a few yards further on.

"Drive home – drive home!" she cried impatiently; and they started on their way.

They had not however gone many paces when, the air being still, Winterborne heard her say, "Stop; tell that man to call the doctor – Mr. Fitzpiers – and send him on to the House. I find I am hurt more seriously than I thought."

The seriousness seemed ludicrous to Winterborne; but he took the message from the groom, and proceeded to the doctor's at once. Having delivered it he stepped back into the darkness, and waited till he had seen Fitzpiers leave the door. He stood for a few minutes looking at the window which, by its light, revealed the room where Grace was sitting; and went away under the gloomy trees.

Fitzpiers duly arrived at Hintock House, whose doors he now saw open for the first time. Contrary to his expectation there was visible no sign of that confusion or alarm which a grave accident to the mistress of the abode would have occasioned. He was shown into a room at the top of the staircase, cosily and femininely draped, where by the light of the shaded lamp he saw a woman of full round figure reclining upon a couch in such a position as not to disturb a pile of magnificent hair on the crown of her head. A deep purple dressing-gown formed an admirable foil to the peculiarly rich brown of her hair-plaits; her left arm, which was naked nearly up to the shoulder,[5] was thrown upwards, and between the fingers of her right hand she held a cigarette,[6] while she idly breathed from her plump lips a thin stream of smoke towards the ceiling.

The doctor's first feeling was a sense of his exaggerated prevision in having brought appliances for a serious case; the next, something more curious. While the scene and the moment were new to him and unanticipated, the sentiment and essence of the moment were indescribably familiar. What could be the cause of it? Probably a dream.

Mrs. Charmond did not move more than to raise her eyes to him, and he came and stood by her. She glanced up at his face across her brows and forehead, and then he observed a blush creep slowly over her decidedly handsome cheeks. Her eyes, which had lingered upon him with an inquiring conscious expression, were hastily withdrawn, and she mechanically applied the cigarette again to her lips.

For a moment he forgot his errand, till suddenly arousing himself he addressed her, formally condoled with her, and made the usual professional inquiries about what had happened to her, and where she was hurt.

"That's what I want you to tell me," she murmured in tones of indefinable reserve. "I quite believe in you, for I know you are very accomplished, because you study so hard."

"I'll do my best to justify your good opinion," said the young man bowing. "And none the less that I am happy to find the accident has not been serious."

"I am very much shaken," she said.

"Oh yes," he replied; and completed his examination, which convinced him that there was really nothing the matter with her, and more than ever puzzled him as to why he had been summoned, since she did not appear to be a timid woman. "You must rest awhile; and I'll send something," he said.

"Oh, I forgot," she returned. "Look here." And she showed him a little scrape on her arm – the full round arm that was exposed. "Put some court-plaster[7] on that, please."

He obeyed. "And now, doctor," she said, "before you go I want to put a question to you. Sit round there in front of me, on that low chair, and bring the candles, or one, to the little table. Do you smoke? Yes? That's right – I am learning. Take one of these; and here's a light." She threw a match-box across.

Fitzpiers caught it, and having lit up regarded her from his new position which, with the shifting of the candles, for the first time afforded him a full view of her face.

"How many years have passed since first we met?" she resumed, in a voice which she endeavoured to maintain at its former pitch of composure, and eyeing him with daring bashfulness.

"*We* met, do you say?"

She nodded. "I saw you recently at an hotel in London, when you were passing through, I suppose, with your bride, and I recognised you as one I had met in my girlhood. Do you remember, when you were studying at Heidelberg, an English family that was staying there, who used to walk –"

"And the young lady who wore a long tail of rare-coloured hair – ah, I see it before my eyes! – who lost her gloves on the Great Terrace – who was going back in the dusk to find them – to whom I said, 'I'll go for them,' and who answered, 'Oh, they are not worth coming all the way up again for.' I *do* remember, and how very long we stayed talking there! I went next morning whilst the dew was on the grass: there they lay – the little fingers sticking out damp and thin. I see them now! I picked them up, and then . . ."

"Well?"

"I kissed them," he rejoined, rather shamefacedly.

"But you had hardly ever seen me except in the dusk?"

"Never mind. I was young then, and I kissed them. I wondered how I could make the most of my *trouvaille*, and decided that I would call at your hotel with them that afternoon. It rained, and I waited till next day. I called, and you were gone."

"Yes," answered she with dry melancholy. "My mother, knowing my face was my only fortune,[8] said she had no wish for such a chit as me to go falling in love with an impecunious student, and spirited me away to Baden.[9] As it is all over and past, I'll tell you one thing; I should have sent you a line had I known your name. That name I never knew till my maid said as you passed up the hotel stairs a month ago, 'There's Dr. Fitzpiers.' "

"Good heaven," said Fitzpiers musingly. "How the time comes back to me! The evening, the morning, the dew, the spot. When I found that you really were gone it was as if a cold iron had been passed down my back. I went up to where you had stood when I last saw you – I flung myself on the grass, and – being not much more than a boy – my eyes were literally blinded with tears. Nameless, unknown to me as you were, I couldn't forget your voice."

"For how long?"

"Oh – ever so long. Days and days."

"Day and days! *Only* days and days? Oh, the heart of a man! Days and days!"

"But, my dear madam, I had not known you more than a day or two. It was not a full-blown love – it was the merest bud – red, fresh, vivid, but small. It was a colossal passion in embryo. It never matured."

"So much the better perhaps."

"Perhaps. But see how powerless is the human will against predestination. We were prevented meeting; we have met. One feature of the case remains the same amid many changes. While you have grown rich,[10] I am still poor. Better than that, you have (judging by your last remark) outgrown the foolish impulsive passions of your early girlhood. I have not outgrown mine."

"I beg your pardon," said she with vibrations of strong feeling in her words. "I have been placed in a position which hinders such outgrowings. Besides, I don't believe that the genuine subjects of emotion do outgrow them; I believe that the older such people get the worse they are. Possibly at ninety or a hundred they may feel they are cured; but a mere threescore and ten won't do it – at least for me, if I live so long."

He gazed at her in undisguised admiration. Here was a soul of souls!

"You speak truly," he exclaimed. "But you speak sadly as well. Why is that?"

"I always am sad when I come here," she said, dropping to a low tone with a sense of having been too demonstrative.

"Then may I inquire why you came?"

"A man brought me. Women are always carried about like corks upon the waves of masculine desires[11] . . . I hope I have not alarmed you; but Hintock has the curious effect of bottling up the emotions till one can no longer hold them; I am often obliged to fly away and discharge my sentiments somewhere, or I should die outright."

"There is very good society in the county, I suppose, for those who have the privilege of entering it."

"Perhaps so. But the misery of remote country life is that your neighbours have no toleration for difference of opinion and habit. My neighbours think I am an atheist, except those who think I am a Roman Catholic; and when I speak disrespectfully of the weather or the crops they think I am a blasphemer."

She broke into a low musical laugh at the idea.

"You don't wish me to stay any longer?" he inquired, when he found that she remained musing.

"No – I think not."

"Then tell me that I am to be gone."

"Why? Cannot you go without?"

"I may consult my own feelings only, if left to myself."

"Well, if you do, what then? Do you suppose you'll be in my way?"

"I feared it might be so."

"Then fear no more. But good-night. Come to-morrow and see if I am going on right. This renewal of acquaintance touches me. I have already a friendship for you."

"If it depends upon myself it shall last for ever."

"My best hopes that it may. Good-bye."

Fitzpiers went down the stairs absolutely unable to decide whether she had sent for him in the natural alarm which might have followed her mishap, or with the single view of making herself known to him as she had done, for which the capsize had afforded excellent opportunity.

Outside the house he mused over the spot under the light of the stars. It seemed very strange that he should have come there more than once when its inhabitant was absent, and observed the house with a nameless interest; that he should have assumed offhand before he knew Grace that it was here she lived; that, in short, at sundry times and seasons the individuality of Hintock House should have forced itself upon him as appertaining to some existence with which he was concerned.

The intersection of his temporal orbit with Mrs. Charmond's for a day or two in the past had created a sentimental interest in her at the time, but it had been so evanescent that in the ordinary onward roll of affairs he would scarce ever have recalled it again. To find her here, however, in these somewhat romantic circumstances, magnified that bygone and transitory tenderness to indescribable proportions.

On entering Little Hintock he found himself regarding that hamlet in a new way – from the Hintock House point of view rather than from his own and the Melburys'. The household had all gone to bed. As he went up stairs he heard the snore of the timber-merchant from his quarter of the building, and turned into the passage communicating with his own rooms in a strange access of sadness.

A light was burning for him in the chamber; but Grace, though in bed was not asleep. In a moment her sympathetic voice came from behind the curtains.

"Edred, is she very seriously hurt?"

Fitzpiers had so entirely lost sight of Mrs. Charmond as a patient that he was not on the instant ready with a reply.

"Oh, no," he said. "There are no bones broken, but she is shaken. I am going again to-morrow."

Another inquiry or two, and Grace said –

"Did she ask for me?"

"Well, I think she did – I don't quite remember; but I am under the impression that she spoke of you."

"Cannot you recollect at all what she said?"

"I cannot, just this minute."

"At any rate, she did not talk much about me?" said Grace with disappointment.

"Oh, no."

"But you did, perhaps," she added, innocently fishing for a compliment.

"Oh, yes – you may depend upon that!" replied he warmly, though scarcely thinking of what he was saying, so vividly was there present to his mind the personality of Mrs. Charmond.

CHAPTER XI

The doctor's professional visit to Hintock House was promptly repeated the next day and the next. He always found Mrs. Charmond reclining on a sofa, and behaving generally as became a patient who was in no great hurry to lose that title. On each occasion he looked gravely at the little scratch on her arm, as if it had been a serious wound.

He had also, to his further satisfaction, found a slight scar on her temple, and it was very convenient to put a piece of black plaster on this conspicuous part of her person in preference to gold-beater's skin,[1] so that it might catch the eyes of the servants, and make his presence appear decidedly necessary, in case there should be any doubt of the fact.

"Oh – you hurt me!" she exclaimed one day.

He was peeling off the bit of plaster on her arm, under which the scrape had turned the colour of an unripe blackberry previous to vanishing altogether.

"Wait a moment, then I'll damp it," said Fitzpiers. He put his lips to the place and kept them there, without any objecting on her part, till the plaster came off easily. "It was at your request I put it on," said he.

"I know it," she replied. "Is that blue vein still in my temple that used to show there? The scar must be just upon it. If the cut had been a little deeper it would have spilt my hot blood indeed!"

Fitzpiers examined so closely that his breath touched her tenderly, at which their eyes rose to an encounter – hers showing themselves as deep and mysterious as interstellar space. She turned her face away suddenly.

"Ah! none of that! none of that – I cannot coquet with you!" she cried. "Don't suppose I consent to for one moment. Our poor, brief, youthful hour of love-making was too long ago to bear continuing now. It is as well that we should understand each other on that point before we go further."

"Coquet! Nor I with you. As it was when I found the historic gloves, so it is now. I might have been and may be foolish; but I am no trifler. I naturally cannot forget that little space in which I flitted across the field of your vision in those days of the past, and the recollection opens up all sorts of imaginings."

"Suppose my mother had not taken me away?" she murmured, her dreamy eyes resting on the swaying tip of a distant tree.

"I should have seen you again."

"And then?"

"Then the fire would have burnt higher and higher. What would have immediately followed I know not; but sorrow and sickness of heart at last."

"Why?"

"Well – that's the end of all love, according to Nature's law. I can give no other reason."

"Oh, don't speak like that!" she exclaimed. "Since we are only picturing the possibilities of that time, don't for pity's sake spoil the picture." Her voice sank almost to a whisper as she added, with an incipient pout upon her full lips, "Let me think at least that if you had really loved me at all seriously, you would have loved me for ever and ever!"

"You are right – think it with all your heart," said he. "It is a pleasant thought, and costs nothing."

She weighed that remark in silence awhile. "Did you ever hear anything of me from then till now?" she inquired.

"Not a word."

"So much the better. I had to fight the battle of life as well as you. I may tell you about it some day. But don't ever ask me to do it, and particularly do not press me to tell you now."

Thus the two or three days that they had spent in tender acquaintance on the romantic slopes above the Neckar[2] were stretched out in retrospect to the length and importance of years; made to form a canvas for infinite fancies, idle dreams, luxurious melancholies, and pretty, alluring assertions which could neither be proved nor disproved.

Grace was never mentioned between them, but a rumour of his contemplated removal from the neighbourhood somehow reached Mrs. Charmond's ears.

"Doctor, you are going away," she exclaimed, confronting him with accusatory reproach in her large dark eyes no less than in her cooing voice. "Oh yes, you are," she went on, springing to her feet with an air which might almost have been called passionate. "It is no use denying it! You have bought a practice at Budmouth. I don't blame you. Nobody can live at Hintock – least of all a professional man who wants to keep abreast of recent discovery. And there is nobody here to induce such a one to stay for other reasons. That's right, that's right – go away!"

"But no – I have not actually bought the practice as yet, though I am indeed in treaty for it. And, my dear friend, if I continue to feel about the business as I feel at this moment – perhaps I may conclude never to go at all."

"But you hate Hintock, and everything and everybody in it that you don't mean to take away with you?"

Fitzpiers contradicted this idea in his most vibratory tones, and she lapsed into the frivolous archness under which she hid passions of no mean strength – strange, smouldering, erratic passions, kept down like a stifled conflagration, but bursting out now here, now there – the only certain element in their direction being its unexpectedness.

If one word could have expressed Felice Charmond it would have been Inconsequence. She was a woman of perversities, delighting in piquant contrasts. She liked mystery, in her life, in her love, in her history. To be fair to her, there was nothing in these which she had any great reason to be ashamed of, and many things of which she might have been proud; but her past had never been fathomed by the honest minds of Hintock, and she rarely volunteered her experiences. As for her capricious nature the people on her estates grew accustomed to it, and with that marvellous subtlety of contrivance in steering round odd tempers that is found in sons of the soil and dependents generally, they managed to get along under her government rather better than they would have done beneath a more equable rule.

Now, with regard to the doctor's notion of leaving Hintock, he had advanced further towards completing the purchase of the Budmouth surgeon's goodwill than he had admitted to Mrs. Charmond. The whole matter hung upon what he might do in the ensuing twenty-four hours. The evening after leaving her he went out into the lane, and walked and pondered between the high hedges, now greenish-white with wild clematis – here called "old-man's-beard" from its aspect later in the year.

The letter of acceptance was to be written that night, after which his departure from Hintock would be irrevocable. But could he go away, remembering what had just passed? The trees, the hills, the leaves, the grass – each had been endowed and quickened with a subtle charm since he had discovered the person and history and, above all, the mood of their owner. There was every temporal reason for leaving: it would be entering again into a world which he had only quitted in a passion for isolation, induced by a fit of Achillean moodiness[3] after an imagined slight. His wife herself saw the awkwardness of their position here, and cheerfully welcomed the purposed change, towards which every step had been taken but the last. But could he find it in his heart – as he found it clearly enough in his conscience – to go away? No.

He drew a troubled breath, and went indoors. Here he rapidly penned a letter, wherein he withdrew, once for all, from the treaty for the Budmouth practice. As the postman had already left Little Hintock for that night he sent one of Melbury's men to intercept a mail-cart on another turnpike-road, and so got the letter off.

The man returned, met Fitzpiers in the lane, and told him the thing was done. Fitzpiers went back to his house musing. Why had he carried out this impulse – taken such wild trouble to effect a probable injury to his own and his young wife's prospects? His motive was fantastic, glowing, shapeless as the fiery scenery about the western sky. Mrs. Charmond could overtly be nothing more to him than a patient now, and to his wife, at the outside, a patron. Yet in the unattached bachelor days of his first sojourn here how highly proper an emotional reason for lingering on would have appeared to troublesome dubiousness. Matrimonial ambition is such an honourable thing!

"My father has told me that you have sent off one of the men with a late letter to Budmouth," cried Grace, coming out vivaciously to meet him under the declining light of the sky, wherein hung, solitary, the folding star.[4] "I said at once that you had finally agreed to pay the premium they ask, and that the tedious question had been settled. When do we go, Edred?"

"I have changed my mind," said he. "They want too much – seven hundred and fifty is too large a sum, – and in short I have declined to go further. We must wait for another opportunity. I fear I am not a good business-man."

He spoke the last words with a momentary faltering at the great foolishness of his act; and as he looked in her fair and honourable face his heart reproached him for what he had done.

Her manner that evening showed her disappointment. Personally she liked the home of her childhood much, and she was not ambitious. But her husband had seemed so dissatisfied with the circumstances hereabout since their marriage that she had sincerely hoped to go for his sake.

It was two or three days before he visited Mrs. Charmond again. The morning had been windy, and little showers had sowed themselves like grain against the walls and window-panes of the Hintock cottages. He went on foot across the wilder recesses of the park, where slimy streams of fresh moisture, exuding from decayed holes caused by old amputations, ran down the bark of the oaks and elms, the rind below being coated with a lichenous wash as green as emerald. They were stout-trunked trees, that never rocked their stems in the fiercest gale, responding to it entirely by crooking their limbs. Wrinkled like an old crone's face, and antlered with dead branches that rose above the foliage of their summits, they were nevertheless still green – though yellow had invaded the leaves of other trees.

She was in a little boudoir or writing-room on the first floor, and Fitzpiers was much surprised to find that the window-curtains were closed and a red-shaded lamp and candles burning, though out of doors it was broad daylight. Moreover a large fire was burning in the grate, though it was not cold.

"What does it all mean?" he asked.

She sat in an easy chair, her face being turned away. "Oh," she murmured, "it is because the world is so dreary outside. Sorrow and bitterness in the sky, and floods of agonised tears beating against the panes. I lay awake last night, and I could hear the scrape of snails creeping up the window glass; it was so sad! My eyes were so heavy this morning that I could have wept my life away. I cannot bear you to see my face; I keep it away from you purposely. Oh! why were we given hungry hearts and wild desires if we have to live in a world like this? Why should Death alone lend what Life is compelled to borrow – rest?[5] Answer that, Dr. Fitzpiers."

"You must eat of a second tree of knowledge[6] before *you* can do it, Felice Charmond."

"Then, when my emotions have exhausted themselves, I become full of fears, till I think I shall die for very fear. The terrible insistencies of society – how severe they are, and cold, and inexorable – ghastly towards those who are made of wax and not of stone. Oh, I am afraid of them; a stab for this error, and a stab for that – correctives and regulations pretendedly framed that society may tend to perfection – an end which I don't care for in the least. Yet for this all I do care for has to be stunted and starved."

Fitzpiers had seated himself near her. "What sets you in this mournful mood?" he asked gently. In reality he thought that it was the result of a loss of tone from staying indoors so much, but he did not say so.

"My reflections. Doctor, you must not come here any more. They

begin to think it a farce[7] already. I say you must come no more. There
– don't be angry with me!" – and she jumped up, pressed his hand,
and looked anxiously at him. "It is necessary. It is best for both you
and me."

"But," said Fitzpiers gloomily, "what have we done?"

"Done – we have done nothing. Perhaps we have thought the more.
However, it is all vexation. I am going away to Middleton Abbey,
near Shottsford, where a relative of my late husband lives, who is
confined to her bed. The engagement was made in London, and
I can't get out of it. Perhaps it is for the best that I go there till all
this is past. When are you going to enter on your new practice,
and leave Hintock behind for ever, with your pretty wife on your
arm?"

"I have refused the opportunity. I love this place too well to
depart."

"You *have?*" she said, regarding him with wild uncertainty. "Why
do you ruin yourself in that way? Great heaven, what have I
done!"

"Nothing. Besides you are going away."

"Oh, yes; but only to Middleton Abbey for a month or two. Yet
perhaps I shall gain strength there – particularly strength of mind – I
require it. And when I come back I shall be a new woman; and you
can come and see me safely then, and bring your wife with you, and
we'll be friends – she and I. Oh, how this shutting up of one's self
does lead to indulgence in idle sentiments! I shall not wish you to
give your attendance to me after to-day. But I am glad that you
are not going away – if your remaining does not injure your prospects
at all."

As soon as he had left the room the mild friendliness she had
preserved in her tone at parting, the playful sadness with which she
had conversed with him, equally departed from her. She became
as heavy as lead – just as she had been before he arrived. Her
whole being seemed to dissolve in a sad powerlessness to do anything,
and the sense of it made her lips tremulous and her closed eyes wet.

His footsteps again startled her, and she turned round.

"I return for a moment to tell you that the evening is going to be fine. The sun is shining, so do open your curtains and put out those lights. Shall I do it for you?"

"Please – if you don't mind."

He drew back the window-curtains, whereupon the red glow of the lamp and the two candle flames became almost invisible under the flood of late autumn sunlight that poured in.

"Shall I come round to you?" he asked, her back being towards him.

"No," she replied.

"Why not?"

"Because I am crying, and I don't want to see you."

He stood a moment irresolute, and regretted that he had killed the rosy passionate lamplight by opening the curtains and letting in garish day.

"Then I am going," he said.

"Very well," she answered, stretching one hand round to him, and patting her eyes with a handkerchief held in the other.

"Shall I write a line to you at —?"

"No, no." A gentle reasonableness came into her tone as she added, "It must not be, you know. It won't do."

"Very well. Good-bye." The next moment he was gone.

In the evening with listless adroitness she encouraged the maid who dressed her for dinner to speak of Dr. Fitzpiers's marriage.

"Mrs. Fitzpiers was once supposed to favour Mr. Winterborne," said the young woman.

"And why didn't she marry him?" said Mrs. Charmond.

"Because you see, ma'am, he lost his houses."

"Lost his houses? How came he to do that?"

"The houses were held on lives, and the lives dropped, and your agent wouldn't renew them, though it is said that Mr. Winterborne had a very good claim. That's as I've heard it, ma'am, and it was through it that the match was broke off."

Being just then distracted by a dozen emotions, Mrs. Charmond sank into a mood of dismal self-reproach. "In refusing that poor man his reasonable request," she said to herself, "I fore-doomed my revived girlhood's romance. Who would have thought such a business matter could have nettled my own heart like this! Now for a winter of regrets and agonies and useless wishes, till I forget him in the spring. Oh! I am glad I am going away."

She left her chamber, and went down to dine, with a sigh. On the stairs she stood opposite the large window for a moment, and looked out upon the lawn. It was not yet quite dark. Half-way up the steep green slope confronting her stood old Timothy Tangs, who was shortening his way homeward by clambering here where there was no road, and in opposition to express orders that no path was to be made there. Tangs had momentarily stopped to take a pinch of snuff, but observing Mrs. Charmond gazing at him he hastened to get over the top out of hail. His precipitancy made him miss his footing, and he rolled like a barrel to the bottom, his snuff box rolling in front of him.

Her indefinite idle impossible passion for Fitzpiers; her constitutional cloud of misery, the sorrowful drops that still hung upon her eyelashes, all made way for the impulse started by the spectacle. She burst into an immoderate fit of laughter; her very gloom of the previous hour seeming to render it the more uncontrollable. It had not died out of her when she reached the dining-room; and even here, before the servants, her shoulders suddenly shook as the scene returned upon her; and the tears of her risibility mingled with the remnants of those engendered by her grief.

She resolved to be sad no more. She drank two glasses of champagne, and a little more still after those; and amused herself in the evening with singing little amatory songs.

"I must do something for that poor man Winterborne, however," she said.

CHAPTER XII

CHAPTER XII

A week had passed, and Mrs. Charmond had left Hintock House. Middleton Abbey, the place of her sojourn, was about twenty miles distant by road, eighteen by bridlepaths and footways.

Grace observed, for the first time, that her husband was restless, that at moments he even was disposed to avoid her. The scrupulous civility of mere acquaintanceship crept into his manner; yet, when sitting at meals, he seemed hardly to hear her remarks. Her little doings interested him no longer, whilst towards her father his bearing was not far from supercilious. It was plain that his mind was entirely outside her life, whereabouts outside it she could not tell; in some region of science possibly, or of psychological literature. But her hope that he was again immersing himself in those lucubrations[1] which before her marriage had made his light a landmark in Hintock, was founded simply on the slender fact that he often sat up late.

One day she discovered him leaning over a gate on Rubdon Hill, the gate at which Winterborne had once been standing, and which opened on the brink of a declivity, slanting down directly into White-Hart Vale, extending beneath the eye at this point to a distance of many miles. His attention was fixed on the landscape far away, and Grace's approach was so noiseless that he did not hear her. When she came close she could see his lips moving unconsciously, as to some impassioned visionary theme.

She spoke, and Fitzpiers started. "What are you looking at?" she asked.

"Oh! I was contemplating our old place of Buckbury, in my idle way," he said.

It had seemed to her that he was looking much to the right of that cradle and tomb of his ancestral dignity; but she made no further observation, and taking his arm walked home beside him almost in silence. She did not know that Middleton Abbey lay in the direction of his gaze.

"Are you going to have out Darling this afternoon?" she asked presently.

Darling, the light-grey mare which Winterborne had bought for Grace, Fitzpiers now constantly used, the animal having turned out a wonderful bargain in combining a perfect docility with an almost human intelligence; moreover, she was not too young. Fitzpiers was unfamiliar with horses, and he valued these qualities.

"Yes," he replied, "but not to drive. I am riding her. I practise crossing a horse as often as I can now, for I find that I can take much shorter cuts on horseback."

He had, in fact, taken these riding exercises for about a week, only since Mrs. Charmond's absence; his universal practice hitherto having been to drive.

Some few days later, Fitzpiers started on the back of this horse to see a patient in the aforesaid Vale. It was about five o'clock in the evening when he went away, and at bedtime he had not reached home. There was nothing very singular in this, though she was not aware that he had any patient more than five or six miles distant in that direction. The clock had struck one before Fitzpiers entered the house, and he came to his room softly, as if anxious not to disturb her.

The next morning she was stirring considerably earlier than he. In the yard there was a conversation going on about the mare; the man who attended to the horses, Darling included, insisted that the latter was "hag-rid";[2] for when he had arrived at the stable that morning, she was in such a state as no horse could be in by honest riding. It was true that the doctor had stabled her himself when he got home, so that she was not looked after as she would have been if the speaker had groomed and fed her; but that did not account for the appearance she presented, if Mr. Fitzpiers's journey had been only where he had stated. The phenomenal exhaustion of Darling, as thus related, was sufficient to develop a whole series of tales about equestrian witches and demons, the narration of which occupied a considerable time.

Grace returned indoors. In passing through the outer room she picked up her husband's overcoat which he had carelessly flung down across a chair. A turnpike ticket[3] fell out of the breast-pocket, and she saw that it had been issued at Middleton Gate. He had therefore visited Middleton the previous night, a distance of at least five-and-thirty miles on horseback, there and back.

During the day she made some inquiries, and learnt for the first time that Mrs. Charmond was staying at Middleton Abbey. She could not resist an inference – strange as that inference was.

A few days later he prepared to start again, at the same time and in the same direction. She knew that the state of the cottager who lived that way was a mere pretext; she was quite sure he was going to Mrs. Charmond.

Grace was amazed at the mildness of the anger which the suspicion engendered in her. She was but little excited, and her jealousy was languid even to death. It told tales of the nature of her affection for him. In truth, her ante-nuptial regard for Fitzpiers had been rather of the quality of awe towards a superior being than of tender solicitude for a lover. It had been based upon mystery and strangeness – the mystery of his past, of his knowledge, of his professional skill, of his beliefs. When this structure of ideals was demolished by the intimacy of common life, and she found him as merely human as the Hintock people themselves, a new foundation was in demand for an enduring and staunch affection – a sympathetic inter-dependence, wherein mutual weaknesses are made the grounds of a defensive alliance. Fitzpiers had furnished none of that single-minded confidence and truth out of which alone such a second union could spring; hence it was with a controllable emotion that she now watched the mare brought round.

"I'll walk with you to the hill if you are not in a great hurry," she said, rather loth, after all, to let him go.

"Do; there's plenty of time," replied her husband.

Accordingly he led along the horse, and walked beside her, impatient enough nevertheless. Thus they proceeded to the turnpike road, and ascended Rubdon Hill to the gate he had been leaning over when she surprised him ten days before. This was the end of her excursion. Fitzpiers bade her adieu with affection, even with tenderness, and she observed that he looked weary-eyed.

"Why do you go to-night?" she said. "You have been called up two nights in succession already."

"I must go," he answered, almost gloomily. "Don't wait up for me." With these words he mounted his horse, passed through the gate which Grace held open for him, and ambled down the steep bridle-track to the valley.

She closed the gate and watched his descent, and then his journey onward. His way was east, the evening sun which stood behind her back beaming full upon him as soon as he got out from the shade of the hill. Notwithstanding this untoward proceeding she was determined to be loyal if he proved true; and the determination to love one's best will carry a heart a long way towards making that best an ever-growing thing.

The conspicuous coat of the active though blanching mare made horse and rider easy objects for the vision. Though Darling had been chosen with such pains by Winterborne for Grace, she had never ridden the sleek creature; but her husband had found the animal exceedingly convenient, particularly now that he had taken to the saddle, plenty of staying power being left in Darling yet. Fitzpiers, like others of his character, while despising Melbury and his station, did not at all disdain to spend Melbury's money, or appropriate to his own use the horse which belonged to Melbury's daughter.

And so the infatuated surgeon went along through the gorgeous autumn landscape of White-Hart Vale, surrounded by orchards, lustrous with the reds of apple-crops, berries, and foliage, the whole intensified by the gilding of the declining sun. The earth this year had been prodigally bountiful, and now was the supreme moment of her bounty. In the poorest spots the hedges were bowed with haws and blackberries; acorns cracked underfoot, and the burst husks of chestnuts lay exposing their auburn contents as if arranged by anxious sellers in a fruit-market. In all this proud show some kernels were unsound as her own situation, and she wondered if there were one world in the universe where the fruit had no worm, and marriage no sorrow.

Her Tannhäuser[4] still moved on, his plodding steed rendering him distinctly visible yet. Could she have heard Fitzpiers's voice at that moment she would have found it murmuring,

" – Towards the load-star of my one desire[5]
I flitted, like a dizzy moth, whose flight
Is as a dead leaf's in the owlet light."

But he was a silent spectacle to her. Soon he rose out of the valley, and skirted a high plateau of the chalk formation on his right, which rested abruptly upon the fruity district of deep loam, the character and herbage of the two formations being so distinct that the calcareous upland appeared but as a deposit of a few years' antiquity upon the level vale.

He kept along the edge of this high, uninclosed country, and the sky behind him being deep violet she could still see white Darling in relief upon it – a mere speck now – a Wouvermans eccentricity[6] reduced to microscopic dimensions. Upon this high ground he gradually disappeared.

Thus she had beheld the pet animal purchased for her own use, in pure love of her, by one who had always been true, impressed to convey her husband away from her to the side of a new-found idol. While she was musing on the vicissitudes of horses and wives, she discerned shapes moving up the valley towards her, quite near at hand, though till now hidden by the hedges. Surely they were Giles Winterborne, with two horses and a cider-apparatus, conducted by Robert Creedle. Up, upward they crept, a stray beam of the sun alighting every now and then like a star on the blades of the pomace-shovels, which had been converted to steel mirrors by the action of the malic acid. She opened the gate when he came close, and the panting horses rested as they achieved the ascent.

"How do you do, Giles?" said she, under a sudden impulse to be familiar with him.

He replied with much more reserve. "You are going for a walk, Mrs. Fitzpiers?" he added. "It is pleasant just now."

"No, I am returning," said she.

The vehicles passed through, the gate slammed, and Winterborne walked by her side in the rear of the apple-mill.

He looked and smelt like Autumn's very brother, his face being sunburnt to wheat-colour, his eyes blue as corn-flowers, his sleeves and leggings dyed with fruit-stains, his hands clammy with the sweet juice of apples, his hat sprinkled with pips, and everywhere about him that atmosphere of cider which at its first return each season has such an indescribable fascination for those who have been born and bred among the orchards. Her heart rose from its late sadness like a released spring; her senses revelled in the sudden lapse back to nature unadorned. The consciousness of having to be genteel because of her husband's profession, the veneer of artificiality which she had acquired at the fashionable schools, were thrown off, and she became the crude country girl of her latent earliest instincts.

Nature was bountiful, she thought. No sooner had she been starved off by Edred Fitzpiers than another being, impersonating bare and undiluted manliness, had arisen out of the earth ready to hand. This was an excursion of the imagination which she did not encourage, and she said suddenly, to disguise the confused regard which had followed her thoughts, "Did you meet my husband?"

Winterborne, with some hesitation: "Yes."

"Where did you meet him?"

"At Calfhay Cross. I come from Middleton Abbey; I have been making there for the last week."

"Haven't they a mill of their own?"

"Yes, but it's out of repair."

"I think – I heard that Mrs. Charmond had gone there to stay?"

"Yes, I have seen her at the windows once or twice."

Grace waited an interval before she went on: "Did Mr. Fitzpiers take the way to Middleton?"

"Yes . . . I met him on Darling." As she did not reply, he added with a gentler inflection, "You know why the mare was called that?"

"Oh yes – of course," she answered quickly.

They had risen so far over the crest of the hill that the whole west sky was revealed. Between the broken clouds they could see far into the recesses of heaven, the eye journeying on under a species of golden arcades, and past fiery obstructions, fancied cairns, logan-stones, stalactites and stalagmites of topaz. Deeper than this their gaze passed thin flakes of incandescence, till it plunged into a bottomless medium of soft green fire.

Her abandonment to the luscious time after her sense of ill-usage, her revolt for the nonce against social law, her passionate desire for primitive life may have showed in her face. Winterborne was looking at her, his eyes lingering on a flower that she wore in her bosom. Almost with the abstraction of a somnambulist he stretched out his hand and gently caressed the flower.

She drew back. "What are you doing, Giles Winterborne!" she exclaimed, with a look of severe surprise.

The evident absence of all premeditation from the act, however, speedily led her to think that it was not necessary to stand upon her dignity here and now. "You must bear in mind, Giles," she said kindly, "that we are not as we were; and some people might have said that what you did was taking a liberty."

It was more than she need have told him; his action of forgetfulness had made him so angry with himself that he flushed through his tan.

"I don't know what I am coming to!" he exclaimed savagely. "Ah – I was not once like this!" Tears of vexation were in his eyes.

"No, now – it was nothing! I was too reproachful."

"It would not have occurred to me if I had not seen something like it done elsewhere – at Middleton lately," he said thoughtfully after a while.

"By whom?"

"Don't ask it."

She scanned him narrowly. "I know quite well enough," she returned indifferently. "It was by my husband, and the woman was Mrs. Charmond. Association of ideas reminded you when you saw me . . . Giles – tell me all you know about that – please do, Giles! But no – I won't hear it. Let the subject cease. And as you are my friend say nothing to my father."

They reached a place where their ways divided. Winterborne continued along the highway which kept outside the copse, and Grace opened a gate that entered it.

CHAPTER XIII

She walked up the soft grassy ride, screened on either hand by
nut-bushes just now heavy with clusters of twos and threes and fours.
A little way on the track she pursued was crossed by a similar one at
right angles. Here Grace stopped; some few yards up the transverse
ride the buxom Suke Damson was visible – her gown tucked up high
through her pocket-hole, and no bonnet on her head – in the act of
pulling down boughs from which she was gathering and eating nuts
with great rapidity, her lover Tim Tangs standing near her engaged
in the same pleasant meal.

Crack, crack, went Suke's jaws every second or two. By an automatic
chain of thought Grace's mind reverted to the toothdrawing scene
described by her husband; and for the first time she wondered if that
narrative were really true, Susan's jaws being so obviously sound and
strong. Grace turned up towards the nut-gatherers, and conquered
her reluctance to speak to the girl, who was a little in advance of Tim.
"Good evening, Susan," she said.

"Good evening, Miss Melbury," (crack).

"Mrs. Fitzpiers."

"Oh yes, ma'am – Mrs. Fitzpiers," said Suke with a peculiar curtsey.

Grace, not to be daunted, continued, "Take care of your teeth,
Suke. That accounts for the toothache."

"I don't know what an ache is, either in tooth, ear, or head, thank
the Lord," (crack).

"Nor the loss of one, either?"

"See for yourself, ma'am." She parted her red lips, and exhibited
the whole double row, full up and unimpaired.

"You have never had one drawn?"

"Never."

"So much the better for your stomach," said Mrs. Fitzpiers in an
altered voice. And turning away quickly she went on.

As her husband's character thus shaped itself under the touch of time, Grace was almost startled to find how little she suffered from that jealous excitement[1] which is conventionally attributed to all wives in such circumstances. But though possessed by none of the feline wildness which it was her moral duty to experience, she did not fail to suspect that she had made a frightful mistake in her marriage. Acquiescence in her father's wishes had been degradation to herself. People are not given premonitions for nothing; she should have obeyed her impulse on that early morning when she peeped from her window, and have steadfastly refused her hand.

Oh, that plausible tale which her then betrothed had told her about Suke – the dramatic account of her entreaties to him to draw the aching enemy, and the fine artistic touch he had given to the story by explaining that it was a lovely molar without a flaw!

She traced the remainder of the woodland track, dazed by the complications of her position. If his protestations to her before their marriage could be believed, her husband had felt affection of some sort for herself and this woman simultaneously; and was now again spreading the same emotion over Mrs. Charmond and herself conjointly, his manner being still kind and fond at times. But surely, rather than that, he must have played the hypocrite towards her in each case with elaborate completeness; and the thought of this sickened her, for it involved the conjecture that if he had not loved her his only motive for making her his wife must have been her little fortune.

Yet here Grace made a mistake, for the love of men like Fitzpiers is unquestionably of such quality as to bear division and transference. He had indeed once declared, though not to her, that on one occasion he had noticed himself to be possessed by five distinct infatuations at the same time.[2] If this were true, his differed from the highest affection as the lower orders of the animal world[3] differ from advanced organisms, partition causing not death but a multiplied existence. He had loved her sincerely, and had by no means ceased to love her now. But such double and treble-barrelled hearts were naturally beyond her conception.

Of poor Suke Damson Grace thought no more. She had had her day.

"If he does not love me I will not love him!" said Grace proudly.

And though these were mere words, it was a somewhat formidable thing for Fitzpiers that her heart was approximating to a state in which it might be possible to carry them out. That very absence of hot jealousy which made his courses so easy, and on which, indeed, he congratulated himself, meant, unknown to either wife or husband, more mischief than the inconvenient watchfulness of a jaundiced eye.

Her sleep that night was nervous. The wing allotted to her and her husband had never seemed so lonely. At last she got up, put on her dressing-gown, and went down stairs. Her father, who slept lightly, heard her descend, and came to the stairhead.

"Is that you, Grace? What's the matter?" he said.

"Nothing more than that I am restless. Edred is detained by a case at Owlscombe in White-Hart Vale."

"But how's that? I saw the woman's husband at Great Hintock just afore bedtime; and she was going on well, and the doctor gone then."

"Then he's detained somewhere else," said Grace. "Never mind me; he will soon be home. I expect him about one."

She went back to her room, and dozed and woke several times. One o'clock had been the hour of his return on the last occasion; but it had passed now by a long way, and still Fitzpiers did not come. Just before dawn she heard the men stirring in the yard, and the flashes of their lanterns spread every now and then through her window-blind. She remembered that her father had told her not to be disturbed if she noticed them, as they would be rising early to send off four loads of hurdles to a distant sheep fair. Peeping out she saw them bustling about, the hollow-turner among the rest; he was loading his wares – wooden bowls, dishes, spigots, spoons, cheese-vats, funnels and so on – upon one of her father's waggons, who carried them to the fair for him every year out of neighbourly kindness.

The scene and the occasion would have enlivened her but that her husband was still absent, though it was now five o'clock. She could hardly suppose him, whatever his infatuation, to have prolonged to a later hour than ten an ostensibly professional call on Mrs. Charmond at Middleton; and he could have ridden home in two hours and a half. What then had become of him? That he had been out the greater part of the two preceding nights added to her uneasiness.

She dressed herself, descended, and went out, the weird twilight of advancing day chilling the rays from the lanterns, and making the men's faces wan. As soon as Melbury saw her he came round, showing his alarm.

"Edred is not come," she said. "And I have reason to know that he's not attending anybody. He has had no rest for two nights before this. I was going to the top of the hill to look for him."

"I'll come with you," said Melbury.

She begged him not to hinder himself; but he insisted, for he saw a peculiar and rigid gloom in her face over and above her uneasiness, and did not like the look of it. Telling the men he would be with them again soon he walked beside her into the turnpike road, and partly up the hill whence she had watched Fitzpiers the night before across the Great White-Hart Valley.

They halted beneath a half-dead oak, hollow, and disfigured with white tumours, its roots spreading out like claws grasping the ground. A chilly wind circled round them, upon whose currents the seeds of a neighbouring lime-tree, supported parachute-wise by the wing attached, flew out of the boughs downward like fledglings from their nest. The vale was wrapped in a dim atmosphere of unnaturalness, and the east was like a livid curtain edged with pink. There was no sign nor sound of Fitzpiers.

"It is no use standing here," said her father. "He may come home fifty ways ... why, look here – here be Darling's tracks – turned homeward and nearly blown dry and hard! He must have come in hours ago without your seeing him."

"He has not done that," said she.

They went back hastily. On entering their own gates they perceived that the men had left the waggons, and were standing round the door of the stable which had been appropriated to the doctor's use.

"Is there anything the matter?" cried Grace.

"Oh, no, ma'am. All's well that ends well,"[4] said old Timothy Tangs. "I've heard of such things before – amongst workfolk, though not amongst your gentlepeople – that's true."

They entered the stable, and saw the pale shape of Darling standing in the middle of her stall, with Fitzpiers on her back, sound asleep. Darling was munching hay as well as she could with the bit in her mouth, and the reins, which had fallen from Fitzpiers's hand, hung upon her neck.

Grace went and touched his hand; shook it, before she could arouse him. He moved, started, opened his eyes, and exclaimed, "Ah, Felice . . . Oh, it's Grace. I could not see in the gloom. What – am I in the saddle!"

"Yes," said she. "How do you come here?"

He collected his thoughts, and in a few minutes stammered as he began dismounting: "I was riding along homeward through the Vale, very, very sleepy, having been up so much of late. When I came opposite Holy Spring the mare turned her head that way as if she wanted to drink. I let her go in, and she drank; I thought she would never finish. While she was drinking the clock of Owlscombe church struck twelve. I distinctly remember counting the strokes. From that moment I positively recollect nothing till I saw you here by my side."

"The name! If it had been any other horse he'd have had a broken neck!" murmured Melbury.

" 'Tis wonderful, sure, how a quiet hoss will bring a man home at such times!" said John Upjohn. "And – what's more wonderful than keeping your seat in a deep slumbering sleep – I've knowed men drowze off walking home from randies where the mead and other liquors have gone round well, and keep walking for more than a mile on end without waking. Well, doctor, 'tis a mercy you wasn't a drownded, or a splintered, or a hanged up to a tree like Absalont[5] – also a handsome gentleman like yerself, as the prophets say."

"True," murmured old Timothy piously, "from the sole of his boots to the crown of his hat there was no blemish in him!"[6]

"Or leastwise you might ha' been a wownded into tatters a'most, and no brother-tradesman to jine your few limbs together within seven mile!"

Whilst this address was proceeding Fitzpiers had dismounted, and taking Grace's arm walked stiffly indoors with her. Melbury stood staring at the horse which, in addition to being very weary, was spattered with mud. There was no mud to speak of about the Hintocks just now – only in the clammy hollows of the Vale beyond Owlscombe, the stiff soil of which retained moisture for weeks after the uplands were dry. Whilst they were rubbing down the mare Melbury's mind coupled with the foreign quality of the mud the name he had heard unconsciously muttered by the surgeon when Grace took his hand – "Felice." Who was Felice? Why, Mrs. Charmond; and she, as he knew, was staying at Middleton.

Melbury had indeed pounced upon the image that filled Fitzpiers's half-awakened soul – wherein there had been a picture of a recent interview on a starlit lawn with a capriciously-passionate woman, who had begged him not to come again in tones whose modulations incited him to disobey. "What are you doing here? Why do you pursue me? Another belongs to you. If they were to see you they would seize you as a thief!" And she had turbulently admitted to his wringing questions that her visit to Middleton had been undertaken less because of the invalid relative than in shamefaced fear of her own weakness if she remained near his home. A triumph then it was to Fitzpiers, poor and hampered as he had become, to recognise his real conquest of this beauty, delayed so many years. His was the passion of Congreve's Millimant, to whom love's supreme delight lay in seeing "that heart which others bleed for,[7] bleed for me."

When the horse had been attended to Melbury stood uneasily here and there about his premises; he was rudely disturbed in the comfortable views which had lately possessed him on his domestic concerns. It is true that he had for some days discerned that Grace more and more sought his company, preferred supervising his kitchen and bake-house with her stepmother to occupying herself with the lighter details of her own apartments. She seemed no longer able to find in her own hearth an adequate focus for her life, and hence, like a weak queen-bee after leading off to an independent home, had hovered again into the parent hive. But he had not construed these and other incidents of the kind till now.

Something was wrong in the dovecote. A ghastly sense beset him that he alone would be responsible for whatever unhappiness should be brought upon her for whom he almost solely lived; whom to retain under his roof he had faced the numerous inconveniences involved in giving up the best part of his house to Fitzpiers. There was no room for doubt that, had he allowed events to take their natural course, she would have accepted Winterborne, and realised his old dream of restitution to that young man's family.

That Fitzpiers could allow himself to look for a moment on any other creature than Grace filled Melbury with grief and astonishment. In the pure and simple life he had led it had scarcely occurred to him that after marriage a man might be faithless. That he could sweep to the heights of Mrs. Charmond's position, lift the veil of Isis,[8] so to speak, would have amazed Melbury by its audacity if he had not suspected encouragement from that quarter. What could he and his simple Grace do to countervail the passions of such as those two sophisticated beings – versed in the world's ways, armed with every apparatus for victory? In such an encounter the homely timber-dealer felt as inferior as a savage with his bow and arrows to the precise weapons of modern warfare.

Grace came out of the house as the morning drew on. The village was silent, most of the folk having gone to the fair. Fitzpiers had retired to bed, and was sleeping off his fatigue. She went to the stable and looked at poor Darling: in all probability Giles Winterborne, by obtaining for her a horse of such intelligence and docility, had been the means of saving her husband's life. She paused over the strange thought; and then there appeared her father behind her.

She saw that he knew things were not as they ought to be, from the troubled dulness of his eye, and from his face, different points of which had independent motions, twitchings, and tremblings, unknown to himself, and involuntary.

"He was detained, I suppose, last night?" said Melbury.

"Oh, yes; a bad case in the Vale," she replied calmly.

"Nevertheless he should have stayed at home."

"But he couldn't, father."

Her father turned away. He could hardly bear to see his whilom truthful girl brought to the humiliation of having to talk like that.

That night carking care sat beside Melbury's pillow, and his stiff limbs tossed at its presence.

"I can't lie here any longer," he muttered. Striking a light he wandered about the room. "What have I done, what have I done for her?" he said to his wife who had anxiously awakened. "I had long planned that she should marry the son of the man I wanted to make amends to; do ye mind how I told you all about it, Lucy, the night before she came home? Ah! but I was not content with doing right, I wanted to do more!"

"Don't raft yourself without good need, George," she replied. "I won't quite believe that things are so much amiss. I won't believe that Mrs. Charmond has encouraged him. Even supposing she has encouraged a great many, she can have no motive to do it now. What so likely as that she is not yet quite well, and doesn't care to let another doctor come near her?"

He did not heed. "Grace used to be so busy every day, with fixing a curtain here and driving a tin-tack there; but she cares for no employment now!"

"Do you know anything of Mrs. Charmond's past history? Perhaps that would throw some light upon things. Before she came here as the wife of old Charmond four or five years ago, not a soul seems to have heard aught of her. Why not make inquiries? And then do ye wait and see more; there'll be plenty of opportunity. Time enough to cry when you know 'tis a crying matter; 'tis bad to meet troubles half-way."

There was some good sense in the notion of seeing further. Melbury resolved to inquire and wait, hoping still, but oppressed between whiles with much fear.

CHAPTER XIV

Examine Grace as her father might, she would admit nothing. For the present, therefore, he simply watched.

The suspicion that his darling child was being slighted wrought almost a miraculous change in Melbury's nature. No man so furtive for the time as the ingenuous countryman who finds that his ingenuousness has been abused. Melbury's heretofore confidential candour towards his gentlemanly son-in-law was displaced by a feline stealth that did injury to his every action, thought, and mood.

He knew that a woman once given to a man for life took, as a rule, her lot as it came, and made the best of it, without external interference; but for the first time he asked himself why this so generally should be done. Besides, this case was not, he argued, like ordinary cases. Leaving out the question of Grace being anything but an ordinary woman, her peculiar situation, as it were in mid-air between two stories of society, together with the loneliness of Hintock, made a husband's neglect a far more tragical matter to her than it would be to one who had a large circle of friends to fall back upon. Wisely or unwisely, and whatever other fathers did, he resolved to fight his daughter's battle still.

Mrs. Charmond had returned. But Hintock House scarcely gave forth signs of life, so quietly had she re-entered it.[1] Autumn drew shiveringly to its end. One day something seemed to be gone from the gardens; the tenderer leaves of vegetables had shrunk under the first smart frost, and hung like faded linen rags; then the forest leaves, which had been descending at leisure, descended in haste and in multitudes, and all the golden colours that had hung overhead were now crowded together in a degraded mass underfoot, where the fallen myriads got redder and hornier, and curled themselves up to rot. The only suspicious features in Mrs. Charmond's existence at this season were two; the first, that she lived with no companion or relative about her, which, considering her age and attractions, was somewhat unusual conduct for a young widow in a lonely country house; the other, that she did not, as in previous years, start from Hintock to winter abroad. In Fitzpiers, the only change from his last autumn's habits lay in his abandonment of night study; his lamp never shone from his new dwelling as from his old.

If the suspected ones met it was by such adroit contrivances that even Melbury's vigilance could not encounter them together. A simple call at her house by the doctor had nothing irregular about it, and that he had paid two or three such calls was certain. What had passed at those interviews was known only to the parties themselves; but that Felice Charmond was under some one's influence Melbury soon had opportunity of perceiving.

Winter had come on. Owls began to be noisy in the mornings and evenings, and flocks of wood-pigeons made themselves prominent again. On a day in February, about six months after the marriage of Fitzpiers, Melbury was returning from Great Hintock on foot through the lane, when he saw before him the surgeon also walking. Melbury would have overtaken him, but at that moment Fitzpiers turned in through a gate to one of the rambling drives among the trees at this side of the wood, which led to nowhere in particular, and the beauty of whose serpentine curves was the only justification of their existence. Felice almost simultaneously trotted down the lane towards the timber-dealer, in a little basket-carriage which she sometimes drove about the estate, unaccompanied by a servant. She turned in at the same place without having seen either Melbury or, apparently, Fitzpiers.

Melbury was soon at the spot, despite his aches and his sixty years. Mrs. Charmond had come up with the doctor, who was standing immediately behind the carriage. She had turned to him, her arm being thrown carelessly over the back of the seat.

They looked in each other's faces without uttering a word, an arch yet gloomy smile wreathing her lips. Fitzpiers clasped her hanging hand, and, while she still remained in the same listless attitude, looking volumes into his eyes, he stealthily unbuttoned her glove, and stripped her hand of it by rolling back the gauntlet over the fingers, so that it came off inside out. He then raised her hand to his mouth, she still reclining passively, watching him as she might have watched a fly upon her dress. At last she said, "Well, sir, what excuse for this disobedience?"

"I make none."

"Then go your way, and let me go mine." She snatched away her hand, touched the pony with the whip, and left him standing there, holding the reversed glove.

Melbury's first impulse was to reveal his presence to Fitzpiers, and upbraid him bitterly. But a moment's thought was sufficient to show him the futility of any such simple proceeding. There was not, after all, so much in what he had witnessed as in what that scene might be the surface and froth of – probably a state of mind which censure aggravates rather than cures. Moreover, he said to himself that the point of attack should be the woman, if either. He therefore kept out of sight, and musing sadly, even tearfully – for he was meek as a child in matters concerning his daughter – continued his walk towards Hintock.

The insight which is bred of deep sympathy was never more finely exemplified than in this instance. Through her guarded manner, her dignified speech, her placid countenance, he discerned the interior of Grace's life only too truly, hidden as were its incidents from every outer eye.

These incidents had become painful enough. Fitzpiers had latterly developed an irritable discontent, which vented itself in monologues when Grace was present to hear them. The early morning of this day had been dull, after a night of wind, and on looking out of the window in the grey grim dawn Fitzpiers had observed some of Melbury's men dragging away a large limb which had been snapped off a beech tree. Everything was cold and colourless.

"My good God!" he said as he stood in his dressing-gown. "This is life!"

He did not know whether Grace was awake or not, and he would not turn his head to ascertain. "Ah, fool," he went on to himself, "to clip your own wings when you were free to soar! . . . But I could not rest till I had done it. Why do I never recognise an opportunity till I have missed it, nor the good or ill of a step till it is irrevocable? . . . I fell in love!"

Grace moved. He thought she had heard some part of his soliloquy. He was sorry – though he had not taken any precaution to prevent her.

He expected a scene at breakfast, but she only exhibited an extreme reserve. It was enough, however, to make him repent that he should have done anything to produce discomfort; for he attributed her manner entirely to what he had said. But Grace's manner had not its cause either in his sayings or in his doings. She had not heard a single word of his regrets. Something even nearer home than her husband's blighted prospects – if blighted they were – was the origin of her mood.

She had made a discovery – one which to a girl of honest nature was almost appalling. She had looked into her heart, and found that her early interest in Giles Winterborne had become revitalised into luxuriant growth by her widening perceptions of what was great and little in life. His homeliness no longer offended her acquired tastes; his comparative want of so-called culture did not now jar on her intellect; his country dress even pleased her eye; his exterior roughness fascinated her. Having discovered by marriage how much that was humanly not great could co-exist with attainments of an exceptional order, there was a revulsion in her sentiments from all that she had formerly clung to in this kind. Honesty, goodness, manliness, tenderness, devotion, for her only existed in their purity now in the breasts of unvarnished men; and here was one who had manifested such towards her from his youth up.

There was, further, that never-ceasing pity in her soul for Giles as a man whom she had wronged – a man who had been unfortunate in his worldly transactions; one who, notwithstanding these things, had, like Hamlet's friend, borne himself throughout his scathing

"As one, in suffering all, that suffers nothing,"[2]

investing himself thereby with a real touch of sublimity. It was these perceptions, and no subtle catching of her husband's murmurs, that had bred the abstraction visible in her.

When her father approached the house after witnessing the interview between Fitzpiers and Mrs. Charmond, Grace was looking out of her sitting-room window, as if she had nothing to do, or think of, or care for. He stood still.

"Ah, Grace," he said, regarding her fixedly.

"Yes, father," she murmured.

"Waiting for your dear husband?" he inquired, speaking with the sarcasm of pitiful affection.

"Oh no – not especially. He has a great many patients to see this afternoon."

Melbury came quite close. "Grace, what's the use of talking like that when you know —? Here, come down and walk with me out in the garden, child."

He unfastened the door in the ivy-laced wall, and waited. This apparent indifference alarmed him. He would far rather that she had rushed in all the fire of jealousy to Hintock House, regardless of conventionality, confronted and attacked Felice Charmond *unguibus et rostro*,[3] and accused her even in exaggerated shape of stealing away her husband. Such a storm might have cleared the air.

She emerged in a minute or two, and they went into the garden together. "You know as well as I do," he resumed, "that there is something threatening mischief to your life, and yet you pretend you do not. Do you suppose I don't see the trouble in your face every day? I am very sure that this quietude is wrong conduct in you. You should look more into matters."

"I am quiet because my sadness is not of a nature to stir me to action."

Melbury wanted to ask her a dozen questions – did she not feel jealous? was she not indignant? – but a natural delicacy restrained him. "You are very tame and let-alone, I am bound to say," he remarked pointedly.

"I am what I feel, father," she repeated.

He glanced at her, and there returned upon his mind the scene of her offering to wed Winterborne instead of Fitzpiers in the last days before her marriage; and he asked himself if it could be the fact that she loved Winterborne now that she had lost him more than she had ever done when she was comparatively free to choose him.

"What would you have me do?" she asked in a low voice.

He recalled his mind from the retrospective pain to the practical matter before them. "I would have you go to Mrs. Charmond," he said.

"Go to Mrs. Charmond – what for?" said she.

"Well – if I must speak plain, dear Grace – to ask her, appeal to her in the name of your common womanhood, and your many like sentiments on things, not to make unhappiness between you and your husband. It lies with her entirely to do one or the other – that I can see."

Grace's face had heated at her father's words, and the very rustle of her skirts upon the box-edging bespoke disdain. "I shall not think of going to her, father – of course, I could not!" she answered.

"Why – don't 'ee want to be happier than you be at present?" said Melbury, more moved on her account than she was herself.

"I don't wish to be more humiliated. If I have anything to bear I can bear it in silence."

"But, my dear maid, you are too young – you don't know what the present state of things may lead to. Just see the harm done a'ready! Your husband would have gone away to Budmouth to a bigger practice if it had not been for this. Although it has gone such a little way it is poisoning your future even now. Mrs. Charmond is thoughtlessly bad, not bad by calculation; and just a word to her now might save 'ee a peck of woes."

"Ah, I loved her once," said Grace with a broken articulation, "and she would not care for me then! Now I no longer love her. Let her do her worst: I don't care."

"You ought to care. You have got into a very good position to start with. You have been well educated, well tended, and you have become the wife of a professional man of unusually good family. Surely you ought to make the best of your position."

"I don't see that I ought. I wish I had never got into it. I wish you had never, never thought of educating me. I wish I worked in the woods like Marty South! I hate genteel life, and I want to be no better than she!"

"Why?" said her amazed father.

"Because cultivation has only brought me inconveniences and troubles. I say again, I wish you had never sent me to those fashionable schools you set your mind on. It all arose out of that, father. If I had stayed at home I should have married —"

She closed up her mouth suddenly and was silent; and he saw that she was not far from crying.

Melbury was much grieved. "What, and would you like to have

grown up as we be here in Hintock – knowing no more, and with no more chance of seeing good life than we have here?"

"Yes. I have never got any happiness outside Hintock that I know of, and I have suffered many a heartache at being sent away. Oh, the misery of those January days when I had got back to school, and left you all here in the wood so happy! I used to wonder why I had to bear it. And I was always a little despised by the other girls at school, because they knew where I came from, and that my parents were not in so good a station as theirs."

Her poor father was much hurt at what he thought her ingratitude and intractability. He had admitted to himself bitterly enough that he should have let young hearts have their way, or rather should have helped on her affection for Winterborne, and given her to him according to his original plan; but he was not prepared for her deprecating those attainments whose completion had been a labour of years, and a severe tax upon his purse.

"Very well," he said with much heaviness of spirit. "If you don't like to go to her I don't wish to force you."

And so the question remained for him still: how should he remedy this perilous state of things? For days he sat in a moody attitude over the fire, a pitcher of cider standing on the hearth beside him, and his drinking-horn inverted upon the top of it. He spent a week and more thus, composing a letter to the chief offender, which he would every now and then attempt to complete, and suddenly crumple up in his hand.[4]

CHAPTER XV

As February merged in March, and lighter evenings broke the gloom of the woodmen's homeward journey, the Hintocks Great and Little began to have ears for a rumour of the events out of which had grown the timber-dealer's troubles.

It took the form of a wide sprinkling of conjecture, wherein no man knew the exact truth. Tantalising phenomena, at once showing and concealing the real relationship of the persons concerned, caused a diffusion of excited surprise. Honest people as the woodlanders were, it was hardly to be expected that they could remain immersed in the study of their trees and gardens amid such circumstances, or sit with their backs turned like the good burghers of Coventry at the passage of the beautiful lady.[1]

Rumour, for a wonder, exaggerated little. There threatened, in fact, in Grace's case as in thousands, the domestic disaster, old as the hills, which, with more or less variation, made a mourner of Ariadne, a by-word of Vashti, and a corpse of Amy Dudley.[2] The incidents were rencounters accidental and contrived, stealthy correspondence, sudden misgivings on one side, sudden self-reproaches on the other. The inner state of the twain was one as of confused noise that would not allow the accents of politic reason to be heard. Determination to go in this direction, and headlong plunges in that; dignified safeguards, undignified collapses; not a single rash step by deliberate intention, and all against judgment.

It was all that Melbury had expected and feared. It was more, for he had overlooked the publicity that would be likely to result, as it now had done. What should he do? Appeal to Mrs. Charmond himself, since Grace would not? He bethought himself of Winterborne, and resolved to consult him, feeling the strong need of some friend of his own sex to whom he might unburden his mind.

He had entirely lost faith in his own judgment. That judgment on which he had relied for so many years seemed recently, like a false companion unmasked, to have disclosed unexpected depths of hypocrisy and speciousness where all had seemed solidity. He felt almost afraid to form a conjecture on the weather, or the time, or the fruit-promise, so great was his self-mistrust.

It was a rimy evening when he set out to look for Giles. The woods seemed to be in a cold sweat; beads of perspiration hung from every bare twig; the sky had no colour, and the trees rose before him as haggard, grey phantoms, whose days of substantiality were passed. Melbury seldom saw Winterborne now, but he believed him to be occupying a lonely hut just beyond the boundary of Mrs. Charmond's estate, though still within the circuit of the woodland. The timber-merchant's thin legs stalked on through the pale damp scenery, his eyes declining on the dead leaves of last year; while every now and then a hasty "ay!" escaped his lips in reply to some bitter mental proposition.

His notice was attracted by a thin blue haze of smoke, behind which arose sounds of voices and chopping: bending his steps that way he saw Winterborne just in front of him.

Though few knew of it, Giles had had a serious illness during the winter; but it just now happened that after being for a long time apathetic and unemployed on that account, he had become one of the busiest men in the neighbourhood. It is often thus; fallen friends, lost sight of, we expect to find starving; we discover them going on fairly well. Without any solicitation, or desire for profit on his part, he had been asked to execute a very large order for hurdles and other copseware, for which purpose he had been obliged to buy several acres of brushwood standing. He was now engaged in the cutting and manufacture of the same, proceeding with the work daily like an automaton.

The hazel-tree did not belie its name to-day. The whole of the copse-wood where the mist had cleared returned purest tints of that hue, amid which Winterborne himself was in the act of making a hurdle, the stakes being driven firmly into the ground in a row, over which he bent and wove the twigs. Beside him was a square, compact pile like the altar of Cain,[3] formed of hurdles already finished, which bristled on all sides with the sharp points of their stakes. At a little distance the men in his employ were assisting him to carry out his contract. Rows of brushwood lay on the ground as it had fallen under the axe; and a shelter had been constructed near at hand, in front of which burnt the fire whose smoke had attracted Melbury. The air was so dank that the smoke hung heavily, and crept away amid the bushes without rising from the ground.

After wistfully regarding the scene a while, Melbury drew nearer, and briefly inquired of Giles how he came to be so busily engaged, with an undertone of slight surprise that Winterborne could recommence thriving, even to this degree, after being deprived of Grace. Melbury was not without emotion at the meeting, for Grace's affairs had divided them, and ended their intimacy of old times.

Winterborne explained just as briefly, without raising his eyes from his occupation of chopping a bough that he held in front of him.

" 'Twill be up in April before you get it all cleared," said Melbury.

"Yes, there or thereabouts," said Winterborne, a chop of the bill-hook jerking the last word into two pieces.

There was another interval; Melbury still looked on, a chip from Winterborne's hook occasionally flying against the waistcoat and legs of his visitor, who took no heed.

"Ah, Giles, you should have been my partner. You should have been my son-in-law," the old man said at last. "It would have been far better for her and for me!"

Winterborne saw that something had gone wrong with his former friend, and, throwing down the switch he was about to interweave, he responded only too readily to the mood of the timber-dealer. "Is she ill?" he said hurriedly.

"No, no." Melbury stood without speaking for some minutes, and then, as though he could not bring himself to proceed, turned to go away.

Winterborne told one of his men to pack up the tools for the night, and walked after Melbury.

"Heaven forbid that I should seem too inquisitive, sir," he said, "especially since we don't stand as we used to stand to one another; but I hope it is well with them all over your way?"

"No," said Melbury, "no."

He stopped, and struck the smooth trunk of a young ash-tree with the flat of his hand. "I would that his ear had been where that rind is!" he exclaimed; "I should have treated him to little compared wi' what he deserves."

"Now," said Winterborne, "don't be in a hurry to go home. I've put some mead down to warm in my shelter here, and we'll sit and drink it and talk this over."

Melbury turned unresistingly as Giles took his arm, and they went back to where the fire was, and sat down under the screen, the other woodmen having gone. He drew out the mead-cup from the ashes, and they drank together.

"Giles, you ought to have had her, as I said just now," repeated Melbury. "I'll tell you why for the first time."

He thereupon told Winterborne, as with great relief, the story of how he won away Giles's father's chosen one – by nothing worse than a lover's cajoleries, it is true; but by means which, except in love, would certainly have been pronounced cruel and unfair. He explained how he had always intended to make reparation to Winterborne the father by giving Grace to Winterborne the son; till the devil tempted him in the person of Fitzpiers and he broke his virtuous vow.

"How highly I thought of that man, to be sure! Who'd have supposed he'd have been so weak and wrong-headed as this! You ought to have had her, Giles, and there's an end on't."

Winterborne knew how to preserve his calm under this unconsciously cruel tearing of a healing wound, to which Melbury's concentration on the more vital subject had blinded him. The young man endeavoured to make the best of the case, for Grace's sake.

"She would hardly have been happy with me," he said, in the dry, unimpassioned voice under which he hid his feelings. "I was not well enough educated: too rough in short. I couldn't have surrounded her with the refinements she looked for, anyhow at all."

"Nonsense – you are quite wrong there," said the unwise old man doggedly. "She told me only this day that she hates refinements and such like. All that my trouble and money bought for her in that way is thrown away upon her quite. She'd fain be like Marty South – think o' that! That's the top of her ambition! Perhaps she's right. Giles, she loved you – under the rind; and what's more she loves ye still – worse luck for the poor maid!"

If Melbury only had known what fires he was recklessly stirring up he might have held his peace. Winterborne was silent a long time. The darkness had closed in round them, and the monotonous drip of the fog from the branches quickened as it turned to fine rain.

"Oh, she never cared much for me," Giles managed to say as he stirred the embers with a brand.

"She did, and does, I tell ye," said the other obstinately. "However, all that's vain talking now. What I come to ask you about is a more practical matter – how to make the best of things as they are. I am thinking of a desperate step – of calling on the woman Charmond. I am going to appeal to her, since Grace will not. 'Tis she who holds the balance in her hands – not he. While she's got the will to lead him astray he will follow – poor unpractical lofty-notioned dreamer – and how long she'll do it depends upon her whim. Did ye ever hear anything about her character before she came to Hintock?"

"She's been a bit of a charmer in her time, I believe," replied Giles, with the same level quietude, as he regarded the red coals. "One who has smiled where she has not loved, and loved where she has not married. Before Mr. Charmond made her his wife she was a play-actress."[4]

"Hey? But how close you have kept all this, Giles! What besides?"

"Mr. Charmond was a rich man engaged in the iron trade in the north – twenty or thirty years older than she. He married her, and retired, and came down here and bought this property."

"Yes, yes – I know all about that. But the other I did not know. I fear it bodes no good. For how can I go and appeal to the forbearance of a woman in this matter who has made cross-loves and crooked entanglements her trade for years? I thank ye, Giles, for finding it out; but it makes my plan the harder that she should have belonged to that unstable tribe!"

Another pause ensued, and they looked gloomily at the smoke that beat about the roof of hurdles through whose weavings a large drop of rain fell at intervals and spat smartly into the fire. Mrs. Charmond had been no friend to Winterborne, but he was manly, and it was not in his heart to let her be condemned without a trial.

"She is said to be generous," he answered. "You might not appeal to her in vain."

"It shall be done," said Melbury, rising. "For good, or for evil, to Mrs. Charmond I'll go."

CHAPTER XVI

At nine o'clock the next morning Melbury dressed himself up in shining broadcloth, creased with folding and smelling of camphor, and started for Hintock House. He was the more impelled to go at once by the absence of his son-in-law in London for a few days, to attend, really or ostensibly, some professional meetings.

He said nothing of his destination either to his wife or to Grace, fearing that they might entreat him to abandon so risky a project; and went out unobserved. He had chosen his time with a view, as he supposed, of conveniently catching Mrs. Charmond when she had just finished her breakfast, before any other business people should be about, if any came. Plodding thoughtfully onward he crossed a glade lying between Little Hintock Woods and the plantation which abutted on the park. The spot being open he was discerned there by Winterborne from the copse on the next hill, where he and his men were working. Knowing his mission the younger man hastened down from the copse and managed to intercept the timber-merchant.

"I have been thinking of this, sir," he said, "and I am of opinion that it would be best to put off your visit for the present."

But Melbury would not even stop to hear him. His mind was fixed, the appeal was to be made; and Winterborne stood and watched him sadly till he entered the second plantation and disappeared.

Melbury rang at the tradesmen's door of the manor-house, and was at once informed that the lady was not yet visible, as indeed he might have guessed had he been anybody but the man he was. Melbury said he would wait, whereupon the young page informed him in a neighbourly way that, between themselves, she was in bed and asleep.

"Never mind," said Melbury, retreating into the court, "I'll stand about here." Charged so fully with his mission he shrank from contact with anybody.

But he walked about the paved court till he was tired, and nobody came to him. He entered the house, and sat down in a small waiting-room, from which he got glimpses of the kitchen-corridor, and of the white-capped maids flitting jauntily hither and thither. They had heard of his arrival, but had not seen him enter, and, imagining him still in the court, discussed freely the possible reason of his calling. They marvelled at his temerity; for though most of the tongues which had been let loose attributed the chief blame to Fitzpiers, these of her household preferred to regard their mistress as the deeper sinner.

Melbury sat with his hands resting on the familiar knobbed thorn walking-stick, whose growing he had seen before he enjoyed its use. The scene to him was not the material environment of his person, but a tragic vision that travelled with him like an envelope. Through this vision the incidents of the moment but gleamed confusedly here and there, as an outer landscape through the high-coloured scenes of a stained window.

He waited thus an hour, an hour and a half, two hours. He began to look pale and ill, whereupon the butler, who came in, asked him to have a glass of wine.

Melbury roused himself, and said "No, no. Is she almost ready?"

"She is just finishing breakfast," said the butler. "She will soon see you now. I am just going up to tell her you are here."

"What, haven't you told her before?" said Melbury.

"Oh, no," said the other. "You see you came so very early."

At last the bell rang: Mrs. Charmond could see him. She was not in her private sitting-room when he reached it, but in a minute he heard her coming from the front staircase, and she entered where he stood.

At this time of the morning Mrs. Charmond looked her full age and more. She might almost have been taken for the typical *femme de trente ans*,[1] though she was really not more than seven or eight and twenty. But the *édition définitive*[2] of her beauty had been reached, even if it were not a little worn.

There being no fire in the room she came in with a shawl thrown loosely round her shoulders, and obviously without the least suspicion that Melbury had called upon any other errand than timber. Felice was, indeed, the only woman in the parish who had not heard the rumour of her own weaknesses; she was at this moment living in a fool's paradise in respect of that rumour, though not in respect of the weaknesses themselves, which, if the truth be told, caused her grave misgivings.

"Do sit down, Mr. Melbury. You have felled all the trees that were to be purchased by you this season, except the oaks, I believe?"

"Yes, yes," said Melbury in a reverie.

He did not take a chair, and she also remained standing. Resting upon his stick he began: "Mrs. Charmond, I have called upon a more serious matter – at least to me – than tree-throwing. And whatever mistakes I make in my manner of speaking upon it to you, madam, do me the justice to set 'em down to my want of practice, and not to my want of care."

Mrs. Charmond looked ill at ease. She might have begun to guess his meaning; but apart from that she had such dread of contact with anything painful, harsh, or even earnest, that his preliminaries alone were enough to distress her.

"Yes, what is it?" she said quickly.

"I am an old man," said Melbury, "whom, somewhat late in life, God thought fit to bless with one child, and she a daughter. Her mother was a very dear wife to me; but she was taken away from us when the child was young; and the child became precious as the apple of my eye to me, for she was all I had left to love. For her sake entirely I married as second wife a homespun woman who had been kind as a mother to her. In due time the question of her education came on; and I said, 'I will educate the maid well, if I live upon bread to do it.' Of her possible marriage I could not bear to think, for it seemed like a death that she should cleave to another man, and grow to think his house her home rather than mine. But I saw it was the law of nature that this should be, and that it was for the maid's happiness that she should have a home when I was gone; and I made up my mind without a murmur to help it on for her sake. In my youth I had wronged my dead friend, and to make amends I determined to give her, my most precious possession, to my friend's son, seeing that they liked each other well. Things came about which made me doubt if it would be for my daughter's happiness to do this, inasmuch as the young man was poor, and she was delicately reared. Another man came and paid court to her – one her equal in breeding and accomplishments; in every way it seemed to me that he only could give her the home which her training had made a necessity almost. I urged her on, and she married him. But, ma'am, a fatal mistake was at the root of my reckoning: I found that this well-born gentleman I had calculated on so surely was not staunch of heart, and that therein lay a danger of great sorrow for my daughter. Madam, he saw you, and you know the rest . . . I have come to make no demands – to utter no threats; I have come simply as a father in great grief about his only child, and I beseech you to deal kindly with my daughter and to do nothing which can turn her husband's heart away from her for ever! Forbid him your presence, ma'am, and speak to him on his duty, as one with your power over him well can do: and I am hopeful that the rent between them may be patched up. For it is not as if you would lose by so doing; your course is far higher than the courses of a professional man; and the gratitude you would win from me and mine by your kindness is more than I can say."

Mrs. Charmond had first rushed into a mood of indignation, on comprehending Melbury's story: hot and cold by turns she had murmured, "Leave me, leave me!" But, as he seemed to take no notice of this, his words began to influence her, and when he ceased speaking she said with hurried breath, "What has led you to think this of me? Who says I have won your daughter's husband away from her? Some monstrous calumnies are afloat – of which I have known nothing until now!"

Melbury started, and looked at her simply: "But surely, ma'am, you know the truth better than I?"

Her features became a little pinched, and the touches of powder on her handsome face for the first time showed themselves as an extrinsic film.

"Will you leave me to myself?" she said with a faintness which suggested a guilty conscience. "This is so utterly unexpected – you obtain admission to my presence by misrepresentation –"

"As God's in heaven, ma'am, that's not true. I made no pretence;

and I thought in reason you would know why I had come. This gossip – "

"I have heard nothing of it. Tell me the gist of it, pray!"

"Tell you, ma'am – not I. What the gossip is, no matter. What really is, you know. Set facts right, and the scandal will right of itself. But pardon me – I speak roughly; and I came to speak gently, to coax you, beg you to be my daughter's friend. She loved you once, ma'am; you began by liking her. Then you dropped her without a reason, and it hurt her warm heart more than I can tell ye. But you were within your right as the superior,[3] no doubt. But if you would consider her position now – surely, surely, you would do her no harm!"

"Certainly I would do her no harm – I –"

Melbury's eye met hers. It was curious, but the allusion to Grace's former love for her seemed to touch her more than all Melbury's other arguments. "Oh, Melbury," she burst out, "you have made me so unhappy! How could you come to me like this! It is too dreadful! Now go away – go, go!"

"I will, and leave you to think," he said, in a husky tone.

As soon as he was out of the room she went to a corner and there sat and writhed, under an emotion in which hurt pride and vexation mingled with better sentiments.

Mrs. Charmond's mobile spirit was subject to these fierce periods of high tide and storm. She had never so clearly perceived till now that her soul was being slowly invaded by a delirium which had brought about all this; that she was losing judgment and dignity under it, becoming an animated impulse only, a passion incarnate. A fascination had led her on; it was as if she had been seized by a hand of velvet; and this was where she found herself – overshadowed with sudden night, as if a tornado had passed.

While she sat, or rather crouched, unhinged by the interview, lunch-time came, and then the early afternoon, almost without her consciousness. Then "a strange gentleman who says it is not necessary to give his name," was suddenly announced.

Felice knew who the strange gentleman was – that Continental follower on whom she had once smiled. But to meet another lover now – the thought made her sick.

"I cannot see him, whoever he may be. I am not at home to anybody."

She heard no more of her visitor; and shortly after, in an attempt to recover some mental serenity by violent physical exercise, she put on her hat and cloak and went out of doors, taking a path which led her up the slopes to the nearest spur of the wood. She disliked the woods, but they had the advantage of being a place in which she could walk comparatively unobserved.

CHAPTER XVII

There was agitation that day in the lives of all whom these matters concerned. It was not till the Hintock dinner-time – one o'clock – that Grace discovered her father's absence from the house after a departure in the morning under somewhat unusual conditions. By a little reasoning and inquiry she was able to divine his errand.

Her husband was absent, and her father did not return. He had, in truth, gone on to Sherton after the interview, but this Grace did not know. In an indefinite dread that something serious would arise out of Melbury's visit by reason of the inequalities of temper and nervous irritation to which he was subject, something possibly that would bring her much more misery than accompanied her present negative state of mind, she left the house about three o'clock, and took a loitering walk in the woodland track by which she imagined he would come home. This track under the bare trees and over the cracking sticks, screened and roofed in from the outer world of wind by a network of boughs, led her slowly on till in time she had left the larger trees behind her and swept round into the coppice where Winterborne and his men were clearing the undergrowth.

Had Giles's attention been concentrated on his hurdles he would not have seen her, but ever since Melbury's passage across the opposite glade in the morning he had been as uneasy and unsettled as Grace herself; and her advent now was the one appearance which, since her father's avowal, could arrest him more than Melbury's return with his tidings. Fearing that something might be the matter he hastened up to her.

She had not seen her old lover for a long time, and too conscious of the late pranks of her heart she could not behold him calmly. "I am only looking for my father," she said in an unnecessary tone of apology.

"I was looking for him too," said Giles. "I think he may perhaps have gone on further."

"Then you knew he was going to the House, Giles?" she said, turning her large tender eyes anxiously upon him. "Did he tell you what for?"

Winterborne glanced doubtingly at her, and then softly hinted that her father had visited him the evening before, and that their old friendship was quite restored; on which she guessed the rest.

"Oh, I am glad indeed that you two are friends again!" she cried.

And then they stood facing each other, fearing each other, troubling each other's souls. Grace experienced acute regret at the sight of these wood-cutting scenes, because she had estranged herself from them; craving, even to its defects and inconveniences, that homely sylvan life of her father which in the best probable succession of events would shortly be denied her.

At a little distance, on the edge of the clearing, Marty South was shaping spar-gads to take home for manufacture during the evenings. Winterborne and Mrs. Fitzpiers stood looking at her in their mutual embarrassment at each other's presence, and while doing so they beheld, approaching the girl, a lady in a dark fur mantle and black hat, having a white veil tied picturesquely round it. She spoke to Marty, who turned and curtsied, and the lady fell into conversation with her. It was Mrs. Charmond.

On leaving her house, Mrs. Charmond had walked on under the fret and fever[1] of her mind with more vigour than she was accustomed to show in her normal moods – a fever which the solace of a cigarette did not entirely allay. Reaching the coppice, she had listlessly observed

Marty at work, when she threw away her cigarette, and drew near. Chop, chop, chop, went Marty's little bill-hook with never more assiduity, till Mrs. Charmond spoke.

"Who is that young lady I see talking to the woodman yonder?" she asked.

"Mrs. Fitzpiers, ma'am," said Marty.

"Oh," said Mrs. Charmond, with something like a start; for she had not recognised Grace at that distance. "And the man she is talking to?"

"That's Mr. Winterborne."

A redness stole into Mary's face as she mentioned Giles's name, which Mrs. Charmond did not fail to notice. "Are you engaged to him?" she asked softly.

"No, ma'am," said Marty. "*She* was once; and I think – "

But Marty could not possibly explain the complications of her thought on this matter – which was nothing less than one of extraordinary acuteness for a girl so young and inexperienced – namely, that she saw danger to two hearts, naturally honest, in Grace being thrown back into Winterborne's society by the neglect of her husband. Mrs. Charmond, however, with the almost supersensory means to knowledge which women have on such occasions, quite understood what Marty had intended to convey; and the picture thus exhibited to her of lives drifting awry, involving the wreck of poor Marty's hopes, prompted her to more generous resolves than all Melbury's remonstrances had been able to stimulate.

Full of the new feeling she bade the girl good afternoon, and went on over the stumps of hazel to where Grace and Winterborne were standing. They saw her approach, and Winterborne said, "She is coming to you; it is a good omen. She dislikes me, so I'll go away."

He accordingly retreated to where he had been working before Grace came, and Grace's formidable rival approached her, each woman taking the other's measure as she drew near.

"Dear – Mrs. Fitzpiers!" said Felice Charmond with some inward turmoil which stopped her speech. "I have not seen you for a long time."

She held out her hand tentatively, while Grace stood like a wild animal on first confronting a mirror[2] or other puzzling product of civilisation. Was it really Mrs. Charmond speaking to her thus? If it was she could no longer form any guess as to what life signified.

"I want to talk to you," said Mrs. Charmond sensitively, for the gaze of the young woman had chilled her through. "Can you walk on with me till we are quite alone?"

Sick with distaste Grace nevertheless complied, as by clockwork, and they moved evenly side by side into the deeper recesses of the woods. They went further, much further than Mrs. Charmond had meant to go; but mental indiscipline hindered her from beginning her conversation, and in default of it she kept walking.

"I have seen your father," she at length resumed. "And – I am much troubled by what he told me."

"What did he tell you? I have not been admitted to his confidence on anything he may have said to you."

"Nevertheless, why should I repeat to you what you can easily divine?"

"True – true," returned Grace mournfully. "Why should you repeat what we both know to be in our minds already?"

"Mrs. Fitzpiers, your husband – "

The moment that the speaker's tongue touched the dangerous subject a vivid look of self-consciousness flashed over her; in which her heart revealed, as by a lightning gleam, what filled it to overflowing. So transitory was the expression that none but a quick-sensed woman, and she in Grace's position, would have had the power to catch its meaning. Upon her the phase was not lost.

"Then you *do* love him!" she exclaimed in a tone of much surprise.

"What do you mean, my young friend?"

"Why," cried Grace, "I thought till now that you had only been cruelly flirting with my husband to amuse your idle moments – a rich lady with a poor professional gentleman whom in her heart she despised not much less than her who belongs to him. But I guess from your manner that you love him desperately; and I don't hate you as I did before . . . Yes, indeed," continued Mrs. Fitzpiers, with a trembling tongue, "since it is not playing in your case at all, but *real* – oh, I do pity you, more than I despise you! For *you* will s-s-suffer most!"

Mrs. Charmond was now as much agitated as Grace. "I ought not to allow myself to argue with you!" she exclaimed. "I demean myself by doing it. But I liked you once, and for the sake of that time I try to tell you how mistaken you are!"

Much of her confusion resulted from her wonder and alarm at finding herself, in a sense, dominated mentally and emotionally by this simple schoolgirl. "I do not love him!" she went on with desperate untruth. "It was a kindness – my making somewhat more of him than one usually does of one's doctor. I was lonely; I talked – well, I trifled with him. I am very sorry if such child's play, out of pure friendship, has been a serious matter to you. Who could have expected it? But the world is so simple here!"

"Oh, that's affectation," said Grace shaking her head. "It is no use – you *love* him. I can see in your face that in this matter of my husband you have not let your acts belie your feelings. During these last four or six months you have been terribly indiscreet, but you have not been insincere; and that almost disarms me."

"I *have* been insincere – if you will have the word – I mean I *have* coquetted, and do *not* love him!"

But Grace clung to her position like a limpet. "You may have trifled with others; but him you love as you never loved another man."

"Oh, well – I won't argue," said Mrs. Charmond, laughing faintly. "And you come to reproach me for it, child?"

"No," said Grace magnanimously. "You may go on loving him if you like – I don't mind at all. You'll find it, let me tell you, a bitterer business for yourself than for me in the end. He'll get tired of you soon, as tired as can be – you don't know him so well as I! – and then you may wish you had never seen him!"

Mrs. Charmond had grown quite pale and weak under this prophecy. It was extraordinary that Grace, whom almost every one would have characterised as a gentle girl, should be of tougher fibre than her interlocutor.

"You exaggerate – cruel, silly young woman," she reiterated, writhing with little agonies. "It is nothing but playful friendship – nothing! It will be proved by my future conduct. I shall at once refuse to see him more – since it will make no difference to my heart, and much to my name."

"I question if you will refuse to see him again," said Grace dryly, as she bent a sapling down. "But I am not incensed against you as you are against me," she added, abandoning the tree to its natural perpendicular. "Before I came I had been despising you for wanton cruelty; now I only pity you for misplaced affection. When Edred has gone out of the house in hope of seeing you, at seasonable hours and unseasonable; when I have found him riding miles and miles across the country at midnight, and risking his life, and getting covered with mud, to get a glimpse of you, I have called him a foolish man – the plaything of a finished coquette. I thought that what was getting to be a tragedy to me was a comedy to you. But now I see that tragedy lies on your side of the situation no less than on mine, and more; that if I have felt trouble at my position you have felt anguish at yours; that if I have had disappointments you have had despairs. Heaven may fortify me – God help you!"

"I cannot attempt to reply to your ravings," returned the other, struggling to restore a dignity which had completely collapsed. "My acts will be my proofs. In the world which you have seen nothing of, friendships between men and women are not unknown; and it would have been better both for you and your father if you had each judged me more respectfully, and left me alone. As it is, I wish never, never to see or speak to you, madam, any more."

Grace bowed, and Mrs. Charmond turned away. The two went apart in directly opposite courses, and were soon hidden from each other by their umbrageous surroundings and by the shadows of eve.

In the excitement of their long argument they had walked onward and zigzagged about without regarding direction or distance. All sound of the woodcutters had long since faded into remoteness, and even had not the interval been too great for hearing them they would have been silent and homeward bound at this twilight hour.

But Grace went on her course without any misgiving, though there was much underwood here with only the narrowest passages for walking, across which brambles hung. She had not, however, traversed this, the wildest, part of the wood since her childhood, and the transformation of outlines had been great; old trees which once were landmarks had been felled or blown down, and the bushes which then had been small and scrubby were now large and overhanging. She soon found that her ideas as to direction were vague – that she had indeed no ideas as to direction at all. If the evening had not been growing so dark, and the wind had not put on its night-moan so distinctly, Grace would not have minded; but she was rather frightened now, and began to strike across hither and thither in random courses.

Denser grew the darkness, more developed the wind-voices, and still no recognisable spot or outlet of any kind appeared, nor any sound of the Hintocks floated near, though she had wandered probably between one and two hours, and began to be weary. She was vexed at her foolishness, since the ground she had covered, if in a straight line, must inevitably have taken her out of the wood to some remote village or other; but she had wasted her forces in countermarches; and now, in much alarm, wondered if she would have to pass the night here.

She stood still to meditate, and fancied that between the soughing of the wind she heard shuffling footsteps on the leaves heavier than those of rabbits or other startled "beasts of beating heart" who lived there. Though fearing at first to meet anybody on the chance of his being a friend, she decided that her fellow-noctambulist, even if a poacher, would not injure her, and that he might possibly be some one sent to search for her. She accordingly shouted a rather timid "Hoi!"

The cry was immediately returned by the other person; and Grace running at once in the direction whence it came beheld an indistinct figure hastening up to her as rapidly. They were almost in each other's arms before she recognised the outline and white veil of her whom she had parted from an hour and a half before – Mrs. Charmond.

"I have lost my way, I have lost my way," cried the latter. "Oh – is it indeed you? I am so glad to meet you or anybody. I have been wandering up and down ever since we parted, and am nearly dead with terror and misery and fatigue!"

"So am I," said Grace. "What shall we do?"

"You won't go away from me?" asked her companion anxiously.

"No, indeed. Are you very tired?"

"I can scarcely move, and I am scratched dreadfully about the ankles."

Grace reflected. "Perhaps, as it is dry under foot, the best thing for us to do would be to sit down for half an hour, and then start again when we have thoroughly rested. By walking straight we must come to a track leading somewhere, before the morning."

They found a clump of bushy hollies which afforded a shelter from the wind, and sat down under it, some tufts of dead fern, crisp and dry, that remained from the previous season, forming a sort of nest for them. But it was cold, nevertheless, on this March night, particularly for Grace, who, with the sanguine prematureness of youth in matters of dress, had considered it spring-time, and hence was not so warmly clad as Mrs. Charmond, who still wore her winter furs.

But after sitting awhile the latter lady shivered no less than Grace as the warmth imparted by her hasty walking began to go off; and they felt the cold air drawing through the holly leaves which scratched their backs and shoulders. Moreover they could hear some drops of rain falling on the trees, though none reached the nook in which they had ensconced themselves.

"If we were to cling close together," said Mrs. Charmond, "we should keep each other warm. But," she added in an uneven voice, "I suppose you won't come near me for the world!"

"Why not?"

"Because – well, you know."

"Yes I will – I don't hate you at all."

They consequently crept up to one another, and being in the dark, lonely, and weary, did what neither had dreamed of doing beforehand – clasped each other closely. Mrs. Charmond's furs consoled Grace's cold face; and each one's body, as she breathed, alternately heaved against that of her companion; while the funereal trees rocked, and chanted dirges unceasingly.

When a few minutes had been spent thus Mrs. Charmond said – "I am so wretched!" in a heavy emotional whisper.

"You are frightened," said Grace kindly. "But there is nothing to fear; I know these woods well."

"I am not at all frightened at the wood; but I am at other things."

Mrs. Charmond embraced Grace more and more tightly, and bowed her head upon that of her companion. The younger woman could feel her neighbour's breathings grow deeper and more spasmodic, as though uncontrollable feelings were germinating.

"After I had left you," Felice went on, "I regretted something I had said. I have to make a confession – I must make it!" she whispered brokenly, the instinct to indulge in warmth of sentiment which had led this woman of passions to respond to Fitzpiers in the first place leading her now to find luxurious comfort in opening her heart to his wife. "I said to you I could give him up without pain or deprivation – that he had only been my pastime. That was absolutely untrue – it was said to deceive you. I could not do it without much pain; and what is more dreadful I cannot give him up – even if I would – of myself alone."

"Why? Because you love him, you mean."

Felice Charmond denoted assent by a movement.

"I knew I was right!" said Grace exaltedly. "But that should not deter you," she presently added in a moral tone. "Oh, do struggle against it, and you will conquer!"

"You are so simple, so simple!" cried Felice. "You think, because you guessed my assumed indifference to him to be a sham, that you know the extremes that people are capable of going to! But a good deal more may have been going on than you have fathomed with all your insight. I *cannot* give him up until he chooses to give up me."

"But surely you are the superior in station and in every way, and the cut must come from you."

"Tchut! Must I tell verbatim, you simple child? Oh, I suppose I must! It will eat away my heart if I do not let out all, after meeting you like this and finding how guileless you are!"

She thereupon whispered a few words in the girl's ear, and burst into a violent fit of sobbing.

Grace started roughly away from the shelter of the furs, and sprang to her feet.

"Oh, my great heaven!" she exclaimed thunderstruck at a revelation transcending her utmost suspicion.[3] "Can it be – can it be!"

She turned as if to hasten away. But Felice Charmond's sobs came to her ear: deep darkness circled her about, the cold lips of the wind kissed her where Mrs. Charmond's warm fur had been, and she did not know which way to go. After the moment of energy she felt mild again, and turned to the motionless woman at her feet.

"Are you rested?" she asked, in what seemed her own voice grown ten years older.

Without an answer Mrs. Charmond slowly rose.

"You mean to betray me!" she said out of the bitterest depths of her soul. "Oh, fool, fool I!"

"No," said Grace shortly. "I mean no such thing. But let us be quick now. We have a serious undertaking before us. Think of nothing but going straight on."

They walked on in profound silence, pulling back boughs now growing wet, and treading down woodbine, but still keeping a pretty straight course. Grace began to be thoroughly worn out, and her companion too, when, on a sudden, they broke into the deserted highway at the hill-top, on which the Sherton man had waited for Mrs. Dollery's van. Grace recognised the spot as soon as she looked around her.

"How we have got here I cannot tell," she said with cold civility. "We have made a complete circuit of Little Hintock. The hazel copse is quite on the other side. Now we have only to follow the road."

They dragged themselves onward, turned into the lane, passed the track to Little Hintock, and so reached the park.

"Here I turn back," said Grace in the same passionless voice. "You are quite near home."

Mrs. Charmond stood inert, seeming appalled by her late admission.

"I have told you something in a moment of irresistible desire to unburden my soul, which all but a fool would have kept silent as the grave," she said. "I cannot help it now. Is it to be a secret, or do you mean war?"

"A secret, certainly," said Grace mournfully. "How can you expect war from such a helpless, wretched being as I!"

"And I'll do my best not to see him. I am his slave; but I'll try."

Grace was naturally kind, but she could not help using a small dagger now.

'Pray don't distress yourself," she said with exquisitely fine scorn. "You may see him as much as you like – for me." Had she been wounded instead of mortified she could not have used the words; but Fitzpiers's hold upon her heart just now was slight.

They parted thus and there,[4] and Grace went moodily homeward. Passing Marty's cottage she observed through the window that the girl was writing instead of chopping as usual, and wondered what her correspondence could be. Directly afterwards she met people in search of her, and reached the house to find all in serious alarm. She soon explained that she had lost her way, and her general depression was attributed to exhaustion on that account.

Could she have known what Marty was writing she would have been surprised.

The rumour which agitated the other folk of Hintock had reached the young girl, and she was penning a letter to Fitzpiers, to tell him that Mrs. Charmond's magnificent pile of hair was made up of the writer's more largely than of her own. It was poor Marty's only card, and she played it, knowing nothing of fashion, and thinking her revelation a fatal one for a lover.

VOLUME III

CHAPTER I

It was at the beginning of April, a few days after the meeting between Grace and Mrs. Charmond in the wood, that Fitzpiers, just returned from London, was travelling from Sherton Abbas to Hintock in a hired carriage. In his eye there was a doubtful light, and the lines of his refined face showed a vague disquietude. He appeared now like one of those who strike the beholder as having suffered wrong in being born.

His position was in truth gloomy, and to his impressible mind it seemed even gloomier than it was. His practice had been slowly dwindling of late, and now threatened to die out altogether, the undaunted old Dr. Jones capturing patients up to Fitzpiers's very door. Fitzpiers knew only too well the latest and greatest cause of his unpopularity; and yet, so illogical is man, the second branch of his sadness grew out of a remedial measure proposed for the first – a letter from Felice Charmond imploring him not to see her again. To bring about their severance still more effectually, she added, she had decided during his absence upon almost immediate departure for the Continent.

The time was that dull interval in a woodlander's life which coincides with great activity in the life of the woodland itself – a period following the close of the winter tree-cutting, and preceding the barking season, when the saps are just beginning to heave with the force of hydraulic lifts inside all the trunks of the forest.

Winterborne's contract was completed, and the plantations were deserted. It was dusk: there were no leaves as yet: the nightingales would not begin to sing for a fortnight; and the Mother of the Months[1] was in her most attenuated phase – starved and bent to a mere bowed skeleton, which glided along behind the bare twigs in Fitzpiers's company.

When he reached home he went straight up to his wife's sitting-room.

He found it deserted, and without a fire. He had mentioned no day for his return: nevertheless he wondered why she was not there waiting to receive him.

On descending to the other wing of the house and inquiring of Mrs. Melbury he learnt with much surprise that Grace had gone on a visit to an acquaintance at Shottsford-Forum, three days earlier: that tidings had on this morning reached her father of her being very unwell there, in consequence of which he had ridden over to see her.

Fitzpiers went up stairs again, and the little drawing-room, now lighted by a solitary candle, was not rendered more cheerful by the entrance of Grammer Oliver with an apron full of wood which she threw on the hearth while she raked out the grate and rattled about the fire-irons, with a view to making things comfortable. Fitzpiers considered that Grace ought to have let him know her plans more accurately before leaving home in a freak like this. He went desultorily to the window, the blind of which had not been pulled down, and looked out at the thin, fast-sinking moon, and at the tall stalk of smoke rising from the top of Suke Damson's chimney, signifying that the young woman had just lit her fire to prepare supper.

He became conscious of a discussion in progress on the opposite side of the court. Somebody had looked over the wall to talk to the sawyers, and was telling them in a loud voice news in which the name of Mrs. Charmond soon arrested his ears.

"Grammer, don't make so much noise with that grate," said the surgeon: at which Grammer reared herself upon her knees and held the fuel suspended in her hand, while Fitzpiers half opened the window.

"She is off to foreign lands again at last – hev made up her mind quite sudden-like – and it is thoughted she'll leave in a day or two. She's been all as if her mind were low for some days past – with a sort of sorrow in her face, as if she reproached her own soul. She's the wrong sort of woman for Hintock – hardly knowing a beech from a woak – that I own. But I don't care who the man is, she's been a very kind friend to me."

"Well – the day after to-morrow is the Sabbath day, and without charity we are but tinkling simples;[2] but this I do say, that her going will be a blessed thing for a certain married couple who remain."

The fire was lighted, and Fitzpiers sat down in front of it, restless as the last leaf upon a tree. "A sort of sorrow in her face, as if she reproached her own soul." Poor, poor Felice!

How her frame must be pulsing under the conditions of which he had just heard the caricature; how her fair temples must ache; what a mood of wretchedness she must be in! But for this mixing up of his name with hers, and her determination to sunder their too close acquaintance on that account, she would probably have sent for him professionally. She was now sitting alone, suffering, perhaps wishing she had not forbidden him to come again.

Unable to remain in this lonely room any longer, or to wait for the meal which was in course of preparation, he made himself ready for riding, descended to the yard, stood by the stable-door while Darling was being saddled, and rode off down the lane. He would have preferred walking, but was weary with his day's travel.

As he approached the door of Marty South's cottage, which it was necessary to pass on his way, she came from the porch as if she had been awaiting him, and met him in the middle of the road, holding up a letter. Fitzpiers took it without stopping, and asked over his shoulder from whom it came.

Marty hesitated. "From me," she said shyly, though with noticeable firmness.

This letter contained, in fact, Marty's declaration that she was the original owner of Mrs. Charmond's supplementary locks, and inclosed a sample from the native stock, which had grown considerably by this time. It was her long contemplated apple of discord,[3] and much her hand trembled as she handed the document up to him.

But it was impossible on account of the gloom for Fitzpiers to read it then, while he had the curiosity to do so; and he put it in his pocket. His imagination having already centred itself on Hintock House, in his pocket the letter remained unopened and forgotten, all the while that Marty was hopefully picturing its excellent weaning effect upon him.

He was not long in reaching the precincts of the manor-house. He drew rein under a group of dark oaks commanding a view of the front, and reflected a while. His entry would not be altogether unnatural in the circumstances of her possible indisposition; but upon the whole he thought it best to avoid riding up to the door. By silently approaching he could retreat unobserved in the event of her not being alone. He dismounted, hitched Darling to a stray bough hanging a little below the general browsing line of the trees, and proceeded to the door on foot.

In the meantime Melbury had returned from Shottsford-Forum. The great court or quadrangle of the timber-merchant's house, divided from the shady lane by an ivy-covered wall, was entered by two white gates, one standing near each extremity of the wall. It had so happened that at the moment when Fitzpiers was riding out at the lower gate on his way to the manor-house, Melbury was approaching the upper gate to enter it. Fitzpiers being in front of Melbury was seen by the latter, but the surgeon, never turning his head, did not observe his father-in-law, ambling up slowly and silently under the trees, though his horse too was a grey one.

"How is Grace?" said his wife, as soon as he entered.

Melbury looked gloomy. "She is not at all well," he said. "I don't like the looks of her at all. I couldn't bear the notion of her staying away in a strange place any longer, and I begged her to let me get her home. At last she agreed to it, but not till after much persuading. I was then sorry that I rode over instead of driving; but I have hired a nice comfortable carriage – the easiest-going I could get – and she'll be here in a couple of hours or less: I rode on ahead to tell you to get her room ready; but I see her husband has come back."

"Yes," said Mrs. Melbury. She expressed her concern that her husband had hired a carriage all the way from Shottsford. "What it will cost!" she said.

"I don't care what it costs!" he exclaimed testily. "I was determined to get her home. Why she went away I can't think! She acts in a way that is not at all likely to mend matters as far as I can see." Grace had not told her father of her interview with Mrs. Charmond, and the disclosure that had been whispered in her startled ear.

"Since Edred is come," he continued, "he might have waited in till I got back, to ask me how she was, if only for a compliment. I saw him go out: where is he gone?"

Mrs. Melbury did not know positively; but she told her husband that there was not much doubt about the place of his first visit after an absence. She had, in fact, seen Fitzpiers take the direction of the manor-house.

Melbury said no more. It was exasperating to him that just at this moment, when there was every reason for Fitzpiers to stay in doors, or at any rate to ride along the Shottsford road to meet his ailing wife, he should be doing despite to her by going elsewhere. The old man went out of doors again; and, his horse being hardly unsaddled as yet, he told Upjohn to re-tighten the girths; he again mounted, and rode off at the heels of the surgeon.

By the time that Melbury reached the park he was prepared to go any lengths in combating this rank and reckless errantry of his daughter's husband. He would fetch home Edred Fitzpiers to-night by some means, rough or fair: in his view there could come of his interference nothing worse than what existed at present. And yet to every bad there is a worse.

He had entered by the bridle-gate which admitted to the park on this side, and cantered over the soft turf almost in the tracks of Fitzpiers's horse, till he reached the clump of trees under which his precursor had halted. The whitish object that was indistinctly visible here in the gloom of the boughs he found to be Darling, as left by Fitzpiers.

"D— him! why did he not ride up to the house in an honest way?" said Melbury.

He profited by Fitzpiers's example: dismounting, he tied his horse under an adjoining tree, and went on to the house on foot, as the other had done. He was no longer disposed to stick at trifles in his investigation, and did not hesitate to gently open the front door without ringing.

The large square hall, with its oak floor, staircase, and wainscot, was lighted by a dim lamp hanging from a beam. Not a soul was visible. He went into the corridor and listened at a door which he knew to be that of the drawing-room; there was no sound, and on turning the handle he found the room empty. A fire burning low in the grate was the sole light of the apartment: its beams flashed mockingly on the somewhat showy Versaillese⁴ furniture and gilding here, in style as unlike that of the structural parts of the building as it was possible to be, and probably introduced by Felice to counteract the fine old English gloom of the place. Disappointed in his hope of confronting his son-in-law here, he went on to the dining-room, which was without light or fire, and pervaded by a cold atmosphere, which signified that she had not dined there that day.

By this time Melbury's mood had a little mollified. Everything here was so pacific, so unaggressive in its repose, that he was no longer incited to provoke a collision with Fitzpiers or with anybody. The comparative stateliness of the apartments influenced him to an emotion, rather than to a belief, that where all was outwardly so good and proper there could not be quite that delinquency within which he had suspected. It occurred to him, too, that even if his suspicion were justified, his abrupt, if not unwarrantable, entry into the house might end in confounding its inhabitant at the expense of his daughter's dignity and his own. Any ill result would be pretty sure to hit Grace hardest in the long run. He would, after all, adopt the more rational course, and plead with Fitzpiers privately, as he had pleaded with Mrs. Charmond.

He accordingly retreated as silently as he had come. Passing the door of the drawing-room anew he fancied that he heard a noise within, which was not the crackling of the fire. Melbury gently re-opened the door to a distance of a few inches, and saw at the opposite window two figures in the act of stepping out – a man and a woman – in whom he recognised the lady of the house and his son-in-law. In a moment they had disappeared amid the gloom of the lawn.

He returned into the hall, and let himself out by the carriage-entrance door, coming round to the lawn-front in time to see the two figures parting at the railing which divided the precincts of the house from the open park.

Mrs. Charmond turned to hasten back immediately that her lover had left her side; and Fitzpiers going onward was speedily absorbed into the duskiness of the trees.

Melbury waited till Mrs. Charmond had re-entered the drawing-room, and then followed after Fitzpiers. He would allow the latter to mount and ride ahead a little way before overtaking him, and giving him a piece of his mind. His son-in-law might possibly see the second horse near his own; but that would do him no harm, and might prepare him for what he was to expect.

The event however, was different from the plan. On plunging into the thick shade of the clump of oaks, he could not perceive his horse Blossom anywhere; but feeling his way carefully along, he by and by discerned Fitzpiers's mare Darling still standing as before under the adjoining tree. For a moment Melbury thought that his own horse, being young and strong, had broken away from her fastening; but on listening intently he could hear her ambling comfortably along a little way ahead, and a creaking of the saddle, which showed that she had a rider. Walking on as far as the small gate in the corner of the park, he met a labourer who, in reply to Melbury's inquiry if he had seen any person on a grey horse, said that he had only met Dr. Fitzpiers.

It was just what Melbury had begun to suspect: Fitzpiers had mounted the mare which did not belong to him in mistake for his own – an oversight easily explicable, in a man ever unwitting in horse-flesh, by the darkness of the spot, and the near similarity of the animals in appearance, though Melbury's was readily enough seen to be the greyer horse by day.

He hastened back, and did what seemed best in the circumstances – got upon old Darling, and rode rapidly after Fitzpiers.

Melbury had just entered the wood, and was winding along the cart-way which led through it, channelled deep in the leaf-mould with large ruts that were formed by the timber-waggons in fetching the spoil of the plantations, when all at once he descried in front, at a point where the road took a turning round a large chestnut tree, the form of his own horse Blossom. Melbury quickened Darling's pace, thinking to come up with Fitzpiers.

Nearer view revealed that the horse had no rider. At Melbury's approach it galloped friskily away under the trees in a homeward direction. Thinking something was wrong, the timber-merchant dismounted as soon as he reached the chestnut, and after feeling about for a minute or two discovered Fitzpiers lying on the ground.

"Here – help!" cried the latter as soon as he felt Melbury's touch;

"I have been thrown off ... But there's not much harm done, I think."

Since Melbury could not now very well read the younger man the lecture he had intended, and as friendliness would be hypocrisy, his instinct was to speak not a single word to his son-in-law. He raised Fitzpiers into a sitting posture, and found that he was a little stunned and stupefied, but, as he had said, not otherwise hurt. How this fall had come about was readily conjecturable: Fitzpiers, imagining there was only old Darling under him, had been taken unawares by the younger horse's sprightliness.

Melbury was a traveller of the old-fashioned sort: having just come from Shottsford-Forum, he still had in his pocket the pilgrim's flask of rum[5] which he always carried on journeys exceeding a dozen miles, though he seldom drank much of it. He poured it down the surgeon's throat, with such effect that he quickly revived. Melbury got him on his legs; but the question was what to do with him. He could not walk more than a few steps, and the other horse had gone away.

With great exertion Melbury contrived to get him astride Darling, mounting himself behind, and holding Fitzpiers round his waist with one arm. Darling being broad, straight-backed, and high in the withers, was well able to carry double, at any rate as far as Hintock, and at a gentle pace.

CHAPTER II

The mare paced along with firm and cautious tread through the copse where Winterborne had worked, and into the heavier soil where the oaks grew: past Great Willy, the largest oak in the wood, and thence towards Tutcombe Bottom, intensely dark now with overgrowth, and popularly supposed to be haunted by the spirits of the fratricides exorcised from Hintock House.

By this time Fitzpiers had quite recovered his physical strength. But he had eaten nothing since making a hasty breakfast in London that morning, his anxiety about Felice having hurried him away from home before dining: as a consequence the old rum administered by his father-in-law flew to the young man's head and loosened his tongue, without his ever having recognised who it was that had lent him a kindly hand. He began to speak in desultory sentences, Melbury still supporting him.

"I've come all the way from London to-day," said Fitzpiers. "Ah, that's the place to meet your equals. I live at Hintock – worse, at Little Hintock! – and I am quite lost there. There's not a man within ten miles of Hintock who can comprehend me ... I tell you, Farmer What's-your-name, that I'm a man of education. I know several languages: the poets and I are familiar friends: I used to read more in metaphysics than anybody within fifty miles; and since I gave that up there's nobody can match me in the whole county of Wessex as a scientist ... Yet I am doomed to live with tradespeople in a miserable little hole like Hintock!"

"Indeed!" muttered Melbury.

Here Fitzpiers, with alcoholic energy, reared himself up suddenly from the bowed posture he had hitherto held, thrusting his shoulders so violently against Melbury's breast as to make it difficult for the old man to keep a hold on the reins.

"People don't appreciate me here!" the surgeon exclaimed; then, lowering his voice, he added softly and slowly, "except one – except one! ... A passionate soul, as warm as she is clever, as beautiful as she is warm, and as rich as she is beautiful. I say, old fellow, those claws of yours clutch me rather tight – rather like the eagle's, you know, that ate out the liver of Pro – Pre –, the man on Mount Caucasus[1] ... People don't appreciate me, I say, except *her*! ... Ah, gods, I am an unlucky man! She would have been mine, she would have taken my name; but unfortunately it cannot be so! I stooped to mate beneath me; and now I rue it."

The position was becoming a very trying one for Melbury, corporeally and mentally. He was obliged to steady Fitzpiers with his left arm, and he began to hate the contact. He hardly knew what to do.

It was useless to remonstrate with Fitzpiers, in his intellectual confusion from the rum and from the fall. He remained silent, his hold upon his companion, however, being stern rather than compassionate.

"You hurt me a little, farmer! – though I am much obliged to you for your kindness . . . People don't appreciate me, I say. Between ourselves, I am losing my practice here; and why? Because I see matchless attraction where matchless attraction is, both in person and position. – I mention no names, so nobody will be the wiser . . . But I have lost her, – in a legitimate sense, that is. If I were a free man now, things have come to such a pass between us that she could not refuse me; while with her fortune (which I don't covet for itself) I should have a chance of satisfying an honourable ambition – a chance I have never had yet! . . . and now never, never shall have probably!"

Melbury, his heart throbbing against the other's backbone, and his brain on fire with indignation, ventured to mutter huskily, "Why?"

The horse ambled on some steps before Fitzpiers replied. "Because I am tied and bound to another by law, as tightly as I am to you by your arm – not that I complain of your arm – I thank you for helping me. Well, where are we? Not nearly home yet? . . . Home, say I. It *is* a home! When I might have been at the other house over there." In a stupefied way he flung his hand in the direction of the park. "I was just two months too early in committing myself. Had I only seen the other first —"

Here the old man's arm gave Fitzpiers a convulsive shake.

"What are you doing?" continued the latter. "Keep still, please, or put me down . . . I was saying that I lost her by a mere little two months! There is no chance for me now in this world, and it makes me reckless – reckless! Unless, indeed, anything should happen to the other one. She is amiable enough; but if anything should happen to her – and I hear she is ill – well, if it *should*, I should be free – and my fame, my happiness, would be insured!"

These were the last words that Fitzpiers uttered in his seat in front of the timber-merchant. Unable longer to master himself, Melbury whipped away his spare arm from Fitzpiers's waist, and seized him by the collar.

"You heartless villain – after all that we have done for ye!" he cried with a quivering lip. "And the money of hers that you've had, and the roof we've provided to shelter ye! – It is to me, George Melbury, that you dare to talk like that!" The exclamation was accompanied by a powerful swing from the shoulder, which flung the young man headlong into the road.

Fitzpiers fell with a heavy thud upon the stumps of some undergrowth which had been cut during the winter preceding. Darling continued her walk for a few paces further, and stopped.

"God forgive me!" Melbury murmured, repenting of what he had done. "He tried me too sorely; and now perhaps I've murdered him!"

He turned round in the saddle, and looked towards the spot on which Fitzpiers had fallen. To his great surprise he beheld the surgeon rise to his feet with a bound, as if unhurt, and walk away rapidly under the trees.

Melbury listened till the rustle of Fitzpiers's footsteps died away. "It might have been a crime, but for the mercy of Providence in providing leaves for his fall," he said to himself. And then his mind reverted to the words of Fitzpiers, and his indignation so mounted within him that he almost wished the fall had put an end to the surgeon there and then.

He had not ridden far when he discerned his own grey mare standing under some bushes. Leaving Darling for a moment, Melbury went forward and easily caught the younger animal, now disheartened at its freak. He made the pair of them fast to a tree, and turning back endeavoured to find some trace of Fitzpiers, feeling pitifully that, after all, he had gone further than he intended with the offender. But though he threaded the wood hither and thither, his toes ploughing layer after layer of the little horny scrolls that had once been leaves, he could not find him. He stood still, listening and looking round. The breeze was oozing through the net-work of boughs as through a strainer; the trunks and larger branches stood against the light of the sky in the forms of writhing men, gigantic candelabra, pikes, halberds, lances, and whatever else the fancy chose to make of them. Giving up the search, Melbury came back to the horses, and walked slowly homeward leading one in each hand.

*

It happened that on the selfsame evening a boy had been returning from Great to Little Hintock about the time of Fitzpiers's
passage home along that route. A horse-collar, that had been left
at the harness-mender's to be repaired, was required for use at
five o'clock next morning, and in consequence the boy had to fetch
it overnight. He put his head through the collar, and accompanied his walk by whistling the one tune he knew, as an antidote
to fear.

The boy suddenly became aware of a horse trotting rather friskily
along the track behind him, and not knowing whether to expect friend
or foe, prudence suggested that he should cease his whistling and
retreat among the trees till the horse and his rider had gone by, a course
to which he was still more inclined when he found how noiselessly they
approached, and saw that the horse looked pale, and remembered
what he had read about Death in the Revelation.[2] He therefore
deposited the collar by a tree, and hid himself behind it. The horseman
came on, and the youth, whose eyes were as keen as telescopes, to his
great relief recognised the doctor.

As Melbury surmised, Fitzpiers had in the darkness taken Blossom
for Darling, and he had not discovered his mistake when he came up
opposite the boy, though he was somewhat surprised at the liveliness
of his usually placid mare. The only other pair of eyes on the spot
whose vision was keen as the young carter's were those of the horse;
and, with that strongly conservative objection to the unusual which
animals show, Blossom, on eyeing the collar under the tree – quite
invisible to Fitzpiers – exercised none of the patience of the older
horse, but shied sufficiently to unseat so second-rate an equestrian as
the surgeon.

He fell, and did not move, lying as Melbury afterwards found him.
The boy ran away, salving his conscience for the desertion by thinking
how vigorously he would spread the alarm of the accident when he
got to Hintock – which he uncompromisingly did, incrusting the
skeleton event with a load of dramatic horrors.

Grace had returned, and the fly[3] hired on her account, though not
by her husband, at the Crown Hotel, Shottsford-Forum, had been
paid for and dismissed. The long drive had somewhat revived her,

her illness being a feverish intermittent nervousness which had more to do with mind than body, and she walked about her sitting-room in something of a hopeful mood. Mrs. Melbury had told her as soon as she arrived that her husband had returned from London. He had gone out, she said, to see a patient as she supposed, and he must soon be back, since he had had no dinner or tea. Grace would not allow her mind to harbour any suspicion of his whereabouts, and her stepmother said nothing of Mrs. Charmond's rumoured sorrows and plans of departure.

So the young wife sat by the fire, waiting silently. She had left Hintock in a turmoil of aversion to her husband, after the revelation of Mrs. Charmond, and had intended not to be at home when he returned. But she had thought the matter over, and had allowed her father's influence to prevail and bring her back; and now somewhat regretted that Edred's arrival had preceded hers.

By and by Mrs. Melbury came up stairs with a slight air of flurry and abruptness.

"I have something to tell – some bad news," she said. "But you must not be alarmed, as it is not so bad as it might have been. Edred has been thrown off his horse. We don't think he is hurt much. It happened in the wood the other side of Tutcombe Bottom, where 'tis said the ghosts of the Brothers[4] walk."

She went on to give a few of the particulars, but none of the invented horrors, that had been communicated by the boy. "I thought it better to tell you at once," she added, "in case he should not – be very well able to walk home, and somebody should bring him."

Mrs. Melbury really thought matters much worse than she represented, and Grace knew that she thought so. She sat down dazed for a few minutes, returning a negative to her stepmother's inquiry if she could do anything for her.

"Ah – yes – please go into the bedroom," Grace said on second thoughts, "and see if all is ready there – in case it is serious." Mrs. Melbury thereupon called Grammer, and they did as directed, supplying the room with everything they could think of for the accommodation of an injured man.

Nobody was left in the lower part of the house. Not many minutes had passed when Grace heard a knock at the door – a single knock, not loud enough to reach the ears of those in the bedroom.

She went to the top of the stairs, and said faintly, "Come up," knowing that the door stood, as usual in such houses, wide open. Retreating into the gloom of the broad landing she saw rise up the stairs a woman whom at first she did not recognise, till her voice revealed her to be Suke Damson, in great fright and sorrow. A streak of light from the partially closed door of Grace's room fell upon her face as she came forward, and it was drawn and pale.

"Oh, Miss Melbury – I would say Mrs. Fitzpiers," she said, wringing her hands. "This terrible news – is he dead? Is he hurted very bad? Tell me; I couldn't help coming – please forgive me, Miss Melbury – Mrs. Fitzpiers, I would say!"

Grace sank down on the oak chest which stood on the landing, and put her hands to her now flushed face and head. Ought she not to order Suke Damson down stairs and out of the house? Her husband might be brought in at any moment, and what would happen? But could she order this genuinely grieved woman away?

There was a dead silence of half a minute or so, till Suke said, "Why don't ye speak? Is he here? Is he dead? If so, why can't I see him – would it be so very wrong?"

Before Grace had answered somebody else came to the door below – a footfall light as a roe's. There was a hurried tapping upon the panel, as if with the impatient tips of fingers whose owner thought not whether a knocker were there or no. Without a pause and possibly guided by the stray beam of light on the landing, the new-comer ascended the staircase as the first had done. Grace started: it was a lady. Grace was sufficiently visible, and the lady came to her side.

"I could make nobody hear down stairs," said Felice Charmond, with lips whose dryness could almost be heard, and panting, as she stood like one ready to sink on the floor with distress. "What is – the matter – tell me the worst! Can he live?"

She looked at Grace imploringly, without perceiving poor Suke, who, dismayed at such a presence, had shrunk away into the shade. Mrs. Charmond's little feet were covered with mud: she was quite unconscious of her appearance now.

"I have heard such a dreadful report," she went on; "I came to ascertain the truth of it. Is he – killed?"

"She won't tell us – he's dying – he's in that room!" burst out Suke, regardless of consequences, as she heard the distant movements of Mrs. Melbury and Grammer in the bedroom at the end of the passage.

"Where?" said Mrs. Charmond; and on Suke pointing out the direction she made as if to go thither.

Grace barred the way.

"He is not there," she said. "I have not seen him any more than you. I have heard a report only – not so bad as you think. It must have been exaggerated to you."

"Please do not conceal anything – let me know all!" said Felice doubtingly.

"You shall know all I know; and indeed you have a perfect right to go in there; who can have a better than either of you?" said Grace with a delicate sting which was lost upon them now, as, ceasing to obstruct the way, she led on to the chamber door, and flung it open.[5] "I repeat, I have only heard a less alarming account than you have heard; how much it means, and how little, I cannot say. I pray God that it means not much – in common humanity. You probably pray the same – *for other reasons*."

Then she regarded them both there in the dim light a while, as they stood dumb in their trouble, staring at the empty bed;[6] not stinging back at her, not heeding her mood. A tenderness spread over Grace like a dew. It was well enough, conventionally, to address either one of them in the wife's regulation terms of virtuous sarcasm, as woman, creature, or thing.[7] But life, what was it, and who was she? She had, like the singer of the Psalm of Asaph,[8] been plagued and chastened all the day long; but could she, by retributive words, in order to please herself, the individual, "offend against the generation," as he would not?

"He is dying, perhaps!" blubbered Suke Damson, putting her apron to her eyes.

In their gestures and faces there were anxieties, affection, agony of heart – all for a man who had wronged them – had never really behaved towards either of them anyhow but selfishly. Neither one but would have well-nigh sacrificed half her life to him, even now. The tears which his possibly critical situation could not bring to her eyes surged over at the contemplation of these fellow-women.[9] She turned to the balustrade, bent herself upon it, and wept.

Thereupon Felice began to cry also, without using her handkerchief, letting the tears run down silently. While these three poor women stood together thus, pitying another though most to be pitied themselves, the pacing of a horse or horses became audible in the court, and in a moment Melbury's voice was heard calling to his stableman.

Grace at once started up, ran down the stairs, and out into the quadrangle as her father crossed it towards the door. "Father, what is the matter with him?" she cried.

"Who, Edred?" said Melbury abruptly. "Matter? Nothing. What, my dear, and have you got home safe? Why, you are better already! But you ought not to be out in the air like this."

"But he has been thrown off his horse!"

"I know; I know. I saw it. He got up again, and walked off as well as ever. A fall on the leaves didn't hurt a spry fellow like him. He did not come this way," he added significantly. "I suppose he went to look for his horse. I tried to find him, but could not. But after seeing him go away under the trees I found the horse, and have led it home for safety. So he must walk. Now, don't you stay out here in this night air."

She returned to the house with her father. When she had again ascended to the landing and to her own rooms beyond, it was a great relief to her to find that both Petticoat the First and Petticoat the Second of her *bien-aimé*[10] had silently disappeared. They had, in all probability, heard the words of her father, and departed, with their anxieties relieved.

Presently her parents came up to Grace, and busied themselves to see that she was comfortable. Perceiving soon that she would prefer to be left alone they went away.

Grace waited on. The clock raised its voice now and then, but her husband did not return. At her father's usual hour for retiring he again came in to see her. "Do not stay up," she said, as soon as he entered. "I am not at all tired. I will sit up for him."

"I think it will be useless, Grace," said Melbury, slowly.

"Why?"

"I have had a bitter quarrel with him. And on that account I hardly think he will return to-night."

"A quarrel? Was that after the fall seen by the boy?"

Melbury nodded an affirmative – without taking his eyes off the candle.

"Yes; it was as we were coming home together," he said.

Something had been swelling up in Grace while her father was speaking. "How could you want to quarrel with him?" she cried suddenly. "Why could you not let him come home quietly, if he were inclined to? He is my husband; and now you have married me to him surely you need not provoke him unnecessarily. First you induce me to accept him, and then you do things that divide us more than we should naturally be divided!"

"How can you speak so unjustly to me, Grace?" said Melbury, with indignant sorrow. "*I* divide you from your husband, indeed! You little think –"

He was inclined to say more – to tell her the whole story of the encounter, and that the provocation he had received had lain entirely in hearing her despised. But it would have greatly distressed her, and he forebore.

"You had better lie down. You are tired," he said soothingly. "Good-night."

The household went to bed, and a silence fell upon the dwelling, broken only by the occasional skirr of a halter in Melbury's stables. Despite her father's advice Grace still waited up. But nobody came.

It was a critical time in Grace's emotional life, that night. She thought of her husband a good deal, and for the nonce forgot Winterborne.

"How these unhappy women must have admired Edred!" she said to herself. "How attractive he must be to everybody; and, indeed, he is attractive." The possibility is that, piqued by rivalry, these ideas might have been transmuted into their corresponding emotions by a show of the least reciprocity in Fitzpiers. There was, in truth, a love-bird yearning to fly from her heart; and it wanted a lodging badly.

But no husband came. The fact was that Melbury had been much mistaken about the condition of Fitzpiers. People do not fall headlong on stumps of underwood with impunity. Had the old man been able to watch Fitzpiers narrowly enough he would have observed that, on rising and walking into the thicket, he dropped blood as he went; that he had not proceeded fifty yards before he showed signs of being dizzy, and, raising his hands to his head, reeled and fell.

CHAPTER III

Grace was not the only one who watched and meditated in Hintock that night. Felice Charmond was in no mood to retire to rest at a customary hour; and over her drawing-room fire at the manor-house she sat as motionless and in as deep a reverie as Grace in her little chamber at the homestead.

Having caught ear of Melbury's intelligence while she had stood on the landing at his house, and been eased of much of her mental distress, her sense of personal decorum had returned upon her with a rush. She descended the stairs and left the door like a ghost, keeping close to the walls of the building till she got round to the gate of the quadrangle, through which she noiselessly passed almost before Grace and her father had finished their discourse. Suke Damson had thought it well to imitate her superior in this respect, and, descending the back stairs as Felice descended the front, went out at the side door and home to her cottage.

Once outside Melbury's gates Mrs. Charmond ran with all her speed to the manor-house, without stopping or turning her head. She entered her own dwelling as she had emerged from it – by the drawing-room window. Everything was just as she had left it: she had been gone about three-quarters of an hour by the clock, and nobody seemed to have discovered her absence. Tired in body but tense in mind she sat down, palpitating, round-eyed, bewildered at what she had done.

She had been betrayed by affrighted love into a visit which, now that the emotion instigating it had calmed down under her belief that Fitzpiers was in no danger, was the saddest surprise to her. This was how she had set about doing her best to escape her passionate bondage to him! Somehow, in declaring to Grace and to herself the unseemliness of her infatuation, she had grown a convert to its irresistibility.

If Heaven would only give her strength; but Heaven never did! One thing was indispensable: she must go away from Hintock if she meant to withstand further temptation. The struggle was too wearying, too hopeless, while she remained. It was but a continual capitulation of conscience to what she dared not name.

By degrees, as she sat on and on, Felice's mind – helped perhaps by the anti-climax of supposing that her lover was unharmed after all her fright about him – grew wondrously strong in wise resolve. For the moment she was in a mood, in the words of Mrs. Elizabeth Montagu,[1] "to run mad with discretion"; and was so persuaded that discretion lay in departure that she wished to set about going that very minute. Jumping up from her seat she began to gather together some small personal knick-knacks scattered about the room, to feel that preparations were really in train.

While moving here and there she fancied that she heard a slight noise out of doors, and stood still. Surely it was a tapping at the window. A thought entered her mind, and burnt her cheek. He had come to that window before; yet was it possible that he should dare to do so now! All the servants were in bed, and in the ordinary course of affairs she would have retired also. Then she remembered that on stepping in by the casement and closing it, she had not fastened the window-shutter, so that a streak of light from the interior of the room might have revealed her vigil to an observer on the lawn. How all things conspired against her keeping faith with Grace!

The tapping recommenced, light as from the bill of a little bird: her illegitimate hope overcame her discretion: she went and pulled back the shutter, determining however to shake her head at him, and keep the casement securely closed.

What she saw outside might have struck terror into a heart stouter than a helpless woman's at midnight. In the centre of the lowest pane of the window, close to the glass, was a human face, which she barely recognised as the face of Fitzpiers. It was surrounded with the darkness of the night without, corpse-like in its pallor, and covered with blood. As disclosed in the square area of the pane it met her frightened eyes like a replica of the Sudarium of St. Veronica.[2]

He moved his lips, and looked at her imploringly. Her rapid mind pieced together in an instant a possible concatenation of events which might have led to this tragical issue. She unlatched the casement with a terrified hand, and bending down to where he was crouching pressed her face to his with passionate solicitude. She assisted him into the room without a word, to do which it was almost necessary to lift him bodily.

Quickly closing the window and fastening the shutters she bent over him breathlessly.

"Are you hurt much, much?" she cried faintly. "Oh, oh, how is this!"

"Rather much – but don't be frightened," he answered in a difficult whisper, and turning himself to obtain an easier position if possible. "A little water, please."

She ran across into the dining-room, and brought a bottle and glass, from which he eagerly drank. He could then speak much better, and with her help got upon the nearest couch.

"Are you dying, Edred?" she said. "Do speak to me!"

"I am half dead," said Fitzpiers. "But perhaps I shall get over it . . . It is chiefly loss of blood."

"But I thought your fall did not hurt you?" said she. "Who did this?"

"Felice – my father-in-law! . . . I have crawled to you more than a mile on my hands and knees – God, I thought I should never have got here! . . . I have come to you – because you are the only friend – I have in the world now . . . I can never go back to Hintock – never – to the roof of the Melburys! Not poppy nor mandragora[3] will ever medicine this bitter feud! . . . If I were only well again –"

"Let me bind your head, now that you have rested."

"Yes – but wait a moment – it has stopped bleeding, fortunately, or I should be a dead man before now. While in the wood I managed to make a tourniquet of some halfpence and my handkerchief, as well as I could in the dark . . . But listen, dear Felice! Can you hide me till I am well? Whatever comes, I can be seen in Hintock no more. My practice is nearly gone you know – and after this I would not care to recover it if I could."

By this time Felice's tears began to blind her. Where were now her discreet plans for sundering their lives for ever? To administer to him in his pain, and trouble, and poverty, was her single thought. The first step was to hide him, and she asked herself where. A place occurred to her mind.

She got him some wine from the dining-room, which strengthened him much. Then she managed to remove his boots, and, as he could now keep himself upright by leaning upon her on one side and a walking-stick on the other, they went thus in slow march out of the room and up the stairs. At the top she took him along a gallery, pausing whenever he required rest, and thence up a smaller staircase to the least used part of the house, where she unlocked a door. Within was a lumber-room, containing abandoned furniture of all descriptions, built up in piles which obscured the light of the windows, and formed between them nooks and lairs in which a person would not be discerned even should an eye gaze in at the door. The articles were mainly those that had belonged to the previous owner of the house, and had been bought in by the late Mr. Charmond at the auction; but changing fashion, and the tastes of a young wife, had caused them to be relegated to this dungeon.

Here Fitzpiers sat on the floor against the wall till she had hauled out materials for a bed, which she spread on the floor in one of the aforesaid nooks. She obtained water and a basin, and washed the dried blood from his face and hands; and when he was comfortably reclining fetched food from the larder. While he ate, her eyes lingered anxiously on his face, following its every movement with such loving-kindness as only a fond woman can show.

He was now in better condition, and discussed his position with her.

"What I fancy I said to Melbury must have been enough to enrage any man, if uttered in cold blood, and with knowledge of his presence. But I did not know him, and I was stupefied by what he had given me, so that I hardly was aware of what I said. Well – the veil of that temple is rent in twain![4] . . . As I am not going to be seen again in Hintock, my first efforts must be directed to allay any alarm that may be felt at my absence, before I am able to get clear away. Nobody must suspect that I have been hurt, or there will be a country talk about me. Felice, I must at once concoct a letter to check all search for me. I think if you can bring me a pen and paper I may be able to do it now. I could rest better if it were done. Poor thing! how I tire her with running up and down!"

She fetched writing materials, and held up the blotting-book as a support to his hand, while he penned a brief note to his nominal wife.

"The animosity shown towards me by your father," he wrote in this coldest of marital epistles, "is such that I cannot return again to a roof which is his, even though it shelters you. A parting is unavoidable, as you are sure to be on his side in this division. I am starting on a journey which will take me a long way from Hintock, and you must not expect to see me there again for some time."

He then gave her a few directions bearing upon his professional engagements and other practical matters, concluding without a hint of his destination, or a notion of when she would see him again. He offered to read the note to Felice before he closed it up; but she would not hear or see it: that side of his obligations distressed her beyond endurance. She turned away from Fitzpiers, and sobbed bitterly.

"If you can get this posted at a place some miles away," he whispered, exhausted by the effort of writing, "at Shottsford, or Port-Bredy, or still better, Budmouth, it will divert all suspicion from this house as the place of my refuge."

"I will drive to one or other of the places myself – anything to keep it unknown," she murmured, her voice weighted with vague foreboding, now that the excitement of helping him had passed away.

Fitzpiers told her that there was yet one thing more to be done. "In creeping over the fence on to the lawn," he said, "I made the rail bloody, and it shows rather too plainly on the white paint – I could see it in the dark. At all hazards it should be washed off. Could you do that also, Felice?"

What will not women do on such devoted occasions? Weary as she was she went – all the way down the rambling staircases to the ground floor, then to search for a lantern, which she lighted and hid under her cloak; then for a wet sponge, and next forth into the night. The white railing stared out in the darkness at her approach, and a ray from the enshrouded lantern fell upon the blood – just where he had told her it would be found. She shuddered. It was almost too much to bear in one day; but with a shaking hand she sponged the rail clean, and returned to the house.

The time occupied by these several proceedings was not much less than two hours. When all was done, and she had smoothed his extemporised bed, and placed everything within his reach that she could think of, she took her leave of him, and locked him in.

CHAPTER IV

When her husband's letter reached Grace's hands, bearing upon it the postmark of a distant town, it never once crossed her mind that Fitzpiers was within a mile of her still. She felt relieved that he did not write more bitterly of the quarrel with her father, whatever its nature might have been; but the general frigidity of his communication quenched in her the incipient spark that events had kindled so shortly before.

From this centre of information it was made known in Hintock that the doctor had gone away, and as none but the Melbury household was aware that he did not return on the night of his accident, no excitement manifested itself in the village.

Thus the early days of May passed by. None but the nocturnal birds and animals observed that late one evening, towards the middle of the month, a closely wrapped figure, with a crutch under one arm and a stick in his hand, crept out from Hintock House across the lawn to the shelter of the trees, taking thence a slow and laborious walk to the nearest point of the turnpike road.

The mysterious personage was so disguised that his own wife would hardly have known him. Felice Charmond was a practised hand at such work, as well she might be; and she had done her utmost in padding and painting Fitzpiers with the old materials of her art[1] in the recesses of that lumber-room.

In the highway he was met by a covered carriage, which conveyed him to Sherton Abbas, whence he proceeded to the nearest port on the south coast, and immediately crossed the Channel.

But it was known to everybody that three days after this time Mrs. Charmond executed her often-deferred plan of setting out for a long term of travel and residence on the Continent. She went off one morning as unostentatiously as could be, and took no maid with her, having, she said, engaged one to meet her at a point further on in her route. After that, Hintock House, so frequently deserted, was again to be let. Spring had not merged in summer when a clinching rumour, founded on the best of evidence, reached the parish and neighbourhood. Mrs. Charmond and Fitzpiers had been seen together in Baden, in relations which set at rest the question that had agitated the little community ever since the winter.

Melbury had entered the Valley of Humiliation[2] even further than Grace. His spirit seemed broken.

But once a week he mechanically went to market as usual, and here, as he was passing by the conduit one day, his mental condition expressed largely by his gait, he heard his name spoken by a voice formerly familiar. He turned and saw a certain Fred Beaucock – once a promising lawyer's clerk and local dandy, who had been called the cleverest fellow in Sherton, without whose brains the firm of solicitors employing him would be nowhere. But later on Beaucock had fallen into the mire. He was invited out a good deal, sang songs at agricultural meetings and burgesses' dinners: in sum, victualled himself with spirits more frequently than was good for the clever brains or body either. He lost his situation, and after an absence spent in trying his powers elsewhere came back to his native town, where, at the time of the foregoing events in Hintock, he gave legal advice for astonishingly small fees – mostly carrying on his profession on public-house settles, in whose recesses he might often have been overheard making country-people's wills for half-a-crown, calling with a learned voice for pen and ink and a halfpenny sheet of paper, on which he drew up the testament, while resting it in a little space wiped with his hand on the table amid the liquid circles formed by the cups and glasses. An idea implanted early in life is difficult to uproot, and many elderly tradespeople still clung to the notion that Fred Beaucock knew a great deal of law.

It was he who had called Melbury by name.

"You look very down, Mr. Melbury – very, if I may say as much," he observed, when the timber-merchant turned. "But I know – I know. A very sad case – very. I was bred to the law, as you know, and am professionally no stranger to such matters. Well, Mrs. Fitzpiers has her remedy."

"How – what – a remedy?" said Melbury.

"Under the new law, sir. A new court was established last year, and under the new statute, twenty and twenty-one Vic., cap. eighty-five,[3] unmarrying is as easy as marrying. No more Acts of Parliament necessary: no longer one law for the rich and another for the poor. But come inside – I was just going to have a nibleykin of rum hot – I'll explain it all to you."

The intelligence amazed Melbury, who saw little of newspapers. And though he was a severely correct man in his habits, and had no taste for entering a tavern with Fred Beaucock – nay, would have been quite uninfluenced by such a character on any other matter in the world – such fascination lay in the idea of delivering his poor girl from bondage, that it deprived him of the critical faculty. He could not resist the ex-lawyer's clerk, and entered the inn.

Here they sat down to the rum, which Melbury paid for as a matter of course, Beaucock leaning back on the settle with a legal gravity which would hardly allow him to be conscious of the spirits before him; though they nevertheless disappeared with mysterious quickness.

How much of the exaggerated information[4] on the then new divorce laws which Beaucock imparted to his listener was the result of ignorance, and how much of dupery, was never ascertained. But he related such a plausible story of the ease with which Grace could become a free woman that her father was irradiated with the project; and, though he scarcely wetted his lips, Melbury never knew how he came out of the inn, or when or where he mounted his gig to pursue his way homeward.

But home he found himself, his brain having all the way seemed to ring sonorously as a gong in the intensity of its stir. Before he had seen Grace, he was accidentally met by Winterborne, who found his face shining as if he had, like the Lawgiver, conversed with an angel.[5]

He relinquished his horse, and took Winterborne by the arm to a heap of rendlewood – as barked oak was here called – which lay under a privet hedge.

"Giles," he said, when they had sat down upon the logs, "there's a new law in the land! Grace can be free quite easily. I only knew it by the merest accident. I might not have found it out for the next ten years. She can get rid of him – d'ye hear – get rid of him. Think of that, my friend Giles!"

He related what he had learnt of the new legal remedy. A subdued tremulousness about the mouth was all the response that Winterborne made; and Melbury added, "My boy, you shall have her yet – if you want her." His feelings had gathered volume as he said this, and the articulate sound of the old idea drowned his sight in mist.

"Are you sure – about this new law?" asked Winterborne, so disquieted by a gigantic exultation which loomed alternately with fearful doubt, that he evaded the full acceptance of Melbury's last statement.

Melbury said that he had no manner of doubt, for since his talk with Beaucock it had come into his mind that he had seen some time ago in the weekly paper an allusion to such a legal change; but, having no interest in those desperate remedies at the moment, he had passed it over.

"But I'm not going to let the matter rest doubtful for a single day," he continued. "I am going to London. Beaucock will go with me, and we shall get the best advice as soon as we possibly can. Beaucock is a thorough lawyer – nothing the matter with him but a fiery palate. I knew him as the stay and refuge of Sherton in knots of law at one time."

Winterborne's replies were of the vaguest. The new possibility was almost unthinkable at the moment. He was what was called at Hintock "a solid-going fellow"; he maintained his abeyant mood, not from want of reciprocity, but from a taciturn hesitancy, taught by life as he knew it.

"But," continued the timber-merchant, a temporary crease or two of anxiety supplementing those already established in his forehead by time, "Grace is not at all well. Nothing constitutional, you know; but she has been in a low nervous state ever since that night of fright. I don't doubt but that she will be all right soon . . . I wonder how she is this evening?" He rose with the words, as if he had too long forgotten her personality in the excitement of her previsioned career.

They had sat till the evening was beginning to dye the garden brown, and now went towards Melbury's house, Giles a few steps in the rear of his old friend, who was stimulated by the enthusiasm of the moment to outstep the more ordinary pace of Winterborne. He felt shy of entering Grace's presence as her reconstituted lover – which was how her father's manner would be sure to present him – before definite information as to her future state was forthcoming: it seemed too nearly like the act of those who rush in where angels fear to tread.[6]

A chill to counterbalance all the glowing promise of the day was prompt enough in coming. No sooner had he followed the timber-merchant in at the door than he heard Grammer inform him that Mrs. Fitzpiers was still more unwell than she had been in the morning. Old Dr. Jones being in the neighbourhood they had called him in, and he had instantly directed them to get her to bed. They were not, however, to consider her illness serious – a feverish, nervous attack, the result of recent events, was what she was suffering from – and she would doubtless be well in a few days.

Winterborne therefore did not remain, and his hope of seeing her that evening was disappointed.

Even this aggravation of her morning condition did not greatly depress Melbury. He knew, he said, that his daughter's constitution was sound enough. It was only these domestic troubles that were pulling her down. Once free she would be blooming again. Melbury diagnosed rightly, as parents usually do.

He set out for London the next morning, Jones having paid another visit and assured him that he might leave home without uneasiness, especially on an errand of that sort, which would the sooner put an end to her suspense.

The timber-merchant had been away only a day or two when it was told in Hintock that Mr. Fitzpiers's hat had been found in the wood. Later on in the afternoon the hat was brought to Melbury's, and, by a piece of ill-fortune, into Grace's presence. It had doubtless lain in the wood ever since his fall from the horse; but it looked so clean and uninjured – the summer weather and leafy shelter having much favoured its preservation – that Grace could not believe it had remained so long concealed. A very little fact was enough to set her fevered fancy at work at this juncture – she thought him still in the neighbourhood, she feared his sudden appearance; and her nervous malady developed consequences so grave that Dr. Jones began to look serious, and the household was alarmed.

It was the beginning of June, and the cuckoo[7] at this time of the summer scarcely ceased his cry for more than two or three hours during the night. The bird's note, so familiar to her ears from infancy, was now absolute torture to the poor girl. On the Friday following the Wednesday of Melbury's departure, and the day after the discovery of Fitzpiers's hat, the cuckoo began at two o'clock in the morning with a sudden cry from one of Melbury's apple-trees, not three yards from the window of Grace's room.

"Oh – he is coming!" she cried, and in her terror sprang clean out from the bed upon the floor.

These starts and frights continued till noon; and when the doctor had arrived and had seen her, and had talked with Mrs. Melbury, he sat down and meditated. That ever-present terror it was indispensable to remove from her mind at all hazards; and he thought how this might be done.

Without saying a word to anybody in the house, or to the disquieted Winterborne waiting in the lane below, Dr. Jones went home and wrote to Mr. Melbury at the address in London he had obtained from his wife. The gist of his communication was that Mrs. Fitzpiers should be assured as soon as possible that steps were taken to sever the bond which was becoming a torture to her; that she would soon be free; and was even then virtually so. "If you can say it *at once* it may be the means of averting much harm," he said. "Write to herself; not to me."

On Saturday he drove over to Hintock, and assured her with mysterious pacifications that in a day or two she might expect to receive some good news.

So it turned out. When Sunday morning came there was a letter for Grace from her father. It arrived at seven o'clock, the usual time at which the toddling postman passed by Hintock: at eight Grace awoke, having slept an hour or two for a wonder, and Mrs. Melbury brought up the letter.

"Can you open it yourself?" said she.

"Oh, yes, yes!" said Grace with feeble impatience. She tore the envelope, unfolded the sheet, and read; when a creeping blush tinctured her white neck and cheek.

Her father had exercised a bold discretion. He informed her that she need have no further concern about Fitzpiers's return; that she would shortly be a free woman; and therefore if she should desire to wed her old lover – which he trusted was the case, since it was his own deep wish – she would be in a position to do so. In this Melbury had not written beyond his belief. But he very much stretched the facts in adding that the legal formalities for dissolving her union were practically settled.

The truth was that on the arrival of the doctor's letter poor Melbury had been much agitated, and could with difficulty be prevented by Beaucock from returning to her bedside. What was the use of his rushing back to Hintock? Beaucock had asked him. The only thing that could do her any good was a breaking of the bond. Though he had not as yet had an interview with the eminent solicitor they were about to consult, he was on the point of seeing him; and the case was clear enough. Thus the simple Melbury, urged by his parental alarm at her danger, by the representations of his companion, and by the doctor's letter, had yielded, and sat down to tell her roundly that she was virtually free.

"And you'd better write also to the gentleman," suggested Beaucock, who, scenting fame and the germ of a large practice in the case, wished to commit Melbury to it irretrievably: to effect which he knew that nothing would be so potent as awakening the passion of Grace for Winterborne, so that her father might not have the heart to withdraw from his attempt to make her love legitimate when he discovered that there were difficulties in the way.

The nervous, impatient Melbury was much pleased with the idea of "starting them at once," as he called it. To put his long-delayed reparative scheme in train had become a passion with him now. He added to the letter addressed to his daughter a passage hinting that she ought to begin to encourage Winterborne, lest she should lose him altogether; and he wrote to Giles that the path was virtually open for him at last. Life was short, he declared; he, her father, was getting old; there were slips betwixt the cup and the lip; her interest in him should be reawakened at once, that all might be ready when the good time came for uniting them.

CHAPTER V

At these warm words Winterborne was much moved. The novelty of the avowal rendered what it carried with it inapprehensible by him all at once. Only a few short months ago completely estranged from this family – beholding Grace going to and fro in the distance, clothed with the alienating radiance of obvious superiority, the wife of the then popular and fashionable Fitzpiers, hopelessly outside his social boundary down to so recent a time that flowers then folded were hardly faded yet – he was now asked by that jealously-guarding father of hers to take courage; to get himself ready for the day when he should be able to claim her.

The old times came back to him in dim procession. How he had been snubbed: how Melbury had despised his Christmas party: how that sweet, coy Grace herself had looked down upon him and his household arrangements, and poor Creedle's contrivances!

Well, he could not believe it. Surely the adamantine barrier of marriage with another could not be pierced like this! It did violence to custom. Yet a new law might do anything. But was it at all within the bounds of probability that a woman who, over and above her own attainments, had been accustomed to those of a cultivated professional man, could ever be the wife of such as he? Since the date of his rejection he had almost grown to see the reasonableness of that treatment. He had said to himself again and again that her father was right: that the ceorl,[1] Giles Winterborne, would never have been able to make such a dainty girl happy. Yet now that she had stood in a position further removed from his own than at first, he was asked to prepare to woo her. He was full of doubt.

Nevertheless, it was not in him to show backwardness. To act so promptly as Melbury desired him to act seemed, indeed, scarcely wise, because of the uncertainty of events. Giles knew nothing of legal procedure; but he did know that for him to step up to Grace as a lover before the bond which bound her was actually dissolved was simply an extravagant dream of her father's overstrained mind. He pitied Melbury for his almost childish enthusiasm, and saw that the ageing man must have suffered acutely to be weakened to this unreasoning desire.

Winterborne was far too magnanimous to harbour any cynical conjecture that the timber-merchant, in his intense affection for Grace, was courting him now because that young lady, when disunited, would be left in an anomalous position, to escape which a bad husband was better than none. He felt quite sure that his old friend was simply on tenterhooks of anxiety to repair the almost irreparable error of dividing two whom nature had striven to join together in earlier days, and that in his ardour to do this he was oblivious of formalities. The cautious supervision of his past years had overleapt itself at last. Hence

Winterborne perceived that, in this new beginning, the necessary care not to compromise Grace by too early advances must be exercised by himself.

There is no such thing as a stationary love: men are either loving more or loving less; but Giles recognised no decline in his sense of her dearness. He had been labouring ever since his rejection and her marriage to reduce his former passion to a docile friendship, out of pure regard to its expediency; but hitherto he had experienced no great success in his attempt.

A week and more passed, and there was no further news of Melbury. But the effect of the intelligence he had already transmitted upon the elastic-nerved daughter of the woods had been much as the old surgeon Jones had surmised. It had soothed her perturbed spirit better than all the opiates in the pharmacopœia.[2] She had slept unbrokenly a whole night and a day. The "new law" was to her a mysterious, beneficent, god-like entity, lately descended upon earth, that would make her as she once had been without trouble or annoyance. Her position fretted her, its abstract features rousing an aversion which was greater than her aversion to the personality of him who had caused it. It was mortifying, productive of slights, undignified. Him she could forget: her circumstances she had always with her.

She saw nothing of Winterborne during the days of her recovery; and perhaps on that account her fancy wove about him a more romantic tissue than it could have done if he had stood before her with all the specks and flaws inseparable from concrete humanity. He rose upon her memory as the fruit-god and the wood-god[3] in alternation: sometimes leafy and smeared with green lichen, as she had seen him amongst the sappy boughs of the plantations: sometimes cider-stained and starred with apple-pips, as she had met him on his return from cider-making in White-Hart Vale, with his vats and presses beside him. In her secret heart she approximated to her father's enthusiasm in wishing to show Giles once for all how she still regarded him.

The question whether the future would indeed bring them together for life was a standing wonder with her. She knew that it could not with any propriety do so just yet. But reverently believing in her father's sound judgment and knowledge, as good girls are wont to do, she remembered what he had written about her giving a hint to Winterborne lest there should be risk in delay, and her feelings were not averse to such a step, so far as it could be done without danger at this early stage of the proceedings.

From being a frail phantom of her former equable self she returned in bounds to a condition of passable philosophy. She bloomed again in the face in the course of a few days, and was well enough to go about as usual.

One day Mrs. Melbury proposed that for a change she should be driven in the gig to Sherton market, whither Melbury's man was going on other errands. Grace had no business whatever in Sherton; but it crossed her mind that Winterborne would probably be there, and this made the thought of such a drive interesting.

On the way she saw nothing of him; but when the horse was walking slowly through the obstructions of Sheep Street, she discerned the young man on the pavement. She thought of that time when he had been standing under his apple-tree on her return from school, and of the tender opportunity then missed through her fastidiousness. Her heart rose in her throat. She abjured all such fastidiousness now. Nor did she forget the last occasion on which she had beheld him in that town, making cider in the courtyard of the Earl of Wessex Hotel, while she was figuring as a fine lady in the balcony above.

Grace directed the man to set her down there in the midst, and immediately went up to her lover. Giles had not before observed her, and his eyes now suppressedly looked his pleasure, without, perhaps, quite so much embarrassment as had formerly marked him at such meetings.

When a few words had been spoken, she said invitingly,[4] "I have nothing to do. Perhaps you are deeply engaged?"

"I? Not a bit. My business now at the best of times is small, I am sorry to say."

"Well, then – I am going into the Abbey. Come along with me."

The proposition had suggested itself as a quick escape from publicity, for many eyes were regarding her. She had hoped that sufficient time had elapsed for the extinction of curiosity; but it was quite otherwise.

The people looked at her with tender interest as the deserted girl-wife
– without obtrusiveness, and without vulgarity; but she was ill-prepared
for scrutiny in any shape.

They walked about the Abbey aisles, and presently sat down. Not
a soul was in the building save themselves. She regarded a stained
window, with her head sideways,[5] and tentatively asked him if he
remembered the last time they were in that town alone.

He remembered it perfectly, and remarked, "You were a proud
damsel then, and as dainty as you were high. Perhaps you are now?"

Grace slowly shook her head. "Affliction has taken all that out of
me," she answered impressively. "Perhaps I am too far the other way
now." As there was something lurking in this that she could not
explain, she added so quickly as not to allow him time to think of it,
"Has my father written to you at all?"

"Yes," said Winterborne.

She glanced ponderingly up at him. "Not about me?"

"Yes."

She saw that he had been bidden to take the hint as to the future
which she had been bidden to give, and the discovery sent a scarlet
pulsation through her for the moment. However it was only Giles who
stood there, of whom she had no fear; and her self-possession returned.

"He said I was to sound you with a view to – what you will
understand, if you care to," continued Winterborne in a low voice.
Having been put on this track by herself, he was not disposed to
abandon it in a hurry.

They had been children together, and there was between them that
familiarity as to personal affairs which only such acquaintanceship
can give. "You know, Giles," she answered, speaking in a very practical
tone, "that this is all very well; but I am in a very anomalous position
at present, and I cannot say anything to the point about such things
as those."

"No?" he said, with a stray air as regarded the subject. He was
looking at her with a curious consciousness of discovery.

He had not been imagining that their renewed intercourse would
show her to him thus. For the first time he realised an unexpectedness
in her, which after all should not have been unexpected. She before

him was not the girl, Grace Melbury, whom he had used to know. Of course, he might easily have prefigured as much; but it had never occurred to him. She was a woman who had been married; she had moved on; and without having lost her girlish modesty, she had lost her girlish shyness. The inevitable change, though known to him, had not been heeded; and it struck him into a momentary fixity. The truth was that he had never come into close comradeship with her since her engagement to Fitzpiers, with the brief exception of the evening encounter on Rubdon Hill, when she met him with his cider apparatus; and that interview had been of too cursory a kind for insight.

Winterborne had advanced, too. Shy though he was, he could criticise her somewhat. Times had been when to criticise a single trait in Grace Melbury would have lain as far beyond his powers as to criticise a deity. And this thing was sure as a result of his criticism: it was a new woman in many ways whom he had come out to see: a creature of more ideas, more dignity, and, above all, more assurance, than the original Grace had been capable of. He could not at first decide whether he were pleased or displeased at this. But upon the whole the novelty attracted him.

She was so sweet and sensitive that she feared his silence betokened something in his brain of the nature of an enemy to her.

"What are you thinking of that makes those lines come in your forehead?" she asked. "I did not mean to offend you by speaking of the time being premature as yet."

Touched by the genuine loving-kindness which had lain at the foundation of these words, and much moved, Winterborne turned his face aside, as he took her by the hand. He was grieved that he had criticised her.

"You are very good, dear Grace," he said in a low voice. "You are better, much better, than you used to be."

"How?"

He could not very well tell her how, and said with an evasive smile, "You are prettier;" which was not what he really had meant. He then remained still holding her right hand in his own right, so that they faced in opposite ways; and, as he did not let go, she ventured upon a tender remonstrance.

"I think we have gone as far as we ought to go at present – and far enough to satisfy my poor father that we are the same as ever. You see, Giles, my case is not settled yet, and if – Oh, suppose I *never* get free! – there should be any hitch or informality!"

She drew a catching breath, and turned pale. The dialogue had been affectionate comedy up to this point. The gloomy atmosphere of the past, and the still gloomy horizon of the present, had been for the interval forgotten. Now, the whole environment came back; the due balance of shade among the light was restored.

"It is sure to be all right, I trust," she resumed in uneasy accents. "What did my father say the solicitor had told him?"

"Oh – that all is sure enough. The case is so clear – nothing could be clearer. But the legal part is not yet quite done and finished, as is natural."

"Oh, no, – of course not," she said, sunk in meek thought. "But father said it was *almost* – did he not? Do you know anything about the new law that makes these things so easy?"

"Nothing – except the general fact that it enables ill-assorted husbands and wives to part in a way they could not formerly do without an Act of Parliament."[6]

"Have you to sign a paper, or swear anything? Is it something like that?"

"Yes, I believe so."

"How long has it been introduced?"

"About six months or a year, the lawyer said, I think."

To hear these two poor Arcadian innocents[7] talk of imperial law would have made a humane person weep who should have known what a dangerous structure they were building up on their supposed knowledge. They remained in thought, like children in the presence of the incomprehensible.

"Giles," she said at last, "it makes me quite weary when I think how serious my situation is, or has been. Shall we not go out from here now, as it may seem rather fast of me – our being so long together, I mean – if anybody were to see us? I am almost sure," she added uncertainly, "that I ought not to let you hold my hand yet, knowing that the documents – or whatever it may be – have not been signed;

so that I – am still as married as ever – or almost. My dear father has forgotten himself. Not that I feel morally bound[8] to any one else, after what has taken place – no woman of spirit could – now, too, that several months have passed. But I wish to keep the proprieties as well as I can."

"Yes, yes. Still, your father reminds me that life is short. I myself feel that it is; that is why I wished to understand you in this that we have begun. At times, dear Grace, since receiving your father's letter, I am as uneasy and fearful as a child at what he said. If one of us were to die before the formal signing and sealing that is to release you have been done – if we should drop out of the world and never have made the most of this little, short, but real opportunity, I should think to myself as I sank down dying, 'Would to my God that I had spoken out my whole heart – given her one poor little kiss when I had the chance to give it! But I never did, although she had promised to be mine some day; and now I never can.' That's what I should think."

She had begun by watching the words from his lips with a mournful regard, as though their passage were visible; but as he went on she dropped her glance.

"Yes," she said, "I have thought that, too. And, because I have thought it, I by no means meant, in speaking of the proprieties, to be reserved and cold to you who loved me so long ago, or to hurt your heart as I used to do at that thoughtless time. Oh, not at all, indeed! But – ought I to allow you – Oh, it is too quick – surely!" Her eyes filled with tears of bewildered, alarmed emotion.

Winterborne was too straightforward to influence her further against her better judgment. "Yes – I suppose it is," he said repentantly. "I'll wait till all is settled. What has your father said in his letters to you?"

He meant about his progress with the petition; but she, mistaking him, frankly spoke of the personal part. "He says – what I have implied. Should I tell more plainly?"

"Oh, no – don't, if it is a secret."

"Not at all. I will tell every word, straight out, Giles, if you wish. He says I am to encourage you. There. But I cannot obey him further to-day. Come, let us go now." She gently slid her hand from his, and went in front of him out of the Abbey.

"I was thinking of getting some dinner," said Winterborne, changing to the prosaic as they walked. "And you, too, must require something. Do let me take you to a place I know."

Grace was almost without a friend in the world outside her father's house: her life with Fitzpiers had brought her no society; had sometimes, indeed, brought her deeper solitude than any she had ever known before. Hence it was a treat to her to find herself again the object of thoughtful care. But she questioned if to go publicly to dine alone with Giles Winterborne were not a proposal due rather to his unsophistication than to his prudence. She said gently, that she would much prefer his ordering her lunch at some place, and then coming to tell her it was ready, while she remained in the Abbey porch. Giles saw her secret reasoning, thought how hopelessly blind to propriety he was beside her, and went to do as she wished.

He was not absent more than ten minutes, and found Grace where he had left her.

"It will be quite ready by the time you get there," he said, and told her the name of the inn at which the meal had been ordered, which was one that she had never heard of.

"I'll find it by inquiry," said Grace, setting out.

"And shall I see you again?"

"Oh, yes – come to me there. It will not be like going together. I shall want you to find my father's man and the gig for me."

He waited on some ten minutes or a quarter of an hour, till he thought her lunch ended, and that he might fairly take advantage of her invitation to start her on her way home. He went straight to The Three Tuns – a little tavern in a side street, scrupulously clean, but humble and inexpensive. On his way he had an occasional misgiving as to whether the place had been elegant enough for her; and as soon as he entered it, and saw her ensconced there, he perceived that he had blundered.

Grace was seated in the only dining-room that the simple old hostelry could boast of, which was also a general parlour on market days: a long, low apartment, with a sanded floor herring-boned with a broom: a wide, red-curtained window to the street, and another to the garden. Grace had retreated to the end of the room looking out upon the latter, the front part being full of a mixed company of dairymen and butchers which had, to be just to him, dropped in since he was there.

She was in a mood of the greatest depression. On arriving, and seeing what the tavern was like, she had been taken by surprise; but having gone too far to retreat, she had heroically entered and sat down on the well-scrubbed settle, opposite the narrow table, with its knives and steel forks, tin pepper-boxes, blue salt-cellars, and posters advertising the sale of bullocks against the wall. The last time that she had taken any meal in a public place it had been with Fitzpiers at the dignified Earl of Wessex Hotel in that town, after a two months' roaming and sojourning at the gigantic hotels of the Continent.

How could she have expected any other kind of accommodation in present circumstances than such as Giles had provided? And yet how unprepared she was for this change! The tastes that she had acquired from Fitzpiers had been imbibed so subtly that she hardly knew she possessed them till confronted by this contrast. The elegant Fitzpiers, in fact, at that very moment owed a long bill at the above-mentioned hotel for the luxurious style in which he used to put her up there whenever they drove to Sherton. But such is social sentiment, that she had been quite comfortable under those debt-impending conditions, whilst she felt humiliated by her present situation, which Winterborne had paid for honestly on the nail.

He had noticed in a moment that she shrank from her position, and all his pleasure was gone. It was the same susceptibility over again which had spoiled his Christmas party long ago.

But he did not know that this recrudescence was only the casual result of Grace's apprenticeship to what she was determined to learn in spite of it – a consequence of one of those sudden surprises which confront everybody bent upon turning over a new leaf. She had finished her lunch, which he saw had been a very mincing performance; and he brought her out of the house as soon as he could.

"Now," he said, with great sad eyes, "you have not finished at all well, I know! Come round to the Earl of Wessex. I'll order a tea there. I did not remember that what was good enough for me was not good enough for you."

Her face faded into an aspect of deep distress when she saw what had happened. "Oh, no, Giles," she said with extreme earnestness: "certainly not. Why do you – say that, when you know better? You *ever* will misunderstand me."

"Indeed, that's not so, Mrs. Fitzpiers. Can you deny that you felt out of place at The Three Tuns?"

"I don't know! . . . Well, since you make me speak, I do not deny it."

"And yet I have felt at home there these twenty years. Your husband used always to take you to the Earl of Wessex, did he not?"

"Yes," she reluctantly admitted. How could she explain in the street of a market-town that it was her superficial and transitory taste which had been offended, and not her nature or her affection?

Fortunately, or unfortunately, at that moment they saw Melbury's man driving vacantly along the street in search of her, the hour having passed at which he had been told to take her up. Winterborne hailed him, and she was powerless then to prolong the discourse. She entered the vehicle sadly, and the horse trotted away.

CHAPTER VI

All night did Winterborne think over that unsatisfactory ending of a pleasant time, forgetting the pleasant time itself. He feared anew that they could never be happy together, even should she be free to choose him. She was accomplished: he was unrefined. It was the original difficulty, which he was too sensitive to recklessly ignore, as some men would have done in his place.

He was one of those silent, unobtrusive beings who want little from others in the way of favour or condescension, and perhaps on that very account scrutinise those others' behaviour too closely. He was not versatile, but one in whom a hope or belief which had once had its rise, meridian, and decline, seldom again exactly recurred, as in the breasts of more sanguine mortals. He had once worshipped her, laid out his life to suit her, wooed her, and lost her. Though it was with almost the same zest, it was with not quite the same hope, that he had begun to tread the old tracks again, and had allowed himself to be so charmed with her that day.

Move another step towards her he would not. He would even repulse her – as a tribute to conscience. It would be sheer sin to let her prepare a pitfall for her happiness not much smaller than the first by inveigling her into a union with such as he. Her poor father was now blind to these subtleties, which he had formerly beheld as in noontide light. It was his own duty to declare them – for her dear sake.

Grace, too, had a very uncomfortable night, and her solicitous embarrassment was not lessened the next morning when another letter from her father was put into her hands. Its tenour was an intenser strain of the one that had preceded it.

After stating how extremely glad he was to hear that she was better, and able to get out of doors, he went on:

"This is a wearisome business, the solicitor we have come to see being out of town. I do not know when I shall get home. My great anxiety in this delay is still lest you should lose Giles Winterborne. I cannot rest at night for thinking that while our business is hanging fire he may become estranged, or in his shyness go away from the neighbourhood. I have set my heart upon seeing him your husband, if you ever have another. Do then, Grace, give him some temporary encouragement, even though it is over-early. For when I consider the past I do think God will forgive me and you for being a little forward. I have another reason for this, my dear. I feel myself going rapidly down hill, and late affairs have still further helped me that way. And until this thing is done I cannot rest in peace."

He added a postscript:

"I have just heard that the solicitor is to be seen to-morrow. Possibly, therefore, I shall return in the evening after you get this."

The paternal longing ran on all fours with her own desire; and yet in forwarding it yesterday she had been on the brink of giving offence.

While craving to be a country girl again, just as her father requested;
to put off the old Eve,[1] the fastidious miss – or rather madam –
completely, her first attempt had been beaten by the unexpected
vitality of that fastidiousness. Her father on returning and seeing the
trifling coolness of Giles would be sure to say that the same perversity
which had led her to make difficulties about marrying Fitzpiers was
now prompting her to blow hot and cold with poor Winterborne.

If the latter had been the most subtle hand at touching the stops[2]
of her delicate soul instead of one who had just bound himself to let
her drift away from him again (if she would) on the wind of her
estranging education, he could not have acted more seductively than
he did that day. He chanced to be superintending some temporary
work in a field opposite her windows. She could not discover what he
was doing, but she read his mood keenly and truly: she could see in
his coming and going an air of determined abandonment of the whole
landscape that lay in her direction.

Oh, how she longed to make it up with him! Her father coming in
the evening – which meant, she supposed, that all formalities would
be in train, her marriage virtually annulled, and she be free to be won
again – how could she look him in the face if he should see them
estranged thus?

It was a fair green afternoon in June. She was seated in the garden,
in the rustic chair which stood under the laurel-bushes, made of
peeled oak branches that came to Melbury's premises as refuse after
barking-time. The mass of full-juiced leafage on the heights around
her was just swayed into faint gestures by a nearly spent wind which,
even in its enfeebled state, did not reach her shelter. All day she had
expected Giles to call – to inquire how she had got home, or something
or other; but he had not come. And he still tantalised her by going
athwart and across that orchard opposite. She could see him as she
sat.

A slight diversion was presently created by Creedle bringing him a
letter. She knew from this that Creedle had just come from Sherton,
and had called as usual at the post-office for anything that had arrived
by the afternoon post, of which there was no delivery at Hintock. She
pondered on what the letter might contain – particularly whether it

were a second refresher for Winterborne from her father, like her own of the morning.

But it appeared to have no bearing upon herself whatever. Giles read its contents; and almost immediately turned away to a gap in the hedge of the orchard – if that could be called a hedge which, owing to the drippings of the trees, was little more than a bank with a bush upon it here and there. He entered the plantation, and was no doubt going that way homeward to the mysterious hut he occupied on the other side of the woodland.

The sad sands were running swiftly through Time's glass;[3] she had often felt it in these latter days; and, like Giles, she felt it doubly now after the solemn and pathetic reminder in her father's communication. Her freshness would pass, the long-suffering devotion of Giles might suddenly end – might end that very hour. Men were so strange. The thought took away from her all her former reticence, and made her action bold. She started from her seat. If the little breach, quarrel, or whatever it might be called, of yesterday, was to be healed up it must be done by her on the instant. She crossed into the orchard, and clambered through the gap after Giles, just as he was diminishing to a faunlike figure under the green canopy and over the brown floor.

Grace had been wrong – very far wrong – in assuming that the letter had no reference to herself because Giles had turned away into the wood after its perusal. It was, sad to say, because the missive had so much reference to herself that he had thus turned away. He feared that his grieved discomfiture might be observed.

The letter was from Beaucock, written a few hours later than Melbury's to his daughter. It announced failure.

Giles had once done that thriftless man a good turn, and now was the moment when Beaucock had chosen to remember it, in his own way. During his absence in town with Melbury, the lawyer's clerk had naturally heard a great deal of the timber-merchant's family scheme of justice to Giles, and his communication was to inform Winterborne at the earliest possible moment that their attempt had failed, in order that the young man should not place himself in a false position towards Grace in the belief of its coming success. The news was, in sum, that Fitzpiers's conduct had not been sufficiently cruel to Grace to enable her to snap the bond. She was apparently doomed to be his wife till the end of the chapter.

Winterborne quite forgot his superficial differences with the poor girl under the warm rush of deep and distracting love for her which the almost tragical information engendered.

To renounce her for ever – that was then the end of it for him, after all. There was no longer any question about suitability, or room for tiffs on petty tastes. The curtain had fallen again between them. She could not be his. The cruelty of their late revived hope was now terrible. How could they all have been so simple as to suppose this thing could be done?

It was at this moment that, hearing some one coming behind him, he turned and saw her hastening on between the thickets. He perceived in an instant that she did not know the blighting news.

"Giles, why didn't you come across to me?" she asked with arch reproach. "Didn't you see me sitting there ever so long?"

"Oh, yes," he said in unprepared, provisional tones, for her unexpected presence caught him without the slightest plan of behaviour in the conjuncture. His manner made her think that she had been too chiding in her speech; and a mild scarlet wave passed over her as she resolved to soften it.

"I have had another letter from my father," she hastened to continue. "He thinks he may come home this evening. And – in view of his hopes – it will grieve him if there is any little difference between us, Giles."

"There is none," he said, sadly regarding her from the face downwards as he pondered how to lay the cruel truth bare.

"Still – I fear you have not quite forgiven me about my being uncomfortable at the inn."

"I have, I'm sure."

"But you speak in quite an unhappy way," she returned, coming up quite close to him with the most winning of the many pretty airs that appertained to her. "Don't you think you will ever be happy, Giles?"

He did not reply for some instants. "When the sun shines on the north front of Sherton Abbey – that's when my happiness will come to me!" said he, staring as it were into the earth.

"But – then that means that there is something more than my offending you in not liking The Three Tuns. If it is because I – did not like to let you kiss me in the Abbey   well, you know, Giles, that it was not on account of my cold feelings, but because I did certainly, just then, think it was rather premature, in spite of my poor father. That was the true reason – the sole one. But I do not want to be hard – God knows I do not," she said, her voice fluctuating. "And perhaps – as I am on the verge of freedom – I am not right, after all, in thinking there is any harm in your kissing me."

"Oh, Heaven!" groaned Winterborne to himself. His head was turned askance as he still resolutely regarded the ground. For the last several minutes he had seen this great temptation approaching him in regular siege; and now it had come. The wrong, the social sin, of now taking advantage of the offer of her lips, had a magnitude, in the eyes of one whose life had been so primitive, so ruled by purest household laws as Giles's, which can hardly be explained.

"Did you say anything?" she asked timidly.

"Oh, no – only that —"

"You mean that it must *be* settled, since my father is coming home?" she said gladly.

"Ah – yes."

"Then why don't you do what you want to?" She was almost pouting at his hesitation.

Winterborne, though fighting valiantly against himself all this while – though he would have protected Grace's good repute as the apple of his eye, was a man; and, as Desdemona said, men are not gods.[4] In face of the agonising seductiveness shown by her, in her unenlightened school-girl simplicity about the laws and ordinances, he betrayed a man's weakness. Since it was so – since it had come to this, that Grace, deeming herself free to do it, was virtually asking him to demonstrate that he loved her – since he could demonstrate it only too truly – since life was short and love was strong – he gave way to the temptation, notwithstanding that he perfectly well knew her to be wedded irrevocably to Fitzpiers. Indeed, he cared for nothing past or future, simply accepting the present and what it brought, deciding once in his life to clasp in his arms her he had watched over and loved so long.

She started back suddenly from his embrace,[5] influenced by a sort of inspiration. "Oh, I suppose," she stammered, "that I am really free? – that this is right? Is there *really* a new law? Father cannot have been too sanguine in saying —"

He did not answer, and a moment afterwards Grace burst into tears in spite of herself. "Oh, why does not my father come home and explain!" she sobbed, "and let me know clearly what I am! It is too trying, this, to ask me to – and then to leave me so long in so vague a state that I do not know what to do, and perhaps do wrong!"

Winterborne felt like a very Cain,[6] over and above his previous sorrow. How he had sinned against her in not telling her what he knew! He turned aside: the feeling of his cruelty mounted higher and higher. How could he have dreamt of kissing her? He could hardly refrain from tears. Surely nothing more pitiable had ever been known than the condition of this poor young thing, now as heretofore the victim of her father's well-meant but blundering policy.

Even in the hour of Melbury's greatest assurance Winterborne had harboured a suspicion that no law, new or old, could undo Grace's marriage without her appearance in public; though he was not sufficiently sure of what might have been enacted to destroy by his own words her pleasing idea that a mere dash of the pen, on her father's testimony, was going to be sufficient. But he had never suspected the sad fact that the position was irremediable.

Poor Grace, perhaps feeling that she had indulged in too much fluster for a mere kiss, even though it had been prolonged an unconscionable time, calmed herself at finding how grave he was.

"I am glad we are friends again anyhow," she said, smiling through her tears. "Giles, if you had only shown half the boldness before I married that you show now, you would have carried me off for your own, first instead of second. If we do marry I hope you will never think badly of me for encouraging you a little, but my father is *so* impatient, you know, as his years and infirmities increase, that he will wish to see us a little advanced when he comes. That is my only excuse."

To Winterborne all this was sadder than it was sweet. How could she so trust her father's conjectures? He did not know how to tell her the truth and shame himself. And yet he felt that it must be done.

To hasten the revelation, however, was beyond even him. What had been begun between them was repeated as they walked, and the afternoon was far advanced before he could actually set about opening her eyes.[7]

"We may have been wrong," he began, almost fearfully, "in supposing that it can all be carried out whilst we stay here at Hintock. I am not sure but that people may have to appear in a public court even under the new Act; and if there should be any difficulty and we cannot marry after all — "

Her cheeks became slowly bloodless. "Oh, Giles," she said, grasping his arm, "you have heard something! What – cannot my father conclude it there and now? Surely, he has done it? Oh, Giles, Giles, don't deceive me. After letting you go on like this – what terrible position am I in?"

He could not tell her, try as he would. The sense of her implicit trust in his honour absolutely disabled him. "I cannot inform you," he murmured, his voice as husky as that of the leaves under foot. "Your father will soon be here. Then we shall know. I will take you home."

Inexpressibly dear as she was to him he offered her his arm with the most reserved air, as he added correctly, "I will take you at any rate into the drive."

Thus they walked on together, Grace vibrating between happiness and misgiving. It was only a few minutes' walk to where the drive ran, and they had hardly descended into it when they heard a voice behind them cry, "Take out that arm!"

For a moment they did not heed, and the voice repeated more loudly and hoarsely:

"Take out that arm!"

It was Melbury's. He had returned sooner than they expected and now came up to them. Grace's hand had been withdrawn like lightning on her hearing the second command.

"I don't blame you, I don't blame you," he said, in the weary cadence of one broken down with scourgings. "But you two must walk together no more – I have been surprised – I have been cruelly deceived – Giles, don't say anything to me; but go away!"

He was evidently not aware that Winterborne had known the truth before he brought it; and Giles would not stay to discuss it with him then. When the young man had gone, Melbury took his daughter indoors to the room he used as his office. There he sat down, and bent over the slope of the bureau, her bewildered gaze fixed upon him.

When Melbury had recovered a little he said, "You are now as ever Fitzpiers's wife. I was deluded. He has not done you *enough* harm.[8] You are still subject to his beck and call."

"Then let it be, and never mind, father," she said with dignified sorrow. "I can bear it. It is your trouble that grieves me most!" She stooped over him, and put her arm round his neck, which distressed Melbury still more.

"I don't mind at all what comes to me," Grace continued; "whose wife I am, or whose I am not. I do love Giles: I cannot help that; and I have gone farther with him than I should have done if I had known exactly how things were. But I do not reproach you."

"Then Giles did not tell you?" said Melbury.

"No," said she. "He could not have known it. His behaviour to me proved that he did not know."

Her father said nothing more, and Grace went away to the solitude of her chamber.

Her heavy disquietude had many shapes; and for a time she put aside the dominant fact to think of her too free conduct towards Giles. His love-making had been brief as it was sweet; but would he on reflection contemn her for forwardness? How could she have been so simple as to suppose she was in a position to behave as she had done! Thus she mentally blamed her ignorance; and yet in the centre of her heart she blessed it a little for what it had momentarily brought her.

CHAPTER VII

Life among the people involved in these events seemed to be suppressed and hidebound for a while. Grace seldom showed herself outside the house, never outside the garden; for she feared she might encounter Giles Winterborne; and that she could not bear.

This pensive intramural existence of the self-constituted nun appeared likely to continue for an indefinite time. She had learnt that there was one possibility in which her formerly imagined position might become real and only one; that her husband's absence should continue long enough to amount to positive desertion. But she never allowed her mind to dwell much upon the thought; still less did she deliberately hope for such a result. Her regard for Winterborne had been rarefied by the shock which followed its avowal into an ethereal emotion that had little to do with living and doing.

As for Giles he was lying – or rather sitting – ill at his hut. A feverish indisposition which had been hanging about him for sometime, the result of a chill caught the previous winter, seemed to acquire virulence with the prostration of his hopes. But not a soul knew of his languor, and he did not think the case serious enough to send for a medical man. After a few days he was better again, and crept about his home in a great-coat, attending to his simple wants as usual with his own hands.

So matters stood when the limpid inertion of Grace's pool-like existence was disturbed as by a geyser.[1] She received a letter from Fitzpiers.

Such a startling letter it was in its import, though couched in the gentlest language. In his absence Grace had grown to regard him with toleration, and her relation to him with equanimity, till she had almost forgotten how trying his presence would be. He wrote briefly and unaffectedly: he made no excuses, but informed her that he was living quite alone, and had been led to think that they ought to be together, if she would make up her mind to forgive him. He therefore purposed to cross the Channel to Budmouth by the steamer on a day he named, which she found to be three days after the time of her present reading.

He said that he could not come to Hintock for obvious reasons, which her father would understand even better than herself. As the only alternative, she was to be on the quay to meet the steamer when it arrived from the opposite coast, probably about half an hour before midnight, bringing with her any luggage she might require; join him there, and pass with him into the twin vessel, which left immediately the other entered the harbour; returning thus with him to his Continental dwelling-place, which he did not name. He had no intention of showing himself on land at all.

The troubled Grace took the letter to her father, who now continued for long hours by the fireless summer chimney-corner, as if he thought it were winter, the pitcher of cider standing beside him, mostly untasted, and coated with a film of dust. After reading it he looked up.

"You sha'n't go," said he.

"I had felt I would not," she answered. "But I did not know what you would say."

"If he comes and lives in England, not too near here, and in a respectable way, and wants you to come to him, I'm not sure that I'll oppose him in wishing it," muttered Melbury. "I'd stint myself to keep you both in a genteel and seemly style. But go abroad you never shall with my consent."

There the question rested that day. Grace was unable to reply to her husband in the absence of an address, and the morrow came, and the next day, and the evening on which he had requested her to meet him. Throughout the whole of it she remained within the four walls of her room.

The sense of her harassment, carking doubt of what might be impending, hung like a cowl of blackness over the Melbury household. They spoke almost in whispers, and wondered what Fitzpiers would do next. It was the hope of every one that, finding she did not arrive, he would return again to France; and as for Grace, she was willing to write to him on the most kindly terms if he would only keep away.

The night passed, Grace lying tense and wide awake, and her

relatives, in great part, likewise. When they met the next morning they were pale and anxious, though neither speaking of the subject which occupied all their thoughts. The day passed as quietly as the previous ones, and she began to think that in the rank caprice of his moods he had abandoned the idea of getting her to join him as quickly as it was formed.

All on a sudden, some person who had just come from Sherton entered the house with the news that Mr. Fitzpiers was on his way home to Hintock. He had been seen hiring a carriage at the Earl of Wessex Hotel.

Her father and Grace were both present when the intelligence was announced.

"Now," said Melbury, "we must make the best of what has been a very bad matter. The man is repenting: the partner of his folly, I hear, is gone away from him to Switzerland, so that chapter of his life is probably over. If he chooses to make a home for ye I think you should not say him nay, Grace. Certainly he cannot very well live at Hintock without a blow to his pride; but if he can bear that, and likes Hintock best, why, there's the empty wing of the house as it was before."

"Oh, father!" said Grace, turning white with dismay.

"Why not?" said he, a little of his former doggedness returning. He was, in truth, disposed to somewhat more leniency towards her husband just now than he had shown formerly, from a conviction that he had treated him over roughly in his anger.

"Surely it is the most respectable thing to do?" he continued. "I don't like this state that you are in – neither married nor single. It hurts me, and it hurts you, and it will always be remembered against us in Hintock. There has never been any scandal like it in the family before."

"He will be here in less than an hour," murmured Grace.

The twilight of the room prevented her father seeing the despondent misery of her face. The one intolerable condition, the condition she had deprecated above all others, was that of Fitzpiers's reinstatement there. "Oh, I won't, I won't see him," she said, sinking down. She was almost hysterical.

"Try if you cannot," he returned moodily.

"Oh, yes, I will, I will," she went on inconsequently: "I'll try"; and jumping up suddenly she left the room.

In the darkness of the apartment to which she flew nothing could have been seen during the next half hour; but from a corner a quick breathing was audible from this impressible creature, who combined modern nerves with primitive emotions,[2] and was doomed by such co-existence to be numbered among the distressed, and to take her scourgings to their exquisite extremity.

The window was open. On this quiet, late summer evening, whatever sound arose in so secluded a district – the chirp of a bird, a call from a voice, the turning of a wheel – extended over bush and tree to unwonted distances. Very few sounds did arise. But as Grace invisibly breathed in the brown glooms of the chamber, the small remote noise of light wheels came into her, accompanied by the trot of a horse on the turnpike road. There seemed to be a sudden hitch or pause in the progress of the vehicle, which was what first drew her attention to it. She knew the point whence the sound proceeded – the hill-top over which travellers passed on their way hitherward from Sherton Abbas – the place at which she had emerged from the wood with Mrs. Charmond. Grace slid along the floor, and bent her head over the window-sill, listening with open lips. The carriage had stopped, and she heard a man use exclamatory words. Then another said, "What the devil is the matter with the horse?" She recognised the voice as her husband's.

The accident, such as it had been, was soon remedied, and the carriage could be heard descending the hill on the Hintock side, soon to turn into the lane leading out of the highway, and then into the "drong" which led out of the lane to the house where she was.

A spasm passed through Grace. The Daphnean instinct[3], exceptionally strong in her as a girl, had been revived by her widowed seclusion; and it was not lessened by her affronted sentiments towards the comer, and her regard for another man. She opened some little ivory tablets[4] that lay on the dressing-table, scribbled in pencil on one of them, "I am gone to visit one of my school-friends," gathered a few toilet necessaries into a hand-bag, and, not three minutes after that voice had been heard, her slim form, hastily wrapped up from observation, might have been seen passing out of the back door of Melbury's house. Thence she skimmed up the garden-path, through the gap in the hedge, and into the mossy cart-track under the trees which led into the depth of the woods.

The leaves overhead were now in their latter green – so opaque, that it was darker at some of the densest spots than in winter time, scarce a crevice existing by which a ray could get down to the ground. But in open places she could see well enough. Summer was ending: in the daytime singing insects hung in every sunbeam: vegetation was heavy nightly with globes of dew; and after showers creeping damps and twilight chills came up from the hollows.

The plantations were always weird at this hour of eve – more spectral far than in the leafless season, when there were fewer masses and more minute lineality. The smooth surfaces of glossy plants came out like weak, lidless eyes: there were strange faces and figures from expiring lights that had somehow wandered into the canopied obscurity; while now and then low peeps of the sky between the trunks were like sheeted shapes, and on the tips of boughs sat faint cloven tongues.

But Grace's fear just now was not imaginative or spiritual; and she heeded these impressions but little. She went on as silently as she could, avoiding the hollows wherein leaves had accumulated, and stepping upon soundless moss and grass-tufts. She paused breathlessly once or twice, and fancied that she could hear, above the sound of her strumming pulse, the vehicle containing Fitzpiers turning in at the gate of her father's premises. She hastened on again.

The Hintock woods owned by Mrs. Charmond were presently left behind, and those into which she next plunged were divided from the latter by a bank, from whose top the hedge had long ago perished – starved for want of sun. It was with some caution that Grace now walked, though she was quite free from any of the commonplace timidities of her ordinary pilgrimages to such posts. She feared no lurking harms, but that her effort would be all in vain, and her return to the house rendered imperative.

She had walked between three and four miles when that prescriptive comfort and relief to wanderers in woods – a distant light – broke at last upon her searching eyes. It was so very small as to be almost sinister to a stranger, but to her it was what she sought. She pushed forward, and the dim outline of a dwelling was disclosed.

The house was a square cot of one story only, sloping up on all sides to a chimney in the midst. It had formerly been the home of a charcoal-burner, in times when that fuel was still used in the county-houses. Its only appurtenance was a paled inclosure, there being no garden, the shade of the trees preventing the growth of vegetables. She advanced to the window whence the rays of light proceeded, and the shutters being as yet unclosed, she could survey the whole interior through the panes.

The room within was kitchen, parlour, and scullery all in one: the natural sandstone floor was worn into hills and dales by long treading, so that none of the furniture stood level, and the table slanted like a desk. A fire burnt on the hearth, in front of which revolved the skinned carcase of a very small rabbit, suspended by a string from a nail. Leaning with one arm on the mantel-shelf stood Winterborne, his eyes on the roasting animal, his face so rapt that speculation could build nothing on it concerning his thoughts, more than that they were not with the scene before him. She thought his features had changed a little since she saw them last. The firelight did not enable her to perceive that they were positively haggard.

Grace's throat emitted a gasp of relief at finding the result so nearly as she had hoped. She went to the door and tapped lightly.

He seemed to be accustomed to the noises of woodpeckers, squirrels, and such small creatures, for he took no notice of her tiny signal, and she knocked again. This time he came and opened the door.

When the light of the room fell upon her face he started; and, hardly knowing what he did, crossed the threshold to her, placing his hands upon her two arms, while surprise, joy, alarm, sadness, chased through him by turns. With Grace it was the same; even in this stress there was the fond fact that they had met again.

Thus they stood,

> "Long tears upon their faces, waxen white
> With extreme sad delight,"[5]

till he broke the silence by saying in a whisper, "Come in."

"No, no, Giles!" she answered hurriedly stepping yet further back from the door. "I am passing by – and I have called on you – I won't enter. Will you help me? I am afraid. I want to get by a roundabout way to Sherton, and so to Exbury. I have a school-fellow there – but I cannot get to Sherton alone. Oh, if you will only accompany me a little way! Don't condemn me, Giles, and be offended! I was obliged to come to you because I have no other help here. Three months ago you were my lover: now you are only my friend. The law has stepped in, and forbidden what we thought of. It must not be. But we can act honestly, and yet you can be my friend for one little hour! I have no other –"

She could get no further. Covering her eyes with one hand, by an effort of repression she wept silent tears, without a sigh or sob. Winterborne took her other hand in both his.

"What has happened?" he said.

"He has come."

There was a stillness as of death, till Winterborne asked, "You mean this, Grace – that I am to help you to get away?"

"Yes," said she. "Appearance is no matter, when the reality is right. I have said to myself, I can trust you."

Giles knew from this that she did not suspect his treachery – if it could be called such – earlier in the summer, when they met for the last time as lovers; and in the intensity of his contrition for that tender wrong, he determined to deserve her faith now at least, and so wipe out that reproach from his conscience.

"I'll come at once," he said. "I'll light a lantern."

He unhooked a dark lantern from a nail under the eaves, and she did not notice how his hand shook with the slight strain, or dream that in making this offer he was taxing a convalescence which could ill afford such self-sacrifice. The lantern was lit and they started.

CHAPTER VIII

The first hundred yards of their course lay under motionless trees, whose upper foliage began to hiss with falling drops of rain. By the time that they emerged upon a glade it rained heavily.

"This is awkward!" said Grace, with a forced little laugh to hide her concern.

Winterborne stopped. "Gracie," he said, preserving a strictly business manner which belied him; "you cannot go to Sherton to-night."

"But I must!"

"Why? It is nine miles from here. It is almost an impossibility in this rain."

"True – *why*," she replied mournfully at the end of a silence. "What is reputation to me?"

"Now hearken," said Giles. "You won't – go back to your –"

"No, no, no! Don't make me!" she cried piteously.

"Then let us turn." They slowly retraced their steps, and again stood before his door. "Now this house from this moment is yours, and not mine," he said deliberately. "I have a place near by where I can stay very well."

Her face had drooped. "Oh," she murmured as she saw the dilemma. "What have I done!"

There was a smell of something burning within, and he looked through the window. The young rabbit that he had been cooking to coax a weak appetite was beginning to char. "Please go in and attend to it," he said. "Do what you like. Now I leave. You will find everything about the hut that is necessary."

"But, Giles – your supper," she exclaimed. "An outhouse would do for me – anything – till to-morrow at daybreak!"

He signified a negative. 'I tell you to go in – you may catch agues out here in your delicate state. You can give me my supper through the window, if you feel well enough. I'll wait a while."

He gently urged her to pass the doorway, and was relieved when he saw her within the room sitting down. Without so much as crossing the threshold himself he closed the door upon her, and turned the key in the lock. Tapping at the window he signified that she should open the casement, and when she had done this he handed in the key to her.

"You are locked in," he said; "and your own mistress."

Even in her trouble she could not refrain from a faint smile at his scrupulousness, as she took the door-key.

"Do you feel better?" he went on. "If so, and you wish to give me some of your supper, please do. If not it is of no importance. I can get some elsewhere."

The grateful sense of his kindness stirred her to action, though she only knew half what that kindness really was. At the end of some ten minutes she again came to the window, pushed it open, and said in a whisper "Giles!" He at once emerged from the shade, and saw that she was preparing to hand him his share of the meal upon a plate.

"I don't like to treat you so hardly," she murmured with deep regret in her words as she heard the rain pattering on the leaves. "But – I suppose it is best to arrange like this?"

"Oh yes," he said quickly.

"I feel that I could never have reached Sherton."

"It was impossible."

"Are you sure you have a snug place out there?" (With renewed misgiving.)

"Quite. Have you found everything you want? I am afraid it is rather rough accommodation."

"Can I notice defects? I have long passed that stage, and you know it, Giles, or you ought to."

His eyes sadly contemplated her face as its pale responsiveness modulated through a crowd of expressions that showed only too clearly to what a pitch she was strung. If ever Winterborne's heart chafed his bosom it was at this sight of a perfectly defenceless creature conditioned by such harsh circumstances. He forgot his own agony in the satisfaction of having at least found her a shelter. He took his plate and cup from her hands, saying, "Now I'll push the shutter to, and you will find an iron pin on the inside, which you must fix into the bolt. Do not stir in the morning till I come and call you."

She expressed an alarmed hope that he would not go very far away.

"Oh, no – I shall be quite within hail," said Winterborne.

She bolted the window as directed, and he retreated. His "snug place" proved to be a wretched little shelter of the roughest kind, formed of four hurdles thatched with brake-fern. Underneath were dry sacks, hay, and other litter of the sort, upon which he sat down; and there in the dark tried to eat his meal. But his appetite was quite gone. He pushed the plate aside, and shook up the hay and sacks, so as to form a rude couch, on which he flung himself down to sleep, for it was getting late.

But sleep he could not, for many reasons, of which not the least was thought of his charge. He sat up, and looked towards the cot through the damp obscurity. With all its external features the same as usual, he could scarcely believe that it contained the dear friend – he would not use a warmer name – who had come to him so unexpectedly and, he could not help admitting, so rashly.

He had not ventured to ask her any particulars; but the position was pretty clear without them. Though social law had negatived for ever their opening paradise of the previous June, it was not without stoical pride that he accepted the present trying conjuncture. There was one man on earth in whom she believed absolutely, and he was that man. That this crisis could end in nothing but sorrow was a view for a moment effaced by this triumphant thought of her trust in him; and the purity of the affection with which he responded to that trust rendered him more than proof against any frailty that besieged him in relation to her.

The rain, which had never ceased, now drew his attention by beginning to drop through the meagre screen that covered him. He rose to attempt some remedy for this discomfort, but the trembling of his knees and the throbbing of his pulse told him that in his weakness he was unable to fence against the storm, and he lay down to bear it as best he might. He was angry with himself for his feebleness – he who had been so strong. It was imperative that she should know nothing of his present state, and to do that she must not see his face by daylight, for its thinness would inevitably betray him.

The next morning, accordingly, when it was hardly light, he rose and dragged his stiff limbs about the precincts, preparing for her everything she could require for getting breakfast within. On the bench outside the window-sill he placed water, wood, and other necessaries, writing with a piece of chalk beside them, "It is best that I should not see you. Put my breakfast on the bench."

At seven o'clock he tapped at her window as he had promised, retreating at once that she might not catch sight of him. But from his shelter under the boughs he could see her very well, when, in response to his signal, she opened the window and the light fell upon her face. The languid largeness of her eyes showed that her sleep had been little more than his own, and the pinkness of their lids, that her waking hours had not been free from tears.

She read the writing, seemed, he thought, disappointed, but took up the materials he had provided, evidently thinking him some way off. Giles waited on, assured that a girl who, in spite of her culture, knew what country life was, would find no difficulty in the simple preparation of their food.

Within the cot it was all very much as he conjectured, though Grace had slept much longer than he. After the loneliness of the night she would have been glad to see him; but appreciating his feeling when she read the request, she made no attempt to recall him. She found abundance of provisions laid in, his plan being to replenish his buttery weekly, and this being the day after the victualling-van had called from Sherton. When the meal was ready, she put what he required outside, as she had done with the supper; and, notwithstanding her longing to see him, withdrew from the window promptly, and left him to himself.

It had been a leaden dawn, and the rain now steadily renewed its fall. As she heard no more of Winterborne, she concluded that he had gone away to his daily work, and forgotten that he had promised to accompany her to Sherton; an erroneous conclusion, for he remained all day, by force of his condition, within fifty yards of where she was.

The morning wore on; and in her doubt when to start, and how to travel, she lingered yet; keeping the door carefully bolted lest an intruder should discover her. Locked in this place she was comparatively safe, at any rate, and doubted if she would be safe elsewhere.

The humid gloom of an ordinary wet day was doubled by the shade and drip of the leafage. Autumn, this year, was coming in with rains. Gazing, in her enforced idleness, from the one window of the living room, she could see various small members of the animal community that lived unmolested there – creatures of hair, fluff, and scale; the toothed kind and the billed kind; underground creatures jointed and ringed – circumambulating the hut, under the impression that, Giles having gone away, nobody was there; and eyeing it inquisitively with a view to winter quarters. Watching these neighbours, who knew neither law nor sin, distracted her a little from her trouble; and she managed to while away some portion of the afternoon by putting Giles's home in order, and making little improvements which she deemed that he would value when she was gone.

Once or twice she fancied that she heard a faint noise amid the trees, resembling a cough; but as it never came any nearer she concluded that it was a squirrel or a bird.

At last the daylight lessened, and she made up a larger fire, for the evenings were chilly. As soon as it was too dark – which was comparatively early – to discern the human countenance in this place of shadows, there came to the window, to her great delight, a tapping which she knew from its method to be Giles's.

She opened the casement instantly, and put out her hand to him, though she could only just perceive his outline. He clasped her fingers, and she noticed the heat of his palm, and its shakiness.

"He has been walking fast, in order to get here quickly," she thought. How could she know that he had just crawled out from the straw of the shelter hard by; and that the heat of his hand was feverishness?

"My dear, good Giles!" she burst out impulsively.

"Anybody would have done it for you," replied Winterborne, with as much matter-of-fact as he could summon.

"About my getting to Exbury?" she said.

"I have been thinking," responded Giles, with tender deference, "that you had better stay where you are for the present, if you wish not to be caught. I need not tell you that the place is yours as long as you like; and perhaps in a day or two, finding you absent, he will go away. At any rate, in two or three days, I could do anything to assist – such as make inquiries, or go a great way towards Sherton-Abbas with you; for the cider season will soon be coming on, and I want to run down to the Vale to see how the crops are, and I shall go by the Sherton road. But for a day or two I am busy here." He was hoping that by the time mentioned he would be strong enough to engage himself actively on her behalf. "I hope you do not feel over-much melancholy in being a prisoner?"

She declared that she did not mind it; but she sighed.

From long acquaintance they could read each other's heart-symptoms like books of large type. "I fear you are sorry you came," said Giles, "and that you think I should have advised you more firmly than I did not to stay."

"Oh, no! dear, dear friend," answered Grace, with a heaving bosom. "Don't think that that is what I regret. What I regret is my enforced treatment of you – dislodging you, excluding you from your own house. Why should I not speak out? You know what I feel for you – what I have felt for no other living man, what I shall never feel for a man again! But as I have vowed myself to somebody else than you, and cannot be released, I must behave as I do behave, and keep that vow. I am not bound to him by any divine law,[1] after what he has done; but I have promised, and I will pay."

The rest of the evening was passed in his handing her such things as she would require the next day, and casual remarks thereupon, an occupation which diverted her mind to some degree from pathetic views of her attitude towards him, and of her life in general. The only infringement – if infringement it could be called – of his predetermined bearing towards her was an involuntary pressing of her hand to his lips when she put it through the casement to bid him good-night. He knew she was weeping, though he could not see her tears.

She again entreated his forgiveness for so selfishly appropriating the cottage. But it would only be for a day or two more, she thought, since go she must.

He yearningly replied, "I – I don't like you to go away!"

"Oh, Giles," said she, "I know – I know! But – I am a woman, and you are a man. I cannot speak more plainly. 'Whatsoever things are pure' – you know what is in my mind,[2] because you know me so well."

"Yes, Gracie, yes. I do not at all mean that the question between us has not been settled by your marriage turning out hopelessly unalterable. I merely meant – well, a feeling – no more."

"In a week, at the outside, I should be discovered if I stayed here; and I think that by law he could compel me to return to him."

"Yes; perhaps you are right. Go when you wish, dear Grace."

His last words that evening were a hopeful remark that all might be well with her yet; that Mr. Fitzpiers would not intrude upon her life, if he found that his presence cost her so much pain. Then the window was closed, the shutters folded, and the rustle of his footsteps died away.

No sooner had she retired to rest that night than the wind began to rise, and after a few prefatory blasts to be accompanied by rain. The wind grew more violent, and as the storm went on it was difficult to believe that no opaque body, but only an invisible colourless thing, was trampling and climbing over the roof, making branches creak, springing out of the trees upon the chimney, popping its head into the flue, and shrieking and blaspheming at every corner of the walls. As in the grisly story,[3] the assailant was a spectre which could be felt but not seen. She had never before been so struck with the devilry of a gusty night in a wood, because she had never been so entirely alone in spirit as she was now. She seemed almost to be apart from herself – a vacuous duplicate only. The recent self of physical animation and clear intentions was not there.

Sometimes a bough from an adjoining tree was swayed so low as to smite the roof in the manner of a gigantic hand smiting the mouth of an adversary, to be followed by a trickle of rain, as blood from the wound. To all this weather Giles must be more or less exposed; how much, she did not know.

At last Grace could hardly endure the idea of such a hardship in relation to him. Whatever he was suffering, it was she who had caused it; he had vacated his house on account of her. She was not worth such self-sacrifice; she should not have accepted it of him. And then, as her anxiety increased with increasing thought, there returned upon her mind some incidents of her late intercourse with him, which she had heeded but little at the time. The look of his face – what had there been about his face which seemed different from its appearance of yore? Was it not thinner, less rich in hue, less like that of ripe Autumn's brother to whom she had formerly compared him? And his voice; she had distinctly noticed a change in tone. And his gait; surely it had been feebler, stiffer, more like the gait of a weary man. That slight occasional noise she had heard in the day, and attributed to squirrels; it might have been his cough after all.

Thus conviction took root in her perturbed mind that Winterborne was unwell, or had been so, and that he had carefully concealed his condition from her that she might have no scruples about accepting a hospitality which by the nature of the case expelled her entertainer.

"My own, own, true I— my dear kind friend!" she cried to herself. "Oh, it shall not be – it shall not be!"

She hastily wrapped herself up, and obtained a light, with which she entered the adjoining room, the cot possessing only one floor. Setting down the candle on the table here she went to the door with the key in her hand, and placed it in the lock. Before turning it she paused, her fingers still clutching it; and pressing her other hand to her forehead she fell into agitating thought.

A tattoo on the window, caused by the tree-droppings blowing against it, brought her indecision to a close. She turned the key, and opened the door.

The darkness was intense, seeming to touch her pupils like a substance. She only now became aware how heavy the rainfall had been and was: the dripping of the eaves splashed like a fountain. She stood listening with parted lips, and holding the door in one hand, till her eyes growing accustomed to the obscurity, discerned the wild brandishing of their arms by the adjoining trees. At last she cried loudly with an effort: "Giles! you may come in!"

There was no answer to her cry, and overpowered by her own temerity, Grace retreated quickly, shut the door, and stood looking on the floor with flushed cheeks. Perhaps he was very well after all.

But this mood was not for long. She again lifted the latch, and with far more determination than at first.

"Giles, Giles!" she cried, with the full strength of her voice, and without any of the shamefacedness that had characterised her first cry. "Oh, come in – come in! Where are you? I have been wicked – I have thought too much of myself! Do you hear? I don't want to keep you out any longer. I cannot bear that you should suffer so. Gi-i-iles!"

A reply? It was a reply! Through the darkness and wind a voice reached her, floating upon the weather as though a part of it.

"Here I am – all right! Don't trouble about me."

"Don't you want to come in? Are you not wet?[4] *I don't mind what they say, or what they think any more.*"

"I am all right," he repeated. "It is not necessary for me to come. Good night! good night!"

Grace sighed, turned, and shut the door slowly. Could she have been mistaken about his health? Perhaps, after all, she had perceived a change in him because she had not seen him for so long. Time sometimes did his ageing work in jerks, as she knew. Well, she had done all she could. He would not come in. She retired to rest again.

CHAPTER IX

The next morning Grace was at the window early. She felt determined to see him somehow that day, and prepared his breakfast eagerly. Eight o'clock struck, and she then remembered that he had not come to arouse her by a knocking as usual, her own anxiety having caused her to stir.

The breakfast was set in its place without. But he did not appear to take it; and she waited on. Nine o'clock arrived, and the breakfast was cold; and still there was no Giles. A thrush, who had been repeating himself a good deal on an opposite bush for some time, came and took a morsel from the plate, bolted it, waited, looked around, and took another. At ten o'clock she drew in the tray, and sat down to her own solitary meal. He must have been called away on business early, the rain having cleared off.

Yet she would have liked to assure herself, by thoroughly exploring the precincts of the hut, that he was nowhere in its vicinity; but as the day was comparatively fine the dread lest some stray passenger or woodman should encounter her in such a reconnoitre paralysed her wish. The solitude was further accentuated to-day by the stopping of the clock for want of winding, and the fall into the chimney-corner of flakes of soot loosened by the rains. At noon she heard a slight rustling outside the window, and found that it was caused by an eft which had crept out of the leaves to bask in the last sun-rays that would be worth having till the following May.

She continually peeped out through the lattice but could see little. In front lay the brown leaves of last year, and upon them some yellowish-green ones of this season that had been prematurely blown down by the gale. Above stretched an old beech, with vast arm-pits, and great pocket-holes in its sides where branches had been removed in past times; a black slug was trying to climb it. Dead boughs were scattered about like ichthyosauri in a museum, and beyond them were perishing woodbine stems resembling old ropes.

From the other window all she could see were more trees, in jackets of lichen and stockings of moss. At their roots were stemless yellow fungi like lemons and apricots, and tall fungi with more stem than stool. Next were more trees close together, wrestling for existence, their branches disfigured with wounds resulting from their mutual rubbings and blows. It was the struggle between these neighbours that she had heard in the night. Beneath them were the rotting stumps of those of the group that had been vanquished long ago, rising from their mossy setting like black teeth from green gums. Further on were other tufts of moss in islands divided by the shed leaves – variety upon variety, dark green and pale green; moss like little fir-trees, like plush, like malachite stars; like nothing on earth except moss.

The strain upon Grace's mind in various ways was so great on this the most desolate day she had passed there that she felt it would be well-nigh impossible to spend another in such circumstances. The evening came at last; the sun, when its chin was on the earth, found an opening through which to pierce the shade, and stretched irradiated gauzes across the damp atmosphere, making the wet trunks shine, and throwing splotches of such ruddiness on the leaves beneath the beech that they were turned to gory hues. When night at last arrived, and with it the time for his return, she was nearly broken down with suspense.

The simple evening meal, partly tea, partly supper, which Grace had prepared, stood waiting upon the hearth; and yet Giles did not come. It was now nearly twenty-four hours since she had seen him. As the room grew darker, and only the firelight broke against the gloom of the walls, she was convinced that it would be beyond her staying power to pass the night without hearing from him or from somebody. Yet eight o'clock drew on, and his form at the window did not appear.

The meal remained untasted. Suddenly rising from before the hearth of smouldering embers, where she had been crouching with her hands clasped over her knees, she crossed the room, unlocked the door, and listened. Every breath of wind had ceased with the decline of day, but the rain had resumed the steady dripping of the night before. Grace might have stood there five minutes when she fancied she heard that old sound, a cough, at no great distance; and it was presently repeated. If it were Winterborne's he must be near her; why, then, had he not visited her?

A horrid misgiving that he could not visit her took possession of Grace, and she looked up anxiously for the lantern, which was hanging above her head. To light it and go in the direction of the sound would be the obvious way to solve the dread problem; but the conditions made her hesitate, and in a moment a cold sweat pervaded her at further sounds from the same quarter.

They were low mutterings; at first like persons in conversation, but gradually resolving themselves into varieties of one voice. It was an endless monologue, like that we sometimes hear from inanimate nature in deep secret places where water flows, or where ivy leaves flap against stones; but by degrees she was convinced that the voice was Winterborne's. Yet who could be his listener, so mute and so patient? for though he argued rapidly and persistently nobody replied.

A dreadful enlightenment spread through the mind of Grace. "Oh," she cried in her anguish as she hastily prepared herself to go out; "how selfishly correct I am always – too, too correct! Can it be that cruel propriety is killing the dearest heart that ever woman clasped to her own!"

While speaking thus to herself she had lit the lantern, and hastening out without further thought took the direction whence the mutterings had proceeded. The course was marked by a little path, which ended at a distance of about forty yards in a small erection of hurdles, not much larger than a shock of corn, such as were frequent in the woods and copses when the cutting season was going on. It was too slight even to be called a hovel, and was not high enough to stand upright in; appearing, in short, to be erected for the temporary shelter of fuel. The side towards Grace was open, and turning the light upon the interior she beheld what her prescient fear had pictured in snatches all the way thither.

Upon the hay within her lover lay in his clothes, just as she had seen him during the whole of her stay here, except that his hat was off, and his hair matted and wild.

Both his clothes and the hay were saturated with rain. His arms were flung over his head; his face was flushed to an unnatural crimson. His eyes had a burning brightness, and, though they met her own, she perceived that he did not recognise her.

"Oh, my Giles," she cried, "what have I done to you!"

But she stopped no longer even to reproach herself. She saw that the first thing to be thought of was to get him indoors.

How Grace performed that labour she never could have exactly explained. But by dint of clasping her arms round him, rearing him into a sitting posture and straining her strength to the uttermost, she put him on one of the hurdles that was loose alongside, and taking the end of it in both her hands, dragged him along the path to the entrance of the hut, and, after a pause for breath, in at the doorway.

It was somewhat singular that Giles in his semi-conscious state acquiesced unresistingly in all that she did. But he never for a moment recognised her; continuing his rapid conversation to himself, and seeming to look upon her as some angel or other supernatural creature of the visionary world in which he was mentally living. The undertaking occupied her more than ten minutes; but by that time, to her great thankfulness, he was in the inner room lying in the bed, his damp outer clothing removed.

Then the unhappy Grace regarded him by the light of the candle. There was something in his look which agonised her, in the rush of his thoughts, accelerating their speed from minute to minute. His soul seemed to be passing through the universe of ideas like a comet: erratic, inapprehensible, untraceable.

Grace's distraction was almost as great as his. In a few moments she firmly believed he was dying. Unable to withstand her impulse, she knelt down beside him, kissed his hands, and his face, and his hair, moaning in a low voice, "How could I? How could I?"

Her timid morality had, indeed, underrated his chivalry till now, though she knew him so well. The purity of his nature, his freedom from the grosser passions, his scrupulous delicacy, had never been fully understood by Grace till this strange self-sacrifice in lonely juxta-position to her own person was revealed. The perception of it added something that was little short of reverence to the deep affection for him of a woman who, herself, had more of Artemis than of Aphrodite[1] in her constitution.

All that a tender nurse could do, Grace did; and the power to express her solicitude in action, unconscious though the sufferer was, brought her mournful satisfaction. She bathed his hot head, clasped his twitching hands, moistened his lips, cooled his fiery eyelids, sponged his heated skin, and administered whatever she could find in the house that the imagination could conceive as likely to be in any way alleviating. That she might have been the cause, or partially the cause, of all this, interfused misery with her sorrow.

Six months before this date a scene, almost similar in its mechanical parts, had been enacted at Hintock House. It was between a pair of persons most intimately connected in their lives with these. Outwardly like as it had been, it was yet infinite in spiritual difference; though a woman's devotion had been common to both.

Grace rose from her attitude of affection, and, bracing her energies, saw that something practical must immediately be done. Much as she would have liked, in the emotion of the moment, to keep him entirely to herself, medical assistance was necessary whilst there remained a possibility of preserving him alive. Such assistance was fatal to her own concealment; but even had the chance of benefiting him been less than it was, she would have run the hazard for his sake. The question was, where should she get a medical man, competent and near?

There was one such man, and only one, within accessible distance: a man who, if it were possible to save Winterborne's life, had the brain most likely to do it. If human pressure could bring him, that man ought to be brought to the sick Giles's side. Though completely stultifying her flight, the attempt should be made.

Yet she dreaded to leave her patient, and the minutes raced past, and still she postponed her departure. At last, when it was after eleven o'clock, Winterborne fell into a fitful sleep, and it seemed to afford her an opportunity.

She hastily made him as comfortable as she could, put on her things, cut a new candle from the bunch hanging in the cupboard, and having set it up, and placed it so that the light did not fall upon his eyes, she closed the door and started, there being now no rain.

The spirit of Winterborne seemed to keep her company and banish all sense of darkness from her mind. The rains had imparted a phosphorescence to the pieces of touchwood[2] and rotting leaves that lay about her path, which, as scattered by her feet, spread abroad like spilt milk. She would not run the hazard of losing her way by plunging into any short, unfrequented track through the denser parts of the woodland, but followed a more open course, which eventually brought her to the highway. Once here, she ran along with great speed, animated by a devoted purpose which had much about it that was stoical; and it was with scarcely any faltering of spirit that, after an hour's progress, she passed over Rubdon Hill, and onward towards that same Hintock, and that same house, out of which she had fled a few days before in irresistible alarm. But that had happened which, above all other things of chance and change, could make her deliberately frustrate her plan of flight, and sink all regard of personal consequences.

One speciality of Fitzpiers was respected by Grace as much as ever: his professional skill. In this she was right. Had his persistence equalled his insight, instead of being the spasmodic and fitful thing it was, fame and fortune need never have remained a wish with him. His freedom from conventional errors and crusted prejudices had indeed been such as to retard rather than accelerate his advance in Hintock and its neighbourhood, where people could not believe that Nature herself effected cures, and that the doctor's business was only to smooth the way.

It was past midnight when Grace arrived opposite her father's house, now again temporarily occupied by her husband, unless he had already gone away. Ever since her emergence from the denser plantations about Winterborne's residence, a pervasive lightness had hung in the damp autumn sky, in spite of the vault of cloud, signifying that a moon of some age was shining above its arch. The two white gates were distinct, and the white balls on the pillars: and the puddles and damp ruts left by the recent rain had a cold, corpse-eyed luminousness. She entered by the lower gate, and crossed the quadrangle to the wing wherein the apartments that had been hers since her marriage were situate, till she stood under a window which, if her husband were in the house, gave light to his bed-chamber.

She faltered, and paused with her hand on her heart, in spite of herself. Could she call to her presence the very cause of all her foregoing troubles? Alas! – old Jones was seven miles off; Giles was possibly dying – what else could she do?

It was in a perspiration, wrought even more by consciousness than by exercise, that she picked up some gravel, threw it at the panes, and waited to see the result. The night-bell which had been fixed when Fitzpiers first took up his residence there still remained; but as it had fallen into disuse with the collapse of his practice, and his elopement, she did not venture to pull it now.

Whoever slept in the room had heard her signal, slight as it was.

In half a minute the window was opened, and a voice said "Yes?" inquiringly. Grace recognised her husband in the speaker at once. Her effort was now to disguise her own accents.

"Doctor," she said, in as unusual a tone as she could command, "a man is dangerously ill in One-Chimney Hut, out towards Delborough, and you must go to him at once – in all mercy!"

"I will, readily."

The alacrity, surprise, and pleasure expressed in his reply amazed her for a moment. But, in truth, they denoted the sudden relief of a man who, having got back in a mood of contrition from erratic abandonment to doubtful joys, found the soothing routine of pro-fessional practice unexpectedly opening anew to him. The highest desire of his soul just now was for a respectable life of painstaking. If this, his first summons since his return, had been to attend upon a cat or dog, he would scarcely have refused it in the circumstances.

"Do you know the way?" she asked.

"Yes," said he.

"One-Chimney Hut," she repeated. "And – immediately!"

"Yes, yes," said Fitzpiers.

Grace remained no longer. She passed through the white gate without slamming it, and hastened on her way back. Her husband, then, had re-entered her father's house. How he had been able to effect a reconciliation with the old man, what were the terms of the treaty between them, she could not so much as conjecture. Some sort of truce must have been entered into, that was all she could say. But close as the question lay to her own life, there was a more urgent one which banished it; and she traced her steps quickly along the meandering trackways.

Meanwhile, Fitzpiers was preparing to leave the house. The state of his mind, over and above his professional zeal, was peculiar. At Grace's first remark he had not recognised or suspected her presence; but as she went on, he was awakened to the great resemblance of the speaker's voice to his wife's. He had taken in such good faith the statement of the household on his arrival, that she had gone on a visit for a time because she could not at once bring her mind to be reconciled to him, that he could not quite believe this neighbour to be she. It was one of the features of Fitzpiers's repentant humour at this date that, on receiving the explanation of her absence, he had made no attempt to outrage her feelings by following her; though nobody had informed him how very shortly her departure had preceded his entry, and of all that might have been inferred from her precipitancy.

Melbury, after much alarm and consideration, had decided not to follow her either. He sympathised with her flight, much as he deplored it; moreover the tragic colour of the antecedent events that he had been a great means of creating checked his instinct to interfere. He prayed and trusted that she had got into no danger on her way (as he supposed) to Sherton, and thence to Exbury, if that were the place she had gone to, forbearing all inquiry which the strangeness of her departure would have made natural. A few months before this time a performance by Grace of one-tenth the magnitude of this would have aroused him to unwonted investigation.

It was in the same spirit that he had tacitly assented to Fitzpiers's domiciliation there. The two men had not met face to face, but Mrs. Melbury had proposed herself as an intermediary, who made the surgeon's re-entrance comparatively easy to him. Everything was provisional, and nobody asked questions. Fitzpiers had come in the performance of a plan of penitence which had originated in circumstances hereafter to be explained; his self-humiliation to the very bass-string was deliberate; and as soon as a voice reached him from the bedside of a dying man his desire was to set to work and do as much good as he could with the least possible fuss or show. He therefore refrained from calling up a stableman to get ready any horse or gig, and set out for One-Chimney Hut on foot as Grace had done.

CHAPTER X

She re-entered the hut, flung off her bonnet and cloak, and approached the sufferer. He had begun anew those terrible mutterings, and his hands were cold. As soon as she saw him there returned to her that agony of mind which the stimulus of her journey had thrown off for a time.

Could he really be dying? She bathed him, kissed him, forgot all things but the fact that lying there before her was he who had loved her more than the mere lover would have loved; had immolated himself for her comfort, cared more for her self-respect than she had thought of caring. This mood continued till she heard quick, smart footsteps without; she knew whose footsteps they were.

Grace sat on the inside of the bed against the wall, holding her lover's hand, so that when her husband entered the patient lay between herself and him. He stood transfixed at first, noticing Grace only. Slowly he dropped his glance; and discerned who the prostrate man was. Strangely enough, though Grace's distaste for her husband's company had amounted almost to dread, and culminated in actual flight, at this moment her last and least feeling was personal. Sensitive femininity was eclipsed by devoted purpose; and that it was a husband who stood there was forgotten. The first look that possessed her face was relief; satisfaction at the presence of the physician obliterated thought of the man, which only returned in the form of a sub-consciousness that did not interfere with her words.

"Is he dying – is there any hope?" she asked.

"Grace!" said Fitzpiers in an indescribable whisper – more than invocating – if not quite deprecatory.

He was arrested by the spectacle, not so much in its intrinsic character – though that was striking enough to a man who called himself the husband of the sufferer's friend and nurse – but in its character as the counterpart of one that had had its run many months before, in which he had figured as the patient, and the woman had been Felice Charmond.

"Is he in great danger – can you save him?" she asked again.

Fitzpiers aroused himself, came a little nearer, and examined Winterborne as he stood. His inspection was concluded in a mere glance. Before he spoke he looked at her contemplatively as to the effect of his coming words.

"He is dying," he said with dry precision.

"What?" said she.

"Nothing can be done, by me or any other man. It will soon be all over. The extremities are dead already." His eyes still remained fixed on her, the conclusion to which he had come seeming to end his interest, professional and otherwise, in Winterborne for ever.

"But it cannot be! He was well a week ago."

"Not well I suspect. This seems like what we call a sequel, which has followed some previous disorder – possibly typhoid – it may have been months ago, or recently."

"Ah – he was ill last year – you are right. And he must have been ill when I came."

There was nothing more to do or say. She crouched down at the side of the bed, and Fitzpiers took a seat. Thus they remained in silence, and long as it lasted she never turned her eyes, or apparently her thoughts, at all to her husband. He occasionally murmured, with automatic authority, some slight directions for alleviating the pain of the dying man, which she mechanically obeyed; bending over him during the intervals in silent tears.

Winterborne never recovered consciousness of what was passing; and that he was going became soon perceptible also to her. In less than an hour the delirium ceased; then there was an interval of somnolent painlessness and soft breathing, at the end of which Winterborne passed quietly away.

Then Fitzpiers broke the silence. "Have you lived here long?" he said.

Grace was wild with sorrow – bitter with all that had befallen her – with the cruelties that had attacked her – with life – with Heaven. She answered at random. "Yes. By what right do you ask?"

"Don't think I claim any right," said Fitzpiers sadly. "It is for you to do and say what you choose. I admit, quite as much as you feel, that I am a vagabond – a brute – not worthy to possess the smallest fragment of you. But here I am, and I have happened to take sufficient interest in you to make that inquiry."

"He is everything to me!" said Grace, hardly heeding her husband, and laying her hand reverently on the dead man's eyelids, where she kept it a long time, pressing down their lashes with gentle touches, as if she were stroking a little bird.

He watched her awhile; and then glanced round the chamber, where his eyes fell upon a few dressing necessaries that she had brought.

"Grace – if I may call you so," he said, "I have been already humiliated almost to the depths. I have come back – since you refused to join me elsewhere – I have entered your father's house – and borne all which that cost me without flinching, because I have felt I deserved humiliation. But is there a yet greater humiliation in store for me? You say you have been living here[1] – that he was everything to you. Am I to draw from that the obvious, the extremest inference?"[2]

Triumph at any price is sweet to men and women – especially the latter. It was her first and last opportunity of repaying him for the slights which she had borne at his hands so docilely.

"Yes," she answered; and there was that in her subtly compounded nature which made her feel a thrill of pride as she did so.

Yet the moment after she had so mightily belied her character she half repented. Her husband had turned as white as the wall behind him. It seemed as if all that remained to him of hope and spirit had been abstracted at a stroke. Yet he did not move, and in his efforts at self-control closed his mouth together as a vice. His determination was fairly successful, though she saw how very much greater than she had expected her triumph had been. Presently he looked across at Winterborne.

"Would it startle you to hear," he said, as if he hardly had breath to utter words, "that she who was to me what he was to you is dead also?"

"Dead – *she* dead?" exclaimed Grace.

"Yes. Felice Charmond is where this young man is."

"Never!" said Grace vehemently.

He went on without heeding the insinuation:[3] "And I came back to try to make it up with you – but ——"

Fitzpiers rose, and moved across the room to go away, looking downwards with the droop of a man whose hope was turned to apathy if not despair. In going round the door his eye fell upon her once more. She was still bending over the body of Winterborne, her face close to his.

"Have you been kissing him during his illness?" asked her husband.

"Yes."

"Since his fevered state set in?"

"Yes."

"On his lips?"

"Yes."

"Then you will do well to take a few drops of this in water as soon as possible." He drew a small phial from his pocket, and returned to offer it to her.

Grace shook her head.

"If you don't do as I tell you you may soon be like him."

"I don't care. I wish to die."

"I'll put it here," said Fitzpiers, placing the bottle on a ledge beside him. "The sin of not having warned you will not be upon my head at any rate, amongst my other sins. I am now going, and I will send somebody to you. Your father does not know that you are here, so I suppose I shall be bound to tell him?"

"Certainly."

Fitzpiers left the cot, and the stroke of his feet was soon immersed in the silence that pervaded the spot. Grace remained kneeling and weeping, she hardly knew how long, and then she sat up, covered poor Giles's features, and went towards the door where her husband had stood. No sign of any other comer greeted her ear, the only perceptible sounds being the tiny cracklings of the dead leaves, which, like a feather bed, had not yet done rising to their normal level where indented by the pressure of her husband's receding footsteps. It reminded her that she had been struck with the change in his aspect; the extremely intellectual look that had always been in his face was wrought to a finer phase by thinness; and a careworn dignity had been superadded. She returned to Winterborne's side, and during her meditations another tread drew near the door, entered the outer room, and halted at the entrance of the chamber where Grace was.

"What – Marty!" said Grace.

"Yes. I have heard," said Marty, whose demeanour had lost all its girlishness under the stroke that seemed almost literally to have bruised her.

"He died for me!" murmured Grace heavily.

Marty did not fully comprehend; and she answered, "He belongs to neither of us now, and your beauty is no more powerful with him than my plainness. I have come to help you, ma'am. He never cared for me, and he cared much for you; but he cares for us both alike now."

"Oh, don't, don't, Marty!"

Marty said no more, but knelt over Winterborne from the other side.

"Did you meet my hus – Mr. Fitzpiers?"

"No."

"Then what brought you here?"

"I come this way sometimes. I have got to go to the further side of the wood this time of the year, and am obliged to get there before four o'clock in the morning, to begin heating the oven for the early baking. I have passed by here often at this time."

Grace looked at her quickly. "Then did you know I was here?"

"Yes, ma'am."

"Did you tell anybody?"

"No. I knew you lived in the hut, that he had gied it up to ye, and lodged out himself."

"Did you know where he lodged?"

"No. That I couldn't find out. Was it at Delborough?"

"No. It was not there, Marty. Would it had been! It would have saved – saved —" To check her tears she turned, and seeing a book in the window-bench took it up. "Look, Marty, this is a Psalter.[4] He was not an outwardly religious man; but he was pure and perfect in his heart. Shall we read a psalm over him?"

"Oh, yes – we will – with all my heart!"

Grace opened the thin brown book, which poor Giles had kept at hand mainly for the convenience of whetting his penknife upon its leather covers. She began to read in that rich, devotional voice peculiar to women only on such occasions. When it was over Marty said, "I should like to pray for his soul."

"So should I," said her companion. "But we must not."

"Why? Nobody would know."

Grace could not resist the argument, influenced as she was by the sense of making amends for having neglected him in the body; and their tender voices united and filled the narrow room with supplicatory murmurs that a Calvinist[5] might have countenanced. They had hardly ended when new and more numerous footfalls were audible; also persons in conversation, one of whom Grace recognised as her father.

She rose, and went to the outer apartment, in which there was only such light as beamed from the inner one. Melbury and Mrs. Melbury were standing there.

"I don't reproach you, Grace," said her father with an estranged manner, and in a voice not at all like his old voice. "What has come upon you and us[6] is beyond reproach, beyond weeping and beyond wailing. Perhaps I drove you to it. But I am hurt; I am scourged; I am astonished. In the face of this there is nothing to be said."

Without replying Grace turned and glided back to the inner chamber. "Marty," she said quickly, "I cannot look my father in the face until he knows the true circumstances of my life here. Go and tell him – what you have told me – what you saw – that he gave up his house to me."

She sat down, her face buried in her hands, and Marty went, and after a short absence returned. Then Grace rose, and going out asked her father if he had talked to Marty.

"Yes," said Melbury.

"And you know all that has happened? I will let my husband think the worst, but not you."

"I do. Forgive me, Grace, for suspecting ye of worse than rashness – I ought to know ye better. Are you coming with me to what was once your home?"

"No. I stay here with *him*. Take no account of me any more."

The tender, perplexing, agitating relations in which she had stood to Winterborne quite lately – brought about by Melbury's own contrivance – could not fail to soften the natural anger of a parent at her more recent doings. "My daughter, things are bad," he rejoined. "But why do you persevere to make 'em worse? What good can you do to Giles by staying here with him? Mind, I ask no questions. I don't inquire why you decided to come here, or anything as to what your course would have been if he had not died, though I know there's no deliberate harm in ye. As for me, I have lost all claim upon you; and I make no complaint. But I do say that by coming back with me now you will show no less kindness to him, and escape any sound of shame."

"But I don't wish to escape it."

"If you don't on your own account cannot you wish to on mine and hers? Nobody except our household knows that you have left home. Then why should you by a piece of perverseness bring down my hairs with sorrow to the grave?"[7]

"If it were not for my husband –" she began, moved by his words. "But how can I meet him there? How can any woman who is not a mere man's creature[8] join him after what has taken place?"

"He would go away again rather than keep you out of my house."

"How do you know that, father?"

"We met him on our way here, and he told us so," said Mrs. Melbury. "He had said something like it before. He seems very much upset altogether."

"He declared to her when he came to our house that he would wait for time and devotion to bring about his forgiveness," said Melbury. "That was it, wasn't it, Lucy?"

"Yes. That he would not intrude upon you, Grace, till you gave him absolute permission," Mrs. Melbury added.

This antecedent considerateness in Fitzpiers was as welcome to Grace as it was unexpected; and though she did not desire his presence, she was sorry that by her retaliatory fiction she had given him a different reason for avoiding her. She made no further objections to accompanying her parents, taking them into the inner room to give Winterborne a last look, and gathering up the two or three things that belonged to her. While she was doing this the two women came who had been called by Melbury, and at their heels poor Creedle.

"Forgive me, but I can't rule my mourning nohow as a man should, Mr. Melbury," he said. "I ha'n't seen him since Thursday se'night, and have wondered for days and days where he's been keeping. There was I expecting him to come and tell me to wash out the cider-barrels against the making, and here was he . . . Well, I've knowed him from table-high; I knowed his father – used to bide about upon two sticks in the sun afore he died! – and now I've seen the end of the family, which we can ill afford to lose, wi' such a scanty lot of good folk in Hintock as we've got. And now Robert Creedle will be nailed up in parish boards 'a b'lieve; and nobody will glutch down a sigh for he."

They started for home, Marty and Creedle remaining behind. For a time Grace and her father walked side by side without speaking. It was just in the blue of the dawn, and the chilling tone of the sky was reflected in her cold, wet face. The whole wood seemed to be a house of death, pervaded by loss to its uttermost length and breadth. Winterborne was gone, and the copses seemed to show the want of him; those young trees, so many of which he had planted, and of which he had spoken so truly when he said that he should fall before they fell, were at that very moment sending out their roots in the direction that he had given them with his subtle hand.

"One thing made it tolerable to us that your husband should come back to the house," said Melbury at last. "The death of Mrs. Charmond."

"Ah, yes," said Grace, arousing slightly to the recollection; "he told me so."

"Did he tell you how she died? It was no such death as Giles's. She was shot – by a disappointed lover. It occurred in Germany. The unfortunate man shot himself afterwards. He was that South Carolina gentleman of very passionate nature, who used to haunt this place to force her to favour him, and followed her about everywhere. So ends the brilliant Felice Charmond – once a good friend to me; but no friend to you."

"I can forgive her," said Grace absently. "Did Edred tell you of this?"

"No; but he put a London newspaper, giving an account of it, on the hall table, folded in such a way that we should see it. It will be in the Sherton paper this week, no doubt. To make the event more solemn still to him he had just before had sharp words with her, and left her. He told Lucy this, as nothing about him appears in the newspaper. And the cause of the quarrel was, of all people, she we've left behind us."

"Do you mean Marty?" Grace spoke the words but perfunctorily. For, pertinent and pointed as Melbury's story was, she had no care for it now.

"Yes. Marty South." Melbury persisted in his narrative, to divert her from her present grief, if possible. "Before he went away she wrote him a letter, which he kept in his pocket a long while before reading. He chanced to pull it out in Mrs. Charmond's presence, and read it out loud. It contained something which teased her very much, and that led to the rupture. She was following him to make it up when she met with her terrible death."

Melbury did not know enough to give the gist of the incident, which was that Marty South's letter had been concerning a certain personal adornment common to herself and Mrs. Charmond. Her bullet reached its billet at last. The scene between Fitzpiers and Felice had been sharp, as only a scene can be which arises out of the mortification of one woman by another in the presence of a lover. True, Marty had not effected it by word of mouth; the charge about the locks of hair was made simply by Fitzpiers reading her letter to him aloud to Felice in the playfully ironical tones of one who had become a little weary of his situation, and was finding his friend, in the phrase of George Herbert, a "flat delight."[9] He had stroked those false tresses with his hand many a time without knowing them to be transplanted, and it was impossible when the discovery was so abruptly made to avoid being finely satirical, despite her generous disposition.

That was how it had begun, and tragedy had been its end. On his abrupt departure she had followed him to the station, but the train was gone; and in travelling to Baden in search of him she had met his rival, whose reproaches led to an altercation, and the death of both. Of that precipitate scene of passion and crime Fitzpiers had known nothing till he saw an account of it in the papers, where, fortunately for himself, no mention was made of his prior acquaintance with the unhappy lady; nor was there any allusion to him in the subsequent inquiry, the double death being attributed to some gambling losses, though in point of fact neither one of them had visited the tables.

Melbury and his daughter drew near their house, having seen but one living thing on their way, a squirrel, which did not run up its tree, but, dropping the sweet chestnut which it carried, cried chut-chut-chut, and stamped with its hind legs on the ground. When the roofs and chimneys of the homestead began to emerge from the screen of boughs, Grace started, and checked herself in her abstracted advance.

"You clearly understand," she said to her stepmother, some of her old misgiving returning, "that I am coming back only on condition of his leaving as he promised? Will you let him know this, that there may be no mistake?"

Mrs. Melbury, who had had some long private talks with Fitzpiers, assured Grace that she need have no doubts on that point, and that he would probably be gone by the evening. Grace then entered with them into Melbury's wing of the house, and sat down listlessly in the parlour while her stepmother went to Fitzpiers.

The prompt obedience to her wishes which the surgeon showed did honour to him, if anything could. Before Mrs. Melbury had returned to the room, Grace, who was sitting on the parlour window-bench, saw her husband go from the door under the increasing light of morning, with a bag in his hand. While passing through the gate he turned his head. The firelight of the room she sat in threw her figure into dark relief against the window as she looked through the panes, and he must have seen her distinctly. In a moment he went on, the gate fell to, and he disappeared. At the hut she had declared that another had filled his place; now she had banished him.

CHAPTER XI

CHAPTER XI

Fitzpiers had hardly been gone an hour when Grace began to sicken. The next day she kept her room. Old Jones was called in: he murmured some statements in which the words "feverish symptoms" occurred. Grace heard them, and guessed the means by which she had brought this visitation upon herself.

One day while she still lay there with her head throbbing, wondering if she were really going to join him who had gone before, Grammer Oliver came to her bedside. "I don't know whe'r this is meant for you to take, ma'am," she said. "But I have found it on the table. It was left by Marty, I think, when she came this morning."

Grace turned her hot eyes upon what Grammer held up. It was the phial left at the hut by her husband when he had begged her to take some drops of its contents, if she wished to preserve herself from falling a victim to the malady which had pulled down Winterborne. She examined it as well as she could. The liquid was of an opaline hue, and bore a label with an inscription in Italian. He had probably got it in his wanderings abroad. She knew but little Italian, but could understand that the cordial was a febrifuge of some sort. Her father, her mother, and all the household were anxious for her recovery, and she resolved to obey her husband's directions. Whatever the risk, if any, she was prepared to run it. A glass of water was brought, and the drops dropped in.

The effect, though not miraculous, was remarkable. In less than an hour she felt calmer, cooler, better able to reflect, less inclined to fret and chafe and wear herself away. She took a few drops more. From that time the fever retreated, and went out like a damped conflagration.

"How clever he is!" she said regretfully. "Why could he not have had more principle, so as to turn his great talents to good account! Perhaps he has saved my useless life. But he doesn't know it, and doesn't care whether he has saved it or not; and on that account will never be told by me. Probably he only gave it to me in the arrogance of his skill, to show the greatness of his resources beside mine, as Elijah drew down fire from Heaven."[1]

As soon as she had quite recovered from this foiled attack upon her life Grace went to Marty South's cottage. The current of her being had again set towards the lost Giles Winterborne.

"Marty," she said, "we both loved him. We will go to his grave together."

Great Hintock church stood at the upper part of the village, and could be reached without passing through the street. In the dusk of the late September day they went thither by secret ways, walking mostly in silence side by side, each busied with her own thoughts. Grace had a trouble exceeding Marty's, that haunting sense of having put out the light of his life by her own hasty doings. She had tried to persuade herself that he might have died of his illness, even if she had not taken possession of his house. Sometimes she succeeded in her attempt; sometimes she did not.

They stood by the grave together, and though the sun had gone down, they could see over the woodland for miles, and down to the vale in which he had been accustomed to descend every year with his portable mill and press to make cider about this time.

Perhaps Grace's first grief, the discovery that if he had lived he could never have claimed her, had some power in softening this, the second. On Marty's part there was the same consideration; never would she have been his. As no anticipation of gratified affection had been in existence while he was with them, there was none to be disappointed now that he had gone.

Grace was abased when, by degrees, she found that she had never understood Giles as Marty had done. Marty South alone, of all the women in Hintock and the world, had approximated to Winterborne's level of intelligent intercourse with Nature. In that respect she had formed his true complement[2] in the other sex, had lived as his counterpart, had subjoined her thought to his as a corollary.

The casual glimpses which the ordinary population bestowed upon that wondrous world of sap and leaves called the Hintock woods had been with these two, Giles and Marty, a clear gaze. They had been possessed of its finer mysteries as of commonplace knowledge; had been able to read its hieroglyphs[3] as ordinary writing; to them the sights and sounds of night, winter, wind, storm, amid those dense boughs, which had to Grace a touch of the uncanny, and even of the supernatural, were simple occurrences whose origin, continuance, and laws they foreknew. They had planted together, and together they had felled; together they had, with the run of the years, mentally collected those remoter signs and symbols which seen in few were of runic obscurity,[4] but all together made an alphabet. From the light lashing of the twigs upon their faces when brushing through them in the dark, they could pronounce upon the species of the tree whence they stretched; from the quality of the wind's murmur through a bough they could in like manner name its sort afar off. They knew by a glance at a trunk if its heart were sound, or tainted with incipient decay; and by the state of its upper twigs the stratum that had been reached by its roots. The artifices of the seasons were seen by them from the conjuror's own point of view, and not from that of the spectator.

"He ought to have married *you*, Marty, and nobody else in the world!" said Grace with conviction, after thinking somewhat in the above strain.

Marty shook her head. "In all our outdoor days and years together, ma'am," she replied, "the one thing he never spoke of to me was love; nor I to him."

"Yet you and he could speak in a tongue that nobody else knew – not even my father, though he came nearest knowing – the tongue of the trees and fruits and flowers themselves."

She could indulge in mournful fancies like this to Marty; but the hard core to her grief – which Marty's had not – remained. Had she been sure that Giles's death resulted entirely from his exposure, it would have driven her well nigh to insanity; but there was always that bare possibility that his exposure had only precipitated what was inevitable. She longed to believe that it had not done even this.

There was only one man whose opinion on the circumstances she would be at all disposed to trust. Her husband was that man. Yet to ask him it would be necessary to detail the true conditions in which she and Winterborne had lived during these three or four critical days that followed her flight; and in withdrawing her original defiant announcement on that point there seemed a weakness she did not care to show. She never doubted that Fitzpiers would believe her if she made a clean confession of the actual situation; but to volunteer the correction would seem like signalling for a truce, and that in her present frame of mind was what she did not feel the need of.

It will probably not appear a surprising statement, after what has been already declared of Fitzpiers, that the man whom Grace's fidelity could not keep faithful was stung into passionate throbs of interest concerning her by her avowal of the contrary.

He declared to himself that he had never known her dangerously full compass if she were capable of such a reprisal; and, melancholy as it may be to admit the fact, his own humiliation and regret engendered a smouldering admiration of her.

He passed a month or two of great misery at Exbury, the place to which he had retired – quite as much misery indeed as Grace, could she have known of it, would have been inclined to inflict upon any living creature, how much soever he might have wronged her. Then a sudden hope dawned upon him; he wondered if her affirmation were true. He asked himself whether it were not the act of an innocent woman whose pique had for the moment blinded her to the contingencies of such an announcement. His wide experience of the sex had taught him that, in many cases, women who ventured on hazardous matters did so because they lacked an imagination gross enough to feel their full force. In this light Grace's bold avowal might merely have denoted the desperation of one who was a child to the realities of obliquity.

Fitzpiers's mental sufferings and suspense led him at last to take a melancholy journey to the neighbourhood of Little Hintock; and here he hovered for hours around the scene of the purest emotional experiences that he had ever known in his life. He walked about the woods that surrounded Melbury's house, keeping out of sight like a criminal. It was a fine evening, and on his way homeward he passed near Marty South's cottage. As usual she had lighted her candle without closing her shutters; he saw her within as he had seen her many times before.

She was polishing tools, and though he had not wished to show himself he could not resist speaking to her through the halfopen door. "What are you doing that for, Marty?"

"Because I want to clean them. They are not mine." He could see indeed that they were not hers, for one was a spade, large and heavy, and another was a bill-hook which she could only have used with both hands. The spade, though not a new one, had been so completely burnished that it was bright as silver.

Fitzpiers somehow divined that they were Giles Winterborne's, and he put the question to her.

She replied in the affirmative. "I am going to keep 'em," she said, "but I can't get his apple-mill and press. I wish I could; it is going to be sold, they say."

"Then I will buy it for you," said Fitzpiers. "That will be making you a return for a kindness you did me." His glance fell upon the girl's rare-coloured hair, which had grown again. "Oh, Marty, those locks of yours – and that letter! . . . But it was a kindness to send it, nevertheless," he added musingly.

After this there was confidence between them – such confidence as there had never been before. Marty was shy, indeed, of speaking about the letter, and her motives in writing it; but she thanked him warmly for his promise of the cider-press. She would travel with it in the autumn season as he had done, she said. She would be quite strong enough, with old Creedle as an assistant.

"Ah! – there was one nearer to him than you," said Fitzpiers, referring to Grace. "One who lived where he lived, and was with him when he died."

Then Marty, suspecting that he did not know the true circumstances, from the fact that Mrs. Fitzpiers and himself were living apart, told him of Giles's generosity to Grace in giving up his house to her at the risk, and possibly the sacrifice, of his own life. When the surgeon heard it he almost envied Giles his chivalrous character. He expressed a wish to Marty that his visit to her should be kept secret, and went home thoughtful, feeling that in more than one sense his journey to Hintock had not been in vain.

He would have given much to win Grace's forgiveness then. But whatever he dared hope for in that kind from the future, there was nothing to be done yet, while Giles Winterborne's memory was green. To wait was imperative. A little time might melt her frozen thoughts, and lead her to look on him with toleration, if not with love.

CHAPTER XII

Weeks and months of mourning for Winterborne had been passed by Grace in the soothing monotony of the memorial act to which she and Marty had devoted themselves. Twice a week the pair went in the dusk to Great Hintock, and, like the two mourners in *Cymbeline*,[1] sweetened his sad grave with their flowers and their tears.

Nothing ever had brought home to her with such force as this death how little acquirements and culture weigh beside sterling personal character. While her simple sorrow for his loss took a softer edge with the lapse of the autumn and winter seasons, her self-reproach at having had a possible hand in causing it knew slight abatement.

Little occurred at Hintock during these months of the fall and decay of the leaf. Discussion of the almost contemporaneous death of Mrs. Charmond abroad had waxed and waned. There was a rumour that her death had resulted less from the shot than from the effect of fright upon her personal condition[2] at the time; but this was never verified. Fitzpiers had had a marvellous escape from being dragged into the inquiry which followed the catastrophe, through the accident of their having parted just before under the influence of Marty South's letter – the tiny instrument of a cause deep in nature.

Her body was not brought home. It seemed to accord well with the fitful fever[3] of that impassioned woman's life that she should not have found a native grave She had enjoyed but a life-interest in the estate, which, after her death, passed to a relative of her husband's – one who knew not Felice, one whose purpose seemed to be to blot out every vestige of her.

On a certain day in February – the cheerful day of St. Valentine[4] – a letter reached Mrs. Fitzpiers, which had been mentally promised her for that particular day a long time before.

Her husband announced that he was living at some midland town, where he had obtained at temporary practice as assistant to a local medical man, whose curative principles were all wrong, though he dared not set them right. He had thought fit to communicate with her on that day of tender traditions to inquire if, in the event of his obtaining a substantial practice that he had in view elsewhere, she could forget the past and bring herself to join him.

There the practical part ended: he then went on:–

"My last year of experience has added ten years to my age, dear Grace and dearest wife that ever erring man undervalued. You may be absolutely indifferent to what I say, but let me say it; I have never loved any woman alive or dead as I love, respect, and honour you at this present moment. What you told me in the pride and naughtiness of your heart I never believed [this, by the way, was not strictly true]; but even if I had believed it, it could never have estranged me from you. Is there any use in telling you – no, there is not – that I dream of your ripe lips more frequently than I say my prayers: that the old familiar rustle of your dress often returns upon my mind till it distracts me? If you could condescend even only to see me again you would be breathing life into a corpse. My pure, pure Grace, modest as a turtle-dove, how came I ever to possess you? For the sake of being present in your mind on this lovers' day, I think I would almost rather have you hate me a little than not think of me at all. You may call my fancies whimsical; but remember, sweet, lost one, that 'nature is fine in love, and where 'tis fine it sends some instance of itself.'[5] – I will not intrude upon you further now. Make me a little bit happy by sending back one line to say that you will consent, at any rate, to a short interview. I will meet you and leave you as a mere acquaintance, if you will only afford me this slight means of making a few explanations, and of putting my position before you. Believe me, in spite of all you may do or feel,

"Your lover always (once your husband),

"E. F."

335

It was, oddly enough, the first occasion, or nearly the first, on which Grace had ever received a love-letter from him, his courtship having taken place under conditions which rendered letter-writing unnecessary. Its perusal, therefore, had a certain novelty for her. She thought that, upon the whole, he wrote love-letters very well. But the chief rational interest of the letter to the reflective Grace lay in the chance that such a meeting as he proposed would afford her of setting her doubts at rest one way or the other on her actual share in Winterborne's death. The relief of consulting a skilled mind, the one professional man who had seen Giles at that time, would be immense. As for that statement that she had uttered in her disdainful grief, which at the time she had regarded as her triumph, she was quite prepared to admit to him that his belief was the true one; for in wronging herself as she did when she made it she had done what to her was a far more serious thing, wronged Winterborne's memory.

Without consulting her father, or any one in the house or out of it, Grace replied to the letter. She agreed to meet Fitzpiers on two conditions, of which the first was that the place of meeting should be the top of Rubdon Hill, the second that he would not object to Marty South accompanying her.

Whatever art, much or little, there may have been in Fitzpiers's so-called valentine to his wife, he felt a delight as of the bursting of spring when her brief reply came. It was one of the few pleasures that he had experienced of late years at all resembling those of his early youth. He promptly replied that he accepted the conditions, and named the day and hour at which he would be on the spot she mentioned.

A few minutes before three on the appointed day found him climbing the well-known hill, which had been the axis of so many critical movements in their lives during his residence at Hintock.

The sight of each homely and well-remembered object swelled the regret that seldom left him now. Whatever paths might lie open to his future, the soothing shades of Hintock were forbidden him for ever as a permanent dwelling-place.

He longed for the society of Grace. But to lay offerings on her slighted altar was his first aim, and until her propitiation was complete he would constrain her in no way to return to him. The least reparation that he could make, in a case where he would gladly have made much, would be to let her feel herself absolutely free to choose between living with him and without him.

Moreover, a subtlist in emotions, he cultivated as under glasses strange and mournful pleasures that he would not willingly let die just at present. To show any forwardness in suggesting a *modus vivendi*[6] to Grace would be to put an end to these exotics. To be the vassal of her sweet will[7] for a time – he demanded no more, and found solace in the contemplation of the soft miseries she caused him.

Approaching the hill-top with a mind strung to these notions, Fitzpiers discerned a gay procession of people coming over the crest, and was not long in perceiving it to be a wedding-party. Though the wind was keen the women were in light attire, and the flowered waistcoats of the men had a pleasing vividness of pattern. Each of the gentler ones clung to the arm of her partner so tightly as to have with him one step, rise, swing, gait, almost one centre of gravity. In the buxom bride Fitzpiers recognised no other than Suke Damson, who in her light gown looked a giantess; the small husband beside her he saw to be Tim Tangs.

Fitzpiers could not escape, for they had seen him; though of all the beauties of the world whom he did not wish to meet Suke was the chief. But he put the best face on the matter that he could, and came on, the approaching company evidently discussing him, and his separation from Mrs. Fitzpiers.[8] As the couples closed upon him he expressed his congratulations.

"We be just walking round the parishes to show ourselves a bit," said Tim. "First we het across to Delborough, then athwart to here, and from here we go to Rubdon and Millshot, and then round by the cross roads home. Home, says I, but it won't be that long. We be off next month."

"Indeed. Where to?"

Tim informed him that they were going to New Zealand. Not but that he would have been contented with Hintock, but his wife was ambitious and wanted to leave; so he had given way.

"Then good-bye," said Fitzpiers; "I may not see you again." He shook hands with Tim and turned to the bride. "Good-bye, Suke," he said, taking her hand also. "I wish you and your husband prosperity in the country you have chosen." With this he left them, and hastened on to his appointment.

The wedding-party re-formed and resumed march likewise. But in restoring his arm to Suke, Tim noticed that her full and blooming countenance had undergone a change. "Hullo! me dear – what's the matter?" said Tim.

"Nothing to speak o'," said she. But to give the lie to her assertion she was seized with lachrymose twitches, that soon produced a dribbling face.

"How – what the devil's this about!" exclaimed the bridegroom.

"She's a little wee bit overcome, poor dear!" said the first bridesmaid, unfolding her handkerchief and wiping Suke's eyes.

"I never did like parting from people!" said Suke as soon as she could speak.

"Why him in particular?"

"Well – he's such a clever doctor, that 'tis a thousand pities we sha'n't see him any more! There'll be no such clever doctor as he in New Zealand, if I should require one; and the thought o't got the better of my feelings!"

They walked on, but Tim's face had grown rigid and pale, for he recalled slight circumstances, disregarded at the time of their occurrence. The former boisterous laughter of the wedding party at the groomsman's jokes was heard ringing through the woods no more.

By this time Fitzpiers had advanced on his way to the top of the hill, where he saw two figures emerging from the bank on the right hand. These were the expected ones, Grace and Marty South, who had evidently come there by a short and secret path through the wood. Grace was muffled up in her winter dress, and he thought that she had never looked so seductive as at this moment, in the noontide bright, but heatless, sun, and the keen wind, and the purplish-grey masses of brushwood around. Fitzpiers continued to regard the nearing picture, till at length their glances met for a moment, when she demurely sent off hers at a tangent and gave him the benefit of her three-quarter face, while with courteous completeness of conduct he lifted his hat in a large arc. Marty dropped behind; and when Fitzpiers held out his hand Grace touched it with her fingers.

"I have agreed to be here mostly because I wanted to ask you something important," said Mrs. Fitzpiers, her intonation modulating in a direction that she had not quite wished it to take.

"I am most attentive," said her husband. "Shall we take to the wood for privacy?"

Grace demurred, and Fitzpiers gave in, and they kept the public road.

At any rate, she would take his arm? This also was gravely negatived, the refusal being audible to Marty.

"Why not?" he inquired.

"Oh, Mr. Fitzpiers – how can you ask?"

"Right, right," said he, his effusiveness shrivelled up.

As they walked on she returned to her inquiry. "It is about a matter that may perhaps be unpleasant to you. But I think I need not consider that too carefully."

"Not at all," said Fitzpiers heroically.

She then took him back to the time of poor Winterborne's death, and related the precise circumstances amid which his fatal illness had come upon him, particularising the dampness of the shelter to which he had betaken himself, his concealment from her of the hardships that he was undergoing, all that he had put up with, all that he had done for her in his scrupulous considerateness. The retrospect brought her to tears as she asked him if he thought that the sin of having driven him to his death was upon her.

Fitzpiers could hardly help showing his satisfaction at what her narrative indirectly revealed, the actual harmlessness of an escapade with her lover, which had at first, by her own showing, looked so grave, and he did not care to inquire whether that harmlessness had been the result of aim or of accident. With regard to her question, he declared that in his judgment no human being could answer it. He thought that upon the whole the balance of probabilities turned in her favour. Winterborne's apparent strength, during the last months of his life, must have been delusive. It had often occurred that after a first attack of that insidious disease a person's apparent recovery was a physiological mendacity.

The relief which came to Grace lay almost as much in sharing her knowledge of the particulars with an intelligent mind as in the assurances Fitzpiers gave her. "Well, then, to put this case before you, and obtain your professional opinion, was chiefly why I consented to come here to-day," said she, when he had reached the aforesaid conclusion.

"For no other reason at all?" he asked ruefully.

"It was nearly the whole."

They stood and looked over a gate ·at twenty or thirty starlings feeding in the grass, and he started the talk again by saying in a low voice, "And yet I love you more than ever I loved you in my life."

Grace did not move her eyes from the birds, and folded her delicate lips as if to keep them in subjection.

"It is a different kind of love altogether," said he. "Less passionate; more profound. It has nothing to do with the material conditions of the object at all; much to do with her character and goodness, as revealed by closer observation. 'Love talks with better knowledge, and knowledge with dearer love.' "

"That's out of *Measure for Measure*,"[9] said she slily.

"Oh, yes – I meant it as a citation," blandly replied Fitzpiers. "Well then, why not give me a very little bit of your heart again?"

The crash of a felled tree in the remote depths of the wood recalled the past at that moment, and all the homely faithfulness of Winterborne. "Don't ask it! My heart is in the grave with Giles," she replied staunchly.

"Mine is with you – in no less deep a grave, I fear, according to that."

"I am very sorry; but it cannot be helped."

"How can you be sorry for me, when you wilfully keep open the grave?"

"Oh, no – that's not so," returned Grace quickly; and moved to go away from him.

"But, dearest Grace!" said he. "You have condescended to come; and I thought from it that perhaps when I had passed through a long state of probation you would be generous. But if there can be no hope of our getting completely reconciled, treat me gently – wretch though I am."

"I did not say you were a wretch, nor have I ever said so."

"But you have such a contemptuous way of looking at me that I fear you think so."

Grace's heart struggled between the wish not to be harsh and the fear that she might mislead him. "I cannot look contemptuous unless I feel contempt," she said evasively, "and all I feel is lovelessness."

"I have been very bad I know," he returned. "But unless you can really love me again, Grace, I would rather go away from you for ever. I don't want you to receive me again for duty's sake, or anything of that sort. If I had not cared more for your affection and forgiveness than my own personal comfort I should never have come back here. I could have obtained a practice at a distance, and have lived my own life without coldness or reproach. But I have chosen to return to the one spot on earth where my name is tarnished – to enter the house of a man from whom I have had worse treatment than from any other man alive – all for you!"

This was undeniably true, and it had its weight with Grace, who began to look as if she thought she had been shockingly severe.

"Before you go," he continued, "I want to know your pleasure about me: what you wish me to do, or not to do."

"You are independent of me, and it seems a mockery to ask that. Far be it from me to advise. But I will think it over. I rather need advice myself than stand in a position to give it."

"*You* don't need advice, wisest, dearest woman that ever lived. If you did . . ."

"Would you give it to me?"

"Would you act upon what I gave?"

"That's not a fair inquiry," said she smiling despite her gravity. "I don't mind hearing it – what you do really think the most correct and proper course for me."

"It is so easy for me to say, and yet I dare not, for it would be provoking you to remonstrances."

Knowing, of course, what the advice would be, she did not press him further, and was about to beckon Marty forward and leave him, when he interrupted her with, "Oh! one moment, dear Grace – you will meet me again?"

She eventually agreed to see him that day fortnight. Fitzpiers expostulated at the interval, but the half-alarmed earnestness with which she intreated him not to come sooner made him say hastily that he submitted to her will – that he would regard her as a friend only, anxious for his reform and well-being, till such time as she might allow him to exceed that privilege.

All this was to assure her; it was only too clear that he had not won her confidence yet. It amazed Fitzpiers, and overthrew all his deductions from previous experience, to find that this girl, though she had been married to him, could yet be so coy. Notwithstanding a certain fascination that it carried with it his reflections were sombre as he went homeward; he saw how deep had been his offence to produce so great a wariness in a gentle and once unsuspicious soul.

He was himself too fastidious to care to coerce her. To be an object of misgiving or dislike to a woman who shared his home was what he could not endure the thought of. Life as it stood was more tolerable.

When he was gone, Marty joined Mrs. Fitzpiers. She would fain have consulted Marty on the question of Platonic relations with her former husband, as she preferred to regard him. But Marty showed no great interest in their affairs, so Grace said nothing. They came onward, and saw Melbury standing at the scene of the felling which had been audible to them, when, telling Marty that she wished her meeting with Mr. Fitzpiers to be kept private, she left the girl to join her father. At any rate, she would consult him on the expediency of occasionally seeing her husband.

Her father was cheerful, and walked by her side as he had done in earlier days. "I was thinking of you when you came up," he said. "I have considered that what has happened is for the best. Since your husband is gone away, and seems not to wish to trouble you, why, let him go, and drop out of your life. Many women are worse off. You can live here comfortably enough, and he can emigrate, or do what he likes for his good. I wouldn't mind sending him the further sum of

money he might naturally expect to come to him, so that you may
not be bothered with him any more. He could hardly have gone on
living here without speaking to me, or meeting me; and that would
have been very unpleasant on both sides."

These remarks checked her intention. There was a sense of weakness
in following them by saying that she had just met her husband by
appointment. "Then you would advise me not to communicate with
him?" she observed.

"I shall never advise ye again. You are your own mistress – do as
you like. But my opinion is that if you don't live with him, you
had better live without him, and not go shilly-shallying and playing
bo-peep.[10] You sent him away; and now he's gone. Very well; trouble
him no more."

Grace felt a guiltiness – she hardly knew why – and made no
confession.

CHAPTER XIII

The woods were uninteresting, and Grace stayed indoors a great deal.
She became quite a student, reading more than she had done since
her marriage. But her seclusion was always broken for the periodical
visit to Winterborne's grave with Marty, which was kept up with pious
strictness for the purpose of putting snowdrops, primroses, and other
vernal flowers thereon as they came.

One afternoon at sunset she was standing just outside her father's
garden, which, like the rest of the Hintock inclosures, abutted into the
wood. A slight footpath led along here, forming a secret way to either
of the houses by getting through its boundary hedge. Grace was just
about to adopt this mode of entry when a figure approached along
the path, and held up his hand to detain her. It was her husband.

"I am delighted," he said, coming up out of breath; and there seemed no reason to doubt his words. "I saw you some way off – I was afraid you would go in before I could reach you."

"It is a week before the time," said she reproachfully. "I said a fortnight from the last meeting."

"My dear, you don't suppose I could wait a fortnight without trying to get a glimpse of you, even though you had declined to meet me! Would it make you angry to know that I have been along this path at dusk three or four times since our last meeting? Well, how are you?"

She did not refuse her hand, but when he showed a wish to retain it a moment longer than mere formality required, she made it smaller, so that it slipped away from him, with again that same alarmed look which always followed his attempts in this direction. He saw that she was not yet out of the elusive mood; not yet to be treated presumingly; and he was correspondingly careful to tranquillise her.

His assertion had seemed to impress her somewhat. "I had no idea you came so often," she said. "How far do you come from?"

"From Exbury. I always walk from Sherton Abbas, for if I hire people will know that I come; and my success with you so far has not been great enough to justify such overtness. Now, my dear one – as I *must* call you – I put it to you: will you see me a little oftener as the spring advances?"

Grace lapsed into unwonted sedateness, and avoiding the question, said: "I wish you would concentrate on your profession, and give up those strange studies that used to distract you so much. I am sure you would get on."

"It is the very thing I am doing. I was going to ask you to burn – or, at least, get rid of – all my philosophical literature. It is in the bookcases in your rooms. The fact is, I never cared much for abstruse studies."

"I am so glad to hear you say that. And those other books – those piles of old plays – what good are they to a medical man?"

"None whatever!" he replied cheerfully. "Sell them at Sherton for what they will fetch."

"And those dreadful old French romances with their horrid spellings[1] of 'filz' and 'ung' and 'ilz' and 'mary' and 'ma foy'?"

"You haven't been reading them, Grace?"

"Oh, no – I just looked into them, that was all."

"Make a bonfire of 'em directly you get home. I meant to do it myself. I can't think what possessed me ever to collect them. I have only a few professional hand-books now, and am quite a practical man. I am in hopes of having some good news to tell you soon, and then do you think you could – come to me again?"

"I would rather you did not press me on that just now," she replied with some feeling. "You have said you mean to lead a new, useful, effectual life; but I should like to see you put it in practice for a little while before you address that query to me. Besides – I could not live with you."

"Why not?"

Grace was silent a few instants. "I go with Marty to Giles's grave. We swore we would show him that devotion. And I mean to keep it up."

"Well, I wouldn't mind that at all. I have no right to expect anything else, and I will not wish you to keep away. I liked the man as well as any I ever knew. In short, I would accompany you a part of the way to the place, and smoke a cigar on the stile while I waited till you came back."

"Then you haven't given up smoking?"

"Well – ahem – no. I have thought of doing so, but" –

His extreme complaisance had rather disconcerted Grace, and the question about smoking had been to effect a diversion. Presently she said firmly, and with a moisture in her eye that he could not see, as her mind returned to poor Giles's "frustrate ghost;"[2] "I don't like you – to speak lightly on that subject, if you did speak lightly. To be frank with you – quite frank – I think of him as my betrothed lover still. I cannot help it. So that it would be wrong for me to join you."

Fitzpiers was now uneasy. "You say your betrothed lover still," he rejoined. "When, then, were you betrothed to him, or engaged, as we common people say?"

"When you were away."

"How could that be?"

Grace would have avoided this; but her natural candour led her on. "It was when I was under the impression that my marriage with you was about to be annulled, and that he could then marry me. So I encouraged him to love me."

Fitzpiers winced visibly; and yet, upon the whole, she was right in telling it. Indeed, his perception that she was right in her absolute sincerity, kept up his affectionate admiration for her under the pain of the rebuff. Time had been when the avowal that Grace had deliberately taken steps to replace him would have brought him no sorrow. But she so far dominated him now that he could not bear to hear her words, although the object of her high regard was no more.

"It is rough upon me – that!" he said bitterly. "Oh, Grace – I did not know you – tried to get rid of me! I suppose it is of no use, but I ask, cannot you hope to – find a little love in your heart for me again?"

"If I could I would oblige you; but I fear I cannot!" she replied, with illogical ruefulness. "And I don't see why you should mind my having had one lover besides yourself in my life, when you have had so many."

"But I can tell you honestly that I love you better than all of them put together, and that's what you will not tell me!"

"I am sorry; but I fear I cannot," she said sighing again.

"I wonder if you ever will?" He looked musingly into her indistinct face as if he would read the future there. "Now have pity, and tell me: will you try?"

"To love you again?"

"Yes; if you can."

"I don't know how to reply," she answered, her embarrassment proving her truth. "Will you promise to leave me quite free as to seeing you or not seeing you?"

"Certainly. Have I given any ground for you to doubt my first promise in that respect?"

She was obliged to admit that he had not.

"Then I think you might get your heart out of that grave," said he, with playful sadness. "It has been there a long time."

She faintly shook her head, but said: "I'll try to think of you more – if I can."

With this, Fitzpiers was compelled to be satisfied, and he asked her when she would meet him again.

"As we arranged – in a fortnight."

"If it must be a fortnight it must!"

"This time at least. I'll consider by the day I see you again if I can shorten the interval."

"Well, be that as it may, I shall come at least twice a week to look at your window."

"You must do as you like about that. Good-night."

"Say 'husband.' "

She seemed almost inclined to give him the word; but exclaiming, "No, no; I cannot," slipped through the garden-hedge and disappeared.

Fitzpiers did not exaggerate when he told her that he should haunt the precincts of the dwelling. But his persistence in this course did not result in his seeing her much oftener than at the fortnightly interval which she had herself marked out as proper. At these times, however, she punctually appeared, and as the spring wore on, the meetings were kept up, though their character changed but little with the increase in their number.

The small garden of the cottage occupied by the Tangs family – father, son, and now son's wife – aligned with the larger one of the timber-dealer at its upper end; and when young Tim, after leaving work at Melbury's, stood at dusk in the little bower at the corner of his inclosure to smoke a pipe, he frequently observed the surgeon pass along the outside track before-mentioned. Fitzpiers always walked loiteringly, pensively, looking with a sharp eye into the gardens one after another as he proceeded; for Fitzpiers did not wish to leave the now absorbing spot too quickly, after travelling so far to reach it; hoping always for a glimpse of her whom he passionately desired to take to his arms anew.

Now Tim began to be struck with these loitering progresses along the garden boundaries in the gloaming, and wondered what they boded. It was, naturally, quite out of his power to divine the singular, sentimental revival in Fitzpiers's heart: the fineness of tissue which could take a deep, emotional – almost also an artistic – pleasure in being the yearning *innamorato*[3] of a woman he once had deserted, would have seemed an absurdity to the young sawyer. Mr. and Mrs. Fitzpiers were separated; therefore the question of affection as between them was settled. But his Suke had, since that meeting on their marriage-day, repentantly admitted, to the urgency of his questioning, a good deal concerning her past levities. Putting all things together, he could hardly avoid connecting Fitzpiers's mysterious visits to this spot with Suke's residence under his roof. But he made himself fairly easy: the vessel in which they were about to emigrate sailed that month; and then Suke would be out of Fitzpiers's way for ever.

The interval at last expired, and the eve of their departure arrived. They were pausing in the room of the cottage allotted to them by Tim's father, after a busy day of preparation, which left them weary. In a corner stood their boxes, crammed and corded, their large case for the hold having already been sent away. The firelight shone upon Suke's fine face and form as she stood looking into it, and upon the face of Tim seated in a corner, and upon the walls of his father's house, which he was beholding that night almost for the last time.

Tim Tangs was not happy. This scheme of emigration was dividing him from his father – for old Tangs would on no account leave Hintock – and had it not been for Suke's reputation and his own dignity Tim would at the last moment have abandoned the project. As he sat in the back part of the room he regarded her moodily, and the fire, and the boxes. One thing he had particularly noticed this evening – she was very restless, fitful in her actions, unable to remain seated, and in a marked degree depressed.

"Sorry that you be going, after all, Suke?" he said.

She sighed involuntarily. "I don't know but that I be," she answered. " 'Tis natural, isn't it, when one is going away?"

"But you wasn't born here as I was."

"No."

"There's folk left behind that you'd fain have with 'ee, I reckon?"

"Why do you think that?"

"I've seen things, and I've heard things; and Suke, I say 'twill be a good move for me to get 'ee away. I don't mind his leavings abroad, but I do mind 'em at home."

Suke's face was not changed from its aspect of listless indifference by the words. She answered nothing; and shortly after he went out for his customary pipe of tobacco at the top of the garden.

The restlessness of Suke had indeed owed its presence to the gentleman of Tim's suspicions, but in a different – and it must be added in justice to her – more innocent sense than he supposed, judging from former doings. She had accidentally discovered that Fitzpiers was in the habit of coming secretly once or twice a week to Hintock, and knew that this evening was a favourite one of the seven for his journey. As she was going next day to leave the country, Suke thought there could be no great harm in giving way to a little sentimentality by obtaining a glimpse of him quite unknown to himself or to anybody, and thus taking a silent last farewell. Aware that Fitzpiers's time for passing was at hand she thus betrayed her feeling. No sooner, therefore, had Tim left the room than she let herself noiselessly out of the house, and hastened to the corner of the garden, whence she could witness the surgeon's transit across the scene – if he had not already gone by.

Her light cotton dress was visible to Tim lounging in the arbour of the opposite corner, though he was hidden from her. He saw her stealthily climb into the hedge, and so ensconce herself there that nobody could have the least doubt her purpose was to watch unseen for a passer-by.

He went across to the spot and stood behind her. Suke started, having in her blundering way forgotten that he might be near. She at once descended from the hedge.

"So he's coming to-night," said Tim laconically. "And we be always anxious to see our dears."

"He *is* coming to-night," she replied with defiance. "And we *be* anxious for our dears."

"Then will you step indoors, where your dear will soon jine 'ee? We've to mouster by half-past three to-morrow, and if we don't get to bed by eight at latest our faces will be as long as clock-cases all day."

She hesitated for a minute, but ultimately obeyed, going slowly down the garden to the house, where he heard the door-latch click behind her.

Tim was incensed beyond measure. His marriage had so far been a total failure, a source of bitter regret; and the only course for improving his case, that of leaving the country, was a sorry, and possibly might not be a very effectual one. Do what he would, his domestic sky was likely to be overcast to the end of the day. Thus he brooded, and his resentment gathered force. He craved a means of striking one blow back at the cause of his cheerless plight, while he was still on the scene of his discomfiture. For some minutes no method suggested itself, and then he had an idea.

Coming to a sudden resolution he hastened along the garden, and entered the one attached to the next cottage, which had formerly been the dwelling of a gamekeeper. Tim descended the path, to the back of the house, where only an old woman lived at present, and reaching the wall he stopped. Owing to the slope of the ground the roof-eaves of the linhay were here within touch, and he thrust his arm up under them, feeling about in the space on the top of the wall plate.

"Ah, I thought my memory didn't deceive me!" he lipped silently.

With some exertion he drew down a cobwebbed object curiously framed in iron, which clanked as he moved it. It was about three feet in length and half as wide. Tim contemplated it as well as he could in the dying light of day, and raked off the cobwebs with his hand.

"That will spoil his pretty shins for'n, I reckon!" he said.

It was a man-trap.[4]

CHAPTER XIV

Were the inventors of automatic machines to be ranged according to the excellence of their devices for producing sound artistic torture, the creator of the man-trap would occupy a very respectable, if not a very high place.

It should rather, however, be said, the inventor of the particular form of man-trap of which this found in the keeper's outhouse was a specimen. For there were other shapes and other sizes, instruments which, if placed in a row beside one of the type disinterred by Tim, would have worn the subordinate aspect of the bears, wild boars, or wolves in a travelling menagerie as compared with the leading lion or tiger. In short, though many varieties had been in use during those centuries which we are accustomed to look back upon as the true and only period of merry England – in the rural districts more especially – and onward down to the third decade of the nineteenth century, this model had borne the palm, and had been most usually followed when the orchards and estates required new ones.

There had been the toothless variety used by the softer-hearted landlords – quite contemptible in their clemency.[1] The jaws of these resembled the jaws of an old woman to whom time has left nothing but gums. There were also the intermediate or half-toothed sorts, probably devised by the middle-natured squires, or those under the influence of their wives: two inches of mercy, two inches of cruelty, two inches of mere nip, two inches of probe, and so on, through the whole extent of the jaws. There were also, as a class apart, the bruisers, which did not lacerate the flesh, but only crushed the bone.

The sight of one of these gins, when set, produced a vivid impression that it was endowed with life. It exhibited the combined aspects of a shark, a crocodile, and a scorpion. Each tooth was in the form of a tapering spine, two and a quarter inches long, which, when the jaws were closed, stood in alternation from this side and from that. When they were open, the two halves formed a complete circle between two and three feet in diameter, the plate or treading-place in the midst being about a foot square, while from beneath extended in opposite directions the soul of the apparatus, a pair of springs, each one being of a stiffness to render necessary a lever or the whole weight of the body when forcing it down.

There were men at this time still living at Hintock who remembered when the gin and others like it were in use. Tim Tangs's great-uncle had endured a night of six hours in this very trap, which lamed him for life. Once a keeper of Hintock woods set it on the track of a poacher, and afterwards, coming back that way forgetful of what he had done, walked into it himself. The wound brought on lockjaw, of which he died. This event occurred during the thirties, and by the year 1840 the use of such implements was well nigh discontinued in the neighbourhood. But being made entirely of iron, they by no means disappeared, and in almost every village one could be found in some nook or corner as readily as this was found by Tim. It had indeed been a fearful amusement of Tim and other Hintock lads – especially those who had a dim sense of becoming renowned poachers when they reached their prime – to drag out this trap from its hiding, set it, and throw it with billets of wood, which were penetrated by the teeth to the depth of near an inch.

As soon as he had examined the trap, and found that the hinges and springs were still perfect, he shouldered it without more ado, and returned with his burden to his own garden, passing on through the hedge to the path immediately outside the boundary. Here, by the help of a stout stake, he set the trap, and laid it carefully behind a bush while he went forward to reconnoitre. As has been stated, nobody passed this way for days together sometimes; but there was just a possibility that some other pedestrian than the one in request might arrive, and it behoved Tim to be careful as to the identity of his victim.

Going about a hundred yards along the rising ground to the right, he reached a ridge whereon a large and thick holly grew. Beyond this for some distance the wood was more open, and the course which Fitzpiers must pursue to reach the point, if he came to-night, was visible a long way forward.

For some time there was no sign of him or of anybody. Then there shaped itself a spot out of the dim mid-distance, between the masses of brushwood on each hand. And it enlarged, and Tim could hear the brushing of feet over the tufts of sour grass. The airy gait revealed Fitzpiers even before his exact outline could be seen.

Tim Tangs turned about, and ran down the opposite side of the hill, till he was again at the head of his own garden. It was the work of a few moments to drag out the man-trap very gently – that the plate might not be disturbed sufficiently to throw it – to a space between a pair of young oaks which, rooted in contiguity, grew apart upward, forming a V-shaped opening between; and, being backed up by bushes, left this as the only course for a foot-passenger. In it he laid the trap with the same gentleness of handling, locked the chain round one of the trees, and finally slid back the guard which was placed to keep the gin from accidentally catching the arms of him who set it, or, to use the local and better word "toiled" it. Having completed these arrangements Tim sprang through the adjoining hedge of his father's garden, ran down the path and softly entered the house.

Obedient to his order, Suke had gone to bed; and as soon as he had bolted the door, Tim unlaced and kicked off his boots at the foot of the stairs, and retired likewise, without lighting a candle. His object seemed to be to undress as soon as possible. Before, however, he had completed the operation a long cry resounded without – penetrating, but indescribable.

"What's that?" said Suke, starting up in bed.

"Sounds as if somebody had caught a hare in his gin."

"Oh no," said she. "It was not a hare, 'twas louder. Hark!"

"Do 'ee get to sleep," said Tim. "How be you going to wake at half-past three else?"

She lay down and was silent. Tim stealthily opened the window and listened. Above the low harmonies produced by the instrumentation of the various species of tree around the premises he could hear the twitching of a chain from the spot whereon he had set the man trap. But further human sound there was none.

Tim was puzzled. In the haste of his project he had not calculated upon a cry; but if one, why not more? He soon ceased to essay an answer, for Hintock was dead to him already. In half a dozen hours he would be out of its precincts for life, on his way to the antipodes. He closed the window and lay down.

The hour which had brought these movements of Tim to birth had been operating actively elsewhere. Awaiting in her father's house the minute of her appointment with her husband, Grace Fitzpiers deliberated on many things. Should she inform her father before going out that the estrangement of herself and Edred was not so complete as he had imagined, and deemed desirable for her happiness? If she did so she must in some measure become the apologist of her husband, and she was not prepared to go so far.

As for him, he kept her in a mood of considerate gravity. He

certainly had changed. He had at his worst times always been gentle
in his manner towards her. Could it be that she might make of him a
true and worthy husband yet? She had married him; there was no
getting over that; and ought she any longer to keep him at a distance?
His suave deference to her lightest whim on the question of his
comings and goings, when as her lawful husband he might show a
little independence, was a trait in his character as unexpected as it
was engaging. If she had been his empress, and he her thrall, he could
not have exhibited a more sensitive care to avoid intruding upon her
against her will.

Impelled by a remembrance she took down a prayer-book, and
turned to the marriage-service.[2] Reading it slowly through she became
quite appalled at her recent offhandedness, when she rediscovered
what awfully solemn promises she had made him at those chancel
steps not so very long ago. She became lost in long ponderings on
how far a person's conscience might be bound by vows made without
at the time a full recognition of their force. That particular sentence,
beginning "Whom God hath joined together," was a staggerer for a
gentle woman of strong devotional sentiment. She wondered whether
God really did join them together. Before she had done deliberating
the time of her engagement drew near, and she went out of the house
almost at the moment that Tim Tangs retired to his own.

The position of things at that critical juncture was briefly as follows.
Two hundred yards to the right of the upper end of Tangs's garden
Fitzpiers was still advancing, having now nearly reached the summit
of the wood-clothed ridge, the path being the actual one which further
on passed between the two young oaks. Thus far it was according to
Tim's conjecture. But about two hundred yards to the left, or rather
less, was arising a condition which he had not divined, the emergence
of Grace as aforesaid from the upper corner of her father's garden
with the view of meeting Tim's intended victim. Midway between
husband and wife was the diabolical trap, silent, open, ready.

Fitzpiers's walk that night had been cheerful, for he was convinced
that the slow and gentle method he had adopted was promising success.
The very restraint that he was obliged to exercise upon himself, so as
not to kill the delicate bud of returning confidence, fed his flame. He

walked so much more rapidly than Grace that, if they continued advancing as they had begun, he would reach the trap a good half minute before she could reach the same spot. But here a new circumstance came in: to escape the unpleasantness of being watched or listened to by lurkers – naturally curious by reason of their strained relations – they had arranged that their meeting for to-night should be at the holm-tree on the ridge above-named. So soon, accordingly, as Fitzpiers reached the tree he stood still to await her.

He had not paused under the prickly foliage more than two minutes when he thought he heard a scream from the other side of the ridge. Fitzpiers wondered what it could mean; but such wind as there was just now blew in an adverse direction, and his mood was light. He set down the origin of the sound to one of the superstitious freaks or frolicsome scrimmages between sweethearts that still survived in Hintock from old-English times; and waited on where he stood till ten minutes had passed. Feeling then a little uneasy his mind reverted to the scream; and he went forward over the summit and down the embowered incline, till he reached the pair of sister oaks with the narrow opening between them.

Fitzpiers stumbled and all but fell. Stretching down his hand to ascertain the obstruction it came in contact with a confused mass of silken drapery and ironwork that conveyed absolutely no explanatory idea to his mind at all. It was but the work of a moment to strike a match; and then he saw a sight which congealed his blood.

The man-trap was thrown; and between its jaws was part of a woman's clothing – a patterned silk skirt – gripped with such violence that the iron teeth had passed through it, skewering its tissue in a score of places. He immediately recognised the skirt as that of one of his wife's gowns – the gown that she had worn when she met him on the very last occasion.

Fitzpiers had often studied the effect of these instruments when examining the collection at Hintock House, and the conception instantly flashed through him that Grace had been caught, taken out mangled by some chance passer, and carried home, some of her clothes being left behind in the difficulty of getting her free. The shock of this conviction, striking into the very current of high hope, was so great that he cried out like one in corporal agony, and in his misery bowed himself down to the ground.

Of all the degrees and qualities of punishment that Fitzpiers had undergone since his sins against Grace first began, not any even approximated in intensity to this. "Oh, my own – my darling! Oh, cruel Heaven – it is too much this!" he cried, writhing and rocking himself over the sorry accessories of her he deplored.

The voice of his distress was sufficiently loud to be audible to any one who might have been there to hear it; and one there was. Right and left of the narrow pass between the oaks were dense bushes; and now from behind these a female figure glided, whose appearance even in the gloom was, though graceful in outline, noticeably strange.

She was in white up to the waist, and figured above. She was, in short, Grace, his wife, lacking the portion of her dress which the gin retained.

"Don't be grieved about me – don't, dear Edred!" she exclaimed, rushing up and bending over him. "I am not hurt a bit! I was coming on to find you after I had released myself, but I heard footsteps; and I hid away, because I was without some of my clothing, and I did not know who the person might be."

Fitzpiers had sprung to his feet, and his next act was no less unpremeditated by him than it was irresistible by her, and would have been so by any woman not of Amazonian strength. He clasped his arms completely round, pressed her to his breast, and kissed her passionately.

"You are not dead! – you are not hurt! Thank God – thank God!" he said, almost sobbing in his delight and relief from the horror of his apprehension. "Grace, my wife, my love, how is this – what has happened?"

"I was coming on to you," she said as distinctly as she could in the half-smothered state of her face against his. "I was trying to be as punctual as possible, and as I had started a minute late I ran along the path very swiftly – fortunately for myself. Just when I had passed between these trees I felt something clutch at my dress from behind with a noise, and the next moment I was pulled backwards by it, and fell to the ground. I screamed with terror, thinking it was a man lying down there to murder me, but the next moment I discovered it was iron, and that my clothes were caught in a trap. I pulled this way and that, but the thing would not let go, drag it as I would, and I did not know what to do. I did not want to alarm my father or anybody, as I wished nobody to know of these meetings with you; so I could think of no other plan than slipping off my skirt, meaning to run on and tell you what a strange accident had happened to me. But when I had just freed myself by leaving the dress behind, I heard steps, and not being sure it was you, I did not like to be seen in such a pickle, so I hid away."

"It was only your speed that saved you! One or both of your legs would have been broken if you had come at ordinary walking pace."

"Or yours, if you had got here first," said she, beginning to realise the whole ghastliness of the possibility. "Oh, Edred, there has been an Eye watching over us to-night, and we should be thankful indeed!"

He continued to press his face to hers. "You are mine – mine again now."

She gently owned that she supposed she was. "I heard what you said when you thought I was injured," she went on shyly, "and I know that a man who could suffer as you were suffering must have a tender regard for me. But how does this awful thing come here?"

"I suppose it has something to do with poachers." Fitzpiers was still so shaken by the sense of her danger that he was obliged to sit awhile, and it was not until Grace said, "If I could only get my skirt out nobody would know anything about it," that he bestirred himself.

By their united efforts, each standing on one of the springs of the trap, they pressed them down sufficiently to insert across the jaws a billet which they dragged from a faggot near at hand, and it was then possible to extract the silk mouthful from the monster's bite, creased and pierced with many holes, but not torn. Fitzpiers assisted her to put it on again; and when her customary contours were thus restored they walked on together, Grace taking his arm, till he effected an improvement by clasping it round her waist.

The ice having been broken in this unexpected manner, she made no further attempt at reserve. "I would ask you to come into the house," she said, "but my meetings with you have been kept secret from my father, and I should like to prepare him."

"Never mind, dearest. I could not very well have accepted the invitation. I shall never live here again – as much for your sake as for mine. I have news to tell you on this very point, but my alarm had put it out of my head. I have bought a practice, or rather a partnership, in the Midlands, and I must go there in a week to take up permanent residence. My poor old great-aunt died about eight months ago, and left me enough to do this. I have taken a little furnished house for a time, till we can get one of our own."

He described the place, and the surroundings, and the view from the windows; and Grace became much interested. "But why are you not there now?" she said.

"Because I cannot tear myself away from here till I have your promise. Now, darling, you will accompany me there – will you not? To-night has settled that?"

Grace's tremblings had gone off, and she did not say nay. They went on together.

The adventure, and the emotions consequent upon the reunion which that event had forced on, combined to render Grace oblivious of the direction of their desultory ramble, till she noticed they were in an encircled glade in the densest part of the wood. The moon, that had imperceptibly added its rays to the scene, shone almost vertically. It was an exceptionally soft, balmy evening for the time of year, which was just that transient period in the May month when beech trees have suddenly unfolded large limp young leaves of the softness of butterflies' wings. Boughs bearing such leaves hung low around, and completely enclosed them, so that it was as if they were in a great green vase, which had moss for its bottom and leaf sides.

The clouds having been packed in the west that evening so as to retain the departing glare a long while, the hour had seemed much earlier than it was. But suddenly the question of time occurred to her.

"I must go back," she said; and without further delay they set their faces towards Hintock. As they walked he examined his watch by the aid of the now strong moonlight.

"By the gods, I think I have lost my train!" said Fitzpiers.

"Dear me – whereabouts are we?" said she.

"Two miles in the direction of Sherton."

"Then do you hasten on, Edred. I am not in the least afraid. I recognise now the part of the wood we are in, and I can find my way back quite easily. I'll tell my father that we have made it up. I wish I had not kept our meetings so private, for it may vex him a little to know I have been seeing you. He is getting old and irritable, that was why I did not. Good-bye."

"But, as I must stay at the Earl of Wessex to-night, for I cannot possibly catch the train, I think it would be safer for you to let me take care of you."

"But what will my father think has become of me! He does not know in the least where I am – he thinks I only went into the garden for a few minutes."

"He will surely guess – somebody has seen me for certain. I'll go all the way back with you to-morrow."

"But that newly done-up place – the Earl of Wessex!"

"If you are so very particular about the publicity I will stay at the Three Tuns."

"Oh no – it is not that I am particular – but I haven't a brush or comb or anything!"

CHAPTER XV

All the evening Melbury had been coming to his door saying, "I wonder where in the world that girl is! Never in all my born days did I know her bide out like this! She surely said she was going into the garden to get some parsley."

Melbury searched the garden, the parsley-bed, and the orchard, but could find no trace of her, and then he made inquiries at the cottages of such of his workmen as had not gone to bed, avoiding Tangs's because he knew the young people were to rise early to leave. In these inquiries one of the men's wives somewhat incautiously let out the fact that she had heard a scream in the wood, though from which direction she could not say.

This set Melbury's fears on end. He told the men to light lanterns, and headed by himself they started, Creedle following at the last moment with quite a burden of grapnels and ropes which he could not be persuaded to leave behind, the company being joined by the hollow-turner and Cawtree who kept the cider-house as they went along.

They explored the precincts of the village, and in a short time lighted upon the man-trap. Its discovery simply added an item of fact without helping their conjectures; but Melbury's indefinite alarm was greatly increased when, holding a candle to the ground, he saw in the teeth of the instrument some frayings from Grace's clothing. No intelligence of any kind was gained till they met a woodman of Delborough, who said that he had seen a lady answering to the description her father gave of Grace, walking through the wood on a gentleman's arm in the direction of Sherton.

"Was he clutching her tight?" said Melbury.

"Well – rather," said the man.

"Did she walk lame?"

"Well 'tis true her head hung over towards him a bit."

Creedle groaned tragically.

Melbury, not suspecting the presence of Fitzpiers, coupled this account with the man-trap and the scream; he could not understand what it all meant, but the sinister event of the trap made him follow on. Accordingly, they bore away towards the town, shouting as they went, and in due course emerged upon the highway.

Nearing Sherton Abbas, the previous information was confirmed by other strollers, though the gentleman's supporting arm had disappeared from these later accounts. At last they were so near Sherton that Melbury informed his faithful followers that he did not wish to drag them further at so late an hour, since he could go on alone and inquire if the woman who had been seen were really Grace. But they would not leave him alone in his anxiety, and trudged onward till the lamplight from the town began to illuminate their fronts. At the entrance to the High Street they got fresh scent of the pursued, but coupled with the new condition that the lady in the costume described had been going up the street alone.

"Faith – I believe she's mesmerised,[1] or walking in her sleep!" said Melbury.

However, the identity of this woman with Grace was by no means certain; but they plodded along the street. Percomb the hairdresser, who had despoiled Marty of her tresses, was standing at his door, and they duly put inquiries to him.

"Ah – how's Little Hintock folk by now!" he said before replying. "Never have I been over there since one winter night some three year ago – and then I lost myself finding it. How can ye live in such a one-eyed place? Great Hintock is bad enough – but Little Hintock – the bats and owls would drive me melancholy-mad![2] It took two days to raise my sperrits to their true pitch again after that night I went there. Mr. Melbury, sir, as a man that's put by money, why not retire and live here, and see something of the world?"

The responses at last given by him to their queries guided them to the building that offered the best accommodation in Sherton – having been enlarged contemporaneously with the construction of the railway – namely, the Earl of Wessex Hotel.

Leaving the others without, Melbury made prompt inquiry here. His alarm was lessened, though his perplexity was increased, when he received a brief reply that such a lady was in the house.

"Do you know if it is my daughter?" asked Melbury.

The waiter did not.

"Do you know the lady's name?"

Of this, too, the household was ignorant, the hotel having been taken by brand-new people from a distance. They knew the gentleman very well by sight, and had not thought it necessary to ask him to enter his name.

"Oh, the gentleman appears again now," said Melbury to himself. "Well, I want to see the lady," he declared.

A message was taken up, and after some delay the shape of Grace appeared descending round the bend of the staircase, looking as if she lived there, but in other respects rather guilty and frightened.

"Why – what the name –" began her father. "I thought you went out to get parsley!"

"Oh, yes – I did – but it is all right," said Grace in a flurried whisper. "I am not alone here. I am here with Edred. It is entirely owing to an accident, father."

"Edred! An accident! How does he come here? I thought he was two hundred mile off."

"Yes; so he is – I mean he has got a beautiful practice two hundred miles off: he has bought it with his own money, some that came to him. But he travelled here, and I was nearly caught in a man-trap, and that's how it is I am here. We were just thinking of sending a messenger to let you know."

Melbury did not seem to be particularly enlightened by this explanation.

"You were caught in a man-trap?"

"Yes; my dress was. That's how it arose. Edred is up stairs in his own sitting-room," she went on. "He would not mind seeing you, I am sure."

"Oh, faith, I don't want to see him! I have seen him too often a'ready. I'll see him another time, perhaps, if 'tis to oblige 'ee."

"He came to see me; he wanted to consult me about this large partnership I speak of, as it is very promising."

"Oh, I am glad to hear it," said Melbury drily.

A pause ensued, during which the inquiring faces and whitey-brown clothes of Melbury's companions appeared in the doorway.

"Then baint you coming home with us?" he asked.

"I – I think not," said Grace, blushing.

"H'm – very well – you are your own mistress," he returned in tones which seemed to assert otherwise. "Good-night;" and Melbury retreated towards the door.

"Don't be angry, father," she said, following him a few steps. "I have done it for the best."

"I am not angry, though it is true I have been a little misled in this. However, good-night. I must get home along."

He left the hotel, not without relief, for to be under the eyes of strangers while he conversed with his lost child had embarrassed him much. His search-party, too, had looked awkward there, having rushed to the task of investigation – some in their shirt-sleeves, others in their leather aprons, and all much stained – just as they had come from their work of barking, and not in their Sherton marketing attire; while Creedle, with his ropes and grapnels and air of impending tragedy, had added melancholy to gawkiness.

"Now, neighbours," said Melbury, on joining them, "as it is getting late we'll leg it home again as fast as we can. I ought to tell you that there has been some mistake – some arrangement entered into between Mr. and Mrs. Fitzpiers which I didn't quite understand – an important practice in the Midland counties has come to him, which made it necessary for her to join him to-night – so she says. That's all it was – and I'm sorry I dragged you out."

"Well," said the hollow-turner, "here be we six mile from home, and night-time, and not a hoss or four-footed creeping thing to our name. I say, we'll have a mossel and a drop o' summat to strengthen our nerves afore we vamp all the way back again? My throat's as dry as a kex. What d'ye say so's?"

They all concurred in the need for this course, and proceeded to the antique and lampless back street in which the red curtain of the Three Tuns was the only radiant object. As soon as they had stumbled down into the room Melbury ordered them to be served, when they made themselves comfortable by the long table, and stretched out their legs upon the herring-boned sand of the floor. Melbury himself, restless as usual, walked to the door while he waited for them, and looked up and down the street.[3]

"I'd gie her a good shaking if she were my maid; pretending to go out in garden, and leading folk a twelve-mile traipse that have got to get up at five o'clock to-morrow," said a bark-ripper; who, not working regularly for Melbury, could afford to indulge in strong opinions.

"I don't speak so warm as that," said the hollow-turner, "but if 'tis right for couples to make a country talk about their separating, and excite the neighbours, and then make fools of 'em like this, why, I haven't stood upon one leg for five-and-twenty year."

All his listeners knew that when he alluded to his foot-lathe in these enigmatic terms, the speaker meant to be impressive; and Creedle chimed in with, "Ah, young women do wax wanton[4] in these days! Why couldn't she ha' bode with her father, and been faithful." Poor Creedle was thinking of his old employer.

"But this deceiving of folks is nothing unusual in matrimony," said Farmer Cawtree. "I knowed a man and wife – faith, I don't mind owning as there's no strangers here, that the pair were my own relations – they'd be at it that hot one hour that you'd hear the poker, and the tongs, and the bellows, and the warming-pan, flee across the house with the movements of their vengeance; and the next hour you'd hear 'em singing 'The Spotted Cow'[5] together as peaceable as two holy twins; yes – and very good voices they had, and would strike in like professional ballet-singers to one another's support in the high notes."

"And I knowed a woman, and the husband o' her went away for four-and-twenty year," said the bark-ripper. "And one night he came home when she was sitting by the fire, and thereupon he sat down himself on the other side of the chimney-corner. 'Well,' says she, 'have ye got any news?' 'Don't know as I have,' says he; 'have you?' 'No,' says she, 'except that my daughter by my second husband was married last month, which was a year after I was made a widow by him.' 'Oh! Anything else?' he says. 'No,' says she. And there they sat, one on each side of that chimney-corner, and were found by the neighbours sound asleep in their chairs, not having known what to talk about at all."

"Well, I don't care who the man is," said Creedle, "they required a good deal to talk about, and that's true. It won't be the same with these."

"No. He is such a projick, you see. And she is a wonderful scholar too!"

"What women do know nowadays!" observed the hollow-turner. "You can't deceive 'em as you could in my time."

"What they knowed then was not small," said John Upjohn. "Always a good deal more than the men! Why, when I went courting my wife that is now, the skilfulness that she would show in keeping me on her pretty side as she walked was beyond all belief. Perhaps you've noticed that she's got a pretty side to her face as well as a plain one?"

"I can't say I've noticed it particular much," said the hollow-turner blandly.

"Well," continued Upjohn, not disconcerted, "she has. All women under the sun be prettier one side than t'other. And, as I was saying, the pains she would take to make me walk on the pretty side were unending! I warrant that whether we were going with the sun or against the sun, uphill or downhill, in wind or in lewth, that wart of hers was always towards the hedge, and that dimple towards me. There was I, too simple to see her wheelings and turnings; and she so artful, though two years younger, that she could lead me with a cotton thread, like a blind ram; for that was in the third climate of our courtship . . . No; I don't think the women have got cleverer, for they was never otherwise."

"How many climates may there be in courtship, Mr. Upjohn?" inquired a youth – the same who had assisted at Winterborne's Christmas party.

"Five – from the coolest to the hottest – leastwise there was five in mine."

"Can ye give us the chronicle of 'em, Mr. Upjohn?"

"Yes – I could. I could certainly. But 'tis quite unnecessary. They'll come to ye by nater, young man, too soon for your good."

"At present Mrs. Fitzpiers can lead the doctor as your mis'ess could lead you," the hollow-turner remarked. "She's got him quite tame. But how long 'twill last I can't say. I happened to be setting a wire[6] on the top of my garden one night when he met her on the other side of the hedge; and the way she queened it, and fenced, and kept that poor feller at a distance was enough to freeze yer blood. I should never have supposed it of such a girl."

Melbury now returned to the room, and the men having declared themselves refreshed, they all started on the homeward journey, which was by no means cheerless under the rays of the high moon. Having to walk the whole distance they came by a footpath rather shorter than the highway, though difficult except to those who knew the country well. This brought them by way of Great Hintock; and passing the churchyard they observed as they talked a motionless figure standing by the gate.

"I think it was Marty South," said the hollow-turner parenthetically.

"I think 'twas; 'a was always a lonely maid," said Upjohn. And they passed on homeward, and thought of the matter no more.

It was Marty, as they had supposed. That evening had been the particular one of the week upon which Grace and herself had been accustomed to privately deposit flowers on Giles's grave, and this was the first occasion since his death eight months earlier on which Grace had failed to keep her appointment. Marty had waited in the road just outside Little Hintock, where her fellow-pilgrim had been wont to join her, till she was weary; and at last, thinking that Grace had missed her and gone on alone, she followed the way to Great Hintock, but saw no Grace in front of her. It got later, and Marty continued her walk till she reached the churchyard gate; but still no Grace. Yet her sense of comradeship would not allow her to go on to the grave alone, and, still thinking the delay had been unavoidable, she stood there with her little basket of flowers in her clasped hands, and her feet chilled by the damp ground, till more than two hours had passed. She then heard the footsteps of Melbury's men, who presently passed on their return from the search. In the silence of the night Marty could not help hearing fragments of their conversation, from which she acquired a general idea of what had occurred, and where Mrs. Fitzpiers then was.[7]

Immediately they had dropped down the hill she entered the churchyard, going to a secluded corner behind the bushes, where rose the unadorned stone that marked the last bed of Giles Winterborne. As this solitary and silent girl stood there in the moonlight, a straight slim figure, clothed in a plaitless gown, the contours of womanhood so undeveloped as to be scarcely perceptible, the marks of poverty and toil effaced by the misty hour, she touched sublimity at points, and looked almost like a being who had rejected with indifference the attribute of sex for the loftier quality of abstract humanism.[8] She stooped down and cleared away the withered flowers that Grace and herself had laid there the previous week, and put her fresh ones in their place.

"Now, my own own love," she whispered, "you are mine, and on'y mine; for she has forgot 'ee at last, although for her you died. But I – whenever I get up I'll think of 'ee, and whenever I lie down I'll think of 'ee. Whenever I plant the young larches I'll think that none can plant as you planted; and whenever I split a gad, and whenever I turn the cider wring, I'll say none could do it like you. If ever I forget your name let me forget home and heaven! . . . But no, no, my love, I never can forget 'ee; for you was a *good* man, and did good things!"

THE END

Preface to 1896 Edition and
Additional Postscript to 1912 Edition

PREFACE

In the present novel, as in one or two others of this series which involve
the question of matrimonial divergence, the immortal puzzle – given
the man and woman, how to find a basis for their sexual relation – is
left where it stood; and it is tacitly assumed for the purposes of the
story that no doubt of the depravity of the erratic heart who feels some
third person to be better suited to his or her tastes than the one with
whom he has contracted to live, enters the head of reader or writer
for a moment. From the point of view of marriage as a distinct covenant
or undertaking, decided on by two people fully cognizant of all its
possible issues, and competent to carry them through, this assumption
is, of course, logical. Yet no thinking person supposes that on the
broader ground of how to afford the greatest happiness to the units
of human society during their brief transit through this sorry world,
there is no more to be said on this covenant; and it is certainly not
supposed by the writer of these pages. But, as Gibbon blandly remarks
on the evidence for and against Christian miracles, 'the duty of an
historian does not call upon him to interpose his private judgment in
this nice and important controversy.'

The stretch of country visible from the heights adjoining the nook
herein described under the name of Little Hintock, cannot be regarded
as inferior to any inland scenery of the sort in the west of England, or
perhaps anywhere in the kingdom. It is singular to find that a worldwide
repute in some cases, and an absolute obliviousness in others, attach
to spots of equal beauty and equal accessibility. The neighbourhood
of High-Stoy (I give, as elsewhere, the real names to natural features),
Bubb Down Hill, and westward to Montacute; of Bulbarrow, Hamble-
don Hill, and eastward to Shaston, Windy Green, and Stour Head,

teems with landscapes which, by a mere accident of iteration, might have been numbered among the scenic celebrities of the century.

T. H.
September 1895.

I have been honoured by so many inquiries for the true name and exact locality of the hamlet 'Little Hintock,' in which the greater part of the action of this story goes on, that I may as well confess here once for all that I do not know myself where that hamlet is more precisely than as explained above and in the pages of the narrative. To oblige readers I once spent several hours on a bicycle with a friend in a serious attempt to discover the real spot; but the search ended in failure; though tourists assure me positively that they have found it without trouble, and that it answers in every particular to the description given in this volume. At all events, as stated elsewhere, the commanding heights called 'High-Stoy' and 'Bubb-Down Hill' overlook the landscape in which it is supposed to be hid.

In respect of the occupations of the characters, the adoption of iron utensils and implements in agriculture, and the discontinuance of thatched roofs for cottages, have almost extinguished the handicrafts classed formerly as 'copsework,' and the type of men who engaged in them.

The Woodlanders was first published complete, in three volumes, in the March of 1887.

T. H.
April 1912.

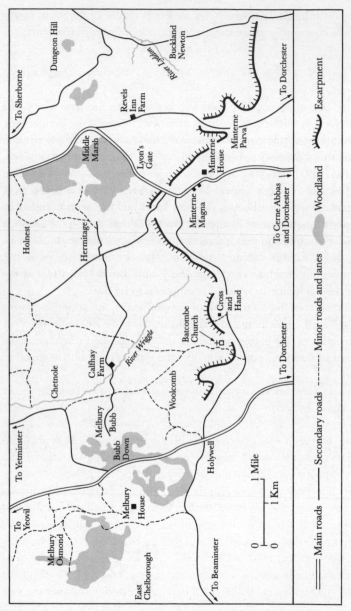

The Location of The Woodlanders

The Location of The Woodlanders

[Place names with inverted commas are fictional names; those without them are real ones.]

The idea of Hardy's 'Wessex' has frequently been assumed to have been exactly mapped by him on to Dorset and its surroundings. But this is not so. The 'truth' of his representation of the countryside is a more imaginative one. It is like that of the Impressionist paintings he saw in 1886 at the British Society of Artists while writing the novel. He refers to them in *The Woodlanders*[1] and he wrote of them at the time:

The impressionist school is strong. It is even more suggestive in the direction of literature than in that of art. As usual it is pushed to absurdity by some. But their principle is, as I understand it, that what you carry away with you from a scene is the true feature to grasp; or in other words, *what appeals to your own individual eye and heart in particular* amid much that does not so appeal, and which you therefore omit to record.[2]

The wealth of detailed and often metaphorical descriptions of the woods and their seasonal changes can thus be regarded as impression-istic not photographic. Similarly, locations of named places may be an amalgam of several actual sites with a general topographical coherence. This coherence is increased in the 1896 and 1912 versions. The names used are sometimes invented; sometimes real, especially for prominent geographical features; and sometimes inventions which echo real names in the area to which a novel relates. For each does, in the sense described above, relate to a definite area on the map of south-west England. In the case of *The Woodlanders*, this is a region north of the town of Dorchester. It lies roughly within a boundary running east from Yeovil to Sherborne; south from Sherborne to Cerne Abbas; north-west from Cerne Abbas to East Chelborough; and north from East Chelborough to Yeovil. It is the quintessence of this landscape that Hardy distils into the woodlands and apple orchards of his narrative.

The question of 'where' in this novel is complicated by the fact that Hardy evidently had in mind one hypothetical location in the early versions;[3] but later, apparently for prudential reasons, made changes to indicate a different siting.

Even in 1887 the 'key' to real places was sought for eagerly. Edmund Gosse seems to have asked about the location of 'Little Hintock' for Hardy wrote to him on 5 April 1887:

It has just occurred to me that in my letter I said *Little* Hintock was Melbury Osmond. I meant *Great* Hintock. Little H. would be a hamlet anywhere within 2 miles of the former.[4]

Melbury Osmond is a town in Dorset just a little to the north-east of East Chelborough and not far from a real Melbury House, the original location of Mrs Charmond's fictitious mansion. This indicates that the novel's 'Rubdon Hill' is equatable with the real Bubb Down and 'Sherton' with Sherborne. The letter also implies that no particular hamlet can be specified as 'Little Hintock'. When the first edition (used here) states that 'Little Hintock' had the old name of 'Hintock St Osmond'[5] this confirms the statement that it relates to an area within two miles of Melbury Osmond. Hardy liked to echo in his fictional names those of places in the area he had in mind.

Though in the early versions the site of Melbury House is the location given to Mrs Charmond's home, its description does not fit the sixteenth-century or Elizabethan manor-house described in the text.[6] The description does, however, fit Turnworth Manor near Blandford.[7] Certainly Hardy avoided the obvious equation with Melbury House – a part-fifteenth-century building which was the home of the Ilchester family. He later used Melbury House (complete with an accurate sketch) under the guise of 'King's Hintock Court' in a 'scandalous' story, 'The First Countess of Wessex' (*Harper's New Monthly Magazine*, December 1889). It is possible that in order to remove the assumption that the adulterous Mrs Charmond and her Melbury House were to be linked to the Ilchesters, Hardy decided to 'change its location' round about 1890. The change of course is theoretical.

In the revised text of 1896 'Rubdon Hill' (alias the real Bubb Down) was changed to High-Stoy Hill. The latter was the real name of a place near a wooded area some distance to the west of the original siting and nearer to the Sherborne–Cerne Abbas main road. This suggests a different location for 'Great Hintock' and 'Little Hintock': just to the west of the Sherborne–Cerne Abbas road. This topography is the one with which most readers are familiar, since the 1912 edition has been the basis of most later editions. The present edition has of course the earlier names and locations which seem to be those from which the descriptions, as opposed to the names used in the narrative, derive. In this sense (only) its topography is the more 'authentic'.

However, the quest for locations (of the 1912 version) has continued. There is evidence from after 1905 that Hardy was prepared to equate 'Great Hintock' with Minterne Magna (Greater Minterne). This suggests an equation of 'Little Hintock' with Minterne Parva (Lesser Minterne). But since the narrative makes clear that 'Little Hintock' is north, not south, of 'Great Hintock', an alternative siting for the former, given by Hermann Lea (1913), is Hermitage (which is to the north).[8] In a sense, however, this is a wild-goose chase since it is clear that originally Hardy at least 'based' his story on the western area of the region under discussion. It seems likely that he was being ironic when he wrote in the 1912 postscript:

I have been honoured by so many inquiries for the true name and exact locality of the hamlet 'Little Hintock' . . . that I may as well confess here once for all that I do not know myself where that hamlet is more precisely than as explained above and in the pages of the narrative. To oblige readers I once spent several hours on a bicycle with a friend in a serious attempt to discover the real spot; but the search ended in failure; though tourists assure me positively that they have found it without trouble, and that it answers in every particular to the description given in this volume. At all events . . . the commanding heights called 'High-Stoy' and 'Bubb-Down Hill' overlook the landscape in which it is supposed to be hid.

A more straightforward statement of the truth seems to be that made in May 1926 when Hardy answered yet another query as to the whereabouts of 'Little Hintock' in relation to a watercolour of Minterne sent by Arthur M. Hind:

As to the spot being the 'Little Hintock' of *The Woodlanders* – that is another question. You will be surprised and shocked at my saying that I myself do not know where 'Little Hintock' is! Several tourists have told me that they have found it, in every detail, and have offered to take me to it, but I have never gone.

However, to be more definite, it has features which were to be found fifty years ago in the hamlets of Hermitage, Middlemarsh, Lyons-Gate, Revels Inn, Holnest, Melbury Bubb, etc. – all lying more or less under the eminence called High Stoy, just beyond Minterne and Dogbury Gate, where the country descends into the Vale of Blackmore.

The topographers you mention as identifying the scene are merely guessers and are wrong . . .[9]

The passage, though it adheres to the 'second (post-1890) siting' of the narrative, stresses mainly the fact that 'Little Hintock' is not a naturalistic representation of a single place. The chief interest therefore of the changes in 1896 and later lies in their attempt to make the relative positions of the fictional places referred to or journeys between them consistent if plotted on a map. This is all the verisimilitude that is aimed at. It is difficult to understand how by doing this Hardy could be said to be 'changing the location'. His 'Wessex' is not a precise recreation of Alfred the Great's kingdom nor of Dorset.

Notes

1. Volume I, chapter IV.
2. *Life*, p. 191.
3. F. B. Pinion, 'The Country and Period of *The Woodlanders*', *Thomas Hardy Yearbook* (1971), pp. 46–55.
4. *Collected Letters*, i.164.
5. Volume I, chapter IV.

6. Volume I, chapter VIII.

7. Pinion (p. 53) has illustrations of both houses which make this clear.

8. Hermann Lea, *Thomas Hardy's Wessex* (London: Macmillan, 1913), p. 108.

9. *Life*, p. 466.

The Law, Marriage and Divorce in The Woodlanders

RELIGIOUS AND CIVIL MARRIAGE

After the engagement between Grace Melbury and Edred Fitzpiers they discuss their wedding. Fitzpiers promptly announces his wishes: 'My inclination is not to be married at the horrid little church here, with all the yokels staring round at us, and a droning parson reading.' He prefers a registry office as a 'quieter, snugger and more convenient place in every way'. Grace is shocked and asks, 'How can I be married except at church, and with all my dear friends around me!' But under pressure from Fitzpiers she acquiesces. Later, when he has to explain away evidence strongly suggesting an affair with Suke Damson, she only agrees to resume the engagement provided they can marry in church.

Grace's objection to a civil marriage is more than a religious one. It was only after the Marriage Act of 1836 that (from 1 July 1837) the option to marry in a specially registered building rather than in an Anglican church became available to those who were not Jews or Quakers or who had a special licence. The insistence on an Anglican church had been thought to discourage some from marrying legally and to contract clandestine marriages instead. However, the registry office connection with the administering of the Poor Law meant that the new civil marriage was disliked by many people. This distaste continued and this type of ceremony remained unpopular with those who saw it as possibly socially inferior. This is evidently part of what Grace Melbury feels when Fitzpiers suggests a less public ceremony in a registry office because he is ashamed of what he sees as her low social origins.

DIVORCE

The Woodlanders, like *Jude the Obscure*, crucially involves the question of divorce. After he has discovered that Grace's husband Edred Fitzpiers has committed adultery, her father Melbury tries to organize a divorce.

He is prompted to do this by the advice of Fred Beaucock 'once a promising lawyer's clerk' who has now 'fallen into the mire'. He assures Melbury that 'Mrs Fitzpiers has her remedy', and then explains:

Under the new law, sir. A new court was established last year, and under the new statute, twenty and twenty-one Vic., cap. eighty-five, unmarrying is as easy as marrying. No more Acts of Parliament necessary: no longer one law for the rich and another for the poor.

This is a clear reference to the legislation of 1857: an Act to Amend the Law relative to Matrimonial Causes in England. Before this date, from the beginning of the eighteenth century, divorce had been possible only by getting an Act of Parliament to dissolve a marriage on the grounds of adultery. In the wife's case, she had to prove that the adultery was aggravated by, for instance, being incestuous. The function of this divorce *a vinculo* was to enable a nobleman whose wife had committed adultery to avoid the risk of having an illegitimate child passed off as his heir. The procedure was costly and therefore rarely used. Between 1840 and 1856 only 24 such Acts were passed. During this pre-1857 period the only alternative to divorce by Act of Parliament was a legal separation (divorce *a mensa et thoro*). After such a separation neither party could remarry and the husband kept his right to all the property that his wife had owned at the time of their marriage or acquired during it. Grounds for this procedure were fornication, adultery, inability to consummate the marriage, or any act of gross cruelty. If the wife obtained the separation, as the innocent party, she was to be provided for. The sum to be allotted for this provision was decided by the judge and was not excessive.

This state of affairs was radically altered by the Act of 1857 (Statute 20 & 21 Vict.). This removed matrimonial jurisdiction from ecclesiastical courts and made divorce available through a new civil court. The grounds for divorce were also extended. The statute laid down:

It shall be lawful for any husband to present a petition to the said court praying that his marriage may be dissolved on the ground that his wife, since the celebration thereof, has been guilty of adultery; and it shall be lawful for any wife to present a petition to the said court praying that her marriage may be dissolved, on the ground that since the celebration thereof her husband has been guilty of incestuous adultery, or of bigamy with adultery, or of rape, or of sodomy or bestiality; or of adultery coupled with such cruelty as without adultery would have entitled her to divorce *a mensa et thoro*, or of adultery coupled with desertion, without reasonable excuse, for two years or upwards.

If the petitioner had condoned adultery, no divorce could be obtained. The number of divorces granted by the civil court under the new Act was 148 in the first ten years.

Clearly this Act of 1857 is the one that Beaucock refers to when he advises Melbury to sue for divorce in the 'new court' under the 'new act'. However, given other evidence in the text as to the supposed date of the events of the story, the date of *c.* 1858 implied by Beaucock's reference to 'last year' is ruled out. Felice Charmond's anonymous American lover says he came to Europe some time after the end of the American Civil War: 1861–5. The interval has been long enough to allow him to become 'Italianized'. This suggests a date in the 1870s. The only significant legislation relating to marriage breakdown that fits this dating is the Matrimonial Causes Amendment Act of 1878. This related to a legal separation being available to a wife whose husband was convicted of an aggravated assault upon her. It also provided for her to receive maintenance and possibly to acquire custody of any children so long as she herself had not committed adultery.

This legislation certainly does not fit the description of that referred to by Beaucock. It is sometimes argued that Hardy intended to imply that the ex-lawyer's clerk is confused because he has been drinking. The narrator leaves the matter open but seems to imply that deception rather than confusion is the cause:

How much of the exaggerated information on the then new divorce laws which Beaucock imparted to his listener was the result of ignorance, and how much of dupery, was never ascertained. But he related such a plausible story of the case with which Grace could become a free woman that her father was irradiated with the project.

Since the grounds for divorce itself were unchanged in the 1870s from those laid down in 1857, Grace cannot become a free woman because Fitzpiers has only committed adultery without aggravating extras such as incest etcetera. The temporary expectation that she and Giles may be able to marry, however, leads her to revive their relationship. While her father and Beaucock are in London attempting to arrange a divorce, Beaucock chooses to reveal the truth secretly to Giles in a letter: 'The news was, in sum, that Fitzpiers's conduct had not been sufficiently cruel to Grace to enable her to snap the bond.' By this extended pivotal episode in the narrative Hardy draws attention forcibly to the double-standard enshrined in the major divorce legislation of the nineteenth century. The inequity was not removed until 1923. It is obvious that Hardy himself knew the relevant legislation and its date. The statute cited by Beaucock, 'twenty and twenty-one Vic.', indicates legislation in the twentieth and twenty-first year of the reign of Victoria who came to the throne in 1837. The plot necessitated a period during which Grace could apparently innocently recognize her love for Giles. This is effected by the device of allowing Beaucock to mislead Melbury; and by *deliberately* omitting to explain the nature of his deception. This leaves it open to various more or less plausible explanations: drunkenness, lack of information, wrong understanding of the facts, or calculated deception for short-term gain.

VOLUME I

CHAPTER I

1. *Little Hintock*: See the 1912 Postscript where Hardy disingenuously claims not to know where this is 'more precisely than as explained above and in the pages of the narrative'. It has been identified with two different Dorset villages: Minterne Parva and Hermitage. Current opinion favours Hermitage, though it is likely that Hardy did not intend to be precise. The first editions of his novels (such as the text used here) did not use locations precisely. Only in the first collected edition (1895–6) did he revise topographical details to suggest more of a correspondence with places in Dorset, though this was not altogether exact. See Appendix II.

2. *some Eastern plain*: It is characteristic of Hardy to see in the worn-out nag the noble lines of Arabian horses, which were renowned for their physique and speed.

3. *by a Dumpy level*: Spirit level used by surveyors to measure elevations. It had a short telescope with a large aperture.

4. *a catenary curve*: A curve created by a rope or chain hanging between two supports not in a vertical line. The description of the reins of the cart in this way is approximate not literal.

5. *waxen woman*: A wax model used to display wigs.

6. *left off his pole*: Percomb has given up the red-and-white striped pole, originally a blood-stained bandage, which was the sign of a barber's shop. He aspires to be regarded as having a superior class of clientele.

7. *dramas of a grandeur and unity truly Sophoclean*: Sophocles (*c.*496–406 BC), the great Athenian tragic dramatist, wrote plays distinguished by the unity of their self-contained plots. He is said to have remarked that he depicted people as they ought to be. His style was dignified without being grandiose. Hardy wrote at the end of 1885: 'a tragedy exhibits a state of things in the life of an individual which unavoidably causes some natural aim or desire to end in a catastrophe when carried out' (*Life*, p. 182).

CHAPTER II

1. *bill-hook*: With this sharp, hook-ended tool Marty is shaping *spar-gads* or hazel rods into *gads* – pointed sticks to hold thatch in place on roofs.

2. *tenure was by copy of court-roll*: A copy of the manorial record was a title to or proof of the holder's tenure. Unlike *lifehold* tenure, it was reasonably secure.

3. *subdue it to what it worked in*: An allusion to Shakespeare's sonnet III, in which the poet speaks of fate having imposed on him a public life 'which public manners breeds'. This has not only stained his reputation but almost corrupted his nature, 'subdu'd/To what it works in, like the dyer's hand'. This means that the work he has been forced to do is degrading. The quotation offers an elaborate contrast to Marty's menial work which has not yet made her hands hard and rough.

4. *an impression-picture*: Hardy's meaning here is clarified by what he wrote in 1886 while completing this novel and after visiting an exhibition of Impressionist pictures at the Society of British Artists: 'The impressionist school is strong. It is even more suggestive in the direction of literature than in that of art . . . their principle is, as I understand it, that what you carry away with you from a scene is the true feature to grasp; or in other words, *what appeals to your own individual eye and heart in particular* amid much that does not so appeal, and which you therefore omit to record' (*Life*, p. 191).

5. *a sovereign*: One of several specific references to money. A sovereign was a one-pound coin. As the pay for one and a half weeks of excessive drudgery it makes a pointed contrast to the sum of £100 a year which in chapter VIII Melbury claims to have spent on his daughter's education and to the £800 that is the price of a new medical practice. See also volume I, chapter IV, note 9.

6. *like the Devil to Dr. Faustus in the penny book*: Faustus, as in Marlowe's play *Dr Faustus* (1594), sold his soul to the devil and enjoyed a life of pleasure before being dragged off to eternal damnation. Marty would know the story from 'penny books' or cheap versions sold by pedlars.

7. *'Tis lifehold*: This is a type of lease on a property which limits tenure to the duration of the lives of specified people. On the death of the last of these the lease lapses and the property reverts to the freeholder. Such leases contrast with the copyhold referred to earlier in this chapter.

CHAPTER III

1. *the ante-mundane Ginnung-Gap*: The great magic void or Norse equivalent of the Chaos thought (for instance, by Milton) to precede the creation of the world. It is therefore said to be *ante-mundane* or 'preceding the world'. Hardy deliberately replaces Christian reference here with the more mysterious Norse mythology. See: Loke (this chapter, note 8), Jarnvid wood (volume I, chapter VII, note 6), and Niflheim (volume I, chapter XIII, note 3).

2. *like Trafalgar line-of-battle ships*: Trafalgar was the battle in which Admiral Nelson defeated Napoleon's fleet in 1805. Line-of-battle ships were those large enough to take part in a major attack and usually had seventy-four or more guns.

3. *thinking of things*: The manuscript and serial here have a more extended dialogue between Melbury and his wife. This version simply compresses it.

4. *turnpike bonds*: Bonds sold to raise funds for the construction and repair of roads.

5. *the ghosts of the Two Brothers*: See volume II, chapter III, for this story.

6. *"buffeting at will by rain and storm"* . . . *celandines*: An allusion to a poem by Wordsworth (1770–1850) called 'The Small Celandine': it is said to be 'buffeted at will by Rain and Storm' (line 12). Like the flower in the poem, Melbury is unable as he grows older to close himself up protectively against life's painful buffetings.

7. *deflowered visage*: The choice of the word 'deflowered' for Marty's cropped head is significant. Loose hair is conventionally associated in nineteenth-century novels with female sexuality or accessibility. The implication here is that Marty has given up all hope of a sexual relationship with the man she loves. At the same time, the cutting off of her beautiful hair to satisfy the vanity of a wealthy coquette is seen as a kind of rape.

8. *ancestral goddess* . . . *Loke*: Sif, the wife of Thor, the Norse god, had her hair cut off by the malicious Loki. She is described as Marty's ancestral goddess because the girl is deflowered of her hair by Percomb. This is one of several references to Norse mythology in the text. See this chapter, note 1 above.

9. *the great web of human doings*: At the time when he was writing this novel, Hardy wrote of a plan (fulfilled much later by his verse drama *The Dynasts*) to expand on these ideas: 'The human race to be shown as one great network or tissue, which quivers in every part when one part is shaken, like a spider's web if touched' (*Life*, p. 183).

10. *the White Sea to Cape Horn*: From Northern Russia to the most southerly part of South America.

CHAPTER IV

1. *like a dead-born child*: In his poem 'To an Unknown Pauper Child', Hardy urges the child

> Breathe not, hid Heart; cease silently,
> And though thy birth-hour beckons thee,
> Sleep the long sleep.

(Poems I, p. 163)

Children are not used as a sign of hope for the future by Hardy. Typical are Fanny Robin's dead baby in *Far from the Madding Crowd*, Tess's short-lived Sorrow, and the three children who die brutally in *Jude the Obscure*.

2. *early Georgian time*: The early eighteenth century when architects designed plain, symmetrical buildings.

3. *intermarriages were of Hapsburgian frequency*: The Hapsburg family, who lasted until the eighteenth century, were over a period rulers of many European countries. Like other such royal families they extended their power by marriages carefully planned to secure the succession to various thrones. The comparison between them and the villagers in Little Hintock suggests by the startling juxtaposition that in spite of differences the human race is the 'great web' described in chapter III above.

4. *arms of ivy . . . sunlight*: In Hardy's poem 'The Ivy-Wife' the ivy speaks of felling a tree by wreathing it with her 'soft green claw' (*Poems* I, p. 75). As the tree falls, however, it drags down the ivy. One of many references in this text to the evolutionary struggle in nature.

5. *taller out of pattens than her mother was in 'em*: Taller without thick-soled clogs than her mother was when wearing them.

6. *a soul's specific gravity*: Specific gravity is a technical expression for the relative heaviness (or density) of any kind or portion of matter. It is here used metaphorically for someone's state of mind on a scale from cheerfulness to depression. Subsequently in this volume there are other similar scientific or material images for states of mind, notably a *Leyden jar* (volume I, chapter XVI, note 4) and pearl-diving (volume II, chapter VI, note 4).

7. *sea of troubles*: This is part of Hamlet's description of the state of life which leads him to contemplate suicide (*Hamlet*, III.i.58). The odd juxtaposition of a scientific metaphor and the literary allusion is the kind of oddity that some critics disapproved of in Hardy's style.

8. *'Who dragged Whom round the walls of What?'*: The right answer is that Achilles dragged Hector's body round the walls of Troy, as described by Homer in

the *Iliad* XXII. This is why Melbury was derided for his homely answer.

9. *a hundred a year*: A very large sum of money. Marty can earn a pound for a week and a half's toil (chapter II above). In Gissing's *The Odd Women* (1893) a lecturer at a London college is paid £150 a year.

10. *The green gig*: A light, two-wheeled one-horse carriage. The means of transport is an indication of social status and financial position. Felice Charmond drives a brougham, a more expensive form of carriage. See volume I, chapter V, note 5 and volume II, chapter X, note 4.

11. *doubtful*: 1887 here omits ' – perhaps a trifle cynical, for that strand was wound into him with the rest' found in the manuscript and serial. It is one of several small changes which turn Giles into a more passive, less tough character. The changes make him into someone less dominant than Grace would like.

CHAPTER V

1. *noted it not*: Manuscript and serial had here 'Neither did he observe what was also the fact, that though he cherished a true and warm feeling towards Grace Melbury, he was not altogether her fool just now'. Another instance of how Giles' character is toned down in this first volume edition.

2. *like an ensign*: Bearer of a regimental standard or flag. This suggests that Giles' tree is a noble emblem but that is not how Grace sees it at this point.

3. *apart from transcendentalism*: An extreme form of a philosophical theory that argues for the identity of, amongst other things, mind and body. Only such extremists as those who held this view could imagine that Grace's outward appearance was identical with her essence.

4. *reductio ad absurdum*: Pushing an argument to its limits in order to show its ridiculous nature. The point seems to be that there is a huge discrepancy between Grace's appearance and her real character. Perhaps this is because she looks like a pretty and conventional girl but, as her later reaction to her husband's adultery shows, she is capable of quite unconventional views.

5. *brougham*: A superior carriage with two or four wheels which seated two or four people. See volume I, chapter IV, note 10.

6. *Olympian creature*: God-like creature. Olympus, the highest mountain in Greece, was said to be the home of the twelve Olympian or highest gods.

7. *Tempe-vale*: Olympus overlooked the Vale of Tempe, here alluded to as the home of ordinary mortals.

CHAPTER VI

1. *a much contrasting scene*: This contradicts what Grace says to her father in volume II, chapter XV about her sense of inferiority at school.

2. *short frocks*: Only girls still young enough to be treated as children could wear short frocks that revealed their ankles.

3. *The world of little things . . . without her presence*: In the poem on his mother's death, 'After the Last Breath', Hardy later writes similarly:

> The lettered vessels of medicaments
> Seem asking wherefore we have set them here;
> Each palliative its silly face presents
> As useless gear.
>
> (*Poems* I, p. 326)

He repeatedly notices the unchanging nature of inanimate things while human beings suffer and decline.

4. *regular terrestrial roll*: The earth's rotation on its axis. See also *Far from the Madding Crowd*, chapter II, when Gabriel Oak is alone at night on Norcombe Hill, there is a similar reference: 'To persons standing alone on a hill during a clear midnight such as this, the roll of the earth eastward is almost a palpable movement. The sensation may be caused by the panoramic glide of the stars past earthly objects . . . or by the better outlook upon space that a hill affords, or by the wind; or by the solitude.'

5. *any common genius*: Either Grammer thinks the word *genius* means 'intellectual' or she regards Fitzpiers as 'the genius of geniuses', not a run-of-the-mill one.

6. *Everything is Nothing*: Possibly a translation of a common formula that God is '*Nichts und alles*' (Nothing and Everything) which is found frequently in the writings of German philosophers. It could be the explanation of Fitzpiers' following remark 'There's only Me and Not Me'. See next note.

7. *There's only Me and Not Me*: From J. G. Fichte's (1762–1814) *Wissenschaftslehre* but Hardy could have found it in Coleridge. Fitzpiers may be glossing it by saying 'Everything is Nothing'. His references to philosophy are pretentious rather than informed. See preceding note.

CHAPTER VII

1. *his shy self-control*: Earlier versions had 'his dry self-control'. Another toning down of Giles' character during revision.

2. *a sudden lapse from the ornate to the primitive on Nature's canvas*: This idea is repeated by Hardy in December 1886 while completing this novel. 'Winter. The landscape has turned from a painting to an engraving: the birds that love worms fall back upon berries: the back parts of homesteads assume, in the general nakedness of the trees, a humiliating squalidness as to their details that has not been contemplated by their occupiers' (*Life*, p. 190).

3. *pari passu*: Keeping pace with.

4. *the depraved crowds of a city slum*: Hardy seems to accept the current theory of 'degeneracy' which argued that generations bred in slums had evolved into creatures who were morally and physically degenerate. This pseudo-scientific view meant that they could be left as they were and attempts made only to improve 'the deserving poor', not this irredeemable residuum. The comment is not one in keeping with Hardy's approach to the poor generally.

5. *The leaf was deformed*: Another reference to the evolutionary struggle in nature as described in chapter III of *The Origin of Species*: 'Hence, as more individuals are produced than can possibly survive, there must in every case be a struggle for existence, either one individual with another of the same species, or with the individuals of distinct species . . .' (ed. J. W. Burrow (Penguin, 1983), p. 117).

6. *Jarnvid wood*: In Norse mythology this wood of iron was the place where wolves were bred. See earlier references, Ginnung-Gap (volume I, chapter III, note 1), Loke (volume I, chapter III, note 8), and later to Niflheim (volume I, chapter XIII, note 3).

7. *philosopher of the Peripatetic school*: The Aristotelian school of philosophy in Athens. Aristotle (384–322 BC) taught in the groves and gymnasium of the Lyceum and there was a covered walk or *peripatos* which gave the school its name. Another story was that Aristotle walked about (Greek *peripatein* – to walk) whilst teaching. Hardy included a comic line-drawing of 'Aristotle delivering his lectures in the shady walks of the Lyceum – Peripatetics' among several (probable date 1885–6) which he made for his wife's niece, Lillian Gifford. The figures are marching match-stick men (reproduced in Millgate, *Thomas Hardy*, opposite p. 272).

8. *by continued compression in infancy*: References to the Chinese practice of binding women's feet to prevent them from growing large are frequently used in the nineteenth century as an image of unnatural restraint imposed on women generally, e.g. in Florence Nightingale's *Cassandra* (1852): 'suffering, "sad" female humanity! What are these feelings which they are taught to consider as disgraceful, to deny to themselves? What form do Chinese feet take when denied their proper development?' (ed. Myra Stark (The Feminist Press, U.S.A., 1979), p. 26). Here the image usually applied to women is, characteristically, applied to trees. See Introduction.

9. *regretted*: In the manuscript and serial this reads 'regretted with some causticity of humour'. Like other alterations during revision, this removes any trace of cynicism from Giles' attitude to the Melburys.

CHAPTER VIII

1. *Hintock House*: The mansion has been identified from its location as Melbury House, home of the Ilchester family.

2. *laps, rolls*: A precise architectural detail referring to the overlapping sheets of lead which were curved into rolls.

3. *mullioned and hooded*: Windows with vertical bars dividing the 'lights' in the windows. Another piece of architectural precision.

4. *They are man-traps*: These were traps for catching poachers who, by stepping on a spring, caused them to close like a mouse-trap. They were out of use by the 1870s but play a significant role in the reunion of the adulterous Fitzpiers and his wife (see volume III, chapter XIII, note 4). Felice's remarks unknowingly look forward to that event, though it is Grace not Fitzpiers who is caught in the mantrap and so 'trapped' by Fitzpiers. Felice's attitude to 'trapping' men is a conventional one not shared by Grace.

5. *a New Sentimental Journey*: Felice Charmond aims to imitate *A Sentimental Journey through France and Italy* (1768) written by Laurence Sterne (1713–68) shortly before he died. Sterne's book used material collected on an eight-month journey.

6. *it was one which . . . neighbours*: The manuscript has here 'which she could not claim either on her own account or on her late husband's. The daughter of an eminent painter, she might have said she could claim more.'

7. *weltbürgerliche*: 'Cosmopolitan, sophisticated, worldly', though in fact she is vulnerable in relation to Fitzpiers.

8. *before a mirror which reflected their faces*: The first of several uses in the text of the mirror image in a dramatic context. Others are Grace's first meeting with Fitzpiers (volume I, chapter XVI) and Grace's fateful encounter with Felice

in the wood (volume II, chapter XIII) when Grace learns that she is Fitzpiers' mistress.

9. *a thousand young fir-trees*: Hardy's poem 'The Pine Planters' expresses Marty South's feelings during this episode. It begins:

> We work here together
> In blast and breeze;
> He fills the earth in,
> I hold the trees.
>
> He does not notice
> That what I do
> Keeps me from moving
> And chills me through.
>
> He has seen one fairer
> I feel by his eye,
> Which skims me as though
> I were not by.
>
> (*Poems* I, p. 328)

CHAPTER IX

1. *Your face is like the face of Moses*: Exodus (34. 29, 35). Hardy uses the same comparison in his poem 'I met a man' where the shining face is that of a man who has seen God speak of the horrors of war (*Poems* II, p. 304). See also volume III, chapter IV, note 5, for another use of this biblical reference.

2. *like Alexandre Dumas and Méry, and Sterne*: The two French writers Alexandre Dumas (1803–70) and François Méry (1797–1866), and Laurence Sterne (1713–68) all wrote books about travel in Europe.

3. *elaborate high tea*: The working-class alternative to dinner in the evening. It is a substantial meal for manual workers. Its elaborateness does not make it appropriate for the would-be middle-class Grace. Hardy's own tastes at his house at Max Gate inclined to 'preferences always for those things (such as cider, kettle-broth, and grilled bacon) associated with, and capable of reviving, the memories of childhood' (Millgate, p. 263).

4. *Beelzebub kind of fork*: Devil's large pitchfork as seen in illustrations of hell.

5. *a bouncing kind of thing?*: 'Festive affair, noisy party'.

6. *mother-law's*: 'Stepmother'. The term was used for mother-in-law and stepmother since both approximated in law to a mother. The use for the latter died out in standard English by the latter part of the nineteenth century.

CHAPTER X

1. *Flemish Last-Suppers*: From an early period the Flemish school of painters paid meticulous attention to accurate representation of detail such as the appearance of fabric. Two of them painted pictures of the Last Supper of Christ and his disciples.

2. *hang-fairs*: Public executions treated as a form of entertainment. They ceased to be public in 1868.

3. *Phrenologists*: Pseudo-scientists who claimed to describe character from the precise contours of an individual's skull. The ignorant Melbury is taken in by this spurious practice.

4. *She may go, oh!*: By 1896 this is replaced by:

> . . . said she,
> A maid again I never shall be
> Till apples grow on an orange tree!

As this makes clear, 'going to the devil' means being seduced.

CHAPTER XI

1. *"taking up" Grace*: Making much of Grace from her higher social position.

2. *post hoc argument*: One which argues that one event causes another just because it is known to have preceded it although there is no valid reason to connect the two.

3. *elevated plane*: Manuscript and serial elaborate Melbury's thoughts in a passage not found here:

He could not forget that Mrs. Charmond had apparently abandoned all interest in his daughter as suddenly as she had conceived it, and was as firmly convinced as ever that the comradeship which Grace had shown with Giles and his crew by attending his party had been the cause.

Matters lingered on thus. And then, as a hoop by gentle knocks on this side and on that is made to travel in specific directions, the little touches of circumstance in the life of this young girl shaped the curves of her career.

CHAPTER XII

1. *Actæonic excitement*: 'The arrogant excitement' of the huntsman. In Greek myth Actaeon was changed into a stag for offending Artemis, the virgin huntress and daughter of the god Zeus, either by boasting that he was a better hunter than she or by seeing her bathing naked. Grace is later referred to as Artemis.

2. *hobbing and nobbing*: 'Consorting familiarly' with someone. From a phrase which originally meant drinking together.

3. *"A perplexing and ticklish possession"* . . . *a Greek poet*: Menander (*c*.342–292 BC) was first known through a large number of sententious quotations from his work. Since the reference is to a daughter who is 'ticklish' or 'unstable, unpredictable', it may refer to one of his plots in which a well-bred girl is seduced; and allude to the unexpected physical attraction Grace feels for Fitzpiers.

4. *Port-Breedy Harbour bonds*: Bonds sold to raise shares for the building of the harbour.

5. *A mere chattel*: This was a term in law for certain possessions and was used metaphorically in the nineteenth century of slaves because they were 'possessions' which could be passed on to an heir.

6. *a dictionary word*: One not used in ordinary speech, such a word as Hardy himself was criticised for using in novels. One reviewer of *Tess of the D'Urbervilles* wrote: 'He is too apt to affect a certain preciosity of phrase which has a somewhat incongruous effect in a tale of rustic life; he is too fond . . . of writing like a man who has been at a great feast of language and stolen the scraps' (R. G. Cox, *Thomas Hardy: the Critical Heritage* (Barnes & Noble: New York, 1970), p. 220). Hardy corresponded with the editors of the *Oxford English Dictionary on Historical Principles* (1884–1928) of which he eagerly bought individual volumes as they appeared. See Introduction.

7. *Can I be a prophet in Hintock?*: In 2 Kings 5, the King of Syria wrongly assumed that the King of Israel is the 'prophet' who can cure leprosy. The true prophet orders that the leper sent by the Syrian king come to him 'and he shall know that there is a prophet in Israel'. He cures the leper. Creedle's assumption of the role is typically ludicrous.

8. *the words of the faithful be only as wind*: Another grandiose misappropriation –

of Job's reproof to those who advise him to accept what God has inflicted on him: 'Do ye imagine to reprove words, and the speeches of one that is desperate, which are as wind?' (Job 6.26).

CHAPTER XIII

1. *a measuring-tape of time by law*: A reference to the lifehold lease on which John South holds tenure of his home from Felice Charmond.

2. *melancholy Gregorian melodies*: Repetitive, unaccompanied liturgical chant of the Roman Catholic Church in Latin. It was named for Pope Gregory the Great (540–604) though it is uncertain whether he had any connection with it.

3. *Niflheim*: According to Norse myth, 'Misty Hell', into which men pass from the world of death and are punished for their misdeeds. See also references to Ginnung-Gap (chapter III, note 1), Loke (chapter III, note 8) and Jarnvid wood (chapter VII, note 6).

4. *tournure*: Fashionable appearance. This suggests some calculated effect had been aimed at.

CHAPTER XIV

1. *the sword of the Lord and of Gideon*: Gideon tricked the Medians, who were oppressing Egypt, into believing that his small army seemed much larger than it actually was. As part of the plan, his men blew trumpets and cried out 'The sword of the Lord and of Gideon' (Judges 7.20). The Medians fled in terror.

2. *de rigueur*: 'Socially appropriate'. An ironic description, given Fitzpiers' less-than-noble conduct.

3. *philosopher*: Not used in the technical sense here (though Fitzpiers studies philosophy) but more loosely to mean a thinker rather than a doer.

4. *a dreamy 'ist of some sort . . . some false kind of ism*: An *'ist* is someone who accepts some sort of *'ism* or fanatical belief or theory. *OED*'s first citation is from Carlyle (1835). It also cites George Eliot (1875): 'We must not take every great physicist or other 'ist for an apostle.'

CHAPTER XV

1. *the divinity who shaped the ends of the Hintock population*: An ironic reference to Felice Charmond's power through the use of Hamlet's assertion that Providence intervened to serve his life: 'There's a divinity that shapes our ends,/ Rough-hew them how we will' (*Hamlet* V.ii.10−11).

2. *face of seven sorrows*: Possibly a reference to the Seven Sorrows of the Virgin Mary, relating mainly to her griefs at the crucifixion of Christ.

3. *Encountering Melbury one day*: 1887 omits an earlier long analysis of Melbury's feelings, including 'He hoped that Giles would of his own accord make some final announcement that he entirely withdrew his pretensions to Grace, and so get the thing past and done with. For though Giles had in a measure acquiesced in the wish of her family, he could make matters unpleasant if he chose to work upon Grace.' This omission is in keeping with the removal of descriptions of Giles that might suggest a more forceful or bitter character.

4. *their plenary absolution*: Unqualified absolution or forgiveness, as in the Catholic expression *plenary indulgence*.

CHAPTER XVI

1. *a Dutch designer of the time of William and Mary*: William and Mary of Orange became king and queen in 1689. They were followed from Holland by architects who created this kind of neat, symmetrical house.

2. *wary grimness induced by the circumstances*: In manuscript and serial this had read: 'wary grimness partly in his character, partly induced by circumstances.' Another change removing any grittiness from Giles' character.

3. *"She moved upon this earth . . . brightness"*: From 'The Revolt of Islam' or 'Laon and Cythna' by Shelley (1792−1822), canto II, stanza 23. Hardy knew the poem well and used a line from it as the epigraph to his last novel *The Well-Beloved* (volume edition, 1897). The poem is a weird version of the French Revolution transferred to an eastern setting where the revolt is organised by an incestuous brother and sister who are finally burnt at the stake.

4. *charged with emotive fluid like a Leyden jar with electric*: A scientific simile (like the specific gravity one earlier) used to describe Melbury's state of mind. The device was made in the eighteenth century by a Dutch scientist, Pieter Van Musschoenbroek, by the modification of a glass jar so that it could store electricity for a short period. Fitzpiers, showing off to Giles, mixes literary, scientific and philosophical references. See also scientific references in volume I, chapter IV, note 6, and volume II, chapter VI, note 4. *OED* cites a similar metaphorical use in 1825: 'she was like a Leyden jar always ready to be let off'.

5. *Spinoza the philosopher says . . . ipsa hominis essentia*: 'The very essence of man' – Baruch Spinoza, philosopher (?1632–77). The implication is that the capacity to love is what makes human beings what they are, in contrast to accidental features, such as that they write novels. The reference is to love of God but Hardy makes Fitzpiers apply it to sexual love. Spinoza in *Ethics* III, prop. 13: *[Amor est] laetitia concomitante idea causae externae*: '[Love of God] is joy accompanied by the thought of an external cause.' Fitzpiers reads philosophy to suit himself.

6. *Socratic* εἰρωνεία: Socratic irony or a way of asking simple but radical questions in order to bring out the deficiencies of an argument.

7. *who hath gathered the wind . . . in a garment?*: The biblical figure in Proverbs 30.4 is expressing trust in God and confessing his own insignificance in a series of rhetorical questions designed to convey God's power: 'Who hath ascended up into heaven, or descended? Who hath gathered the wind in his fists? Who hath bound the waters in a garment?'

VOLUME II

CHAPTER I

1. *'Ch*: This archaic form of *ich*, 'I', is mentioned by Hardy in answer to questions by Edmund Gosse in 1889: 'This and kindred words, e.g. – "Ich woll", "er woll", etc. are still used by old people in N.W. Dorset and Somerset (*vide* Grammer Oliver's conversation in "The Woodlanders" . . . I heard "Ich" only last Sunday; but it is dying rapidly' (*Life*, p. 232).

2. *ten pounds*: A large sum to Grammer Oliver, though it is only one-tenth of what Melbury spent in a year on his daughter's education. See volume I, chapter IV, note 9.

3. *my holy cross*: The cross made by the illiterate as a signature, used instead of a name and regarded here as a way of swearing on Christ's cross.

4. *er*: 'he'. See note 1 above.

5. *a remorseless Jehovah of the sciences*: Like the God of the Old Testament, Fitzpiers seems to Grace to be ruthlessly exacting what is his due.

6. *the zodiac of the intellectual heaven*: A savagely ironic use of the image of the astrological signs of the zodiac to indicate that Fitzpiers is a dabbling dilettante who sees himself as rapidly encompassing all intellectual disciplines. Like the claims of the astrologer his belief about his intellectual range is spurious.

7. *rank literatures of emotion and passion*: Fitzpiers, it is suggested, has a taste for romantic or salacious novels and poetry. In volume III, chapter XIII, he forbids Grace to read his French books.

8. *matériel of science*: Scientific equipment.

9. *the Muses*: Goddesses who were said to inspire music, literature and dance. Here literature is referred to.

10. *glued up by frozen thawings*: 'Closed by the freezing of their opening bud'. In 'In a Drear-nighted December', Keats (1795–1821) speaks of the branches of a once-green tree:

> The north cannot undo them,
> With a sleety whistle through them,
> Nor frozen thawings glue them
> From budding at the prime. (St. 1)

Keats is stressing the resilience of nature, but Hardy uses the phrase to describe trees mistakenly budding too early. This event is something not understood by Fitzpiers and it is one of many references to his inability to read what he sees in the landscape. See Introduction.

11. *the settle*: The settle was a wooden seat with a high back and wings to keep out draught.

CHAPTER II

1. *mural tomb*: *Mural* means here either set into a wall or backed on to a wall.

2. *in the glass*: This, like the two other significant confrontations (between Grace and Felice), involves a mirror or the image of a mirror. See volume I, chapter VIII, note 8.

3. *something very fiendish in the compact*: For Grammer Oliver and Grace, Fitzpiers seems like the devil tempting Faustus to sell his soul, just as the barber Percomb seemed to Marty.

4. *Nature has at last recovered her lost union with the Idea!*: The Platonic 'Ideal' was said to be perfect and eternal and for ever separate from its shadow in the imperfect world of nature.

5. *a transcendental philosopher*: A thinker who believed that the physical and the ideal might coincide. Several of these are mentioned in the novel: Schleiermacher, Spinoza, and Shelley (who used their ideas).

6. *Idealism*: This refers to any system of thought in which the object of external perception is said to consist in the ideas of the perceiving mind.

CHAPTER III

1. *the recreative character of such acquaintance*: This had read less cynically in manuscript and serial: 'the ethereal nature of my regard'.

2. *vulgar intimacy*: Again in manuscript and serial this was more innocently, 'vulgar flirtation'.

3. *"little toilette"*: The name for the preparation of a victim's head for the guillotine. The hair on the back of the head was moved or shaved to leave the neck bare.

4. *this patronising lady*: Used in the older sense of someone who bestows patronage (support or gifts) on another.

5. *unaccountable tendency to tearfulness*: The first indication of Fitzpiers' effect on Grace, always described in physical terms. See also volume II, chapter VI, notes 5 and 6, and volume II, chapter VII, notes 4 and 5.

6. *New Year's Day, Old Style*: Until 1752 the new year began on 25 March. In that year it was changed to 1 January.

7. *curers*: Workers who treated the tree bark so as to preserve it.

8. *Crusoe's island*: Robinson Crusoe in Defoe's novel of that name, published in 1719, is shipwrecked on an island uninhabited except by one native. Money would of course be useless there.

9. *cardinal virtues*: Schleiermacher in *On Religion: Speeches to its Cultured Despisers*, Speech 2: 'To intuit the world and to have religion, man must first have found humanity, and he finds it only in love and through love.' The four virtues go back to Aquinas' attempts to combine ancient Greek virtues with the Christian virtues of Faith, Hope, Charity/Love. Again Fitzpiers secularizes.

10. *According to Schleiermacher*: Friedrich Schleiermacher (1768–1834), one of the several idealist philosophers referred to in the novel. He believed that individuals should act in the highest interests of society as a whole. It is therefore ironic that Fitzpiers cites as a model a thinker who values the selflessness that the doctor strikingly lacks.

CHAPTER IV

1. *Idea . . . substance*: The ideal and reality had fused in Grace. See chapter II above, note 4.

2. *old Midsummer eve*: 24 June; here, *eve* means not 'the day before' but 'the evening of the day itself'.

3. *the hole-digging*: Hardy wrote earlier on 8 June 1871 in his Personal Notebooks: 'On old Midsummer-noon dig a hole in the grass plot, and place your ear thereon precisely at 12. The occupation of your future husband will be revealed by the noises heard' (Richard H. Taylor, *The Personal Notebooks of Thomas Hardy* (London: Macmillan 1979), p. 10).

4. *the evil one*: A circumlocution to avoid naming the devil.

5. *sowing of hemp-seed*: Usually done to increase fertility but here to raise apparitions of their future husbands.

6. *he captured her*: One of several references to Fitzpiers 'capturing' Grace, as earlier in the clearing when she screams and at the end of the novel when she has been caught in the man-trap.

7. *"Oh, come in from the foggy, foggy dew"*: The refrain of a folk-song in which the lover invites his sweetheart into bed and she becomes pregnant. Here gender roles are changed and Suke Damson invites Fitzpiers.

8. *It was daybreak . . . Little Hintock*: This sentence is found in the manuscript but omitted from the serial as too sexually explicit.

CHAPTER V

1. *Satan . . . with his hour-glass*: A confusion of Satan with the figure of Father Time and his hour-glass which symbolizes life ebbing away. So this is doubly threatening.

2. *the failure of the Southern cause . . . returned*: This helps fix the supposed date of events in the novel as some years after 1865. The Southern States lost the American Civil War which lasted 1861–5. The date is apparently at odds with what Beaucock later says about the 'new divorce' law which seems to refer to the Divorce Act of 1857 (see volume III, chapter IV, note 3) but this is explainable. See Appendix III.

CHAPTER VI

1. *the spring-tide of a sentiment*: A spring-tide occurs after the full moon which causes the water level to rise to its maximum height.

2. *Family?*: i.e. do her social origins matter? Fitzpiers himself is given a social background which later textual changes made increasingly aristocratic. Social class is important to the narrative and at various stages Hardy modified the rank of Mrs. Charmond and Fitzpiers. See Note on the History of the Text.

3. *that huntsman-fellow*: The man who spoke rudely to Grace because he assumed her to be of a lower social class than himself. See volume I, chapter XII, note 1.

4. *like ... a plunge for a pearl ... temperature*: Another scientific comparison to capture an emotional state. See also references to specific gravity (volume I, chapter IV, note 6) and the Leyden jar (volume I, chapter XVI, note 4).

5. *an almost psychic influence*: One of several references to the fact that Grace is strongly attracted sexually by Fitzpiers. *Psychic* means physical as in *OED*'s 1889 citation: 'The psychic, or animal, man, is the natural man of this present age.'

6. *like a dram*: A small measure of neat spirit. Fitzpiers affects Grace physically as strong drink might. See also volume II, chapter III, note 5, and volume II, chapter VII below, notes 4 and 5.

7. *experienced*: Omitted here are the words found in manuscript and serial ' – still more if she reflected on the silent, almost sarcastic criticism apparent in Winterborne's air towards her': a further toning down of Giles' character.

CHAPTER VII

1. *romantical family*: 1912 adds here: 'Why on his mother's side he's connected with the long line of the Lords Baxby of Sherton.'

2. *a high, perusing life*: An intellectual life.

3. *crochet capital*: Ornate head of a Gothic column usually in the shape of curling foliage. Another typically precise architectural detail.

4. *the strange influence*: A second reference to the fact that Grace is powerfully affected physically by Fitzpiers' presence. He gives her 'a fearful consciousness of hazard'. See volume II, chapter III, note 5, and volume II, chapter VI, notes 5 and 6 above and volume II, chapter VII, note 5 below.

5. *fearful consciousness*: See preceding note.

6. *Galen, Hippocrates, and Herophilus . . . hermetical*: Three physicians of ancient times whom it was customary to regard as the founders of medicine: the Greeks Galen (AD 129–199) and Hippocrates (*c*.460–*c*.370 BC); and the Alexandrian Herophilus (first half of the third century BC). *dogmatic*: Working from what are supposed to be established principles of medicine; *empiric*: Experimental, working by trial and error with respect to the effectiveness of the remedy; *hermetical*: Using magical remedies not based on reasoning.

7. *the Interpreter's which well-nigh choked the Pilgrim*: In *Pilgrim's Progress* (Part I) by John Bunyan (1628–88), Christian the pilgrim arrives at a dusty parlour in the House of the Interpreter (the Holy Spirit as interpreter of the Gospel). A man sweeps up the dust which 'began so abundantly to fly about, that Christian had almost therewith been choked' but a damsel sprinkles it with water. The Interpreter explains that the dust is the sin of unregenerate man and the water is the Gospel which redeems him. The comparison is made to stress the rigour of the Melburys' preparation for Fitzpiers. It is also ironically underlining the fact that the latter is no would-be virtuous pilgrim.

CHAPTER VIII

1. *the incident in the wood*: This is later replaced in 1895 by 'the intimacy established in the hayfield'.

CHAPTER IX

1. *when the fair apples . . . sky*: From a marriage song in 'Songe to Aella' (stanza 33) by Thomas Chatterton (1752–70). It is clearly appropriate to this scene. Chatterton pretended to have found 'The Rowley poems' in a fifteenth-century manuscript which, in fact, he had forged. At first he was believed and one poem was published, but by 1770 he had committed suicide.

2. *the youthful Chatterton*: A later reading is 'the marvellous Chatterton', a quotation from Wordsworth's poem, 'Resolution and Independence' (ll. 43–4) which sees him as an instance of poets who start in gladness but end in 'despondency and madness'. This change may indicate that a parallel is being made between the poet and Giles.

3. *If I forget*: From the poem 'Two Points of View' by Hardy's friend Edmund Gosse (1849–1928). The first point of view is Giles', the second Grace's. Hardy wrote to Gosse on 8 October 1886: 'I quote you in the current number of

Macmillan – or rather misquote you for I altered one word to make lines suit the circumstances of the story.' He changed 'lord' to 'queen' (*Letters*, I, p. 153).

4. *that fellow*: 'lout'. *OED* cites Disraeli (1826): 'This is some vile conspiracy of your own, fellow.'

5. *locum tenens*: Stand-in for doctor or clergyman.

6. *tanner*: Someone who cured hide; *exciseman*: local collector of excise duties on liquor.

7. *like a handwriting on the wall*: What Mrs Charmond has said seems to Fitzpiers to prophesy accurately his failure. At Belshazzar's feast (Daniel 5) a man's hand appears and writes mysterious words on the wall. Daniel rightly interprets them as foretelling Belshazzar's downfall because of his pride and idolatry.

8. *supersubtle*: 'Over-subtle', a rare word possibly taken from Iago's disparaging description of Desdemona as 'a supersubtle Venetian' (*Othello*, I.iii.348–9).

9. *Board of Guardians*: A board appointed by Justices of the Peace to administer poor relief in a parish. The medical care of paupers would be in their gift.

10. *the Union*: The Poorhouse.

11. *eight hundred pounds*: Eight times the annual sum paid for Grace's education and many times Marty's annual wages.

CHAPTER X

1. *levelled*: 1912 adds here: 'According to the landlords' principle at this date of getting rid of cottages wherever possible.'

2. *the great November gale of 1824*: A reference to an actual event, long remembered.

3. *Chesil Bank*: A long pebble beach stretching westwards from Portland Bill (The Isle of Slingers in *The Well-Beloved*) to Abbotsbury.

4. *phaeton*: A fashionable, light, four-wheeled carriage for two used from the eighteenth century onwards. See references earlier to *gig* and *brougham* and volume I, chapter IV, note 10.

5. *naked nearly up to the shoulder*: A clear indication of a woman who flaunts her sexuality. Though her accident accounts for her being not formally dressed, the dressing-gown is by literary convention also indicative of a state of undress and hence sexual accessibility.

6. *she held a cigarette*: Another mark of a 'fast' or loose-living woman. Cigarette is the name of a bold and promiscuous woman in *Under Two Flags* (1867) by Ouida (1839–1908). At her first appearance she is described as having 'an arch, brilliant, kitten-like face, so sunny, so *mignon*, and those scarlet lips like a bud of camellia that were never so handsome as when a cigarette was between them' (chapter XV).

7. *court-plaster*: A silk-covered dressing for a small wound.

8. *my face was my only fortune*: A reference to the old song 'My face is my fortune, sir, she said'.

9. *Baden*: The fashionable spa town.

10. *you have grown rich*: Earlier this was 'you are still rich', one of the alterations which indicates a lower social origin for Mrs. Charmond than in earlier versions.

11. *like corks upon the waves of masculine desires*: Felice Charmond always takes a conventional view of women as helpless sexual objects at the mercy of men and bent only on trapping a man. See her earlier reference to 'man-traps' in volume I, chapter VIII, note 4, and Introduction.

CHAPTER XI

1. *gold-beater's skin*: An unobtrusive flesh-coloured dressing. Gold leaf was used in its preparation.

2. *Neckar*: The river at Heidelberg.

3. *a fit of Achillean moodiness*: Achilles was the chief hero on the Greek side in the Trojan War, noted for his fierce temper and unpredictability. When he sulked in his tent after a quarrel with Agamemnon, the Greeks were driven back to their ships and almost defeated. It is typical of Fitzpiers to see his own petulance as an almost noble peccadillo.

4. *the folding star*: The evening star, so-called from 'folding time' when cattle were driven into the fold or pen for the night.

5. *Why should Death alone lend what Life is compelled to borrow – rest?*: An allusion to stanza 21 of 'Adonais', a poem by Shelley (1792–1822) on the death of Keats in 1821, in which he is said to take 'his fill/Of deep and liquid rest' (stanza 7). Hardy paraphrases here the line 'death, who lends what life must borrow' (stanza 21).

6. *a second tree of knowledge*: The first tree of knowledge was the one from which Adam and Eve ate the forbidden fruit in the Garden of Eden. The context here suggests that the second tree is death. Fitzpiers is right in his would-be flattering prediction: Felice's restlessness lasts until she is murdered.

7. *to think it a farce*: 'A piece of play-acting' – they don't believe that she needs him as a doctor. This is one of several references to the theatricality of Felice Charmond and Fitzpiers. See Introduction.

CHAPTER XII

1. *lucubrations*: 'Night-studies'.
2. *"hag-rid"*: Ridden by a witch; such riding of humans was thought to produce nightmares.
3. *A turnpike ticket*: A ticket received on payment of a toll at a gate on a turnpike road.
4. *Tannhäuser*: In a sixteenth-century legend Tannhäuser, a medieval poet, is lured into the arms of Venus where he spends years in sensual abandon. After seeking but failing to receive absolution from the Pope, he returns to his pleasures in despair. Hardy probably knew the story from the erotic poem 'Laus Veneris' by Swinburne (1837–1909) which dramatizes it. Clearly Felice Charmond is the Venus to Fitzpiers' Tannhäuser.
5. *"Towards the load-star of my one desire"*: From 'Epipsychidion' (1821), a poem by Shelley (1792–1822) describing a passionate search for the eternal image of Beauty in the earthly form of women. It is addressed to Emilia Viviani 'Now Imprisoned in the Convent of −'.
6. *a Wouvermans eccentricity*: Philips Wouwerman (1619–68), a Dutchman who frequently painted horses. It has been suggested by James Gibbs (cited in *The Woodlanders*, ed. D. Kramer (Oxford, 1985), p. 294) that this refers to a work by this painter, *A View on a Seashore, with Fishwives offering Fish to a Horseman*, in which there is a 'back view of a white horse against a vast sky'.

CHAPTER XIII

1. *how little she suffered from that jealous excitement*: An early indication of Grace's unconventional reactions to her husband's infidelity, seen more clearly in her treatment of his two mistresses in volume III, chapter II.
2. *possessed by five distinct infatuations at the same time*: Multiple infatuations recur in Hardy and are the subject of *The Well-Beloved* (volume edition, 1897).
3. *If this were true . . . lower orders of the animal world*: Possibly an ironic reference to Chapter Five of Darwin's *Origin of Species*, 'Laws of Variation': where he refers to 'the very general opinion of naturalists, that beings low in the scale of nature are more variable than those which are higher' (ed. J. W. Burrow (Penguin, 1983), p. 187). See also Hardy's poem 'So Various' which, after describing a dozen different men that the listener might have encountered, concludes:

> Now . . . All these specimens of man,
> So various in their pith and plan,
> Curious to say
> Were *one* man. Yea,
> I was all they.
>
> (*Poems*, III, p. 208)

4. *All's well that ends well*: An innocent remark but a pointer to the fact that all is *not* well. In Shakespeare's play of this name, a love triangle is resolved when Helena, who loves the reluctant Bertram, manages to procure him as a husband by replacing Diana (whom he loves) at a midnight assignation. Their marriage, though superficially satisfactory, matches the fragile reconciliation of Fitzpiers and Grace.

5. *Absalont*: In 2 Samuel 18.9–17, David's beloved son, Absalom, is lifted from his horse by an overhanging tree and slain by his enemies while hanging there.

6. *no blemish in him!*: Timothy misquotes scripture: 'But in all Israel there was none to be so much praised as Absalom for his beauty: from the sole of his foot even to the crown of his head there was no blemish in him' (2 Samuel 14.25).

7. *"that heart which others bleed for"*: From the heroine Millamant's cynical song in *The Way of the World* by William Congreve (1670–1729): 'If there's delight in love, 'tis when I see/That heart which others bleed for, bleed for me' (III.i.422–3).

8. *lift the veil of Isis*: 'Sacrilegiously look into sacred mysteries'. Isis was the great Egyptian goddess and symbol of female fertility, sometimes equated with Demeter or Aphrodite. Her cult was a mystery religion. Another indication that the woodlanders perceive Felice Charmond as a kind of divinity because of her power in their lives. At the same time the allusion is to her abundant sexuality.

CHAPTER XIV

1. *re-entered it*: After this the manuscript and serial had three paragraphs not reprinted in Hardy's lifetime in which Melbury goes to church and watches Felice and Fitzpiers. A glance from Fitzpiers which causes her to blush makes Melbury realize that there is more than flirtation involved between them – 'a threatening conclusion'. Perhaps Hardy felt that this episode took away from the drama of the later incident in volume III, chapter 2, where Fitzpiers unwittingly makes clear to Melbury his sexual liaison.

2. *"As one, in suffering all, that suffers nothing"*: She sees him, as Hamlet sees Horatio, as a rock of stability (*Hamlet*, III. ii.64). It is high praise. Referring to the death of his father in 1892, Hardy wrote 'that the character of Horatio in *Hamlet* was his father to a nicety', and in Hardy's copy of that play his father's name and the date of his death are written opposite the following lines:

> Thou hast been
> As one in suffering all that suffers nothing;
> A man that fortune's buffets and rewards
> Hast ta'en with equal thanks.
>
> (*Life*, p. 262)

3. *unguibus et rostro*: With claws and bill.

4. *For days . . . in his hand*: This incident is not found in the manuscript.

CHAPTER XV

1. *the good burghers of Coventry . . . beautiful lady*: According to legend, Godiva, wife of the ruler of Mercia, agreed to ride naked through Coventry if her husband would withdraw a tax imposed on the citizens (*burghers*). All of them, except Peeping Tom, obeyed her instruction to stay indoors with their windows shut. The naked Godiva represents the liaison of Fitzpiers and Felice – too blatant to be ignored.

2. *a mourner of Ariadne, a by-word of Vashti, and a corpse of Amy Dudley*: Ariadne, daughter of King Minos of Crete, saved the life of her lover Theseus after he killed the bull-headed man or Minotaur, but he deserted her on the Isle of Naxos. *Vashti*, wife of King Ahasuerus, was discarded by her husband, who took Esther as his queen because Vashti refused his summons to come and display her beauty before his court (Esther 1–2). *Amy Dudley*, wife of Queen Elizabeth's favourite, Robert Earl of Leicester, died in mysterious circumstances. It was said that he had murdered her in order to be able to marry the Queen. So all three are famous symbols of women rejected by husbands or lovers.

3. *like the altar of Cain*: It was because God rejected the sacrifice of Cain, 'a tiller of the ground', but accepted that of his brother, Abel, 'a keeper of sheep', that Cain killed Abel (Genesis 4.2–8). The allusion is to the bitter rejection of Giles, not to the murder.

4. *she was a play-actress*: Refers to an early nineteenth-century view of actresses. In *The Half Sisters* (1848) a male character explains: 'I would never marry an artiste of any grade. A woman who makes her mind public, or exhibits herself in any way . . . seems to me little better than a woman of nameless class . . . for that is publishing both mind and body too' (Book II, 18–19).

CHAPTER XVI

1. *femme de trente ans*: Used to indicate an age of perfect maturity in a woman. Balzac's novel *Une femme de trente ans* (1831) refers to Madame d'Aiglemont, a woman of thirty who has irresistible attractions for a young man since she is said to lack the illusions and inexperience of 'a young girl'. The latter yields and needs to be guided whereas the older woman chooses, which is flattering, and also instructs. So the woman of thirty flatters the man psychologically as well as sexually. Felice does not, however, remain in control of Fitzpiers in this way.

2. *édition définitive*: Technical term for an authoritative and final edition of a literary text. Similarly Felice has reached her point of physical perfection.

3. *within your right as the superior*: Even when overwrought, Melbury still believes that her rank privileges Felice to reject Grace if she pleases.

CHAPTER XVII

1. *fret and fever*: Used as a set phrase in the nineteenth century but here involving an allusion to Keats' 'Ode to a Nightingale', where the world-weary speaker wishes to fade away and forget 'The weariness, the fever and the fret/Here, where men sit and hear each other groan' (ll. 23–4).

2. *like a wild animal on first confronting a mirror*: The third use in the text of the mirror image in a dramatic encounter. See volume I, chapter VIII, note 8.

3. *suspicion*: 1896 inserts here 'He's had you!'. See Note on the History of the Text.

4. *and there*: 1912 adds 'kissing each other almost unintentionally'. The addition stresses, as do others, Grace's feeling of fellowship with the other women who have been her husband's mistresses.

VOLUME III

CHAPTER I

1. *the Mother of the Months*: In 'Atlanta in Calydon' by Swinburne (1837–1909), the phrase is used of the moon.

2. *tinkling simples*: a confusion of 1 Corinthians 13.1: 'Though I speak with the tongues of men and of angels, and have not charity, I am become as sounding brass, or a tinkling cymbal.' The last phrase means an empty sound. Another of the rustics' distortions of scripture.

3. *apple of discord*: Marty's letter about Mrs Charmond buying her hair is designed to make trouble between her and Fitzpiers. So it is compared to the golden apple inscribed 'for the most beautiful' which, in the Greek story, Paris had to give to one of three beautiful goddesses, Hera, Athena or Aphrodite. His choice of Aphrodite ultimately led to the Trojan War.

4. *Versaillese furniture*: Ornate furniture of the eighteenth century associated with the French palace of Versailles.

5. *the pilgrim's flask of rum*: A flask suspended round the traveller's neck by a cord attached to it.

CHAPTER II

1. *Pro — Pre . . . Caucasus*: In his stupefied state Fitzpiers cannot remember the name of Prometheus, said in Greek myth to have offended the god Zeus and been chained to a rock in the Caucasus as a punishment. An eagle daily ate his liver which grew again for the next day's torment. This is how Fitzpiers now sees his marriage to Grace.

2. *Death in the Revelation*: The pale horse reminds the boy of the horse in Revelation 6.8: 'And I looked, and behold a pale horse: and his name that sat on him was Death, and Hell followed with him.'

3. *the fly*: Light one-horse carriage let out on hire as a cab.

4. *the ghosts of the Brothers*: See volume II, chapter III.

5. *flung it open*: 1896 adds here 'Wives all, let's enter together!' See Note on the History of the Text and see this chapter, note 7 below.

6. *empty bed*: By 1896 this reads 'empty bed, staring at it, and at his night-shirt lying on the pillow', in line with the increasing explicitness of later revisions. See Note on the History of the Text.

7. *the wife's regulation terms . . . woman, creature, or thing*: All these words could have a contemptuous use. *Woman*, as now, used as a term of address was abusive. *OED* quotes 1860, 'Will you hold your tongue, woman?'; and 1888, 'Though the duke was a weak creature, his position was strong'; and 1860, 'To accept the sovereignty of a thing like Henry of Valois . . .'.

8. *the Psalm of Asaph*: Psalm 73.14: 'For all day long have I been plagued/And chastened every morning.' Like the speaker in the Psalm, Grace will *not* 'offend against the generation by seeking retribution'.

9. *fellow-women*: 1896 adds 'whose relations with him were as close as her own without its conventionality'.

10. *bien-aimé*: 'Well-beloved' ironically used, later to be the title of Hardy's late novel (*The Well-Beloved* volume, 1897).

CHAPTER III

1. *the words of Mrs. Elizabeth Montagu* (1720–1800): A female intellectual and member of the Bluestocking Circle. She held a salon and was herself a minor author.

2. *Sudarium of St. Veronica*: The cloth with which, according to legend, Veronica wiped the face of Christ on the journey to Calvary. It was said that the imprint of his features was left on the cloth.

3. *Not poppy nor mandragora*: Refers to Iago's comment when he has induced Othello to believe that his wife has been unfaithful – 'Not poppy, nor mandragora/Nor all the drowsy syrups of the world,/Shall ever medicine thee to that sweet sleep/Which thou owed'st yesterday' (III.iii.334–7). Ironically it is Fitzpiers, the unfaithful husband, who refers to himself in this theatrical way.

4. *the veil of that temple is rent in twain*: In Matthew 27.51 these words are used to describe what happened at the time of Christ's crucifixion. When he died '. . . behold, the veil of the temple was rent in twain from the top to the bottom; and the earth did quake, and the rocks rent'. The same image is later used by Jude in *Jude the Obscure* (1895) to describe his separation from Sue Bridehead: 'Then let the veil of our temple be rent in two from this hour!' (Book VI, chapter III). Both examples secularize the quotations.

CHAPTER IV

1. *her art*: Alludes both to the fact that Felice was once an actress and to her practice of painting her face with cosmetics. See also volume II, chapters II and V, for references to the theatricality of Fitzpiers, Grace, Felice's foreign lover and her time as an actress; and see also Introduction.

2. *the Valley of Humiliation*: In *Pilgrim's Progress* by John Bunyan (1628–88), the pilgrim Christian goes into the Valley of Humiliation and meets the dreaded Apollyon and with God's help survives a fight with him (Part I).

3. *the new statute, twenty and twenty-one Vic., cap. eighty-five*: This was the Divorce and Matrimonial Causes Act of 1857 which for the first time allowed divorce without an individual Act of Parliament. Men could divorce their wives for a single act of adultery; women had to prove in addition to adultery some aggravating cause such as cruelty, incest, sodomy or bestiality. Other references in the novel suggest that a later law of 1878 is involved. So does the allusion to the American Civil War (1861–5) being over (see volume II, chapter V, note 2). So Beaucock is either ill-informed or deliberately misleading Melbury by referring to a law which was not new but some twenty years old. See next note.

4. *exaggerated information*: On the new divorce laws. The question of whether Grace can divorce Fitzpiers solely for adultery hinges on the 1857 law. Clearly she could not because he had given her no 'aggravating cause' (see previous note). Beaucock is evidently claiming that the arrangements for separation (not divorce) in the 1878 law are new conditions for divorce.

5. *his face shining . . . with an angel*: In Exodus 34.29 and 35, this is how Moses is described as he comes down from Mount Sinai with the two stone tablets inscribed with God's laws. See also volume I, chapter IX, note 1, for a use of the same biblical reference.

6. *where angels fear to tread*: In *An Essay on Criticism* by Alexander Pope (1688–1744) he speaks of St. Paul's as a place of resort and gossip: 'there they'll talk you dead:/For Fools rush in where Angels fear to tread' (ll. 597–8). He refers both to the sacred location and to the rash opinions offered on serious subjects.

7. *the cuckoo*: Traditionally the symbol that a husband had an unfaithful wife since the cuckoo suggested an intruder in the nest.

CHAPTER V

1. *the ceorl*: An earlier form of the word 'churl' alluding to its ancient sense of *the lowest class* – 'a member of the lowest class of freeman (as opposed to serfs)'.

2. *all the opiates in the pharmacopoeia*: A book listing all medicines with directions for their preparation and identification. 'Previous to 1863 three pharmaco-poeias were extant in Great Britain, *viz*. those of the colleges of physicians of London, Edinburgh and Dublin. In 1863 a *British Pharmacopoeia* was compiled' (*OED*, 1866).

3. *the fruit-god and the wood-god*: The Roman god of orchards is Vertumnus; the wood god is possibly Faunus.

4. *invitingly*: More explicit than the manuscript and serial reading – 'archly'.

5. *She regarded . . . with her head sideways*: Replaced in 1912 by: 'She regarded a high marble tomb to the last representative of an extinct earldom, without a thought that it was the family with which Fitzpiers was maternally connected, and with her head sideways.'

6. *it enables ill-assorted husbands and wives to part in a way they could not formerly do without an Act of Parliament*: An unambiguous reference to the terms of the Divorce Act of 1857. See volume III, chapter IV, note 3 for a discussion of the dating of the novel. See also Appendix III.

7. *Arcadian innocents*: Arcadia was a region of Greece in the Peloponnese, idealized by the Roman poet Virgil (70–19 BC) in his *Eclogues* as the setting of idyllic country life. Grace and Giles are the child-like inhabitants of this unreal place.

8. *Not that I feel morally bound*: An astonishingly unconventional view at a time when, since she was not divorced, she would generally be thought to be morally bound to Fitzpiers.

CHAPTER VI

1. *to put off the old Eve*: Eve is here a symbol of erring womanhood, though in Grace's case the errors have only been her misjudgment of the value of Giles and Fitzpiers, brought about by a snobbish education.

2. *touching the stops*: The stops on an organ are a set of graduated pipes producing tones of the same quality.

3. *through Time's glass*: Time's symbol of an hour-glass through which the sands of time run quickly. See earlier reference to Felice's foreign lover looking like Time with an hour-glass (volume II, chapter V, note 1).

4. *as Desdemona said, men are not gods*: Desdemona's attempt to explain away Othello's jealousy as the result of other worries oppressing him: 'Nay, we must think, men are not gods,/Nor of them look for such observancy/As fits the bridal' (*Othello* III.iv.149–51). Hardy uses it to mean that men succumb easily to sexual temptation.

5. *embrace*: 1912 'long embrace and kiss'.

6. *like a very Cain*: Like a man who had murdered his brother (Genesis 4.8).

7. *To hasten . . . eyes*: This passage describing repeated kisses is not found in either manuscript or serial.

8. *He has not done you enough harm*: He has only committed adultery and not added a further offence such as bigamy, incest, rape, et cetera, which would make it possible for a woman to divorce her husband after 1857.

CHAPTER VII

1. *as by a geyser*: As by a hot-water spring shooting up into the air.

2. *who combined modern nerves . . . primitive emotions*: This is like a reviewer's description of Sue Bridehead, a 'New Woman', which Hardy quotes in the 1912 Postscript to *Jude the Obscure* as 'the intellectualized, emancipated bundle of nerves that modern conditions were producing, mainly in cities'.

3. *The Daphnean instinct*: Daphne was a nymph and huntress who, in Greek legend, wanted no lovers. Fleeing from the amorous Apollo, she prayed for help and was turned into a laurel bush.

4. *some little ivory tablets*: Stiff sheets to write on.

5. *"Long tears . . . delight"*: From 'A Ballad of Life' (stanza 6) by Swinburne (1837–1909). The poem describes the ecstatic delight of those who hear in the poet's dream a lady's lute playing and singing.

CHAPTER VIII

1. *I am not bound to him by any divine law*: An astonishingly unconventional statement for a woman to make of a husband, however unfaithful, in the late nineteenth century. It is however consistent with Grace's reaction to the appearance of Fitzpiers' two mistresses at his bedside when they hear that he is injured.

2. *I cannot speak more plainly. 'Whatsoever things are pure' – you know what is in my mind*: In 1912 this read: 'I cannot speak more plainly. I yearn to let you in, – but you know what is in my mind.'

3. *As in the grisly story*: A traditional element in ghost stories is the ghost that cannot be seen but which touches the living person or causes them to feel cold. The description of the storm does resemble that in 'The House of Usher' by Edgar Allan Poe (1809–49) but in which there is no invisible spectre, only a woman who breaks out of the coffin into which she has accidentally been nailed while still alive, to drag her brother to his death with her.

4. *wet*: 1896 adds after this 'Come to me!', evidently a directly sexual invitation. In 1912 it becomes 'Come to me, dearest!'

CHAPTER IX

1. *more of Artemis than Aphrodite*: Artemis is the daughter of the god Zeus in Greek mythology. She was identified with the Roman goddess Diana, the virgin huntress. Aphrodite, Greek goddess of beauty, love and fertility, equated with the Roman Venus. This description of Grace as more inclined to chastity than love does not fit with the earlier stress on her physical susceptibility to Fitzpiers. See the reference to Actaeon who pursued Artemis in volume I, chapter XII, note 1.

2. *the pieces of touchwood*: soft white substance into which wood is converted by fungi.

CHAPTER X

1. *living here*: 1896 adds, to make it franker, 'with him'.

2. *the extremest inference?*: That she is Giles' mistress.

3. *the insinuation*: That Giles is in heaven but Felice in hell.

4. *a Psalter*: In making the women read from the book of psalms, Hardy suggests a human value in this kind of ceremony, though it is noteworthy that they read from a text which relates to the human condition generally and is not specifically Christian. This is typical of his avoidance of Christian references with Christian implications in this text. They are put on a par with allusions to Classical and Norse mythology.

5. *that a Calvinist*: A Calvinist would be expected to think praying for the dead useless and wrong. Calvin (1509–64) broke away from the Roman Catholic church in *c*.1533 and set up his own sect in an attempt to purify and reform the church.

6. *What has come upon you and us*: To this is added in 1896 'through your giving up yourself to him'.

7. *bring down my hairs . . . to the grave*: Jacob's rebuke to his son, Reuben, who wishes to take his youngest brother Benjamin as a hostage to Egypt: 'My son shall not go down with you . . . if mischief befall him by the way in the which ye go, then shall ye bring down my gray hairs with sorrow to the grave' (Genesis 42.38).

8. *a mere man's creature*: See volume III, chapter II, note 7.

9. *a "flat delight"*: In 'Vanitie II' by George Herbert (1593–1633) the phrase is used to describe earthly as opposed to heavenly pleasure. But Fitzpiers is merely finding that his affair with Felice has become stale with time.

CHAPTER XI

1. *Elijah drew down fire from Heaven*: Elijah, the prophet, in 2 Kings 1.1–16 draws down fire to destroy the soldiers of Ahaziah in order to prove that he is a man of God. What in Elijah was the result of divine instruction is in Fitzpiers caused by arrogance.

2. *his true complement in the other sex*: This is echoed by the idea found repeated in *Jude the Obscure*, which Phillotson alludes to when he says of Jude and Sue that 'They seem to be one person split in two' (Book IV, chapter iv).

3. *hieroglyphs*: This means that the woodland is a set of cryptic signs which only the initiated can decode – a recurrent theme in the novel. See Introduction.

4. *runic obscurity*: Runes made up the earliest Germanic alphabet and were Roman letters modified into angular forms so that they could be carved into wood or stone. With a few exceptions they died out long before the Norman Conquest in 1066. They became a symbol later of something difficult to interpret.

CHAPTER XII

1. *the two mourners in Cymbeline*: In *Cymbeline* IV.ii.219ff, the heroine Imogen's brothers strew her grave with flowers and tears when they wrongly believe her dead. The comparison with Giles is made because of her innocence and integrity.

2. *her personal condition*: This means that she was pregnant and it is not found in the manuscript or serial.

3. *fitful fever*: Macbeth says of Duncan that 'After life's fitful fever he sleeps well' (III.ii.23).

4. *St. Valentine*: 14 February is the feast of St Valentine, an obscure Roman martyr. It is associated with courtship and specifically the choice of a lover, perhaps because of the earlier pagan festival of Lupercalia on 15 February, perhaps because of a connection with springtime.

5. *"nature is fine . . . some instance of itself"*: An elaborately inappropriate use of Laertes' speech in *Hamlet* when he meets his sister Ophelia, now mad: 'Nature is fine in love; and where tis fine/It sends some precious instance of itself/After the thing it loves' (IV.v.158–60). *Fine* means 'sensitive' and the lines suggest that Ophelia's madness matches her desperate love for Hamlet. Fitzpiers uses them wilfully to imply that his letter is a sign of deep love.

6. *modus vivendi*: Way of life.

7. *vassal of her sweet will*: A cliché that might have come from a conventional Valentine card.

8. *Mrs. Fitzpiers*: This way of referring to Grace marks the new distance between husband and wife.

9. *out of* Measure for Measure: See III.ii.140–41 of the play where the disguised duke of Vienna, Angelo, is defending himself against Lucio's slanders that he is a lecherous drunkard. Lucio has claimed to know and love the duke and this is how he is answered. Fitzpiers again uses a high-flown allusion in a trite way by claiming to have learnt to know and love Grace better. In fact, her apparent boldness in taking a lover excites him.

10. *playing bo-peep*: Teasing someone by alternately hiding and peeping out at them.

CHAPTER XIII

1. *dreadful old French romances with their horrid spellings*: Fitzpiers' response suggests that these were parts of his library too salacious for Grace to read.

2. *"frustrate ghost"*: In 'The Statue and the Bust' by Browning (1812–89) the narrative tells how a statue of a medieval duke looks up to the window of a married woman whose carved bust looks down on him. The pair loved each other but never consummated their love. The poem sees this as a failure:

Stake your counter as boldly every whit,
Venture as warily, use the same skill,
Do your best, whether winning or losing it,

If you choose to play! – is my principle.
Let a man contend to the uttermost
For his life's set prize, be it what it will!

The counter our lovers staked was lost
As surely as if it were lawful coin:
And the sin I impute to each frustrate ghost

Is – the unlit lamp and the ungirt loin,
Though the end in sight was a vice, I say.

(ll. 238–48).

The clear parallel with Giles and Grace hints that Hardy shares this sense of pointless wasted life.

3. *yearning innamorato*: pining lover.

4. *It was a man-trap*: This harks back to Felice's comment to Grace about 'man-traps' (volume I, chapter VIII, note 4), though ironically it is the man who traps the woman rather than the other way round as Felice expected.

CHAPTER XIV

1. *quite contemptible in their clemency*: Hardy's sarcasm here indicates a distaste for physical cruelty also seen in his hostility to blood sports when he expresses his horror at the fact 'that so-called educated men should be encouraged to harass and kill for pleasure feeble creatures by mean stratagems', and slaughter-house practices – 'that they should be dark dens of cruelty . . .' (*Letters* III, p. 238).

2. *the marriage-service*: At this period Hardy's own view of marriage was far from reverent and in *Jude the Obscure* (1895) he specifically derides the marriage vows (made by Jude and Arabella) that Grace is so moved by: '. . . the two swore that at every other time of their lives till death took them, they would assuredly believe, feel, and desire precisely as they had believed, felt, and desired during the few preceding weeks. What was as remarkable as the undertaking itself was that nobody seemed at all surprised at what they swore' (Book I, chapter ix).

CHAPTER XV

1. *she's mesmerised*: Literally hypnotized, allegedly by the 'animal magnetism' of the hypnotist. The practice was devised by an Austrian physician, Franz Anton Mesmer (1734–1815), and claimed to induce, amongst other things, insensibility to pain. Figuratively it meant 'fascinated', but here it seems to be accurate in relation to Fitzpiers' influence over her which was strongly stressed earlier.

2. *melancholy-mad!*: Mad with grief or misery. Dickens in *Hard Times* (1854) uses the epithet ironically of factory machinery which he describes as 'melancholy-mad elephants' (Book I, chapter 11) and says: '. . . the piston of the steam-engine worked monotonously up and down, like the head of an elephant in a state of melancholy madness' (Book I, chapter 5).

3. *down the street*: By 1896 this read: ' "Well – he's her husband," Melbury said to himself, "but it's a forlorn hope for her; and God knows how it will end. But let her bear in mind that the woman walks and laughs somewhere at this very moment whose neck he'll be coling next year as he does hers to-night; and as he did Felice Charmond's last year; and Suke Damson's the year afore!" '

4. *wax wanton*: 'Grow fickle or unpredictable'.

5. *'The Spotted Cow'*: In *Tess of the D'Urbervilles*, chapter III, Tess's mother sings two lines from this. It tells of a girl looking for a lost cow lured away by a seducer who claims to have seen it 'down in yonder lane'. His trick is successful and 'I've lost my spotted cow' subsequently becomes her way of calling her lover. The song is a dialogue between the two.

6. *setting a wire*: Setting a trap for rabbits and hares.

7. *Mrs. Fitzpiers then was*: 1912 reads 'Mrs. Fitzpiers was that time in the arms of another man than Giles.'

8. *the loftier quality of abstract humanism*: Marty is a symbol of humanity at its morally highest level. *OED* quotes for 1888, 'According as he [man] raises his intellectual and moral nature to the levels of higher and higher humanism'.

GLOSSARY

Words glossed are not exclusively dialectal.

Abbreviations
a. adjective
advb. adverb
conj. conjunction
pa.t. past tense
phr. phrase
prep. preposition
pron. pronoun
p.p. past participle
pr.p. present participle
pr.t. present tense
sb. substantive/noun
sb.pl. substantive/noun plural
vb. verb

abeyant, a.	dormant, latent
a-croupied, p.p.	crouched
agues, sb.pl.	fever, fit
antemundane, a.	existing before the creation of the world
apple-blooth, sb.	apple-blossom
ashlar, sb.	square-cut stone
athwart, advb.	across (usually transversely)
baint, vb. + neg.	are not
beater, sb.	watch with a loud tick
beck, sb.	nod
bide (about), vb.	remain, continue, wait, sojourn
bien-aimé, sb.	beloved

bill-hook, sb.	knife or chopper with hook end
blade, sb.	fellow
blanching, a.	whitening with age
bode, p.p.	stayed
bouncing, a.	frisky, lively
brake-fern, sb.	bracken
brougham, sb.	one-horse closed carriage with two or four wheels
bruckle, a.	uncertain, shaky
bucks, sb.pl.	young fellows
calcareous, a.	composed of or containing lime-stone
carcase, sb.	body, person
carking, a.	worrying, haunting
'ch, pron.	I
chiel, sb.	child
chimmer, sb.	room
cock-watching, a.	awake at dawn
conjuncture, sb.	circumstance, meeting
conterminous, a.	with the same limits
copse-ware, sb.	products made from branches
court-roll, sb.	record held in connection with a manor, containing details of tenure for tenants or copyholders; copy = tenant's title deeds
crib-framing, sb.	making of troughs or mangers
criddled, p.p.	curdled
cross-loves, sb.pl.	illicit loves
deplored, pa.t.	lamented for
despite, sb.	injury
die, sb.	dice
dog-knobs, sb.pl.	two supports for burning logs or coals
dram, sb.	small draught
drong, sb.	a narrow way between two hedges or walls
'ee, pron.	you
eft, sb.	small lizard
embayed, a.	steeped, suffused
ensign, sb.	standard bearer
er, pron.	he

fay, vb.	succeed, fare, prosper
febrifuge, sb.	cooling drink
flitches, sb.pl.	sides of bacon
fond, a.	desirable, cherished
foot-passenger, sb.	pedestrian
for 'n, phr.	for him
(in a) freak, phr.	in a capricious mood
fruit promise, sb.	likely harvest
fugleman, sb.	well-drilled soldier used as a model for others and placed in front of a regiment
gad, sb.	stout stick
garniture, sb.	ornament, trimming
gied, , pa.t.	given
gig, sb.	light, two-wheeled one-horse carriage
gin-trap, sb.	mechanical trap
gizzard, sb.	in phr. *fret one's gizzard*: worry
gloaming, sb.	dusk, twilight
glutch (down), vb.	swallow, choke down
grapnels, sb.pl.	clawed instrument for seizing or holding an object
green, a.	in phr. *fret his heart green*: make himself heartsick
hag-rid, a.	oppressed in mind, troubled
hang-fairs, sb.pl.	public executions
heart-symptoms, sb.pl.	feelings, emotions
het, vb.	cut (across to)
hidebound, a.	narrow, cramped
hollow turner, sb.	wood-worker who makes hollow vessels
hollow turnery, sb.	making of hollow wooden vessels
homealong, advb.	homewards
hopper (of the mill), sb.	receiver through which grain passes into the mill
huffed, pa. t.	offended
hurdle, sb.	open frame with horizontal bars used in fences
ingathering, sb.	harvest
intramural, a.	indoor
jine, vb.	join

kex, sb.	dry hollow stem of a plant
knee-jints, sb.pl.	knee joints
larries, sb.pl.	excitements
let-alone, a.	passive
lewth, sb.	shelter
libration, sb.	wavering
linhay, sb.	open-fronted shed with lean-to roof
lipped, pa.t.	mouthed
lucubrations, sb.pl.	nocturnal studies
make, sb.	quantity produced
mawn-baskets, sb.pl.	large, round baskets with handles
meridional, a.	running due north–south
moiling, pr.p.	toiling, drudging
mossel, sb.	bite to eat
mother-in-law, sb.	stepmother
mouster, vb.	get ready
mullioned, a.	with windows with vertical bars dividing panes
nater, sb.	nature
natomy, sb.	subject for medical dissection
nesh, a.	delicate
nipperkin, sb.	small vessel containing less than half-a-pint
paled, a.	fenced
pattens, sb.pl.	thick-soled shoes or clogs
perruquier, sb.	wig-maker
phaeton, sb.	four-wheeled, light, open carriage
plaitless, a.	ungathered, unpleated
playward, a.	playful
pomace, sb.	apple pulp
pouts, sb.pl.	in phr. *in the pouts*: piqued
projick, sb.	prodigy
raft, vb.	trouble, disturb
randys, sb.pl.	noisy revels
randyvoo, sb.	noisy merrymaking, spree
rencounters, sb.pl.	meetings, rendezvous
reticulations, sb.pl.	networks
rozums, sb.pl.	strange stories or sayings